Elizabeth Jane Howard was born in March 1923. After training at the London Mask Theatre School she played with a repertory theatre in Devon and at Stratford-on-Avon. During this period she also modelled and worked for the BBC.

In 1947 she left the theatre to become a secretary. Subsequently she started to review and edit books and to write her own novels. In 1950 she was awarded the John Llewellyn Rhys Memorial Prize for her first book *The Beautiful Visit*.

Her books include *The Long View*, a Book Society choice, *The Sea Change*, *After Julius*, *Odd Girl Out* and *Mr Wrong*, a collection of short stories. Her novel, *Getting It Right*, was winner of the 1982 Yorkshire Post Novel of the Year Award. She has also edited *The Lovers' Companion: The Pleasure, Joys and Anguish of Loving*.

Elizabeth Jane Howard's most recent novel is *The Light Years*, the opening volume of her new trilogy, *The Cazalet Chronicle*.

Elizabeth Jane Howard

The Beautiful Visit

Pan Books
in association with Jonathan Cape

First published 1950 by Jonathan Cape Ltd
This edition published 1990 by Pan Books Ltd,
Cavaye Place, London SW10 9PG
9 8 7 6 5 4 3 2
© Elizabeth Jane Howard 1950
ISBN 0 330 31554 4

Printed in England by Clays Ltd, St Ives plc

To Robert Aickman

I woke because the fur wrapped round me had slipped off my feet, which were cold. As I moved to cover them, there was a loud creak and I discovered that my waist was encircled with a heavy leather belt. This was not at all usual, and drawing the fur up to my chin I lay back again to think. If it came to that, I did not usually sleep in a fur rug. Lying there, the ridiculous thought occurred to me that I had just been born. She was born with a girdle round her waist, they would say, to account for her misadventures. This is the kind of absurd notion one has when half awake; but for some minutes I lay still, waking; enjoying the exquisite detachment and emptiness of my mind.

It was not dark nor light, but a very fresh early grey air, and above me I could see small round windows, uncurtained. *Round* windows! I looked down again and saw, a few yards away, a pair of shining black boots which appeared never to have been worn. I was on the floor. I stretched out my left arm to touch it, and I was wearing a heavy gauntlet. The floor seemed to be shivering, or perhaps it was I who shivered. Listening, I heard a faint indescribable sound, an unhurrying rush, a sound of quiet, continuous, monotonous movement. I imagined the noise one makes walking through long dry grass; a little water spilt on to stone from some height; the distant drum-like murmur of a crowd ceaselessly conferring. Surely I must be the only person in the tremendous silence lying outside the small sound I could hear. I felt alone, warm and alone, in a desert or in outer space.

At this, my mind pricked up its senses and drawing the fur closely round me, I sat huddled on the floor and stared at the two round windows which were now a perceptibly paler grey.

After a moment, I rose stiffly to my feet and went to a window. There was nothing to be seen but a limitless wash of sea, breaking, and glinting where it broke, like steel. Above it was a paler empty stretch of sky, divided from the sea by a straight, faint, silver line. This whole round picture quivered, dipped a little, sustained the decline, and then rose again so that the original proportions of two-thirds sea, one-third sky were visible. This, very generally speaking, was where I was: but why? where was I going? and how did I come to be here at all?

I walked softly to the door, opened it, and looked out. There was nothing but a dim narrow passage: I hesitated a moment, then closing the door again, stood with my back to it, surveying the cabin where I had been sleeping. Catching sight of the boots again, I drew back the fur and looked down at myself. I was not reassured by my clothes, but clothes in which one had slept all night are not very re-assuring. There was a perfectly good bed in one corner. Why had I not slept in that? I went to look at the bed. Lying in the middle of it were two fat marbled exercise books.

I remembered everything: remembered who I was and felt imprisoned with the knowledge that I was not free and new and empty as I had been when I woke on the floor. I stared at the two books which contained my life. I took them and sat beneath one of the windows, intending only, I think, to glance at them for the contrast they provided to my present circumstances. After all, I had little idea what would happen next. My life loomed before me, as wide with chance as it had been the day I was born.

CHAPTER ONE

I was born in Kensington. My father was a composer. My mother came from a rich home, and was, I believe, incurably romantic. She married my father, despite the half-hearted protestations of her family, who felt that to marry a musician was very nearly as bad as to marry into trade, and far less secure. I imagine their protestations were half-hearted, because she was, after all, their seventh daughter; and if they had been at all vehement in their disapproval I cannot imagine my mother sticking to her decision. At any rate, her family, after attending the wedding (there are pictures of all my aunts looking sulky, righteous, and incredibly tightly laced, on this occasion), washed their hands of her, which was far the cheapest, and from their point of view, the most moral attitude to adopt. It was certainly the cheapest. My father was not a good composer, he was not even successful; and my mother had no idea of money (or music). She had four of us in as many years, and I was the fourth. We would all wear passed on clothes until our nurse would no longer take us near the shops, and our contemporaries laughed at us; and then suddenly, in the drawing-room, would hang rich fiery brocade curtains; or perhaps there would be a party, and we would have new muslin frocks with velvet sashes; worn for that one occasion, and outgrown long before the next. I always remember my mother as pretty, but ceaselessly exhausted by her efforts to keep the increasing number of heads above water.

We had the usual childhood, with governesses, and interminable walks in Kensington Gardens. We soon learned that most people's fathers were not composers, and we boasted about ours to the other children we met on our walks: affected a knowledge and love for music which we did not feel, and held prearranged conversations about it for the benefit of these richer and generally more fortunate friends. We were intelligent, and they were impressed. It all helped us to bear the lack of parties, seaside holidays and expensive toys.

Eventually, of course, my two brothers went away to school, and I was left at home with my sister. In all the years we grew up together, only two things stand out in my mind. The first was our poverty. I do not think we were exactly poor, but we had, as we were continually told, a position to keep up. I think the situation was complicated by the fact that my father and mother had quite different positions in mind; with the result that we oscillated hopelessly just out of reach of either.

The second was music. Music dominated our lives ever since I can remember. We were forced to listen to it for hours on end in silence; sometimes for a whole afternoon. My garters were often too tight; I used to rub under my knees, and my father would frown, and play something longer, and even less enjoyable. He was a tired, disgruntled little man; ineffectually sarcastic, and haunted by a very bad digestion, which made him morose and incapable of enjoying anything. I think even he got sick of music sometimes, but not until he had left it too late to start anything else: and my mother, I think, would have been finally shattered if he had presented her with any alternative.

Occasionally, his work would be performed; we would all go and there would be desperate little parties in the Green Room afterwards, with a lot of kissing, and frenziedly considered praise.

We were all made to learn the piano; but I was the only one who survived the tearful lessons with an enormous woman, who lisped, adored my father, and ambled into unwieldy rages at our incompetence. Also the chill, blue-fingered hour of practice before breakfast, choked the others' less dogged aspiration. After some years, my father suddenly added another hour on to this practice, and began to superintend it. He used to stand over me while I raced through easier passages of Mozart, or perhaps exercises of

Bülow, asking me difficult questions which were larded with sarcastic similies I was far too resentful and afraid to comprehend.

I remember us getting steadily poorer. There were eventually no parties, except at tea-time, when my mother would perforce entertain her more distant relations, who patronized her, and suggested alterations in the household which she had neither energy nor means to allow.

The house smelt of dusty carpets and forgotten meals; of grievance and misfortune. There was cracked white paint on all the window sills, and there were slimy slips of soap in the basins. The drawing-room degenerated to a dining, living and schoolroom; with the remains of furniture for all three purposes. There were yellowing pictures of us on the mantelpiece; languid, and consciously cultivated. The glass bookcase with cracked panes held rows of dull dark volumes which nobody wished to read. I remember the sunlight, sordid and unwelcome on my mother's sofa; and her head drooping over the arm. Her hair was always parted in the middle, strained back, and escaping in brittle strands round her ears. She seemed perpetually struggling with an enormous round work basket, writhing with grey and brown socks which gaped for attention. I can remember no colour that I can describe: no change of tempo. In the studio, the pianos stopped and started with monotonous regularity when my father resorted to teaching. For several years there was a great jar of dusty crackling beech leaves. I remember odd ends of braid round the piano stools, which shivered when pupils banged the door, as they invariably did. It was a very heavy door. Upstairs there were wide draughty passages covered with small faded mats over which one slid or tripped. My mother's bedroom was filled with huge and reputedly valuable pieces of furniture: but her remnants of jewellery winked sadly in worn white velvet; her silver-topped brushes were always tarnished; there were innumerable bent hairpins in cracks between the floorboards; and the whole room was impregnated with the brisk improbable smell of my father's shaving soap (there was always a soft grey foam on his brush). There were a great many gilt mirrors about the passages, all spotted and blurred with damp, like the passages themselves. We had a tiny garden, surrounded by black brick walls, filled with straggling grass and silent fleeting cats. I do not recall anything else very much.

My elder sister put up her hair, and began going down to dinner. The boys were always away, and I did not, in any case, like them very much. I was horribly lonely. I read everything I could lay my hands on, which was little; grew too fast; and, above all, longed for something to happen.

My sister began going to church a great deal and I found a purple Bible with silver clasps in her bedroom. She was out and I was amusing myself with her room and private things. There were a crucifix, a rosary and a few books on religious subjects smugly bound in red and gold. Was she a Roman Catholic? I didn't know anything about her; if I caught her eye at meals or in the evening she would smile, remotely gentle, and go on eating or sewing, delicately withdrawn. Her speech was carefully non-committal and she didn't talk to me much beyond asking me if I was going to wash my hair or telling me to help our mother.

I opened the drawers of her dressing-table. Her underclothes were beautifully embroidered, all white and folded, made by herself. Her boots were polished, with no broken laces. Above them in the wardrobe her dresses hung wasted with waiting; with no one to take them out into the air. They were chiefly white, mauve, dark blue and grey, with shoulders flopping sulkily off the hangers. The mauve was pretty: I had never worn mauve. It had hundreds of little buttons made of itself. I took it out of the wardrobe. It swayed a little, and suddenly I was unhooking my skirt, tearing my blouse under the arms as I wrenched it over my head, my long hair catching on the hooks, and then standing in my petticoat looking down at my ugly black shoes and stockings. I laid hands on the mauve frock. The buttons were awfully difficult to do up. I couldn't manage the one in the middle of my back at all. I twisted like a flamingo and heard the taut cotton cracking. Just about to crack I hoped. Not actually torn. I turned to a long thin mirror by the bed. My petticoat was not long enough and there was a line like a let-down hem. The dress fitted me. How clean and trim and old. I looked into the glass and said: 'I love you, Edward,' several times. My hair was wrong; he would laugh. I rushed to the dressing-table, the tight mauve skirts primly resisting, and succeeded after some agonizing moments with hairpins in twisting a bun at the back of my head. 'Good afternoon, Lavinia,' I said, advancing on the mirror. 'Good afternoon.' And I curtsied. At that moment my sister came into the room. I saw her face in the mirror. I turned round quickly so that she should not see the gap with the undone buttons. I was very frightened and afraid the gap would make her more angry. I hated her for coming in. No harm, I kept repeating to myself, only one frock, no harm.

'I hate my clothes,' I said. 'I didn't choose this house. I can't start life in it. This is so pretty.'

She shut the door, and began taking off her gloves from slim smooth white hands, fingers unpricked because she always wore thimbles when she worked.

'Will you take if off now? I don't want it too crushed,' she said.

I was struggling with the buttons when she glided forward and I felt her fingers regularly neat, releasing them, down to my waist. I pulled the dress over my head. She took it from me in silence and replaced it on its hanger in the wardrobe. I reached for my skirt and she said, 'Have you been trying on all my clothes?'

She saw the drawers open. I bent over my skirt ashamed. She sat down and talked. She would not have minded me trying on her clothes with her there, she said. But did I not feel it a little wrong to come to her room when she was out, to play with her private possessions? 'If I had known you were going to do that I should have asked you to wash your hands.' And she laughed pleasantly.

I looked at my hands. They were grey and clumsy. I felt they had only become dirty for her to see.

'We must try and remember that things don't matter.' She

was leaning forward. 'I know jealousy is hard. I have suffered from it myself' (with a weary reminiscent little smile). 'But there are other things so much more important and so little time to set sufficient values. Life is hard for us all in different ways.'

She talked for a long time in the same quiet assured unemotional voice. There was a lot about God and trying to live a good life, peace of mind, acceptance of what was given, examples, final reward, and back to not prying unasked into other people's things: and an absolute passion of disagreement grew in me.

'I split the frock,' I said.

'That is a pity. But I expect it can be mended. I am not angry. It's quite all right.'

'I've got to go. I promised to sort the laundry,' I said. I couldn't bear her voice any more.

'Well we'll say no more about it. Agreed?' And she rose suddenly and kissed my cheek. I left her room quickly and ran into mine. 'Don't forget the laundry,' I heard her voice daintily energetic as I shut my door.

My passion broke and I sat on the floor clutching my knees and repeating her words so that I could fight them more clearly in my mind. Things must matter. Everything existed because someone had once thought it important. Nobody gave me this house, nobody could love it; if you were peaceful you never wanted to change. I wanted every single simple thing to be different. I should not mind people looking at my clothes if they were nice. There *wasn't* anyone to help. If helpful people didn't care about beautiful stuffs and colours, sounds and more people, then they weren't any use to me. But there was nobody to help me here. Hot resentful tears fell down into my hands. Everything was dirty, dusty and grey; no clear colour; no piercing sound; and at tea everything would be the same. Nobody worth their salt ever had much peace of mind. I wasn't jealous of her. Good Lord no. And I repeated 'Good Lord' aloud in a pompous self-satisfied manner enjoying its rounded scorn. It was a mistake to put me in this house. I wasn't suited to it. I couldn't even cry any more, but my nose was hot and full: horrid. I got up to search for a handkerchief and rooted for hours among bits of string; postcards; a broken watch; a ring out of a cracker; a musty lavender bag, all dust and spikes; a shoelace; elastic; a ninepenny Nelson; a little pink china pig with a chipped ear; a balloon, soft, and curiously unpleasant to touch; an envelope bursting with stamps; a penwiper; and, at last, a handkerchief, grey, but folded. I shook it out, and it smelt of dolls' houses and the water out of their tea cups. I blew my nose and sat down.

'I am against everybody,' I said.

Nothing changed.

'Everybody and everything. I don't like it, I'm going to change.' The gaping drawer reminded me. A lot of those things were too childish to keep. I had outgrown them. I would throw away everything I hated. Everything in my room.

But it was tea-time.

Two days later I was still in the midst of my private revolution. My room was chaotic and each night when I went to bed the bloated waste-paper basket reminded me of more to purge. The family took no notice of me, which was comforting as there would only have been an incredulous banality about their comments. I eventually made my room unsentimentally bare; hardly belonging to me, and only resentfully part of the house. All the books and toys that had verged on grown-up possessions were gone, and it took me no time to find a handkerchief. That was not as enjoyable as I had expected; but I persevered and sorted my clothes into heaps of the unwearable, mendable, and usable. The mending took several days; I got bored and relegated many garments to the first heap.

The next thing was to find new people. I started walking in Kensington Gardens by myself, watching the people, and trying to find someone to suit my needs. This accomplished, I intended taking the person home to tea with me. The Round Pond seemed the most likely spot, because people stopped to feed the birds, or watch the yachts, or simply the minnows. I was afraid to speak to anyone. Each day I resolved to take the plunge but I was determined that it should be thoroughly done and there was a private rule that the person had to be taken to tea. I saw one girl: very pretty, carrying a little blue book, and gazing at the swans. She sat down on a seat and I watched her, fascinated. She had enormous brown eyes with very long lashes and moth-like eyebrows. She opened the little blue book, and a stupid duck which was walking on the grass and gravel, moved, hasty and eager, like a shop attendant, thinking about bread I suppose. It waited, then walked to the water and slid in, swimming smugly away as though it never hurried greedily up to seats at all. The girl stopped reading and looked up pensively. The sun was setting, and gold was slipping uncertainly off the trees and water and her hair. It was very calm; the yachts were lying on the pond, with their sails shivering still; and the gardens were blue in the distance with the tree trunks dark, like legs seen from a basement window. On the Broad Walk a leisurely stream of perambulators rolled homewards; stiff gaiters to unbutton and peel off fat frantic legs and square white feeders to be tied round hundreds of warm pink necks. A clock struck four, and the swans arched their necks for the sound to pass through. A minnow floated on its side in the water, its mouth opening: it was going to die. The girl shut her book and walked away, and I had not spoken to her. I imagined her walking back to a neat beautiful home with friends all coming to a wonderful tea. She did not walk towards my gate. 'She would never have liked me,' I said. 'She would not have come home.' The thought cheered me for the loss of her. She was only a speck among the trees already. It didn't matter, there were so many people. It was just a pity to let anyone go. All the way home I imagined her walking with me, telling me many new and exciting things about how to live, so that tea with the family would be a waste of her. It was cold by the time I reached home; the lamps were being lit in the streets, and the piano sounded in petulant bursts as I stood on the door step. My father was giving a lesson. My sister was wearing her mauve frock.

After tea I darned black stockings and ironed my hair ribbons.

The next day I went to the Round Pond half hoping, half expecting to see the girl with the blue book. It was a fresh, cold day and she was not there. I stood in front of the water: a little tufted duck dived and came up gleaming with secret pleasure. Beside me was a tall old man, very neat and black, with a stick.

'Water water everywhere nor any drop to drink,' he said suddenly. I turned to him.

> 'The very deep did rot: Oh Christ!
> 'That ever this should be!'

he went on rapidly with great emphasis.

'I know it all by heart,' he said. Then suddenly: 'Do you know where that came from, young lady?'

'Coleridge. *Ancient Mariner*,' I mumbled. My governess had read it with me.

'Quite right. Exactly right. Not many young people nowadays know that sort of thing. Great poetry. I know it all by heart.' And he walked away lifting his hat. A dog ran after him sniffing, but he took no notice and walked faster.

Nothing else happened that day. I told my family at tea about the old man, and they received it with the expected mild surprise. My father had written a choral work which was to be performed at Christmas, and they were all absorbed with being a composer's family.

We went to a concert that evening. We always contrived to look poor, cultured, and apart at these functions. The programme was chamber music, mostly Schubert and Brahms. I could never listen to chamber music for more than an hour; after which I began to count people's heads; still, bald, hatless, swaying, thrown back, shrunk forward between the shoulders, sunk on the hands, erect, anguished, emotional, ecstatic; my father stern and bored, and my mother acquiescently rapt; my sister prettily still; and I, I wondered what I looked like. I shut one eye and squinted. No good. There were red plush and gold paint; fat naked little boys in biscuit-coloured relief. The platform was a pale blue semi-circle, with the players impressively still, driving their instruments with a delicate force and deliberation. We went to see the players afterwards. They were dazed and friendly, their hands wrung and their faces stretched with answering good-will.

Going home was the nicest.

CHAPTER TWO

I still walked in the Gardens, but I did not feel any less lonely.

One windy day there were kites between the Orangery and the Pond. I went to the slope and stared upward at three of them. They were half proud, half fearful; soaring with wild little tugs at their strings. I watched their joy at a moment's release in the dropping wind's fantasy; their floating in the second's calm before they were off again; sinuous and wild, and captive all the time. I looked down, too far of course, to the ground and saw muddy tufted grass and a pair of black boots. Enormous boots. A boy. An old boy; nearly as old as I. His suit was dirty, his breeches tight, his sleeves too short, and his wrists red and bony. He was very intent on his kite; his eyes were screwed up with the sky and staring cold; his dark hair ruffled up by the wind into a square crest. He had a large Adam's apple which reminded me of five notes and then down a fifth on a piano. I stood a little nearer and stared again at the kite because he was so intent upon it. I was suddenly possessed of a desire to have been flying it with him; for his winding in to be by our mutual consent, because we had other things to do, planned together. The kite was almost in; it was pink and yellow, with ribs dark and delicate against the sky; and he was winding fast, his fingers hard and capable against the string. His eyes came down to earth, and he glanced at me just as the kite hit the ground with a thin papery thud.

'Can I look at it?'

'What?'

'Your kite. Can I look at it?'

'If you like.' He watched the kite in my hands indifferently.

'Did you make it?'

'No.' I knew he wished he had.

'Do you often fly it?'

'No.'

I gave it back to him.

'I've stopped because of the wind,' he volunteered.

'It's dropping.' My mouth was very dry.

'I'm going home now. Good-bye.' He started off, the kite perched in his arms. 'I'll be here tomorrow if you want to see it fly properly.' He was going.

'I say,' I called. 'I say. Would you like to come home to tea?'

He stopped. It was up to him. I saw his eyes faintly curious and defensive, and I longed for him to come.

'What's your name?'

I told him.

'How old are you?'

I told him.

'All right,' he said; and we set off down the Broad Walk.

'Will your family wonder where you are?'

'Oh no. I shouldn't get any tea anyhow. They're against me at the moment. I don't agree with them.'

I digested that in silence.

'My father's a doctor,' he added as an explanation.

'I see,' I said. 'What school do you go to?'

'I don't. I've been expelled.'

I didn't know what to say.

'How awful.'

'It jolly well is. I didn't like it much there but it's worse at home.'

'Why did they?'

'Partly because of God.' He stopped and transferred the kite from one arm to the other. 'And partly because of games.'

'I didn't know they could expel you for them.'

'Oh well it wasn't just them. They just started it. I was a bad influence anyway,' he said with some pride.

'How do you start being an influence?'

'Why?' He stopped and regarded me again suspiciously. 'I

don't think it would be easy for you. You might be a good influence of course. Girls always want to be that. But I shouldn't advise you to try. It's no good deliberately trying to influence anyone. My English master taught me that. It's about all I learned at school. You mustn't try and change other people. It's never good for them in the end. At school they want the masters to change everyone. And they want the boys to be sure of being everyone. He wouldn't and I wasn't and so he left and I was expelled.'

'Where is he now?'

'Edinburgh. With his family. They aren't pleased. I get letters from him. I'll show you if you like. You seem sensible.'

'Oh I am,' I said.

'We'd better sit down. Letters are too difficult standing up.'

We sat on a black bench. He took a crumpled envelope out of his pocket, and unfolded the letter. The writing was slanting and very difficult.

'– decision is not simple. Man's ultimate purgatory could be fraught with endless decisions; the consequences unknown and terrible even with knowledge – ' a blank which I couldn't read, ending with – 'and he spent twenty years deciding that, incomplete though it is – ' unreadable again – 'therefore assess yourself freely with sincerity and courage and tackle the main problem of what you want to be; once you are at all sure, nothing should stop you. Until then it is just strife for the sake of self-expression, a grisly means to achieve no positive end. I hope – '

The boy didn't turn over the page but folded it away back into the envelope and his pocket. 'The rest is just about writing and what to read,' he said.

I was paralysed. It was the first time I found myself facing something about which I had never thought, and was quite incapable of judging even generally, good from bad.

'He means, if you are going to change be sure why, and know what you want to change into, or else it would be like throwing your clothes away and being naked.'

'But if you want to change,' I said. 'If you want everything to be different, it's because the old things are dreary and dead and *anything* else would be new to you.'

'Not necessarily good though.'

'Supposing you wanted them new at all costs? Surely sometimes anything different would be better?'

'To think or to do?'

'I can't separate them,' I said.

He looked at me rather scornfully. 'I don't think you can. But don't you see by renouncing anything blindly without substitute you expose yourself to any fool or foolishness.'

'But supposing you hate everything that is in you,' I cried desperately, 'and you've never had a chance to know anything else, you only know you must change, what do you do then? You have to throw things away.' A litter of fairy books and dolls' clothes flung across my mind.

'You can read can't you?' he demanded fiercely. 'And talk to people. Learn, listen, and find out, and then choose.' And he went on in stern little spurts of energy and knowledge, serious, even sententious, but it didn't seem that then; only marvellous and rather frightening that one could be my age and know so much, and then be so fierce, and excited and serious about it.

My thoughts were like shillings in a pool, glittering and blurred, shimmering to the groping finger and always deeper and more elusive, until you think that perhaps there isn't a shilling at all, it seems so far out of reach. I floundered and the words wouldn't come. He forced me relentlessly into corners, and I felt the back of my neck getting hot, and warm little shivers down my spine. I didn't tell him about myself lest he should scorn what then seemed to me such childish endeavour. He raced on through religion, came triumphantly to blasphemous conclusions. Education was stabbed with a ferocity I had never before encountered; until it lay a bewildered mess of Latin, historical dates and cricket stumps. And then the older generation was subjected to a vitriolic attack: such remorseless contempt, such despairing anger, such a thunder of criticism was broken over their meek, bald and bun-like heads that I was dumb at the death of so large a body; trembling with anxious rapture of choice and the still distance of freedom.

He stared at the gravel, his talk calming. The kite lay between us on the bench, its paper stretched between the struts, breathing and rucked a little in the breeze. I had not attempted to argue or deny, I was quite incapable of either; it just seemed to me that my solitude was at an end; and his talk, his spate of words were rushing, like liquid, into my mind.

'What about *your* parents?' he said, suddenly lifting his head.

'Oh they – I have the same trouble.'

'Do they stop you doing things?'

'No, not exactly. There's nothing for them to stop.'

'What does your father do?'

'He writes music.'

'Oh, that should make it simpler for you.'

'I don't think it does. Anyway I don't think he thought much about it being simple for anyone when he started. There isn't much money and my mother's always tired.'

'I'm cold,' he said and rose to his feet. 'You're cold too,' looking down on me. It was an impersonal remark but I blushed and rose with a murmuring denial. It was blue grey, and the Gardens were nearly empty. We walked home almost in silence, and apprehension superseded the excitement I had known on the bench with the letter and the kite.

Lights were showing from houses, but mine was dark. I noticed the paint bubbled and peeling off the plaster, and the windows powdered and dull with dust.

We went in to tea.

'Do you always keep your door open?'

'Yes. It saves so much time.' My teeth were chattering and I didn't want to talk.

'I like that.' He put the kite on two chairs in the hall.

'Do you want to wash?'

He looked surprised, and urged me on down the passage.

The dining-room was terribly near. I prayed that they wouldn't all be there. They would put down their cups and their bread and look up, all towards the door, at him, and at me, and back to him again, and there would be a stealthy concert against speaking first, an awkward calm, which I must clumsily break. I opened the door. They put down their cups.

'He's come to tea,' I said, and turned to him blocking their sight. 'I can't remember your name.'

'Michael Latham,' he muttered as though it meant nothing, and he had learned it by heart.

'Come and sit down, Michael. Milk and sugar, Michael?' My mother wielded the tea-pot.

My father resumed his reading of *Blackwood's Magazine*. Michael stared at him. My sister lowered her eyes and scraped strawberry jam neatly with her knife. I could think of nothing to say. There was an exhausted pupil swallowing tea with a pale film; it was cold, and he had been too nervous and depressed to drink it, until he had felt sure that attention was diverted from him and his tremendous, thick, white hands. Michael ate an enormous tea, punctuated by monosyllabic replies to my mother's and sister's small inquisitive advances. He seemed fascinated by my father, watching him timidly and bending his head abrupt and shy if my father turned a page or stirred his tea.

How to escape and where? My brothers always seemed to manage it when they had friends to tea. They clattered with one purposeful rush to their large bedroom, where they remained for the evening. If, for any reason, I had ever gone into their room, they were always to be found standing in a conspiratorial group, quite silent and apparently doing nothing, frozen like animals at an unavoidable intrusion; hostile, scarcely breathing, with some secret purpose deep in their minds. I could not take Michael upstairs; I knew that for some reason my parents would not like it.

'Are you going to use the studio?' I asked my father. The pupil wriggled and hid his hands with a desperate little grin.

'I have to play something over once. Why?'

'I thought that if it was empty it would be a good place for us to go,' I said.

'Do you want somewhere to play?'

'No. It doesn't matter.'

'Well I want somewhere to play and I can't move my toys about as you can.' And he went on reading.

I saw Michael furiously kneading his bread, with shining eyes. There was a meek little silence; my mother was filling the tea-pot and we were all eating our tea, regardless of anything but our little personal movements.

I knew that if we were to escape I must get up and know where we were to go.

Better get on with it. I rose to my feet and in the same instant I heard Michael say, 'Could I hear you play, sir?'

My father looked up, a little pleased. 'Certainly, if you like.'

My heart thudded and I felt very cold. There was a general movement and I found myself in the studio, my father at the piano, with Michael and the pupil in appreciative attitudes. He played for two hours, and then Michael left. He stopped being shy with my father, thanked him with a great jerk of enthusiasm, and shook his hand twice very quickly. I walked with him down the steps to the gate.

'Well thank you,' he said. 'I loved hearing your father play. You never told me how good he was. I wish my family were like that.'

I was silent.

'Music whenever you like and no one minding who you bring home. Marvellous. Thank you very much. Good-bye.' And he went off with his kite.

I walked slowly back up the path. I would go upstairs, and perhaps I would cry a little because it finished a feeling more quickly and it would be easier to start again. It would be better to stay alone for a bit in order to know how to talk about it at dinner. I was tired; my legs felt heavy and the sides of my forehead ached. In the hall I met my sister who smiled discreetly, as though she knew the secret wrong thing, and suggested I lay the table for dinner. So I did. The girl who cooked helped me with fat pasty sighs, pushing her mauve fingers through her greasy hair and saying 'Yes Miss' while she smeared boards and tables with a grey stringy cloth. I filled the water jug from the cold tap in the scullery which roared out in an angry gush, leaving me with little round cold drops on my arms and chin; wiped the jug with a cloth; and carried it into the dining-room, where it left a little dim damp rim afterwards hidden by a cork mat. I edged the blue glass mustard pot out of its silver frame, rinsed the malevolent brown crust with my fingers, half expecting it to sting; and mixed the fresh yellow powder to an appealing cream. Then I shook the leather strap on which hung an assortment of Swiss cow bells, which wrangled among themselves, dreary and at the same time fierce, dying away into one surprisingly clear sweet note as they settled into a trembling silence.

There was only just time to tear with a comb at my hair before we sat down. They wanted to know all about him. How I had found him. Where he lived, what his father did, and whether he had any brothers or sisters. The worst of it was that they behaved quite nicely, especially my father, whose comments on his intelligence were unbarbed with sarcasm. I was surprised to find how little I knew of Michael, but I took a secretly spiteful delight in evading any question the answer to which I knew. They asked if he was coming again, and I realized that unless I went to watch his kite tomorrow I could not secure him. I said I didn't know and the talk frittered away to our usual subjects.

I was not alone until I went to bed, and by then I did not want to cry, I did not even feel sad; there was only an exhausted irritation about the whole episode culminating in a dreary uncertainty about whether to see him tomorrow. I had wanted him so desperately to bring his life to me, and he had identified himself with mine; I had thought he would bring a new air into the house, and he had merged with my family until I was again alone.

'I won't go tomorrow.' The thought gave me a queer little

tinge of pride. 'He may come again by himself. Or he may not.'

Two tears came out of my eyes. I fell asleep and dreamed that I was having tea at Michael's house, which had pink and yellow walls. His father wrote me two hundred prescriptions in very slanty handwriting, which we administered to an enormous shy man and I kept putting my tongue out at Michael, until he burst into tears and washed all the bottles with a grey cloth.

CHAPTER THREE

Michael did not come again, and I had no chance to mind, or to renew my search for anyone else, because a week later I was asked, or rather my sister was asked, to stay with a family who were spending the Christmas holidays at their home in the country. The family were some distant connection of my mother's, and my sister did not want to go. My mother wrote refusing for her, and received a telegram a day later which said: 'Send another daughter.' Telegrams in my family meant that you had died or missed a train, so it caused a stir. My father surprisingly decreed that I should go; so my mother worried over collars and stockings and my sister looked generously aloof. I was at first excited, and then appalled at the enormity of the adventure, never having stayed anywhere by myself before. And now for a whole ten days I should be surrounded by people I did not know, with new rooms, food, furniture, and country. I knew guests at parties had to do what was planned for them, although they were given the mockery of a choice; they had to pretend to enjoy it; their time was never their own until they were in bed in their new room.

Whenever I could consider the visit calmly, I realized, of course, that this was my chance, the chance for which I had longed; to get right away from my family and see new people and a different life. I was to go in a week from the telegram. As the days fled by I was less and less able to think calmly about it, and prayed that something, anything would happen to prevent it.

My mother took me shopping and bought me a red dress with black braid; a dark blouse; half a dozen stiff collars; a long thin jersey; and a pair of thick shoes. I was very quiet and did not argue over her choice of colours. She looked at me once in an unusually penetrating manner, and then led me to another part of the shop where she bought a beautiful frock, of rose-coloured silk, with knife thin pleating round the hem and foaming soft lace at the neck; a perfectly grown-up dress. She said that now I was sixteen I must put up my hair.

The dress fitted without any alteration, and my mother seemed gently pleased. She smiled and said would I like it? 'There is sure to be a party and I want you to look nice,' she said.

The pleasure of the frock, its glowing colour, its delicate silky polish under my fingers, its grace and beautifully fitting silk, was so sharp that my eyes were liquid; I felt myself blushing deeply and couldn't speak for enchantment.

'I don't think we need try any more,' my mother was saying to the assistant, and they went out of the little room. When they came back, I was still standing, staring at myself in the dress. When I had taken it off, the assistant swung the frock with a delicious rustle over her arm.

'Thank you. It's beautiful. The most beautiful frock. Thank you.'

They both smiled. I had never seen my mother so much alive, and I felt a little thrill of sympathy as a cord between us: as though we had some private vague plan. I must glitter and be decked and the reason was clouded and hidden: only they knew a little, I not at all. The assistant went away for wrappings and a pair of pink shoes: we were left alone, with the frock on the counter between us.

'Yes, it's a pretty frock. I hope you have a good time in it,' said my mother.

She seemed almost wistful. Suddenly I thought of red carpets under glass porches; men in top hats with dark green silk umbrellas helping her out of carriages to the golden luxury of a house filled with lights and tiny little pink ices and a great shining hard floor on which to dance in a rose-coloured frock – all the things I imagined she had had before she married my father. She fingered the frock and I could feel her looking ahead for me into those ten days, and beyond, as though I were a pebble to be dropped into water and she an exhausted outside ripple from the pebble before. I was filled with a pity and distaste for her life, and the ten days suddenly became significant and timeless. I touched the frock: there was a heavy sweet taste in my mouth and the resistance of panic mounting to a recklessness so that I couldn't bear to be silent.

'I can't go. I don't want to go. Don't make me. Say I'm ill. I *am* ill. I shall be ill if I go. I can't be ill in a strange house. It wouldn't matter if you said I couldn't go. Please mother I can't go away' ... My voice stopped. I was crying tears on to the frock, soaking little dark pink circles; and in a minute the assistant would come back. I felt a handkerchief soft in my hand; I smelt lavender water, and the warm sweet smell of my mother: which made it much worse. I couldn't speak, or stop crying: and then I was in the fitting-room again, sitting on a round chair, blowing my nose, and feeling incredibly stupid and sad. My mother was treating me as a child; holding my shoulders, and seeming beautiful and necessary again; saying that she understood, but of course I must go, and things were nice once you had started them, and I should soon be back, and so sad that it was over. Now I must stop crying and come home and be pleased about my frock. So I stopped and we went home. I didn't feel less terrified about going away, only a little relieved that my mother knew, and I was not entirely alone with my fears.

CHAPTER FOUR

I was not ill. The morning arrived when I came down from my room with its bare dressing-table and my small trunk packed and strapped in the middle of the floor; and was enjoined to eat a good breakfast.

My father took me to the station. I know I felt faintly apologetic in the midst of my apathy; he disliked trains; they made him nervous. He found me a corner seat in a second-class carriage which possessed a large old lady who looked at me with inquisitive kindness, assuring my father of her protection.

'Well,' said my father. 'You know where you have to get out?' I nodded.

'Got something to read?' I shook my head. There was a lump in my throat.

'Well, you can amuse yourself looking out of the window. Your luggage is at the back of the train.' He edged out of the carriage, and looked up the platform, at the clock, I guessed.

'Don't wait,' I said. I wanted him to very much, but he nodded, offered me his pale grey face to kiss, almost smiled, and was gone.

I opened my bag, containing a new leather purse, my ticket, one sovereign, and sixpence for the porter; shook out my handkerchief and blew my nose. It had begun. I stared out of the window and wondered whether everyone in the station had travelled alone and how much they had minded. The old lady suddenly offered me a pear drop which I accepted. It was rather common to eat sweets in a train in the morning but I was afraid she would be hurt.

The old lady asked me where I was going, and what did I do at home, and whether I liked animals; and then told me about herself. She told me nearly her whole life, because the train started quite soon, and she never stopped talking. Her life was very dull; mostly about how animals loved her and how much her sister disapproved, because her sister was very religious, and didn't believe that animals had souls and went to heaven. It all seemed pretty dull to me, or else she never told me the interesting bits. She had always lived in one house; and now she was left with her sister, whom I don't think she liked; their father having been a clergyman who died of a stroke when he was quite old. That was a horrible bit: she described his face and muttering with no one able to understand a word he said. They had nursed him devotedly, until one day when he sat up, said 'Thank God,' and died.

We were in the country by then. There was fine drizzling rain, so that houses looked remote, mysterious and too small; and the cows in the fields lay and waited like sofas on a pavement; patient, uncomfortable and somehow rakish. The train stopped four times, but it was never my station, and the old lady didn't get out; until I began to think that she didn't have a station, but simply lived on pear drops in a train and told people about animals.

The old lady eventually said that my station was next. I tidied my hair, and looked in my purse to see if the sixpence was still there.

The train stopped, and I got out. The old lady said I was sure to enjoy myself, young people always did, and settled herself back in her corner seat.

I collected my trunk and it was wheeled outside the small station by a porter. I could see no one to meet me at all. It was cold and still raining; and I began to feel very frightened again. The rain dripped off the scalloped edges of the platform roofs and gathered in sullen little puddles on the gravel; the tree trunks looked black and slippery like mackintosh. The porter asked me where I was going. I told him The Village, whereupon he said They thought the train came fifteen minutes later than she do, they'll be along, well miss he'd be leaving me. So there was nothing for it but to give him the sixpence and wait.

They came at last, a boy and a girl, in a pony trap.

'How long have you been waiting?'

32

'Not very long.'

'Mother's fault again. She's hopeless about trains. She simply makes up the time they arrive and it's always wrong. Last week we were half an hour early.'

The boy shouted:

'Joe. I want a hand with this trunk. Here I'll find him.' He disappeared.

The girl smiled encouragingly.

'Get in. It's no drier, but at least there's a seat.' I climbed up clumsily and sat beside her.

'My name's Lucy,' she said. 'What's yours?'

I told her.

'It was jolly nice of you to come. I hate staying with people, don't you?' For a moment I was outfaced.

'I've never done it before, but I thought I would hate it.'

She flicked the whip across the pony's back. 'You won't by tomorrow. Keep still you. We have great fun these holidays. Lots of people. We're having a dance on Christmas Eve. I hope you've got a frock.'

'Yes, I did bring one.'

'Good. How old are you?' I told her. 'I'm just sixteen too. Can you skate?'

My heart sank. 'No. I'm afraid not.'

'Well you needn't. I hate it, it hurts your ankles.' She stretched out a long thin boot. 'But Gerald adores it.'

'Is he your cousin?'

'My brother. I have two sisters and two brothers but the whole place is full of cousins.'

'Is there any ice for skating?'

'Not yet. But Gerald says there will be. He's always right about things he likes. He's awfully good at it. He simply skims about. Lovely to watch.' She turned her thin, pale pink face to me eager and friendly. 'What do *you* like?'

'I don't know yet.'

'Oh well,' she said cheerfully, 'there's lots to do. The great thing is not to mind doing it till you've tried. Here comes Gerald.'

My trunk was hoisted in and we set off; Lucy driving, with Gerald a watchful critic.

'I shall tell mother about that train. She really ought to know better. Can you skate?'

'No,' I said. 'But I'd love to learn.'

Lucy gave me a brilliant smile; I smiled back, and it was delightful.

'Look where you're going, Lucy.'

'Gerald thinks only men can drive and talk. Women are so lucky to be allowed to drive at all that they certainly shouldn't speak or enjoy it. Their poor little minds aren't capable of thinking about two things at once. *Don't* Gerald.' They were laughing, the trap was all over the road, and I felt much happier.

'It's easy,' I thought, 'staying with people is easy;' then thought of the house and unknown family and shivered a little because I was wet.

'Cold?' said Lucy. Large drops of rain slipped down her face and thin arched nose, and watered her silky-gold strands of hair. Her eyes seemed almost transparently wet, so darkly grey, clear and alive.

'Of course she's cold. We're all cold *and* hungry. Hurry up Lucy, think of lunch.'

We trotted through a silent streaming village, into a drive, with an elegant iron gate swung back and embedded in brilliant soft grass; round a gentle curve edged with iron railings, to the sweep before the house: a square cream-coloured house, with large square windows and green shutters; a magnificent cedar tree like a butler, old, indispensable and gloomy; and curls of smoke, the colour of distance, creeping sedately up out of the squat mulberry chimneys.

We walked slowly past the house through an arch into a cobbled courtyard, surrounded by buildings, which smelled of moss and leather, hot wet animals, and a curiously pungent clean smell that I afterwards learned was saddle soap. A white-haired man limped out of a loose box and took the pony's head. He looked very fierce, until I realized that one eye stared out sideways unwinking like a parrot. Gerald helped me out. 'Parker will bring your trunk.'

We walked back through the arch, pushed open the green front door, and were in the large hall. I shall never forget the smell of that house. Logs, lavender and damp, the old scent of a house that has been full of flowers for so many years that the very pollen and flower pots stay behind intangibly enchanting – candles and grapes – weak aged taffeta stretched on the chairs – drops of sherry left in fragile shallow glasses – nectarines and strawberries – the warm earthy confidential odour of enormous books and butterfly smell of the pages, a combination of leather and moth – dense glassy mahogany ripe with polishing and the sun – guns and old coats – smooth dead fur on the glaring sentimental deers' heads – beeswax, brown sugar and smoke – it smelled of everything I first remember seeing there, and I shall never forget it.

We hurried along a passage into the drawing-room. It was very full of people. Lucy took my hand, and led me up to a thin delicate woman who was sitting bolt upright in a tall thin armchair, doing an intricate and incredibly ugly piece of embroidery in a wooden frame stuck with nails and festooned with strands of coloured wool.

'Here she is. This is my mother,' said Lucy. Lucy's mother had a pair of mild blue eyes and a blue-veined hand with rings that dug into my fingers.

'You are Mary's eldest daughter?' she said. As I had never heard my mother called Mary I kept politely silent.

'No, Mother, she came last week.'

'Ah yes. Then *I* know who you are.'

'And you were quite wrong about the train, Mother.'

'Nonsense. Here she is. How could I have been wrong?'

A gong boomed.

'Lunch?' said Lucy's mother. 'Come with me. Wash your hands, people. Mind the jigsaw.'

A boy got up from beside its fragments. 'That is Mary's eldest son,' said Lucy's mother triumphantly, as she rose from her chair, scattering little balls of wool, heavy decorative thimbles, and tiny crumpled white handkerchiefs over the carpet.

We went to lunch, after washing our hands in a flower sink in the passage. We sat at an enormous table with a bowl of Christmas roses. At first, I had a confused impression of boys and girls, with Lucy's mother carving cold mutton neatly and fast at one end, and an oldish man, who came in last with a glass of sherry, at the other. Then I began trying very hard to sort them out; their brown hands, freckles, fair heads, dark eyes. In a moment we seemed to have reached the fruit pie (with too much sugar on it); streaks of clear crimson juice round hectic shining mouths; small hands crushing nutcrackers, the nut escaping with a teasing bounce; chairs scraping back; and older hands crumbling bread in the ensuing peace. The first meal, a ceremony I had been dreading for weeks, was over, and when I counted the meals that remained, as I had so miserably counted them many times before, it was already with an entirely new and welcome regret that they could be so easily numbered.

CHAPTER FIVE

After lunch I was taken to my bedroom, which was small, square, and white, with dark wood and a gorgeous carpet, a Lord Mayorish carpet, rich, and somehow vulgar. There was a second door in one corner.

Out of the window I could see a wide gravel path, flower beds, a long slanting lawn drifting into distant long grass down the slope to a lazy winding river, with reeds, and moorhens in an ungraceful hurry. Rising beyond the river were a field or park, picked out with big casual trees; and a copse at the top of a gentle crest, held together, it seemed, by railings, like an elastic band round a bunch of twigs. Above this a grey sky was framed on either side by scarce bony trees, which were distorted high up, with dense dark jagged nests.

'Rooks,' said Lucy behind me.

'How did you know I was looking?'

'I didn't. But you would have asked me. People always ask what they are. Come out. You'd better get some thicker shoes.'

'I'd better unpack.'

'Nanny'll do it. Just get your boots out.' We struggled over the trunk.

'Are you awfully rich?' I asked as it opened.

'Good heavens, I don't know. Papa wouldn't tell me, because he won't give me a new saddle unless it's a side saddle. I would like to ride like a boy, but it's not delicate. Life for women is terribly unfair, you know.' She sat on the floor holding her knees, earnestly sad.

'Is that what it is?'

'How do you mean?'

'Well, things haven't felt right to me for some time now. Years really,' I added, feeling old and extravagant about

37

my life. 'But I didn't think of it being worse for women.'

'Of course it is!' cried Lucy energetically. 'Who gets the best ponies? The boys. Or they get a horse and we have to rattle about on little grass-fed creatures with no wind. If Papa has an expedition and only a few may go, it's always the boys. They're always allowed to learn things first. Fishing and driving; and they shoot, but Papa says I may not. And their clothes are so much more suitable. When I was fourteen I cut off my hair and there was a fearful row . . .'

'Right off?'

'Up to here,' she placed her fingers just below her ears. 'It was very uneven. I did it with Nanny's cutting-out scissors. But of course I had to grow it again. And everyone laughed. Except Gerald. He thought I looked jolly fine.'

All my clothes and possessions seemed strange and far away; belonging to my home and London, and even to the train; but not to me and this house. Boots at the bottom, of course. I plunged.

'And chocolate pudding,' burst Lucy. 'They always get second helpings of that. Girls aren't supposed to mind about food. Except fruit. It's all right to like fruit. Sometimes I can hardly bear it. Still, we do go to bed at the same time. And Gerald says I have beautiful hands. He'd trust me with his own horse, he says.'

'Has he got one?'

'Not yet. But he would. Look, I'll get Nanny to come and do your clothes.'

Lucy was amazing, I thought. She seemed to have done so many things and yet she was no older than I. Perhaps it was living in the country. She came back with Nanny, who shook hands with me and called me Miss.

'We're going for a walk, Nanny.'

'Change your shoes, then.'

'They're changed. I didn't change them for lunch.'

'All that mud over the carpet. How many times have I told you . . .'

'Hundreds of times, Nanny. I forgot. She still thinks I'm seven.'

'Well, you behave like seven. You're the worst of the lot,' said Nanny adoringly.

'I'll change them for tea like anything. I'm afraid we've rumpled the trunk. Come on,' she added to me.

'Let her get her coat on. Whatever will the poor young lady think?'

'Oh, is that your frock? How lovely!'

'Leave go of it, Miss Lucy. Run and get your jacket. Be quick now. You'll have to be back before tea because I've that blouse to try on.'

'Nanny, you simply ruin my life.'

'Anyone would think I was cruel to her.' Lucy had gone for the jacket. 'I've put your stockings in the drawer.'

'Nanny, could I wash?' Her eye, which had looked at Lucy with such loving despair and pride, and at me so calmly shrewd and appraising as if she could assess my manners at meals by the way I parted my hair and tied my laces, was instantly active and commanding. I could see her managing all the little crises of countless children with tremendous certainty and devotion, keeping life easy and natural and safe, always watching, now that they were grown up, for the rare casual moments when they might need her a little. I began to realize Lucy and the house, and understand the security and affection which shot through the air like light.

'Of course, Miss, I'll take you. Miss Lucy should have thought. There you are. The other's that little door on the right,' and she padded tactfully away.

We went downstairs.

'I know,' said Lucy. 'We'll take Elspeth.' She opened a door and we entered a library with enormous leather chairs.

'Elspeth.' No sound. '*Elspeth*.' There was a faint scuffle. We crossed the room and by the window in one of the enormous chairs was a girl crumpled up and weighed down by a great book with coloured plates. She shook her hair back.

'Elspeth. You are hiding. Come out. Leave your old caterpillars.'

'Oh, don't.'

'Why?'

'Don't tell them about there being caterpillars. They think it's just butterflies. They say caterpillars aren't nice for girls.'

'Oh, they won't know. Come out, we're going to the wood.'

'I'd rather stay.'

'You can't read all day. We might build a house. They'll find you here and send you out anyway, so you'd much better come with us.'

'Oh all right.' She got up and the book slid to the floor with a fat, heavy bang. 'Oh!'

'You haven't hurt it.'

'I have! Oh I have. There's a page crumpled.' Her eyes filled with tears and spurted out.

'Don't cry on the leather anyway. Remember what happened to Gerald's stamp album. The marks all went puffy and dull.'

'Put it away for me. I can't stop.' Lucy put it away.

'Look here,' she said severely. 'You can easily stop. I've smoothed the page.' She went close to Elspeth. 'You look *stupid*. Your face will go puffy and dull like leather.'

Elspeth took the antimacassar off the back of the chair and wiped her face. 'I've stopped,' she said calmly.

'Well get your coat and hurry up.' Elspeth went.

'Now we'll *have* to build a house. She loves them,' said Lucy.

'What kind of a house?' It sounded rather childish. I didn't think I'd enjoy it much.

'Oh, a log house. You'll see.'

Elspeth came back and we set off. It had stopped raining; there was a grey stillness, and my nose felt cold immediately.

Elspeth must have been about fourteen, although her face was older. She was very bony, with thin clear skin stretched over the bones, making her look taut and breakable. She walked beside us with a little hop without speaking except when Lucy asked her a question to which she replied 'No', very firmly, thereby shattering any further advances. But her silence was not so much unfriendly as absorbed, so that it didn't spoil anything.

When we left the lawn for the long grass, little silver drops leapt from each blade as our shoes shuffled through. The river was very still as though the last moorhen hurrying across had cleared the scene for some exciting action. I could hear the rooks now, fluttering about their messy nests. We turned left, and walked under their trees. There was a damp velvety path covered with leaves, either slimy and curled as though each had died in a separate little agony; or older and rotted to delicate silvery skeletons. The path was edged with ragged rhododendra, massed, and hiding the sudden rustle of some bird. We were in single file, Lucy, and me, and Elspeth hopping very slowly behind. We came to a wooden bridge over the river, mossy and overgrown; there were brown lily leaves in the water, and the noisy uneven drip from the trees disturbed the grey of the river. The other side of the bridge we were in grass again.

'Where are the others?'

'Gone to fetch Deb,' said Lucy.

'Who is Deb?'

'My sister. She's been staying with cousins. She's very beautiful.'

'Have they all gone to fetch her?'

'Only Gerald and Tom. And Elinor. The others are in the house. Aunt Edith has a cold and my mother doesn't go out much in winter. Papa will be riding. He likes best to ride by himself. Do you ride? Oh I suppose you don't. What do you *do* in London?'

'Not very much.'

'Your papa is a painter, isn't he?'

'He writes music.'

'All the time?'

'No. Every now and then. He teaches it, too.'

'You cannot teach people to write music, can you?'

'No,' said Elspeth.

'Elspeth, you don't know anything about it.'

'I do. A girl at school wrote a song. It just came. No one taught her.

'She wasn't a proper writer. One song!' said Lucy scornfully.

'He doesn't teach people to write it. He teaches people to play it,' I said.

'Can you teach people to write it though?'

'I don't know,' I said truthfully. I felt embarrassed. Of course I should have known.

'You can't teach people anything that matters,' said Elspeth surprisingly.

'Of course you can, Elspeth.' Lucy was very shocked. 'Books and things. People always learn like that. Think of schools. You ought to know that. You're always reading.'

'It saves a certain amount of time. I couldn't get enough species together in my head unless there were books.'

'She's showing off. You read lots of fairy tales.'

'I don't.'

'You do.'

'I hardly ever read them. I read books out of the library.'

'Don't be silly. It doesn't matter what you read anyway.'

'It does matter what I read.'

'The trouble with you is,' said Lucy very gravely, 'that you take yourself far too seriously for your age. You simply can't go about being so old *and* crying. Do *you* read a lot?'

'Well, a bit,' I said cautiously.

'You don't read just to talk about reading anyway. I hardly ever read. It depends whether you need it. I like moving about.'

We were quite close to the wood which was striped with different trees; dark, aloof and inviting.

'I never like starting a wood,' said Elspeth.

There was a small iron gate. We went in. It did feel rather like going into a place that easily might belong to someone who resented our feet and our voices. A blackbird flew low, chattering dramatically.

'Where are we going?'

'To the middle,' said Lucy. 'There's a clearing with a bank.'

I looked up at the sky streaked with branches and suddenly thought of Michael and his kite. He would like Elspeth and scorn Lucy, and he was the kind of awful person whom it was difficult not to believe, so perhaps it was a good thing he wasn't there.

'Is Rupert coming?' asked Elspeth.

'He's coming for the dance. Just for Christmas; otherwise he has to work.'

'Who is Rupert?'

'Rupert Laing. His father was at school with Papa. He always comes in the holidays.'

'He sounds mysterious and rich.'

'Why?'

I didn't know why I'd said that. How silly. How very very silly.

'How odd. He is mysterious. I don't think he's rich. You'll see. He looks into the back of you, and he makes very silly jokes.'

There was a silence. Rupert was finished. To me he was just an appalling embarrassment and Lucy and Elspeth had explored his character and whereabouts sufficiently to leave him alone.

'Here we are,' said Lucy.

It was a clearing, a hollow, filled with Spanish chestnut suckers, reddish brown, with shining sharp bumps. We sat down on the rubble of leaves and moss.

'Now,' said Elspeth.

'All right,' said Lucy. 'But you can't expect a house every time you go for a walk.'

Elspeth rolled on the ground clutching her knees; then leaped up and walked slowly, darting down for a silvery stick. One was too long and she bit it. It snapped in half, and she bit it again in a rage and stamped it into the leaves.

'It wouldn't have been strong enough,' said Lucy. 'I'll help.' And she, too, joined in the collecting. I sat, feeling miserable and stupid. I had no idea what they were doing.

'We collect sticks,' said Lucy.

'We collect special *useful* sticks,' said Elspeth, pouncing in time to her words. I smiled foolishly and sat still. They put eight sticks upright and firm in the ground, two and two in a square. Then they laid thinner sticks in between to make

43

walls, which crept up slowly with uneven ends. I stared at the ground, a tear dropped on to a leaf, tap, and it overbalanced; oh horror, I was going to cry, and for no reason I filled my hands with earth and squeezed, ground the tears out of my eyes; tap, tap, tap, they seemed endless. It was terrible to be sixteen and cry in a wood.

'You're crying,' said Lucy, concerned, and they both came and stood in front of me looking down. 'What's the matter?'

I looked up and snatched bravely. 'I'm a bit homesick, that's all.'

'Oh,' said Lucy. She squatted. 'Bad luck. You needn't be. Have you got a handkerchief?'

'Yes.' Really, I couldn't use other people's handkerchiefs. Elspeth stared. I blew my nose.

'Poor you,' said Lucy. 'Do you want to go home?'

'Only a bit.' I didn't at all, but once you cried you had to sound brave about it.

'Bad luck,' said Lucy again, very helpless. 'Would you like to go back to tea?'

'You'd better finish your house first. I'm all right.'

'Will you help us then?'

'You'll have to show me what to do,' I said patronizingly.

'I'm never homesick,' said Elspeth.

'You don't get the chance to be,' said Lucy fiercely.

I got up.

'Promise you won't tell the others I cried.'

'I promise,' said Lucy. 'Go on, Elspeth.'

'Honour bright,' said Elspeth carelessly, and turned away.

It was a beautiful house. The walls were about a foot high, with a gap in one wall for a door. There was the intricate job of constructing a flat roof which did not imperil the shaky structure. We laid slender strips across, then bark and moss on top of them. Elspeth wanted leaves; but they would not lie flat, and snapped and crumbled maliciously weak, so we gave them up, and between the twigs crammed smoky dry moss in wedges. We scraped the ground flat round the house and Elspeth started to make a fence; but got bored, and found a slug. It was under a bit of loose bark, and was grey and oily, with a brilliant orange front. 'If I look at it long I shall be sick.'

'Don't be silly, Elspeth. Don't look at it.'

'It's moving,' said Elspeth, horrified.

'I can't think why you mind them if you like caterpillars.'

'Caterpillars are dry.' She loved watching it really. 'Anyway, it's such a slimy shape.'

'Better kill it,' said Lucy.

'No, don't kill it. It's a horrible poor thing.'

'They eat the vegetables.'

'It couldn't walk as far as the vegetables. Ugh, it doesn't walk. It crawls. It sort of slimes along. Lucy, there are probably lots of them. I may have sat on one. Have I, Lucy?'

'Oh, my goodness! An enormous one!' Lucy examined her skirt in mock horror, then turned her round.

'Don't cry, baby, of course you haven't. Can't you take a joke?'

'Can't always risk a joke.'

'The house is finished,' I said. I had been patting and poking the roof. It was beautiful, and it looked so useful and necessary that I wanted to have it and take it away. It was finished and we stood round it. Even Lucy was touched by its complete sweetness.

'The best we've ever made,' said Elspeth.

They had done it before. It was so new to me that I couldn't bear to think of that. I suggested we go, and we left the house to its first night's adventure.

We were through the gate again, on the grass, staring at the misty dusk ahead and the little orange sparks glowing from the house down the slope.

'Let's run,' said Elspeth.

We took hands and ran down the slope; past when we were breathless, until our running became almost frightening, although enjoyable because we were together. The ground was uneven, and I watched it (I was not as used as the others to running on a field). When I looked up, the bony trees were high above us; the river gleamed like a wide snake asleep; the windows were paler gold broken by their frames; and the black creeper clinging to the house made it seem a wonderful place to receive us for the end of the day. We were panting, Elspeth had not run all the leaves out of her hair, and the lights shone in our eyes.

Upstairs, Lucy showed me her room. There were two beds and a coat lay at the end of one.

'Deb's back,' said Lucy joyfully.

I did not see Deb until tea. She was beautiful, and it was obvious that they all adored her. She sat between Gerald and her mother, and I saw him turn the plate round so that the cake with the large cherry was nearest her. She took it so easily that I knew she had always had the cherries. Elspeth told her about the house; Elspeth's father about a horse; and she turned from one to another radiant; recounting her visit with a kind of brilliant modesty, infecting us with her success and happiness, and enriching all their tales with her attention and concern so that one watched her, wholly enchanted. She was quite beautiful; triangular eyes with flecks of green, shining dark hair, a thin pointed mouth, pointed eyebrows to match, and a skin so milky pale that if you were to touch it it would hardly be there. I could not take my eyes off her. I sat and watched her neck twisting (she wore a tight gold chain round the hight collar of her blouse), and neat head above it. I sat and watched until my fingers were cramped in the handle of my tea-cup and Lucy leaned forward and said *'Isn't* she lovely!' in a warm rush. Everyone laughed. Her mother said 'Nonsense.' I flushed. Deb sat quite still, half smiling and not at all shy.

After tea, we all went to the morning-room which everyone left in a joyful state of confusion. The jigsaw was still on the floor, half completed; it was very big, and Toby, the fat little boy, would allow no one to touch it but himself. He was very slow and immersed in fitting pink roses all over a thatched cottage. When Lucy found the door, he growled and crossed the room with his hands in his pockets in a solemn rage, and one tuft of hair sticking straight up from the crown of his head.

Lucy's mother said, 'Don't dear,' calmly. She was embroidering a hideous peacock with exquisite deliberation; admiring Elspeth's butterfly transfers, crooked and smeared in a large scrap book; reminding Gerald and Lucy about the names of ponies (they were absorbed with an old collection of plaited horses' hair kept, with labels attached, in a weak cardboard box); advising Deb over colours for her cross stitch, who, I noticed, listened charmingly and never took the advice; hearing Elinor's poem that she was learning, and being quite unruffled when the recital always stuck in the same place; then talking to me, asking me about my mother, and my sister and brothers, what I did, and which I liked best, town or country; making everything I'd done seem important and interesting, so that I could not imagine why it had all seemed empty before.

'I think it is very brave of you to come,' she said. 'Come along, darling, finish the roses.' Toby came and smiled a beautiful slow smile, shook himself like a puppy, and fell on the floor beside his great work. 'He does it over and over again. No, darling, a *host* of golden daffodils. Start again to yourself. And are your brothers all at the same school? That must be nice. Punch he was called, Lucy dear. The funny pink pony with a brindled tail who used to flybuck.'

'Strawberry roan,' they chanted, and Gerald wrote another little ticket.

'All right, Toby, I won't do it but you should try and finish the edges first. And do you play the piano? You must play to us some time. Not today; wait until there are a lot of us and then we can dance. We all want to hear you. Well, darling, call it a Tortoiseshell, and do another with more water for a Painted Lady. Will you ring the bell, dear? I want to speak about Aunt Edith's sarsaparilla. No, Toby, that bit is lost. Blue, Deb, like the other side; or red like the border; you'll find them both in my Indian Bag.' Deb abstracted a thread of green with a charming smile.

Feeling completely part of the great warm untidy room I asked if after all I might play the piano. Of course I might. I played a rather scratchy piece of Scarlatti, and remember feeling faintly shocked when no one paid the slightest atten-

47

tion. Elspeth had just upset her transfer water and was mopping it up with a skein of pale blue wool, and Elinor was half-way through the daffodils, still holding her breath for the last verse. However, I found it much nicer from the playing point of view; it was much more enjoyable to approve and criticize oneself, to play back, as it were, only to one's own ears. I stopped after a bit. There was a great dark picture above my head, with the canvas gleaming like oily water at night. It was of a man, surly with health, in a pink coat, holding a riding crop with both hands and leaning forward a little. He looked irritable and impatient, as though sitting anywhere but on a horse was a woman's job; and now he was dead, I felt he was very dead, and condemned to listen to any music I cared to make, with only the welter of mainly feminine ploys beyond as relief. A maid came and drew the curtains all round the bay window and at my side by the piano. She moved on tip-toe and answered Lucy's mother about sarsaparilla with a kind of gasping lightness as though it were only respectful to use the very edge of herself, her toes and fingers and the front of her throat. She was very neat and pretty.

Deb rose from her work and strolled over to me. 'Come and change for dinner with me,' she said. She was leaning over the piano, provocative and friendly, with a 'come and see what I've got' look.

Lucy heard.

'The bell hasn't gone,' she said. Their mother laughed.

'You know how Deb loves to potter. Run along.'

As if Deb would run. No, she would glide unhurried, preferably, I thought, down smooth paths banked by pinks and delphinia, or glassy floors flocked with people less beautiful than she making a wide lane for her, she accepting it. We left together, with a little laughing demur at the door which ended in my holding it for her and turning the glass knob carefully, shutting us out together. Half-way down the passage she stopped and dabbled her fingers in a large Chinese bowl.

'Lavender,' she said stretching out her fingers to me. I

copied her. We went straight to the room with the two beds.

'I have to share it with Lucy. Sit down, I'll show you my jewellery. Wait, I'll shut the door.'

She sped to it. I sat and watched the room in comfort. Lucy slept there, but I could now see that it was certainly not shared; it was Deb's room. The pictures, the large pink roses flopping over the white chintz curtains; the dressing-table delicately shrouded in muslin with petulant frills, topped by a slender elegant rosewood mirror; the fat white beds, and heavy jug and basin with kingfishers on it; all assumed a pretty significance, unique and personal to Deb; Deb's possessions, Deb's elegance, and her rich careless charm. She was kneeling by a little cabinet with two doors which swung back to disclose a pile of shallow drawers of blushing yellow wood. There were eleven, and I knew the first six were hers.

'Which belong to Lucy?'

'Those at the bottom. I have one extra.' And she smiled very sweetly.

They were stiff to pull and the knobs were too dainty for use. I was very pleased at being right about the drawers. It is a wonderful feeling to guess anything about a person and hear aloud that you were right. It made me feel stronger with Deb. Suddenly the drawer flew open almost too far so that it swayed and disclosed rows of pink and yellow shells neatly placed on flat cotton wool.

'Wrong drawer,' said Deb crossly.

The jewel drawer slid open with ease; she dropped down to it and then, straightening casually, flung a handful of jewels in my lap, so suddenly that they weighed my skirt down between my knees. She rose, leaving the drawer bare and gaping like someone who has had a great surprise.

'Look at them,' she said impatiently, seeing me. 'I'm going to change my dress.' She opened her wardrobe, and ran her hands through her frocks in a nervous and affected manner.

There were a pearl brooch shaped in a crescent; a turquoise heart; a locket on a golden chain. There were a string of corals; a topaz brooch with elaborate gold work round it; a large and beautiful ring with garnets and pearls and a

49

minute turquoise in the middle; a golden cross on another chain; and a thin wavering bracelet with moonstones. There was also a brooch with a miniature of a lady, placid and fragile, with grey powdered hair, a fresh complexion, a tiny little dark red mouth, and pale blue eyes which looked out with an air of sprightly indifference.

'I don't like that one,' said Deb. 'An aunt left it to me. It's a clumsy old thing. I don't take it away when I stay in houses. Do you enjoy paying visits?'

'This is the first I've ever paid.'

'Well, are you enjoying it? I do. I enjoy *all* the times I stay away. More and more I enjoy it,' with a voluptuous little sigh.

'Do you always go by yourself?'

'Usually. Do you? Are you enjoying yourself now?'

'Oh yes. Much more than I thought.'

That pleased her, and she began unpinning her hair as though it were a direct reward.

'You seem to have had a lovely time,' I said.

She paused, her face full of a thousand unknown moments, smiled a little, shook herself, and turned to receive my curiosity.

'There was a dance,' she said. I did not perceive the significance of this remark, but I gave an understanding smile of encouragement.

'Do you dance much in London?' she asked abruptly.

'No, not much.' I felt that I could hardly afford never to have danced at all.

'Do you know why I am unpinning my hair?' I shook my head. 'In a minute I shall tell you. There.' And suddenly there it was; pouring down her back; flocked and tumbling, swinging round each shoulder; clinging to her head but escaping in tendrils round her ears. She seized a white brush.

'Now,' she said. 'I'll tell you. If you are interested. You are interested, aren't you?' with a questioning dart at me.

'Yes,' I said. 'Oh yes, I am.' She laughed; of course she knew I was. 'Will there be time?'

'We can have more talks,' she said, settling comfortably

down to her monologue. 'Something very exciting has just happened to me. We have always lived here and as you can see nothing would be likely to happen here that could afford one any real amusement. That is why I have always longed to go away and one is only allowed to do so in order to pay visits. And even then ... but this time ...' She broke off holding the brush against her head.

'You must listen and not watch me. But – am I beautiful? I don't want you to say so unless you think I am. *Am* I?' She leaned forward a little. She was sitting on the floor holding her knees, her face tilted towards me. I complied. There was such compelling charm, such charming desire, that I had no alternative, although I was embarrassed into inadequacy. She seemed satisfied, however, and leaned back with a little sigh.

'You don't know how important it is for me yet. It all happened in this last fortnight. I was staying with cousins. Very distant cousins of Papa's. We had an awfully jolly time.' She paused again, forcing me to an unbearable impatience. She had the quality of making one feel that anything she said was almost unbearably interesting. 'We rode a great deal. I don't know why it was so pleasant. New people, I suppose. And it was a lovely house. I had met Roland before but we hadn't noticed each other. It is extraordinary how one does not realize at once about the most important person in one's life. Everyone adores him; but I – this is the point, and a very great secret, only I must tell someone – I love him. I told him.'

'Was he pleased?'

She opened her lovely eyes, incredulously.

'Of course. We both love each other. I shall marry him, but my parents don't know yet. We aren't going to tell them. Roland agrees that there should be some secrecy about anyone's love. Don't you think so?'

'I don't know much about it.'

'I'll tell you. We decided at the dance. Before, I hadn't been so sure that Roland really loved me. But half-way through a dance he suddenly waltzed me away and into the hall, threw a man's coat round my shoulders and we stole out through a door in the passage, and down a path with a high hedge. I was shivering, but I wasn't cold. Then he took my face and kissed me. I wasn't frightened at all. I watched the leaves black against the moon. I put my arms round him and then there was a cloud across the moon and I couldn't watch the leaves. He's wonderful. He said that he loved me and asked me to marry him. He is sure our families would approve, we are such very distant cousins, and I think so, too, although of course they will say we are too young. Isn't it extraordinary that they can say that when they haven't the faintest notion how much we love each other? Roland has got to get settled in his job.'

'What does he do?'

'He works in the City. He hates it, and as soon as he has thought of something else he's going to do it, if it doesn't make our future uncertain. But I shouldn't mind what he did as long as I could be with him. Do you know he tried to pull down my hair? Isn't that odd? He said it would seem more possible, more real to him, if he saw my hair down, I should seem to belong to him more. That reminds me. Look.'

She had a pair of golden scissors, shaped in some curious way like a stork. I can only remember the wings and neck impossibly graceful and twisted.

'Cut some off for me. He wants it. I can't cut it myself. I can't cut hair.'

I was terrified.

'I've never cut hair. Couldn't you get Nanny to do it?'

'She'd want to know why. What are you thinking of? This is a secret.'

I took the scissors.

'Why does he want it?'

'To keep, of course. People always do that. Didn't you know?'

'Have you some of his hair?'

'No. No, I haven't. Roland's hair isn't the kind one keeps.

It's too thin – fine,' she added. And then honesty got the better of her and she said, 'Besides it isn't a *very* interesting colour. *Please* cut it for me.'

'How much do I cut?' I still felt nervous.

Deb seemed nonplussed. 'I don't know. I've never actually done this before. How much do you think he would like?'

'All of it, I should say. Growing.' I was holding a lock, feeling rather proud to be with her.

'Silly thing,' she laughed, delighted. 'Cut what you like.' I grasped the lock firmly and hacked away, the little scissors protesting, squeaking weakly until they collapsed on air with a final gasp.

'There.' I held it up.

'Yes.' She seemed doubtful. 'It's left a funny end and I don't know whether he'll want quite so much. Still it will be a surprise.' She folded it away in crumpled tissue paper and pushed it into one of the shallow drawers. 'Good. I knew you'd help me.' A bell rang. 'Time to dress.'

'What shall I wear?' I had never changed for dinner in my life, and I suddenly felt rather tired, and afraid of new things.

'Oh, a frock. I shall wear this.' She pulled out a mass of dull green silk. 'See you at dinner.'

In my room, I wrenched off my clothes. My hands were cold and I began to worry about the way to the dining-room and always being called Mary, and Nanny noticing my hair, newly washed and utterly out of control. There was a gleaming brass jug standing in my basin, the steam very white and noticeable in the cold room. Better warm my hands. The jug was very heavy and I slopped some water on the marble washstand and nearly chipped the basin.

I washed my face and neck and hands, using an unyielding new cake of soap, rubbed myself dry, first with a rough scratching bath towel, and finally with a fragile slip of linen with embroidered initials that became bumpy as the cloth grew wet. I stepped into the red frock with black braid. I should be late, and they would all have gathered in the drawing-room, or worse still, be sitting in their places at table, all waiting for me to come into the room. Thank goodness Nanny was coming; I could never have managed all the buttons up the back. I pulled my hair down, and was breaking the teeth of my comb when Nanny came in. She started by fastening my buttons with huge cold fingers and ended by doing my hair with an impeccable parting and a bun so tight that the hairs were strained and tweaking behind my ears. She noticed that I had a hole in one of my stockings, so I changed them. My shoes were rather tight and slippery. Nanny cleaned my brush with the comb and clicked her tongue over the broken teeth, but I was still immeasurably grateful to her. She was a perfect woman. She sent me down tidy and assured and luxurious. She would draw the stocking together, and I need have no fears about being late. I think she must have been understanding enough to have encompassed the world she served, Deb and Lucy's world, and that house and their friends, and wise enough never to venture further so that she always remained mistress of every situation she encountered. Dressing for dinner held the same importance for her as it did for me. She was infinitely kind.

Dinner was long and gay, ending with oranges and nuts and a sip of port because I had never tasted it before. It burned my tongue, but it was a beautiful colour. Deb smiled at me, sweetly conspiratorial. I told Gerald about Michael although he wasn't very interested except in the expelling part. He told me much more about his school than my brothers had ever vouchsafed about theirs. He was very anxious to assure me of the narrowness of his own escape from expulsion, and my interest and surprise must have pleased him, as he grew bright red and very friendly.

After dinner we played charades. I'd played them before, but this was different. I was picked by Gerald to act. We jostled out into the hall, which was flickering with a dying fire; and everyone talked simultaneously with choleric speed, decrying and applauding each other's efforts without apparently interrupting their own flow of ideas; collecting walking sticks, summer hats, overcoats, and Nanny's glasses the while. I could think of nothing, my self-conscious apprehension rose in my throat, and my heart bumped against my new red dress as I took refuge in weak general approval.

It was not so terrible. I was to be a shop assistant, which entailed an apron, secured from a maid who giggled and resisted at first, investing our designs with a delicious mixture of wickedness and importance. I was to arrange the hats on the piano, and Gerald was to bring Deb, his wife, to choose one; and at one point I must implore her to observe the back, so they told me again and again. Gerald went to clear the scene, and we heard the impatience of our audience through the door. He came back. Deb was not ready, but finally floated down the stairs in a long white fringed shawl with her hair miraculously different. I was pushed forward. Nervously, I arranged the hats and waited. Nothing happened, and I was deeply conscious that my audience now knew as much of the situation as I did. In a minute I should forget the bit about the back of Deb's head. I surveyed the hats. 'That looks stylish,' I said aloud, and felt the quickening of attention in the room. Emboldened, I selected an old straw hat with artificial roses pinched together, and tried it on. At that moment Gerald and Deb came in and from then on the whole charade went with a swing. The audience guessed it, of course, but nobody cared as long as enough people dressed up, and the waits between the scenes were not interminable.

We went to bed at eleven o'clock, general good-nights being exchanged in the drawing-room. Lucy took me up to my room and left me tired and happy. I had just undressed when there was a tap on my door.

'Oh,' she said. 'About the wood. I mean what you said in it. Of course I haven't told anyone, but are you all right now?'

'Yes, quite all right, thank you.'

'I just wanted to know.' We were both rather embarrassed.

'Well, good, I just wanted to know,' she repeated, and then

clumsily, she kissed me, my ear and a good deal of hair.

'Good night,' she said, and smiled, brightly sweet.

'Good night,' I replied.

Having fumbled with the gas lamp, which shot up like a train coming towards me, then subsided, I felt my way into bed.

The sheets were cold and different; there was a knife edge of air cutting through the crack of window and it was very silent. Lying there, I reviewed the day which had begun with getting up, my trunk bumping corners down the stairs, and a choking tasteless breakfast (travellers' pride, someone had said). My father's rough blue cheek; the carriages upholstered like short thick grass; my mouth sore from the pear drop; rain; cows; people, black purposeless specks since I never saw them achieve their destinations; the gate open, the door shut, the hedge reached; arriving, waiting for the trap; cold, damp and apprehension, Lucy, Gerald, the whip making a greasy line on the pony's heavy coat, Lucy's smile, laughing; then the house, and the parrot's eye of the groom. Lucy's mother; the smell, oh yes the smell; lunch, a gleaming table and Deb; Nanny, and the darling little house. I dwelled on that until it became almost animate. I had enjoyed it so much. Perhaps we should go and see if it were still there; whether it had stood the weather and the night and the silence – of course it would be noisy in a wood I supposed, rather frightening. I remembered running in the dusk, and the sparks of windows, orange, like the slug. Deb, and her cherries at tea, what a secret I knew, all about an engagement; her hair, her jewels. There must be stars in the sky, should I look at them? I remembered the high hedge and the moon. What extraordinary things happened to other people!

Still, I notice them, I notice a good deal more than some people, and something exciting must happen to me. Lucy kissed me, she must like me. I love it: I want this time to last. I don't care if nothing else happens; I'll have this as my loveliest time. Really, it's only a beginning, I'm sixteen. I want everything, every single thing.

In the dark, almost asleep, I embraced the wonderfully welcome unknown; slept, hugging every change, and all the time I had, with this one lovely day, slipping out of my body into my mind.

CHAPTER SIX

That was the beginning of the best Christmas that I remember. I think one of the most delightful aspects of the house was that it was made up of fascinating ceremonies and expeditions. They made every day and moment taut with excitement or sprawling with pleasure: the house accepted me, and the people unfolded like tulips.

The mornings were exquisite: beginning with pure white mist on the ground, which had been secretly inlaid with sparkling hard frost, glittering and twinkling like stars in a morning sky, as the palely elegant sun rose and devoured the drops, broke the ice-like paper on the river, and touched the copse to red with its spidery rays. Porridge poured down our throats like molten lead, heating us for the day. Other people's breakfasts seem so infinitely richer than one's own; even their marmalade seems rarer, and the toast is a different shape. Then there were things like honey and mushrooms and pears that I had never before eaten for breakfast. And what were we going to do today? Lucy's mother always asked.

'Picnic.'

'Silly, far too cold.'

'I'm going to ride. Gerald, shall you ride?'

'I don't know. Where's this ice?'

'Papa, who is to have Tufty?'

'Someone has to get holly for the church.'

'It's not a good year for holly.'

Elspeth opened her eyes wide. 'It's an excellent year for holly.'

Well *you* find it. *You* find enough for the pulpit and all the windows.'

'Papa, who is to have Tufty? Gerald had him last time.'

'Elinor, run up and ask Aunt Edith whether she'd like half a pear. Wait a minute, take it.'

'Who's going to the village?'

'The vicarage children are pining to play French and English.'

'*Papa*. Please may I ride Tufty? In a snaffle. I won't hurt his mouth. May I? Papa, please.'

'I'll take you.'

'Oh!' Lucy was delighted.

'And what's Toby going to do?'

'Balloons,' he answered, and plunged into his milk.

'What about the vicarage children?'

'Gerald can ride Golden Plume.'

'Oh!' Lucy was rather dashed. 'Gerald, you lucky thing. May I tomorrow?'

'You're having Tufty . . . When creeping murmur and the something dark. Seven letters.'

Lucy's mother paused. 'Whispering. No. I don't know, dear. I never can do the Double Acrostic. It's a quotation . . . Now,' she summed us all up. 'Gerald and Lucy are riding. Gerald, run and tell Parker. Elspeth's going to get holly, and you're all going to play French and English with the vicarage children before tea. I can't help it, my dears, think of their poor mother. Pouring, darling, pouring dark.' And so on.

I spent the day with several of them. I watched Lucy go off for her ride, radiant, on a wicked black pony who sidled about like a crab with a grin; and then collected holly with Elspeth, who talked much more when one was alone with her. Climbing a gate she stood on the top bar, apparently quite comfortable, and slashed at the holly, throwing down branches to me.

'What are you going to do when you're grown up?' was her opening gambit.

'I don't know.'

'Don't know! You'll have to think soon, won't you? You're nearly grown up now.'

'Yes.' I must think I supposed. 'What are *you* going to do?'

'I shall keep a small *zoo*,' she said stretching out for a

branch, 'and – hold my legs, will you? – I shall write a great many books. They will be about different things.'

'What sort of things?'

'Mostly about people. I want to find out where they start being different. Now you' – she sat down on the gate swinging her legs – 'now you're quite different from Lucy. And Gerald and Lucy are more alike than any of us. And I'm different again.'

'What about Elinor?'

'She's a wishy-washy little thing,' she said impatiently. Elinor was far older than Elspeth, at least fifteen, so I was impressed. 'She is so careful to be the same as other people. She can't think beyond her school. And she does her Holiday Task. Poetry.'

'Perhaps she likes poetry.'

'She doesn't know anything about it. It's the Task. In the summer holidays it was painting blackberries. Well, she did it. So that they'll be pleased with her at school. She just wants to be a mother and have babies.' This seemed to me a lot to want, but Elspeth was so scornful that I didn't dare say so. 'And if you ask her who she wants to marry, she doesn't say a pirate or a lord or anything interesting like that, she simply says a nice man. Well, I *ask* you. She says she wants to live in London because they have nice clothes. I said, now that *you*'ve come she can see there's nothing in that, is there? You don't have specially nice clothes. I mean, they're all right, but not feathers and things.'

'You could have feathers if you wanted them. You don't like Elinor.'

'Not much, I like older people. I like people to be ahead of me.'

'What about Deb?'

'Deb.' Elspeth considered her. 'Well, she's different. I mean you can't decide about Deb. Because the moment you start, you think, well, she's beautiful, so it means you can't count the bad things she does much, and the good things seem better. Deb wants what she thinks is everything, but she can't see very far. So really they're fairly dull things and she'll get them, I should think. Now you'd want far harder things.'

'What?'

She considered me wisely, with her head a little on one side.

'I don't *know* you.'

'Do you like me?'

'I think so, you're rather pretty. Good heavens, I didn't mean to embarrass you.'

'It's all right,' I mumbled, feeling a fool. It had been such a very stupid question. No one had ever said anything like that. 'You're cold,' Michael had said, and now, 'You're pretty, rather pretty.' Some awful fascination led me on. I gripped the gate.

'Elspeth, in what way am I pretty?' It must be an important thing to know, because Deb had minded so much. 'It's not as silly as it sounds. At least, I've never thought about it before, but it seems suddenly to matter. I don't know many people. So I haven't asked anyone else. I don't do things very well. I want to start, and if I were pretty – rather pretty – it ought to help, oughtn't it? I mean a person should have something interesting or nice about them. I play the piano a bit, but not well enough to count. I seem to have so much *less* than other people. It's an awful feeling, because you have it by yourself just as much as with other people. So in what way would you say I was pretty?' I stopped. Everything I had said sounded inexpressibly foolish.

Elspeth regarded me a moment in silence. Then in a clear voice with a hint of scorn in it she said, 'You're really worrying about whether you'll get married. *I* don't know whether you will. It seems such a queer thing to worry about. But I've noticed that quite sensible girls do. Boys don't. It just happens to them.'

'I don't think I am.'

'Well then you're worrying about whether people will like you. That's silly too. You shouldn't mind so much. *Deb* doesn't.'

I was stung. 'She does. She minds very much.'

Elspeth looked at me curiously.

'*Does* she?' she said softly, and jumped off the gate in silence. We picked up the branches and in a bewildered way I almost hated Elspeth. Why had she said that Deb didn't mind? Why was she so sure? Giving me her advice! Of course I had asked for it. She was only a child, much younger than I. She was in her own surroundings, that was all; she was at ease, but where would she not be? In my limited experience I could think of nowhere. Of course she read books ... Supposing that was important. No, Lucy didn't read. She had said so. What was it?

'What's the time?' Elspeth broke in. 'I wish *I* had a watch. It's practically the only thing I want. I've asked for one for Christmas. Come on, lunch.' Her hands were covered with scratches and full of holly. 'It *is* lovely, isn't it?' she said. She looked purely delighted.

'Sorry I asked you such silly questions.'

'That's all right. I enjoy it really. They say I'm pompous, but I don't care. It comes out of me like that.'

'Do you always live here?'

'Yes, at present. My mother is dead.' She said it easily, looking at me, but her eyes suddenly went quite flat.

I didn't say anything, and seconds later she turned her head a little towards me, gratefully, as though she were acknowledging my silence.

Walking along a track up a hill, we came upon a cottage. It was yellow, with a low untidy thatch, and it had two stunted elms beside it. A woman stood in the open door. She wore a vast blue-flowered overall. Her hair was done in a hard bun at the back. She was holding a large baby with a grey face and pale curls and *he* was holding a painted horse by its tail, loosely, so that the head swung against the woman.

'Hello, Mrs Druid,' said Elspeth. At this, three more children suddenly appeared from among the cabbages. They stared.

'Good morning, Miss,' said Mrs Druid.

'We've been collecting holly.'

'I see you 'ave.'

'For the church.'

'Ah,' said Mrs Druid.

'How's George?' said Elspeth. Mrs Druid shook the baby gloomily.

'Better than he should be. He 'ad a ball of wool yesterday. Didn't you, George?'

George became convulsed over her shoulder and the horse flapped wildly.

'He eats things,' said Elspeth regarding him with respect.

'It was only a little ball. Last week he eat arf a page of Druid's paper, didn't you, George?'

George hung motionless like seaweed.

'He ate a lot of soap once and she couldn't wash any of them,' said Elspeth to me. One of the children giggled and fell over a hen.

'It didn't upset him at *all*,' said Elspeth with awe.

'Can't keep 'is dinner down though,' said Mrs Druid unexpectedly. 'Just picks at it. Still we can't 'ave everything. Can we, George?' She laughed comfortably and pulled his legs down like the weights of a grandfather clock.

'Oh well,' said Elspeth. 'I hope he'll grow out of it.'

'We're getting used to it,' said Mrs Druid, and she laughed again.

'Well, good-bye,' said Elspeth.

Mrs Druid banged George enthusiastically on the back by way of farewell and disappeared into her cottage. The three children ran like rabbits to the gate and watched us up the hill. They were still there when we descended the other side, out of sight.

'It's always worth stopping to see her,' said Elspeth.

'Doesn't he get frightfully ill?'

'Good Lord, no. He's not like other people at all. That's why I always talk to her.'

When we got back, I found Toby squatting on the top landing, beside four balloons, tied to the banisters by long pieces of string. He could let them down to the ground floor and then haul them up. He looked very pleased and secret and didn't speak at all. Lucy called me. She was sitting in the day nursery, with her feet in a tub. Nanny was rubbing her arm with some stuff out of a bottle.

'I fell off twice,' she said. She looked white but triumphant.

'Goodness, did it hurt?'

'Oh yes.'

'Of course it did. You should have had a good cry before you got on again. You're not a boy you know.'

'That doesn't make the slightest difference, Nanny. Can I take my feet out?'

'I don't hold with your riding a pony with tricks like that. You might have broken a bone and then where would you have been, with the dance coming on and all?'

'Nanny, never *mind*.' Lucy was very near to tears. 'You go on down,' she said, and I went.

The vicarage children came at half-past three. They were very punctual and clean and pugnacious. There were two boys and a girl. They had ordered the game and they lost no time in organizing it. They picked sides with various agressive comments on our potential running powers. I had never played the game before. After ten minutes' confusion I had a stitch in my side and had not managed to collect either a handkerchief or Lucy, now quite cured of her falls, and prisoner.

The vicarage children charged and shouted and hurled insults and won the game. It was agreed that we should play something else, and while Gerald and the elder boy were deciding, the other two children chased each other and fought, with panting fury, any of us who stood in their way.

Eventually, no other game determined, we reverted to French and English. This time, however, Gerald forced them to pick the sides evenly. It was quite an effort, although he was at least three years older than the elder boy. Our tea bell rang, just as I had distinguished myself by a spectacular capture of Gerald, who yelled 'Well done!' as he roared back to his side. I felt proud, and was just settling down to enjoy the game.

' 'Fraid we must go,' said Gerald.

'Mother said we could stay to tea as soon as we were asked,' said the girl, eyeing Lucy firmly. Good heavens, I thought, they must be awful indoors. They were the sort of children that one only visualized in the open. The training of generations rose to aid Lucy and she answered gallantly enough.

'Well, of course, do come to tea.' We all moved towards the house.

'Although, you know,' I heard Elspeth say to one of them, 'we don't really want you to tea in the least. Lucy was only being polite.'

Whether we wanted them mattered not at all, I realized. They all washed at once, turning on and off the taps with wet grey hands, leaving the soap with black cracks, and a high-water mark all round the basin which Elspeth cleaned with the nail brush in silent indignation. Elspeth was a very particular child.

At tea they ate an enormous amount; the girl spilt her milk; and the boys had an argument. Lucy's mother was admirable. After the opening courtesies, she took no further notice, and even told one of them to leave a chocolate biscuit for his brother. When we left the table, the floor was thick with crumbs round their places.

'Still, it was a nice rest for their poor mother,' said our charitable hostess. She asked me whether I had written to my mother. 'Don't you think it would be a good idea?' she said. I felt myself blushing, and she showed me to a desk with pens and ink in silver stands, and pale grey paper with the address upon it in white.

'Dearest Mother . . .' What could I tell her? She had hoped I would have a good time. How far her hopes were excelled already! Strangely, my happiness made her further removed; it was harder to write than I had thought possible.

'I am arrived here quite safely. Everyone is very kind, and Mrs Lancing sends you her love. It is very cold. This morning I went picking holly for the church with a girl called Elspeth. Last night we played games and this afternoon the vicarage children came to tea.'

I thought a bit and then added, 'There is going to be a dance so I shall wear my frock, so thank you for buying it for me. I am having a lovely time. Your affectionate daughter.'

That night I had a very real and frightening dream. I was dancing in my pink frock, dancing quite safely with Elspeth. At the end of a passage stood Michael; much taller than he really was, with his arms out like a tree. The nearer I danced to him the larger he was and the further away he seemed. Then I noticed Rupert whom I had never seen, on a hill. I was so frightened of Michael that I picked up my skirts and ran cold and breathless nearer and nearer to Rupert, until I was quite up to him; and then I was in a wood, with no light to be seen, groping and stumbling in the dark, with Michael's laugh outside. I felt that the whole wood was Rupert, although I could not find him. The branches clung to me like arms and the leaves smothered me like a face, but I still called desperately for Rupert, pushing him away in my struggle. I must move on, get somewhere, but I did not know where I was going. When I woke, my heart was pounding in the silent room, and perspiration streamed down between my breasts. I lay stiff and still until the blackness of the window softened to a deep grey, bringing with it a faint sense of relief. I was freezing cold. I unplaited my hair, pulled it round my shoulder for warmth, and slept.

Christmas began to make itself felt. There was a tremendous expedition to the nearest town for the purpose of buying presents. Lucy's mother became the source of all secrets, all desires and inventions were exposed to her, and she sat giving gentle practical advice, smiling at everything, laughing at no one, keeping all secrets equally well. I accompanied Deb on the expedition. She spent nearly all her money on a watch chain for her Roland, and we packed and dispatched it together. That accomplished, she seemed to have no further interest in either her plans or mine; buying all her presents with careless speed, and giving me perfunctory advice in my schemes. She did not play games like the rest of them, and I found her more difficult. Occasionally, she collected me for some confidence or other, but she neither expected nor desired any return on my part.

Gerald tested the ice every day with growing confidence. I had one fateful riding lesson with Lucy and Parker. It was all right while the pony walked, but when it was clicked and encouraged to trot, I bit my tongue and lost a stirrup. Nothing was said about the venture, but it was mutually agreed that one could not learn to ride in ten days unless one showed some aptitude.

We suffered several visits from the vicarage children whose names I found were inappropriately enough, Vivian, Cecil and Bunty. They were aggressive and awe inspiring. They wore heavy clasp knives on leather belts round their waists, and always one of them was suffering from some frightful self-inflicted wound. They came through hedges, instead of over gates, and they usually entered any building by the first floor. One of them was always stuck at the top of a tree, while the other two pelted him with chestnuts or stones, in a heartless endeavour to get him down at all costs. They were permanently and terribly hungry; and they ate almost anything, from cow cake to frost-bitten blackberries. They ran everywhere, and only stayed in one place in order to fight. Their favourite pastimes were frightening each other, and giving other people terrible shocks. I think they were curiously devoted, or at any rate dependent, one always needing the others to carry out some complicated scheme. I cannot imagine how their poor parents existed under their rule. It must have been like living with a minor storm, on the brink of revolution, with a cloud of locusts.

Parcels kept arriving by post. There was mistletoe in the hall, under which Elspeth solemnly kissed me. Nanny ironed all our best clothes. Nobody was allowed into the library, which someone said was piled to the ceiling with presents. Great curly chrysanthemums stood in the hall, yellow and white, and smaller bronze-red ones, rambling and ragged, all smelling sweetly burnt.

Three days before Christmas the ice bore. Gerald broke

the news at breakfast, and immediately after we were wrapping up for skating. I had learned in that short time to like any new venture, since new ventures were no longer initiated by me as a desperate resort against boredom and solitude. Gerald had brought a broom with which he carefully swept a large slice of the river, while we sat on the banks surveying the green-grey ice. Lucy helped me put on a pair of skates. They seemed tight; although she assured me that that gave one support.

'Now,' she said. 'Hold on to me and walk.'

I staggered down to the edge of the river. Lucy embarked and held out her hands. 'You'll soon get used to it.' Kind Lucy! My gratitude made me brave. Of course I sat down pretty hard in a moment, though the others skimmed about like butterflies. Seeing Deb coming across the grass, with some difficulty I got to my feet. Lucy took my arm and soon I was lurching along, she urging me to take long steps, and supporting me when I lost my balance.

Learning to skate is much the same for everyone: it is enough to say that before the morning was over I was able to move up and down the river with quick uneven steps alternating with a drunken roll, that I fell down with painful regularity, and that getting to my feet with nothing to help me presented its usual problems. My ankles ached badly, and it became sad to see the others racing about, cutting figures and dancing together. I was encouraged by Deb's very reserved enjoyment; she glided about for an hour with Gerald, then repaired to the house. I sat on the bank and watched them all. Elspeth seemed intent on speed; she shot up and down the swept strip, her knees bent and her face thrust forward, so that I could almost see the air being cut away by her, like the pictures of steamers with a white wave in front. Elinor was very little more advanced than I, or so it seemed. She painstakingly cut a figure of eight, over and over again. Lucy and Gerald were the best; they leapt about and he showed her complicated steps and turns, they laughed a lot, and once they collided and stood holding each other's elbows, when their laughter died, they looked at each other, and rubbed noses to make it easy and usual again. Lucy's mother came to watch with a bag of peppermints. She fed us like birds because our gloves were too thick to manage for ourselves. 'Don't get cold,' she said to me. She came back again later, bringing Toby, who skated like a duck in a hurry, quickly and easily from side to side. He said he didn't like it, but he stayed.

After lunch I packed my presents with Deb, whose parcels were all small and neat, wrapped in white paper and tied with silver cord.

'What will you do when you go back to London?' she asked.

'Just be at home. There's nothing much to do there.'

'Oh!' She glanced at me incuriously.

'It's awfully dull there. It's not a bit like being here. There's so much to do.'

'Yes, but that's only because it's different. Think of doing them for years.'

'I should like it. There are more people here. I mean you do things together.'

'I like one person at a time,' she answered absently, smoothing a piece of tissue paper.

'You like parties, too.'

'Yes, I like them well enough. If I were in London I should have many more.'

You would, of course, I thought. London would change for you, never present itself in an everyday manner for you. But that would be the same wherever you went.

'Surely you meet a lot of people there?'

'Oh well, musicians and people who like music.'

'I should love that. What are they like?'

'They are my parents' friends,' I answered stiffly, as though it was impossible for me to explain my parents' friends.

'Well?' She was impatient. 'Are you not old enough to like them?'

'I don't notice them.' I was ashamed and irritated and it was not even true. 'They don't talk to me much.'

'Of course, I suppose they wouldn't.' She had the half resentful respect the world has for an artist, that I already
knew so well.

'Do you like music?' I asked.

'I like waltzes. Chopin,' she added as if to excuse her
frivolous choice.

'Oh, but other kinds of real music. Don't you like that?'

'I don't know what you mean, real music. I like songs and
music for dancing. But I don't see the point of the other
kind.' I looked smugly shocked. 'Well, can *you* tell me the
point of it? What *is* the point?'

'To – to listen to – and enjoy.'

'How do you enjoy it, if you don't see the point of it?' she
persisted, mischievously intent.

'Well, flowers,' I said lamely. 'They haven't much point
and you enjoy them.'

'They smell,' she said indignantly. 'And they are pretty
colours.'

'I don't suppose musicians care much for flowers,' I said,
uncertainly, but it served my point to say so.

'But flowers are useful. You can wear them and they make
rooms look nice. There's nothing useful about music.'

'I suppose people have special enjoyments, and they don't
need them to be useful. It's just luck if you like beautiful
things.'

'I adore beautiful things,' she said.

'Not all . . .' I began.

'But I just like to like them. I don't want to have to be
clever to like them.' She threw a little parcel on the heap and
touched her hair.

I realized then how self-consciously I admired the things I
thought it right to admire. We were silent for a time and I
was sorting desperately the things that I *knew* I liked. I did
not get very far, because I liked everything about that house
and nothing about mine; and yet many things were the
same. I dismissed the whole problem because Deb interrupted me with some comment on our activity.

When we went to tea, I met Toby on the stairs. He was

very warm and smelt of toast. There was a huge chocolate cake and everyone was hungry from skating. I sat next to Elinor, who left her icing to the end, and ate it very thoughtfully. Everyone was gay and peaceful. Suddenly in the middle of tea the door opened and two young men appeared.

'Rupert!' cried Lucy.

There was much confusion, people got to their feet, with littles cries of delighted surprise, and there was a spasm of excitement. I had leisure to observe, and watched Rupert because I had a natural curiosity about him. The other young man might have been his shadow. Rupert walked forward, kissed his hostess's hand, straightened himself and smiled faintly.

'How did you come, my dear boy?'

'We motored. Ian had a motor. By the way, this *is* Ian.'

'How long did it take?'

Gerald wore a keenly professional look.

'Well we had a puncture or so.'

'Who drove?'

'I drove and the wretched Ian sat and mended tyre after tyre.'

'Introduce me to Ian,' said Lucy's mother calmly.

'Mrs Lancing. The Lady of the House, and my, our, admirable hostess. This is Ian Graham.'

'Have you come to stay?'

The young man was dreadfully embarrassed and Rupert had turned away to shake hands with Lucy's father. Ian was thin and fair. He blushed, and murmured something, rubbing his hands which were white with cold.

'We're delighted to have you. Sit down. Elspeth ring for some more tea. Sit by me,' this to Ian. 'Now I must introduce you. This is my husband. This is Deborah, my eldest daughter, Lucy, Elinor, and Elspeth, who is their cousin. Toby, my youngest, Gerald ...' She continued round the large table. Rupert followed these introductions with a jerk of his eyes; to Deb he threw a mocking smile of admiration, and then when Mrs Lancing stopped he came to me, and by reason of her silence, he stared a little. Ian seemed too confused to speak. He was very shy and kept looking at his hands.

'And who is that?'

'Good gracious I forgot.'

I was duly introduced, Mrs Lancing explaining that I had been sitting too close to her, thus stalling the flood of shame in me that Rupert's faintly insolent remark had induced. They sat down.

'How do you come by a motor car?' Mr Lancing rarely spoke.

'Well Ian is my only rich friend. We bought it this morning, because I don't like trains and he's very fond of me. And of course once we'd bought it, he had to come too, and I knew you'd like him so that was that.'

'Why didn't you drive if it was your motor car?'

'He doesn't like cars,' said Rupert calmly as he slashed a piece of cake.

'Rupert how selfish of you. You are so selfish. Give Ian some cake.'

'He doesn't like cake either.'

'Stop telling us what he doesn't like. It's horrid for him.'

The tea arrived.

'Deborah,' said Rupert lovingly. She arched her neck and looked at him inquiringly.

'Sweet Deb, how do you manage to keep it up?'

'Keep what up?'

'Your beauty.'

She was defiantly silent.

'Rupert, stop it,' cried Mrs Lancing. 'You are an impudent boor.'

He grinned sweetly.

'Well it's true. Ian don't you think she . . .?'

'It's no use,' said Lucy's mother. 'Every year when you go away I resolve never to have you again and then you write me such an enchanting Collins that I find it impossible to deprive myself of the chance of another.'

'Ho, you shouldn't do things for gain.'

'You shouldn't speak with your mouth full,' said Elspeth severely.

'When you reach my age you can do the most awful things and no one will stop you. They merely shudder and hold up their hands.'

Toby suddenly shuddered and held up his hands, so funnily that everyone laughed. He relapsed into a silent little boy and took no notice.

'What awful things have you been doing?'

'Nothing much. Why haven't you got a dog in this house? It's all wrong, I found myself in that hall, and nobody knocked me down, or licked my face. I was awfully disappointed.' His narrow eyes screwed up. 'But the chrysanthemums smelled a treat. Ian was at Cambridge with me,' he added suddenly.

'I should have thought people stopped you doing things far more when you were old,' said Elspeth.

'Oh no,' I said. 'Only then you don't want to do them.'

Rupert looked at me.

'Well, well,' he said softly.

'We've been skating,' said Gerald after a pause.

'There's going to be a dance.'

'I say how marvellous.' Ian choked in his tea.

'Pat him on the back. He's very young.'

'Awful chap,' spluttered Ian.

'Oh I'm beyond the pale. Far beyond it,' said Rupert gravely, and for a moment he looked sad and obsessed. 'I hope you're surprised to see me,' he said, after a moment.

'You're conceited too.'

'I suppose you think we've all been *gasping* for you,' said Lucy cheerfully.

'I didn't say pleased. You're all so kind that I imagine you pleased about anyone. I prefer to engender surprise. Shock. Startlement.' His angular eyebrows shot up and he looked fiercely at Toby who grinned resentfully.

'Ha,' said Rupert. 'I really annoyed him.' He said it with a sort of satisfaction.

CHAPTER SEVEN

Two days later I was in the library with Elspeth. There was a smell of books seldom opened, or perhaps it was Elspeth's hair. I remember we were kneeling on the window seat and there was a little snow on the ground outside. Rupert put his head round the door.

'Come for a walk?'

Elspeth wriggled. 'You come here and talk.'

'No, I want a walk. And I didn't mean you.'

'All right.' I scrambled off the seat.

Elspeth caught my skirt. 'You don't want to go.'

'Why not?'

She pursed her lips. 'We were looking at books.'

Suddenly I did not want her to come too.

'Hurry up,' said Rupert. I ran to change. When I was ready he was still standing in the door and Elspeth was sulking, and trying not to laugh. I said good-bye to her and she did not answer whereupon Rupert slammed the door.

'Silly little creature.'

We strode up the drive, our feet barely marking the speckled ground.

'She's clever.'

'Only compared with the other people in the house.'

'Of course she may prove intelligent later on,' he said after a pause, then glancing at me. 'Don't look so shocked. Does intelligence mean so much to you?'

'I don't know,' I said truthfully.

'Oh I hoped you knew. I hoped you would say that intelligence was the distinction you needed and admired in your friends. That you would throw away beauty, charm and riches for so precious a commodity as intelligence. What would you say it was anyway?'

'What?' This was going to be a startling walk.

'Intelligence.'

'Untrained knowledge?'

He threw back his head and laughed loudly. 'What a damn silly thing to say. But she doesn't rise,' he said in mock surprise a moment later. I felt he was teasing, provoking me into a reply, but I was better able to hold my ground with silence. We strode on up the hill, with the snow flakes slipping down towards us, dark against the milky sky, and suddenly shining white as they fell into our landscape.

'Do you like all this?' I indicated the country before us.

'Yes,' he said. 'But I couldn't live in it for long. I am drawn to the Metropolis. The lights, music and the people. There isn't enough to do here.'

'Much more than in London, I think,' I said warmly.

'What? One can farm, or be a gentleman of leisure and I have neither inclination nor means.'

'What do you do in London?'

'Nothing now. I was to be a doctor.'

'Were you expelled?'

'No I left,' he answered quite seriously, as though I had used the right word.

'Why did you leave?'

'That's the trouble. I don't know. I never stop anything merely for something else. Hence these awful gaps, when I come to sneer and vegetate in the country, with a crowd of people who give me the benefit of the doubt through sheer ignorance.'

'Where do you live?'

'I did live in a horrible room in Gloucester Road. Last week I left it in the morning in a fog and I shan't go back now.'

'Have you left all your things there?'

'Some of them. I didn't want them you know.' He seemed amused.

'I have been throwing things away too.'

'And where do you intend going?'

'Going?' I repeated. 'I hadn't thought. I just want to do something.'

75

'You do. What do you want to do?'

'I don't know.'

'Ah,' he said. 'We neither of us know.' His comfort in the fact communicated itself to me.

'What could I do?'

'Come and keep house for me.'

'Oh *no*.'

'What vehemence. You asked me what you should do. I imagine like most girls you have made a passionate resolve to be needed. You've thought of being a nun, a nurse, the wife of a blind man. Surely my housekeeper is the next step? Or is there someone else? Have you dedicated yourself to some other aimless youth?'

'I want to help myself.'

'Hooray!'

'I don't like being teased. I was serious.'

'I knew you were. I like teasing people.'

'Well you shouldn't.'

'I only tease people I like.'

'You shouldn't do just what you like to people.'

'Not to do what I like to people would be pretending. If you're to housekeep for me I should see you every day and however much I liked you I couldn't keep up the pretence. That would be like marriage.' He said the last with such extraordinary bitterness that I was startled into continuing the conversation which I had before begun to regret.

'What do you mean "like marriage"?'

'I forgot. You probably think that married people love each other.'

'I hadn't thought anything about it.' Suddenly I was remembering my father padding away to his studio after meals, and my mother settling with a whimpering little sigh, to her darning. 'I thought they ceased to consider it.'

'They pretend,' he said fiercely after a moment, 'so hard that there isn't time for anything else.'

'They have their house, children, work. I don't think they consider it,' I said.

'Do they honestly love each other then?'

'No.'

'Do they admire each other?'

'No.'

'Enjoy each other's company?'

'Not much.'

'Like each other?'

'Oh, I don't know.' I felt inexpressibly sad.

'Poor little thing. That's why you're so concerned with doing something. You get away. They're finished. You can't do anything for them.'

At once the whole universe rocked for me, leaving what had been an accepted supposition an abyss of uncertainty and fear. The shock of realizing that Rupert knew I had been speaking of my parents, breaking down as it did such necessary reserve, paralysed me. It did not occur to me that he was generalizing out of personal bitterness; that therefore this awful statement could be fought, could be disproved or rejected. (I was at an age when if anyone said something with sufficient certainty I was forced to believe them and suffer accordingly.) I looked at Rupert; he was only one person. He was still striding along with his head bent; a little cut on his cheek, furtive and crimson. The cut made me feel surer. Suddenly I could speak and my own voice gave me courage.

'There's no need to marry anyone unless you love them. Of course there might be mistakes, but that's nothing to do with pretending. A great many people may be utterly content. You don't know all the people. Enough people then,' I added, feeling his laugh about to break.

We had turned off the lane into a bridle path, edged with dead blackberries, mottled hips and crackling grass stiffened by frost.

'Let's see who's in the best position to generalize. How many married couples do you know intimately?'

I was not be caught again. 'Not many. How many do you know?'

'Not many. But I'm older than you so that my "not many" means more. Therefore I am better able to judge about marriage than you, and until you're my size of mind you must accept any statement I care to make.'

'People aren't an even age. I am older than you in some ways.'

'Darling little creature, I was teasing you. Still able to quarrel about who's the oldest. Not very old yet,' he said in mock despair.

'I don't believe you about marriage.'

'I was warning you.'

'I don't want to be warned. I *shall* love someone and I *shall* marry them. I will manage myself,' I said sullenly.

'Hooray, you have thought everything out.'

The path was now skirting a wood, a copse. The older trees were felled and lying in reckless attitudes, their bark blistering and ragged like wallpaper.

'I'm tired,' I said.

He glanced at me. 'We won't argue any more. I won't tease you.'

'I'm tired. Really,' I repeated, some instinct telling me how to get the better of him.

'Right.' He lifted me in his arms, over a ditch, and into the wood where he seated me on a log.

'How old are you?'

'Sixteen.'

'Ah yes. Sixteen, and there you sit, cold and tired and teased past all endurance.'

I looked up at him. He seemed kind. I was still aching and wondering what I should think alone, with my thoughts uncoloured by his interruptions.

'Nothing is certain,' I said rather shakily.

'What a desperate little remark. Yes, we need to believe some things.'

'You don't leave much.'

'There are too many things for belief,' he said sadly. 'The world's too full. It has extended beyond any single mind. There are so many Gods, so many people, so many ideas, so many creeds and convictions. We have simply to choose.'

'How do we do that?'

I felt him groping along my thoughts with the fingers of his mind. 'Don't try to find out what is generally right. That's mere condonement, *not* personal acceptance, which means feeling, thinking and knowing until that belief will live with you from sheer love.' He seemed to be telling himself. He finished suddenly. He sat down and pulled out a pipe. 'And now, may I smoke this?'

I nodded, I did more or less understand him, and felt calmer.

'Your family are musicians aren't they?'

'My father.' I stared at his long bony hands loosely clasped round his knees.

'I've heard some of his work. Influenced by Schumann isn't he?'

'Everyone says that.'

'I'm sorry.' He was mocking again.

'Everybody is influenced by someone.'

He bowed and a long lock of hair fell over his face.

'I should like to come and see them.'

'No you wouldn't.'

'Yes, I shall accompany you on your day off, to visit your family.'

'*No.*'

'But what deadly secret have you to hide that you are so positive?'

'No secret.' I stared again at his hands. 'I'll come and see you.'

'You will?'

'Wherever you are living.'

'You *want* to be my housekeeper?'

'Rupert, I ...' Did he really mean that? What did he expect me to say?

'I suppose it would be rather improper.' I looked up at the sound of his voice and found him watching my face. 'Did you think I was furtively asking you to be my mistress?'

I had very little idea of what being a mistress implied, but I felt the blood rushing to my face; a wild desire to escape and stop everything or be someone else. He took both my hands in his: I looked down at them warmly folded, and then back to his face again, and still I couldn't speak. He stared at me intently; and there was such a depth of honesty in his eyes that my self-consciousness melted as my face cooled, and I was unafraid.

'That wasn't very kind of me. Of course you didn't. I'm afraid you can't even be my housekeeper. But you shall come to tea, or whenever you haven't anywhere else to go, and want to come. I'll tell you where I am, when I know, so that you won't forget.'

'I won't.'

'Now I'm going to kiss you to finish things off because we must go home.'

He took my face in his hands and bent his head. I put my arms round his neck; his hair felt silky at the back.

'What a convulsive little gesture,' he said and kissed me. His lips were cool and firm; and when he stopped, my mouth felt strange, separate and alive.

He held out his hand, pulled me to my feet, and we set off out of the wood, back down the mysterious dead path to the road.

The snow was falling more thickly, into our faces, but I did not mind it. I was in an unquestioning exhilarated mood where I needed no more or less of the road and snow and company than was provided.

Half-way home we found a young cat, almost a kitten. It followed us desperately, falling behind and then running round our feet, its ears flattened with dislike of the weather. Rupert insisted on buttoning it into his coat in spite of my saying that cats always found their way home.

'Nonsense,' he said decisively. 'Almost as silly a saying as the one about the English always being kind to animals.'

I felt rebuffed and faintly jealous. The cat was secure and drew the warmth of Rupert's presence away from me. Instantly my mood deserted me. I felt really tired; my legs ached, my boots rubbed my heels, and my skirts were heavy and dank.

The village appeared, its street ribbed with wheel tracks,

and my knowledge of Rupert slipped away as we approached it.

'Nearly home,' said Rupert cheerfully. 'We'll have an enormous scorching tea. You'll feel rested, warm and tired and full of food. It's the best part of a walk.'

Numb with a lack of reality I turned towards the house.

CHAPTER EIGHT

I remember lying rigid on my back having been sent to rest on the afternoon before the dance.

Nanny had drawn the curtains, and padded away to mull the afternoon suitably for the others. Telling me to have a nice rest, she shut the door. There ensued the most still and lasting silence. This is how to lie I thought when one is dead. Stiff and narrow amid complete silence. A cock crowed and I jumped out of bed and drew back the curtains again. I remember Rupert had looked at us at lunch, at Deb, at Lucy and at me, agreeing that we should rest, and the thought flitted across my mind, that we were to emerge from the artificial dusk of our rooms to dance a few hours in the light, like butterflies, for his pleasure.

I became very sad lying there because I could not imagine what was to happen after the dancing, when I went home. My pride would never let things be the same; so there would be decisions to make, life to be wielded, and too many people drifting with time to watch. I thought of my sister; she had refused this visit; she had no desire for anything new: she could sew and read and go to church, and for walks, and stay the same size, and complete herself within that tiny sphere. I wanted things before I knew what they were. I wondered what Rupert would do when he went back to London. I had not asked him. There were so many things I had wanted to ask him, but had not dared or had forgotten. The time I had spent with him had been choked with talk, and yet now it felt so short. Of course one would not have had one's fill of anybody in a single afternoon. Perhaps he would not want to talk to me again. I numbered on my fingers the few days left. Christmas could not count, it needed the day for itself. I tried to imagine Rupert with my father. They would talk about music, of course; my father's face would light up, and he would use boyish exclamations coined in his youth. Rupert would be perfectly at home. I would sit and watch them both and occasionally Rupert would smile at me. But the house! I could not bear Rupert to see the house. He was fastidious. The dirt and decay would not please him. I could never let him come there. I would not see him at all. I must wait for him to invite me. It was not possible to collect people just because you wanted them. If you were a woman, you must wait until they came to you.

The doctrine vaguely dissatisfied me: I got out of bed again to look for a book and found *The Wide Wide World*. It was full of very interesting information, and religion, and a little girl cried on nearly every page.

The house was warm and polished, with clusters of flowers in pots, which were scrubbed like sand to the fingers. The dining-room had long tables with white cloths to the floor; lines of glasses, and heaps of little spoons tangled and gleaming like fishes. The great room where we were to dance was lined with chairs, the floor bare, waiting to be furnished with people.

'Roland is coming,' said Deb.

'And I shall have Rupert,' I thought to myself with a little arrow of excitement. 'It will be quite different from the wood. I shall wear my beautiful frock and it is a dance.' And all the while I dressed I was conscious of a new delight in preparing myself for a single person's approbation.

I had bathed and was drawing my heavy bronze silk stockings up my legs. They unrolled with a beautiful smooth precision over the bony whiteness, collecting my limbs in elegant silken lines. I pointed my toe. Really they were a good shape. It was perfectly sensible to admire them, since nobody else would see them. I pulled down my petticoat. I was to brush my hair for Nanny to put it up. Deb having invited me to her room I planned to ask her for a piece of jewellery to wear on my frock. I dipped my finger in water and smoothed my eyebrows until they were finely narrow like Deb's. When I looked in the mirror, a new face looked back, with little shadows lying on the bones, and enormous eyes startled with excitement. I felt very beautiful then; the fear of being newly grown up and not knowing things slipped away because I could praise my own appearance from perfect intimacy with its shortcomings. The pink frock was laid out on the bed, with the pointed pink shoes beside it. I scratched the soles with scissors, and my finger suddenly blossomed a thin line of blood, with a drop on the pink strap of the shoe. I rubbed the strap with my flannel. It would not show, but the little moist circle was disquieting.

Nanny did my hair superbly with a narrow plait over the top of my head and the rest drawn waxen smooth. I raised my hands in bewildered delight.

'Don't touch it now,' Nanny said. 'Are you wearing any ornament in it?'

Despair engulfed me. 'I haven't got anything,' I stammered. Impossible, of course, I must wear something; it looked so stiff and bare. Deb swept into the room.

'You never came to see me.' She looked at my head and hopeless face below it. 'That's lovely, Nanny. It suits you. Wait a minute. Nanny, fetch my roses like an angel. The little pink ones.' When they came she fastened them into the edge of my plait. 'There,' she said. 'Three little pink roses.' Our eyes met, amused and grateful. 'All right?' she said. 'Nanny my stockings again,' and flung something misty across the room. So those were the stockings one wore for dancing. Mine were hopeless thick things – still they would not show. How absurd I had been. Nanny had disappeared. Deb was particularly charming to me. 'Let's put on your frock. Have you a locket?'

'No.'

'Come into my room. I'll lend you one.'

I rustled after her feeling gracious and at least twenty years old in my dress. She slung the turquoise heart on a chain, and fastened it round my neck where it lay brilliantly in the hollow of my throat.

'Now sit on a chair while I dress.'

She looked wonderful of course, and she loved to be

watched. I recollect yards and yards of pale yellow in an enormous skirt trimmed with green velvet ribbons. 'He likes green,' she said complacently as she fastened that colour neatly round her white neck. I watched her fasten green leaves in her hair, green velvet round her wrists; slip her feet into green slippers; tweak her shoulders, stroke her skirts and preen, and smile at me in the glass, all with a calm contented efficiency. This was really her life.

'Find out what Nanny is doing. I don't want her to come in here suddenly.'

Nanny was doing Elspeth's hair.

'Elspeth always cries when her hair is done. It takes ages.' From the back of a drawer she took a box of powder and carefully powdered her nose. 'Have some.' I leaned forward. 'I'll do it for you. Shut your eyes.' A fine dust descended on me, gathered in the corners of my eyes and mouth. She put the powder away. 'There it is if we want it,' she said with a gleam and again I had the feeling of a conspiracy. She pinched her cheeks and bit her lips and the colour flowed into them. Then she took a minute handkerchief gritty with lace, and shook out two little drops of lavender water. This time I was not included.

'Women can't wear the same scent,' she said, half apologetically. 'How do I look?'

'Wonderful.'

'You are awfully pretty too,' she said generously.

We rose from our chairs, shook out our skirts, and descended.

Dinner was an unsubstantial affair; a dream of half-eaten dishes and desultory anticipation. Nobody's mind came to the surface; nobody wanted to eat, but it was too old and established a custom to be foregone. Elspeth sat next to me absently eating nuts. She was in crimson velvet, with puff sleeves showing her childish arms with a little stream of delicate blue veins in the crook running down to her wrists. Her evening was darkened with the knowledge that she was to go to bed at half past ten. 'Although I sleep very little nowadays,' she said with scornful eyes and a quivering mouth.

Before the meal, we had been into the morning room, where Rupert was admiring Mrs Lancing's pearls and Aunt Edith sat in black velvet with a marvellous white silk shawl the fringes of which caught in her chair. Mrs Lancing had admired us, and Rupert had said 'Beautiful,' very firmly, with his eyes on Deb.

After the meal we were finally inspected by Nanny, Deb again powdered her nose, and we stood in the drawing-room, at one end of which the orchestra was now grouped, surrounded with hothouse ferns. There were sounds of the first people arriving. Lucy waltzed me across the room to the entrance where Mrs Lancing stood, with Deb frowning at us. The first announcement sounded absurd in the empty room when everyone could see who the arrivals were. Two plain girls wearing queer short dresses of peacock blue and hair tied back with enormous bows of the same colour, advanced nervously to be introduced.

'Their mother believes in Freedom of Movement,' muttered Lucy viciously in my ear. Rupert came in announcing himself in a loud unnatural voice which made the footmen shuffle sheepishly.

Then scores of guests arrived: girls in white and pink, and blue; boys in Eton suits; men, very young in evening dress; mothers, in lace and pearls; fathers, military men, with stiff legs and walking sticks; red-faced men curiously light on shiny black feet, good riders, sportsmen, all prepared for a festivity that would become the ladies, the objects of their chivalry, tolerance and affection; thin spare men of uncertain age laughing with nervous goodwill and rubbing their hands. (Surely men couldn't be shy?) Amid the hum of conversation Gerald handed out programmes with tiny pencils and tassels. I was introduced to a number of men who booked dances. I wondered when I should dance with Rupert and whether Roland had arrived: yes that must be Roland, tall and fair and close to Deb. I left four dances free for Rupert. He would of course forget to book them; would see me standing, and assume that we had planned those dances. He would put his arm round me; we should glide away in silence, and perhaps look at each other a moment later to acknowledge our understanding.

Upstairs, Nanny would be hovering with pins and combs and a needle, ready for any feminine emergency. And elsewhere supper was prepared; the slices of lemon floating sideways in the jugs of cup; the trifles quivering on their plates: everything was ready. The first dance. And the second. Learning the things one said; the general form of the conversation; dancing with good dancers and with bad, abandoning oneself to the delight of the movement, or admiration, tentative and clumsy ('those roses are ripping'): or the choking flood of panic when one could not interest one's partner with any of the opening remarks so newly learned – the floor, the orchestra, skating, Christmas, the hospitality of the Lancings. Dreary little pools of silence, broken by an apology ('So sorry.' 'My fault.'). The fifth dance. Rupert dancing with Deb, then with Mrs Lancing herself. Elspeth being sent to bed with a jelly. Rupert, his arms folded, leaning against the wall talking to another man. Dancing with Roland, and Deb smiling her approval. An uneasy little conversation on Deb's beauties. The sixth dance.

I went upstairs to tidy my hair. One could not walk into the room and say 'Rupert take me in to supper,' as Deb had done. Lucy was standing impatiently while Nanny whipped up a frill on her skirt. 'Who's taking you in to supper?'

'I don't know.'

'Oh.'

Poor Lucy was so kind that she was easily unhappy.

'It's all right,' I said carefully.

'You've had lots of partners haven't you?' said Lucy with an eager reassuring smile.

'Oh *yes*. I'm having a lovely time. Are you?'

'Of course,' she said simply. 'It's a dance.'

'Down you go,' said Nanny. We went.

'I think Roland is rather unhappy,' whispered Lucy. 'I shall talk to him,' and she sped away, her coffee-coloured skirts flying round her neat ankles. Why was not Deb having supper with Roland? Why had it not been I who had smiled up at Rupert so affectionately, and commanded him to take me in to supper? Only a third of the evening gone.

Mrs Lancing introduced me to a sturdy young man in spectacles. Mr Fielding. 'You both like music,' she said firmly and left us.

'What sort of music do you like?'

'Oh, different things. What do you like?'

'Oh, any music really.'

'What about a little supper?'

'That would be lovely.'

We had supper. Gerald was hilarious with several men friends and a girl in yellow who giggled at everything he said and ate a great deal. Mr Fielding politely supplied me with food. Music died a natural death between us and we had nothing further to say to one another. Deb and Rupert were not there. How strange. Lucy and Roland were discussing the feeding of ponies for hunting. The cup was very cool and a little bitter, and I was desperately thirsty. A clock struck eleven. Mr Fielding was joining in the general conversation. I murmured something about a handkerchief and left him. In the hall I paused. My face was burning hot and I longed to cool it. I opened a door leading on to the garden and slipped out. There was a watery moon galloping across the sky. I heard footsteps, a low laugh, a murmured protesting denial, and then silence. The moon slipped thinly behind a feathery cloud and out the other side, rakish and gleaming. I stood a moment uncertain, then shut myself into the house again, and after wandering round the hall, seated myself half-way up the stairs.

They came in by the same door, as I had known they would, he holding it for her, she with his coat round her shoulders. All exactly as she had told me.

I was above them and they did not see me, but Lucy and Roland came out of the supper-room facing me.

'Hullo,' said Lucy, but Roland saw Deb.

'I was looking for you,' he said and moved forward uncertainly.

'Were you?' said Deb. 'Well here I am, come and give me a drink.' She sounded sharp and a little nervous. As she moved to Roland she saw me, through the banisters and tilted her head. I saw a spot of colour on her cheekbones, her eyes narrowed, sparkling through the black fringe of lashes, and a tendril of hair curling down her neck. 'You there, too?'

'I was having a rest.'

She nodded, and went away with Roland. I could feel Rupert watching me and rose to my feet. He met me at the bottom of the stairs.

'May I have the honour of dancing with you?'

Dust and ashes; I swallowed.

'There isn't any dancing, they're having a rest too,' said Lucy cheerfully. 'But I expect they'll start soon,' she added kindly. 'I'm going to have an ice,' and she went.

'Would you like an ice?'

'No thank you.'

'Would you like to go on resting here? Hullo, you've got Deb's turquoise heart.'

My fingers clutched the heart, there was an ache in my throat. I nodded.

'Does that mean you *would* like to sit here?'

I shook my head and turned away. He caught my wrist and a large tear fell on his hand.

'I cannot allow you to turn away from me in tears,' he said, and pulled me back.

He looked hard at me for a second and fumbled in his pockets. 'Damn, I never have one.' He smoothed my cheeks with his fingers and then licked them, and seeing my surprise he said seriously, 'I like your tears very much. Now, I'll decide what to do, since you can do nothing but cry.'

We went to the dance room. It was almost empty. The orchestra were sitting waiting their appointed time to start again. Rupert left me and talked to them.

'We are going to dance by ourselves. Now, if you've a handkerchief I think you'd better use it.'

'I haven't.'

'You people who weep never have,' he said.

We danced in silence and alone. He was a very much better dancer than I, which afforded me a peculiar delight. People joined us in the end and when it was over Rupert said he was starving and I must come and watch him eat. 'I shall sup off cold chicken and tears.' He piled a plate and said, 'Now we sit on the stairs. Take this, and I'll join you.' He returned with a pink ice. 'For you. Now, are you happy?'

'I don't know.'

'You shouldn't say that. When people ask you whether you're happy, they don't require a serious answer. Unless you are a person who takes happiness very seriously.'

'I do.'

'I'll ask you in five years whether you meant that.'

I spooned my ice in silence.

'But I think you meant yourself,' he added, 'which is a very different thing.'

I wanted to change the subject. 'Doesn't Deb look beautiful tonight?'

'Now, now, none of that,' he said sharply. 'I've given you every chance to recover gracefully from your tears.'

Again I had the naked sensation of having my mind laid bare for his understanding.

'You see,' he said. 'If one is unhappy for a good reason one does not mind exposure so much. But if one suffers because one is young and absurd, silence and secrecy are preferable, and should be supported.'

'Am I young and absurd?'

'You are young and absurd.'

I stared ahead of me, my hands in my lap, finding it easier now that he said that. A wave of gratitude to him loosened my tongue.

'It was silly of me to mind.' He was silent. 'You see I went into the garden and I knew it was you. It was silly of me to mind,' I repeated.

'It was very silly of you.'

'I should have realized that it didn't make any difference.'

'To what?'

'To, to what you said on the walk,' I said weakly.

'I cannot understand how a moment's moonlight dallying in the garden with Deb is connected with anything I said to you on a walk.'

'I thought you didn't care.'

'Care?'

'About me,' I faltered. This was getting worse every moment.

'But I don't.' He sounded thoroughly startled. 'Listen. We had a very nice walk, and I enjoyed your company. You are not only young and absurd, which is enjoyable but commonplace; you are other things. Deb is other things too and she is enjoyable in a different way.' I could see he laughed at his own choice of words. 'But neither of these minor, these very minor events deserve the complications with which you would honour them. You are both charming and I enjoy you both, and perhaps you enjoy me which makes it better still, but we none of us need to make things larger than they are. In fact you must not be a creator of situations.'

'You didn't mean what you said?'

'Of course I did. I was, if I remember, extremely earnest, and dictatorial. But I am a talker. I talk like that all the time. You mustn't let the idea of a young girl going into a garden getting kissed under a moon and instantly becoming engaged to be married get too strong a hold on you. You've been reading the wrong sort of books. And as you cannot prevent Deb being more beautiful than you, you must accept it and not damage yourself by jealousy in so ridiculous a manner. And now if you dare to cry I shall shake you and be so unkind that you're irritated into stopping.'

There was a pause while I struggled with my feelings: shame, astonishment and chagrin, but strangely no resentment towards him. He had, I suppose, an innate understanding for what was bearable and what was not, and the gift of saying brutal things with a mixture of honesty and ease that took the sting out of them.

'You liked being kissed didn't you?'

I nodded.

'Good, that was honest. Some things can be very nice when

they happen once. It isn't necessary to ensure that they are repeated indefinitely before one can begin to value them.' I recognized this gentle piece of mocking and felt calmer.

'Do you know how old I am?'

I didn't know.

'I'm twenty-three.'

I had not imagined him as any particular age, but had felt sure he was more. I took a deep breath. 'Remarkable,' I said ironically.

'I always planned to be remarkable at twenty-three,' he answered. 'So you can laugh. Come and do it in front of a lot of people. I am sure they would be surprised.' And we went back to the dance.

People began to go at twelve o'clock and by half past the dance was finished. We were left supping warm milk, and exclaiming contentedly over the success of the evening.

Upstairs, Deb drew me into her room.

'I shall not marry Roland after all. It would be the greatest mistake. I'll tell you about it tomorrow if you like. Sleep well.'

CHAPTER NINE

I don't know why I should have expected life to be different at home, but I did. I had imagined so strongly that it would be, without any clear idea what form the change would take, that for a few days I lived in my imagination, the food tasted new, and even my father's pupils were more interesting. Gradually, the exhilaration of my holidays ebbed away. I had written a stilted little letter to Mrs Lancing, expressing my gratitude, which set the seal on the visit, and finally finished it in my mind. My sister showed no curiosity about my adventures, and to my mother I remained unduly silent. One of my brothers began teaching at a preparatory school in Kent and the other was at a Training College. They were shadows. I knew they thought us very dull and they avoided bringing their friends to the house.

I determined to educate myself, and joined a library. The young lady who attended to my needs overawed me. I had approached her with a tentative inquiry hoping that she would assign me some particular book, and thus relieve me of the responsibility of choosing. But she flung out her arms in different directions and said Travel, Fiction, Biography and Religious with a detached generosity which it was impossible to refuse. I thanked her and walked away. Travel, I thought; I should know about other countries; it would widen and improve my mind. I selected *Ten Weeks in Northern Italy* by May something or other, illustrated by the author. I returned to the assistant and laid it uncertainly on the counter.

'You're allowed three books you know,' she said.

I hastened away. A biography. I searched until my neck ached and the names of the books before me had no separate meaning. In the end I chose the Memoirs by a lady-in-waiting at some obscure Ducal court in Germany. I chose it because it was bound in crimson leather with gold lettering and the colour pleased me. And then in a nervous little rush I seized *Wuthering Heights*, the first book that caught my eye from the rows of fiction. With these, I returned to my assistant, not a little pleased with myself. While she was writing my name and address, I asked her stupidly whether the books were good.

'I don't know,' she said. 'You've serious tastes, haven't you? I should think that would be interesting.' She flicked back the cover of the Memoirs. 'But that other's classic, isn't it?'

'Do you read much?'

'I like a nice novel. But by the time I finish here I'm ready for a good time. I like a bit of fun in the evenings myself.' She was called away by an old gentleman. 'Back in a minute.'

She had a fleeing bouncing figure as though she were set on springs. The wide belt at her waist pulled her in, so that it seemed she must spring out above it. She wore a white blouse with a black ribbon at the neck, and a black ribbon at the back of her head. Her hair was very light brown, almost green, and sprang out round her face in enormous puffs. She had large pale blue eyes set rather close together, and a mouth that reminded me of two little sausages. When she came back to me she smiled, and showed unexpectedly neat teeth with a gold stopping flashing a signal of friendliness. She had great good humour about her. I remember her so well because we became close friends. We did not talk any more that day; she was busy and I was shy, but I was attracted by the ease with which she did her work, and the evident satisfaction she had in her appearance.

Ten Weeks in Northern Italy was written in the form of letters to her father by a very religious woman. The book was adorned with uneasy little pen drawings and filled with watery raptures over the beauties of the landscape and buildings. After two chapters, I wondered how it was possible to see so much in so short a space of time. The Italians were regarded as odd and amusing and I gathered that they were chiefly there to be admired for their picturesque appearance. Were all Italians picturesque, I wondered? Why did they not talk at all? I supposed that the author knew no Italian. I left the book after the third chapter, with a confused impression of mountains, churches and lakes.

My mother made some efforts at that time to introduce me to people of my own age. There was a cousin called Mary who was very short sighted and sang. We never had much to say to each other. I went to tea with her. She enjoyed the luxury of a sitting-room into which we self-consciously shut ourselves and talked about music and my father's works, and her ambitions. I chiefly remember the cloying hygienic smell of the lozenges she sucked, and the persistence with which one stuck to my handkerchief where I had hidden it.

I read the Memoirs to the end, feeling guilty about Northern Italy. They were very dull, and chiefly concerned the sayings of the Duchess and the occasional events which took place in her life; which apart from the birth of an incredible number of children, were very few.

I went back to the library several times and talked to Miss Tate. She recommended me a good novel; about a nun in olden times, she said. I enjoyed it enormously. The nun had a unique capacity for combining a truly noble spirit and the power to get what she wanted. She finally turned out not to be a nun at all, and fainted into the arms of a crusading knight, where she remained during the last two pages of the book. I was much affected by the story but I felt sure that my enjoyment proved of how little use the book was to my education.

I asked Miss Tate to have tea with me in a teashop. I was afraid to ask her home lest it be a repetition of Michael. She talked a great deal about her life at home. Her father was a draper, hence the selection of ribbons she wore on her white blouses; and her brother was in the army. She told me at first that her mother was dead, but later said that she had run off with a conjurer, and nobody knew where she was.

'Wasn't your father terribly unhappy?'

'I expect he was put out at first, but he has his life all right, just the same. There's the shop and he plays bowls. He's president of his club. Mother went off when I was ten so I don't remember her much and auntie came and brought us up, till she and father had a quarrel. She left then, and took all the spoons with her. Father was put out, they were a wedding present from his sister and auntie went right back to Bexhill and never said a word. Still it was nice while it lasted.' She very often finished a story with some gay enigmatic phrase of this kind, throwing back her head and laughing afterwards, her gold stopping glinting and a tear in the corner of her eye. She asked me perfunctorily about myself and seemed impressed that my father wrote music. She condoled with me easily about the dullness of my life and gave me the impression that she thought I was too good for it, that I had a devil up my sleeve which would betray itself to her own admiration. 'Go on now,' she would say, 'I bet you laughed.' And 'If only they knew.' She asked me if I had ever been in love, and I lied and said once but that he had gone away. I remember a sincere pang as I said this for something unknown. I asked her about herself and she bridled and said she liked a bit of fun, no harm in it; and for some extraordinary reason I imagined her putting on her stockings. In spite of her appearance she had a delicate regard for her health and suffered from a series of unaccountable headaches, turns and suffocations which always manifested themselves at some crisis in her life. 'I felt awful,' she would say rolling her eyes. 'I didn't know how I was going to get through. Still you never know till you try.' She would cram fat white hands into gloves, fumble with the buttons, and be getting along, leaving half a cake on her plate. Through her I became acquainted with Charlotte M. Yonge and Dickens.

I wrote twice to Lucy and once to Deb, but received no reply.

It was early spring and my sister was engaged in organizing a stall for a Church Bazaar. The promise of a long but peaceful summer loomed ahead.

One day Miss Tate (whose other name was Agnes) said, 'Why don't you take a job? Or do you like it as you are?'

'No,' I said. 'I'd love to work.'

'*I* like it. Then you know where you are. When to work and when to play. Still they say all work and no play makes Jack a dull boy,' she laughed.

'What could I do?' I stared hopefully at her. She was so gay and sure, I depended on her exuberance.

'Well, you might come here. Or wouldn't you like it?' She was very well aware that we lived in different ways and generally treated me with a kindly concern, never feeling very sure that I could do things for myself. She liked and expected ineptitude.

'Oh yes. Is there a place for me?'

'The other girl left last week. Trouble at home.' She rolled her eyes. 'Oh dear, some people. But Mr Simmons, he's our manager, he's on the look out.'

'Where is he?'

'Better ask your parents first. You don't want trouble.'

'They won't mind,' I said defiantly.

She eyed me protectively.

'You ask first. Don't want any nastiness, not with summer coming on.'

'Summer?'

'My father stops me going out in the evening if he's put out.'

'I don't think mine would do that.'

'You haven't gone against them,' she said wisely. 'You talk it over. It's nine to six, three-quarters of an hour for lunch. Saturday afternoon off. Two pounds a week. I'd show you round. You'd soon pick it up, with an education.'

Two pounds! An enormous amount of money.

'What a lot.'

'Don't make a mistake. Depends how far you have to make it go. You tell me tomorrow. Bye-bye.'

I went home with a beating heart. As soon as I was out of the shop I realized the wisdom of her remarks about my family. It would be terrible to have started and be ignominiously hauled back. Two pounds. I would even be able to buy flowers. But supposing my father refused to allow me. I wondered how Agnes spent her money. Perhaps she had to buy her clothes with it. Well I could pay for my clothes and surely my parents would be pleased. They could not object to my earning some part of my living. We were desperately short of money. My mother had darned my stockings herself, when I was out, to make up for not buying me new ones; and when I had thanked her she had flushed and promised to afford them in a month. Perhaps if I earned enough money we could even paint the house bright shiny cream like the others. I must choose a moment when my sister was not there. We sat through tea and cleared it away. My father went to his studio. My sister sat firmly in the room embroidering a boot bag. I had decided to approach my mother alone. The opportunity did not come, and I grew more and more nervous and despairing of success.

My sister went to bed very early after supper: I think she read in her bedroom. But fate persisted against me and my father for once did not go to his studio, but elected to play patience with me. For twenty minutes we played; I growing more and more distrait and stupid. Finally I dropped a whole pack of cards on the floor.

'What is the matter with you?' asked my father. I knelt, fumbling and groping to pick them up, and then I knew I must have courage to tell them.

'I should like to start ...' My voice was cracked and squeaky. I began again with a deep breath. 'I have been thinking that perhaps it would be a good thing if I had a job, work of some kind.' There was a short silence. They looked at me expectantly.

'Well,' I said. I remember sketching a feeble little gesture with my hands as I waited for their reply.

'And what work would you consider taking up?' My father was at his dryest and most sarcastic. I hated him then.

'Of course I know that I cannot do anything. I haven't been taught.' I was speaking to my mother. The irony of placating her with my uselessness escaped me at the time. 'But I thought there are things I could do, learn to do, that aren't very difficult, if you had no objection to my trying.'

'You have plenty to do at home,' said my father.

'No,' I said. 'I haven't.' The firmness of my voice surprised us all. 'There is a vacancy in a library near here. I thought I might apply for it. Two pounds a week. The hours are from nine until six with three-quarters of an hour off for lunch, and half a day on Saturday.'

'How did you find all that out?'

'Somebody told me.'

'Have you been making friends with people who work there?'

'One of them.' I stared at my father defiantly. 'I should like it very much. I could earn enough money to buy my clothes.' My mother winced. 'Or to buy anything we wanted,' I added ashamed that I had hurt her.

My father laughed. 'My dear little girl, it's out of the question. Poor though we are, I could not think of you slaving in a shop in order to relieve us.'

'It wouldn't be slaving. I should love it. Oh please let me go. I'm tired of doing nothing. I'm tired of trying to fill up my life with little events, and remaining so useless. I should like to earn money and feel that I could do a proper job like other people.'

'That is all very well, but I'm afraid that the job cannot be in a library.'

'Why not? What is the difference between working there, and anywhere else?'

'There is a difference,' he reiterated stubbornly. 'But perhaps we might find other work for you. Why do you not help your sister with her stall?'

'Oh *that*. That's not what I mean. It is done for fun. For charity. In a few weeks it would be over. I want a real job that would go on, where I could earn money.'

'I'm afraid I cannot allow you to work in a library.' He appealed to my mother. 'Don't you agree?'

'I think it would probably be a mistake.'

'You see, dear,' he went on awkwardly to me, 'the girls who work there are different from you. They would resent your coming there, they would feel that you did not need the money and they would naturally resent it. It would not be fair.'

'But we do need it.' I was terrified of crying and the fear made me reckless and cruel. 'We do need money. Our house is never painted. We never have new curtains or enough clothes. We're always having to consider before we buy things. We only have one servant and the house is too big for her to keep it clean. We don't have holidays unless someone asks us to stay. Tom and Hubert never bring their friends back here because it's so dull and they can have better times somewhere else. We used to have parties with candles on the table and fruit in a big dish. And concerts when people came. Soon no one will ask us to stay because they'll have forgotten we exist. I'm getting older; I want to know things and see more people. This is something for me, not you, you needn't think about it.'

'You are overwrought. Go to bed now and we'll talk about it in the morning.'

'You won't, you won't.' My voice was shaking and I was crying. 'You'll forget, on purpose. Just because you've got some silly class prejudice you'll try to stop me going.'

'You are being very thoughtless and unkind. We have done the best we can for you, and you are making the worst of it. I think staying with your rich friends in the country has had a very bad effect on you.'

'I am sure we could find a nice place where you could work,' said my mother, and I saw how she was suffering from the situation and how desperately she wanted it to stop before I could say more things that would hurt her and enrage my father.

I went to my room without a word, and sitting on my bed I heard the low hum of my parents' voices below, rising and falling for a good two hours. I undressed. I was still and cold and I knew that I had lost. The thought of complete rebellion never entered my head.

My mother came into my room that night, and bent over me.

'Are you all right, dear?'

'Yes.'

'Father was upset. He is very tired these days.'

I reached out my arms and hugged her, so fiercely that she was almost frightened although a little pleased.

'I didn't mean it about the clothes. I just said it because I wanted to go so much.'

The chance had slipped from my fingers on to the floor finally into the past. She sat on the edge of my bed and promised that she would find me something to do, stroking my hair nervously all the while. She said that she understood how I felt, that she had been like that, and one of those unaccountable tales came out that one's parents sometimes tell one, utterly inconsistent with the idea one has of them and fascinating for that very reason. I loved her very much and she lulled me into acquiescence through the content I had in that feeling. But I went to sleep pondering on the doctrine of 'You shall not do what you like,' wondering how many more people lived under its grey sinuous rule.

CHAPTER TEN

The next morning my father treated me as though the night before had never happened; and I was grateful to him.

I also had leisure to reflect that he was after all not deliberately trying to thwart me, that he was obeying a code laid down by generations; and in a flash of understanding I realized how poverty must strengthen it.

Agnes's sympathy fell sweetly on my ears when we had lunch together. She never stored things up as I did, but felt most thoroughly and strongly any feeling she had until it was finished, and had no false pride about admitting the change of her mood. 'Oh, I felt like that yesterday, but least said soonest mended,' she would say and I profited by the buoyancy of her nature.

A week later, I started taking two children out for walks in Kensington Gardens every afternoon. They lived in a large crimson house in our road, and were part of a big family. My mother had met them, in the midst of various charitable functions. The two mothers arranged the walks. I went to see the other mother, who said that she must pay me for the time and trouble. I became proud and stupid and refused the offer saying that I liked walks and it was no trouble. I think I had a subconscious desire to make the job of my parents' choosing unsatisfactory to myself, to render it amateur and ladylike and so nurse a grievance.

'Nonsense, my dear,' she said. 'I shall have to pay a governess. You can talk French to them if it makes you feel any better about it.' I thought of the endless limitations of my French and we both laughed. It was finally arranged at the rate of two shillings an afternoon. The children were a boy and a girl aged seven and five. Their names I remember were William and Anne. I grew fond of them and nervously proud of my responsibility. Of course it was boring at times:

William would become without warning exceedingly unmanageable, throw stones at the ducks and put his boots in the water, or throw them at me if I attempted to pull him away from the edge. Anne was a good little thing, content to walk sedately telling me the most astonishing lies.

'Are you tired?' I asked her one day.

'Not much. But I walk seven miles you know every morning.' She also said she had hot strawberries for tea every day. I believed her in the beginning; the little pink face with the candid blue eyes, and the quiet convincing calm of her manner made her difficult to disbelieve: until one day when she announced that Nanny slept with a big axe in her bed to chop off their heads if they were naughty; and that some being called Mr Sykes rode her tricycle round the nursery at night.

'That cannot be true,' I implored William aghast.

'Oh no. She just says that.'

'It is quite well true.' She shrugged her minute shoulders and walked on, quelling any moral reasoning upon which I might have embarked.

On wet days I played with them in their schoolroom. The Victorian house had large rooms with high ceilings, and dark flamboyant wallpapers, except in the children's quarters, which were in pale green paint. The schoolroom had 'Scenes from History' pictures stuck in a frieze on the walls and glazed. I remember officers, standing almost bolt upright on their horses (which were invariably rearing), as they urged on their men to relieve some fort or other; the picture being decorated with little orange sparks surrounded by puffs of smoke which represented the shells bursting. There were the Crusaders; the Battle of Bosworth; the Battle of Hastings, with Harold staggering, an arrow exactly in the middle of his eye; the signing of Magna Charta; Canute in an enormous chair with the waves rippling delicately over his big pointed feet; Agincourt; Henry VIII surrounded most improbably by all his wives at once; Queen Elizabeth prancing over Raleigh's cloak; Charles II hiding in an oak tree in bright sunlight; Nelson dying, ghastly pale by the light of a flickering lantern – I have forgotten the rest, but I was fascinated at the time. The children, of course, had grown up with them, and never looked at, or even saw them. The elder children were at schools, but there was a baby in long white lace clothes, and a child of three, both in charge of a Nanny. The family was well-to-do; the father having managed some industry in the north, and settled in London when his fortune was made. They had wonderful teas, I remember.

On Sundays the children walked with their parents, and I was free. I met them once on a Sunday and was for some reason incredibly embarrassed; they seemed like different people although they were perfectly friendly.

I planned to give my mother a length of silk for a dress, as thick and heavy as it was possible to buy. I knew that I could not bear to buy clothes for myself after my cruel outburst on the lack of them. After one visit to the shop I realized that it would be another month before I had the necessary sum.

My family never inquired about Agnes Tate, and as I did not bring her home the friendship prospered on the few hours allotted to it. (Agnes had only her lunch hour to spare.) I had met at the library a young man with pale hair and a lisp. I had not liked him, his voice and his choice of words being too intellectually effusive for my young Spartan mind, but he had been kind about books, selecting, encouraging and asking my opinion, in a manner which I later realized could only be described as woman to woman.

Agnes had laughed at me with careless admiration. We had to be very careful not to talk too much while she was working, as it displeased Mr Simmons, who would sidle towards us like a crab, scratching his right ear where he kept his pencil.

And then something happened in the middle of this calm. We were sitting in the park, Agnes and I, eating cherries.

'Why don't you come out on the spree one night?' she said.

'With you?'

'With me and some friends. Unless you like to bring anyone yourself.'

I knew she meant a man and there was no one to take.

'I'd love to,' I said guardedly. 'Where would we go?'

'Might go to a show and have a bit of supper. Or walk in the park. You leave that to me.'

I was rather frightened. 'I haven't anyone to bring.'

'Don't you have any friends?'

'They're in the country, except you.'

'Oh *me*. I meant men friends. Funny idea keeping them so far away. Tell you what. I'll ask my friend to bring a friend.'

'I don't need one. I could go with you.'

'Go on, you are awful. Wouldn't my friend be pleased! He works in a big place. He'll find someone.'

'What about my family?'

'Tell them you're going to a concert. Something fancy.' She imitated someone playing the violin. 'That'll fetch them. They won't know.' A sense of adventure seized me.

'I'll tell them I'm going out with a friend I met in the country.'

'That's it,' she said and looked at my watch. 'Oo, I must be getting back. I'll let you know.'

Two days later she said it was all right for Thursday night, if that suited me. We were to meet in the Gardens at seven o'clock under Queen Victoria's statue. 'Arthur is bringing a friend,' she said. 'They work together. I said you wanted a bit of fun and didn't get out much. His friend's older than Arthur, he knows his way about.'

I was filled with vague misgivings.

'What'll you wear?'

'I don't know. What shall you wear?'

'I'll wear a skirt and my new piqué. And I shall take a coat. I trimmed my straw last week and father'll lend me some gloves. Don't dress too fine,' she added, rather anxiously.

'I haven't got anything fine. Would a cotton frock be all right?'

'What's it like?'

'Pale green. Trimmed with white. I haven't a hat though.'

'I'll lend you one. I'll bring it tomorrow. You'll have to put something on it.'

'Oh Agnes, you *are* kind.'

'You'll have me embarrassed next. You'd better get a green ribbon to match. It's a dove straw.'

'What are we going to do?'

'Arthur doesn't know yet. He's asking his friend. It's much better to let the men plan. After all, they pay.' The financial aspect had not occurred to me.

'Will it cost very much?' I faltered. Surely it could not be right to let a completely unknown man pay for my supper.

'They can manage. After all they choose to do it. They get something out of it too. Arthur's friend hasn't got a friend and he wants to meet you. I told Arthur what you were like.'

What had she said I wondered.

'Is Arthur in love with you?'

'Goodness me what a leading question,' she giggled. 'We've passed an evening in the park from time to time.'

Passed an evening in the park. And we were meeting in the park. Still Agnes would be there. It must be all right really. I went home planning what to tell my parents.

She gave me the hat next day, and I spent an anxious half hour choosing ribbon. Wide green petersham, and, as an afterthought, a strip of artificial daisies. I showed them to Agnes, who approved.

'Tell you what. I'll trim it for you. I like doing it.'

I was filled with gratitude.

It was Tuesday evening. I told my mother that a girl I had met at the Lancings' had asked me to a concert and supper.

'Did she write to you?'

'No, I met her, quite by chance in the street.'

My mother was appeased and I was delighted with my easy success.

Wednesday passed in a fever of anticipation. Agnes brought me the hat and told me that Arthur's friend was called Mr Harris, Edward Harris, and that we were going to a musical. I had no idea what a musical was, but did not dare display my further ignorance.

'Then we'll have supper,' she said. 'Arthur says they're going to do it in style.'

On Thursday I took the children up to Queen Victoria's statue and sat beneath it, hardly able to believe that in a few hours' time I should be there under such different circumstances. The day was very fine and hot with a threat of thunder. Suppose it should rain. The afternoon crept by loaded with doubts and fears. I took the children back, and was unusually helpful to my mother in order to pass the time.

'Where is your friend staying?' she said suddenly.

'I am meeting her in the park.'

'If you do not know where she lives, you may need a cab home. Have you money?'

'No – yes.'

'Which do you mean?'

'I have money.' My mother said nothing, but when I went to my room, I found three shillings on the dressing-table. I brushed my hair and wished that I could wear my pink frock. There was a little sick feeling of excitement, and I found it impossible to stop shivering as I stared at the frock, my shoes, a handkerchief and the hat. I must conceal the hat; put it on when I was away from the house. My mother would be sure to ask where I had bought it, and then when it disappeared mysteriously after this evening, she would want some explanation. It was oppressively hot. I had no face powder. I tried some talc in the bathroom but it turned me a greenish white, and meant washing my face again.

At a quarter to seven I slipped out of the house, calling good-bye to my mother. Her voice, shouting, 'Don't be late', floated away from me. At the corner, I put on my hat and fastened it by two immense hatpins with white heads. Then lifting my skirts I ran up Victoria Road, until the heat and my age reminded me to stop. It would be better to let the others arrive first. Ten to seven ... I had plenty of time. I walked along, alternately feeling the back of my hair, tucking in any stray wisps, and looking down at my frock. An old man who was airing his dog, watched me anxiously. I felt his eyes on the back of my head after I had passed, and looked round. He was standing facing me. I should never have turned back. When he saw me he stared at the pavement, grunted and continued his walk. I hastened up the Broad Walk, emptier than in the day time, but sprinkled with couples, slowly pacing, their faces turned to each other. There was a tall ragged boy pulling a cart on iron wheels. He looked at me and grinned. 'Don't be late for 'im. 'E mightn't wite.' I flushed angrily. Horrid little boy.

I arrived at the statue at two minutes to seven. There was no one there: I was early after all. I sat down and smoothed my gloves, beset by anxiety. Suppose Agnes had been laughing at me and had never intended to come.

Seven o'clock struck. There was one yacht becalmed on the pond. People were beginning to drift towards the entrance of the park. Agnes was too good-natured to deceive me so cruelly. Would they come from the right or the left? I must not look too eagerly for them. Two minutes past seven. Time slept. I watched the sky, a golden blue, the white-edged clouds scalloped like lace, the great trees heavy with green, the biscuit-coloured paths stretching in every direction and accentuated by the low black railings over which William loved to jump, the coarse green grass worn bare in patches, the line of pink may trees planted each side of my bench and filling the air with a rich common sweetness ...

'Hullo,' said Agnes.

I looked up. She was standing before me, a young man on either arm. She introduced us. 'You were day-dreaming,' she said. 'Make room for us.'

They sat down, Arthur one side and Edward on the other. 'We're going to Gilbert and Sullivan. *The Mikado*. You know.'

'How lovely.'

The two young men seemed tongue-tied, Arthur blushing whenever Agnes looked at him and Edward staring straight in front of him with his arms folded. Edward was obviously older than the others, and was possessed of a fine black moustache and grey eyes which caught mine from time to time. Once he took out a purple silk handkerchief with which he blew his nose, whereupon Agnes jumped and said he gave her such a fright. We laughed and the situation settled itself. Agnes talked to Arthur and I was left to Edward. We both made strenuous efforts, but we were desperately shy. He, I think seeing my awkwardness, replied to my questions with patronizing little bursts to prove that it was more than his own. I asked him about his job and whether he liked it, and he said it 'was all right for the time being'. He asked me whether I had ever seen *The Mikado*, and was pleased when I said no; assured me that it was quite amusing, and said that he knew a nice little place for supper afterwards.

Agnes and Arthur giggled and chattered and provided an enviable contrast to our stilted efforts.

'Well, we ought to be going,' said Arthur. He was a fair spry man, very young, with a fresh complexion. We started walking. Agnes told them how she and I had met, and we all laughed and said how lucky it was. Edward offered me his arm in a friendly manner and I felt gratified that everything was going so well.

We stopped an omnibus and went on top, as the evening continued so finely in our favour. It was cool and refreshing and we admired the Albert Memorial. Edward, becoming more expansive, told me about Kew Gardens and Richmond, and the fair on Hampstead Heath. Knightsbridge was alive with hansom cabs like upright beetles, trotting towards Piccadilly.

'I like to see a bit of life,' said Agnes, and we all agreed with her. Here I was, going to an opera. I had always been promised a Gilbert and Sullivan but the promise had never been fulfilled and I had no conception of what form the entertainment would take.

We had jostled off the omnibus, nearly too late, and were now walking four abreast. Arthur bought a rose from an old flower seller; and Edward, after a moment's hesitation, selected a little bunch of violets and presented them to me. They were soft and cool and smelt faintly of purple mist. From that moment I was really happy. I had never been given flowers, and the violets were perfect to me. I turned on Edward, stammering with gratitude, and embarrassed the poor man considerably, although the others laughed with pleasure to see me so easily pleased. Edward took my arm rather more firmly and said it was nothing, nothing at all, and they suited me. 'You're rather like a violet yourself, I should say.' He then choked so badly that he had to use the purple handkerchief. We arrived at the theatre with time to spare and watched the people pouring into the building. Edward said that you could tell where they would sit by their clothes. Agnes pointed out real lace and well cut gowns with professional discernment. The carriages drove to the entrance; a footman alighted and let down the steps; the gentlemen, in black and white, sprang out to assist the ladies, who stepped down, settled themselves on the pavement like birds, and walked proudly in talking and laughing.

'I should love to go in a carriage like that,' said Agnes to me. I did not tell her that I had, and that sitting with one's back to the horse made one feel sick, but enjoyed the illusion and freedom of the spectacle, leaning on Edward's arm.

We were seated in the pit. 'Lovely seats,' Agnes whispered excitedly to me as we settled ourselves and broke the seals on the two programmes. Edward leaned over me to share mine. Our shoulders pressed together. Once he looked at me, I smiled, he went on looking, and I felt that he admired me, thought I was pretty. I smiled again recklessly disarming. He leaned over the violets pinned on my frock. 'Do they smell?' I lowered the programme into my lap. He sniffed and murmured something softly that I did not hear. The lights went down and the orchestra struck up with the overture.

The curtain went up noiselessly and at a tantalizing speed and I heard myself gasp with excitement and delight. Edward covered my hand with his own, large and hard, and irresistibly comforting.

We took the air in the interval. It was dusky, and we walked in couples, up and down outside the theatre, saying very little. My head was full of tunes, glorious racy tunes, that came to the expected and desired ending, with pleasing and reassuring certainty. The acting was wonderful. Several times a song had been sung again which made me feel that I had seen the whole act twice.

Agnes and I repaired to a cloak-room to preen. It was crowded and presided over by an old woman who exulted in the overcrowdedness with a blowsy delight. 'They must think we're fairies,' I heard Agnes say, and we giggled. She lent me some face powder and I returned rejuvenated with gritty eyelashes.

It was unbearable to find the opera at an end, the singers standing in a line, bowing, and giving one a final chance to take an agonized farewell of their charms.

We reeled into the street, discussing what we had liked best, and Edward leading the way to our supper place. Arthur hummed one of the tunes and Agnes supplied the words. 'For he's going to marry Yum-Yum, Yum-Yum.' We marched in time.

I had not left the theatre, or the scene, the black-haired women with fluttering hands, the large fat man who followed the Mikado himself, the exotic and improbable colour which had pervaded the whole evening – I was in a dream, with only Edward's presence between me and reality. He did not talk, and I assumed that his mood was like mine; that our consciousness of each other was only a recognition of our mutual feeling. I wanted to walk for ever in silence, on his arm. We stopped. I had never been in a public house in my life. Edward pushed open the swing door marked 'Saloon Bar', and we entered. It was full of people. Edward spoke to the man behind the counter, who nodded, raised the flap, and ushered us to the back of the room, through a pair of deep red curtains, into a passage, and finally into a much smaller room, with a table and a large window looking on to the street. 'They know me here,' said Edward, and I think we were all impressed. We sat down. The window had coarse net curtains which showed the dark shapes of people passing in the street. The ceiling was encrusted with a repeated pattern of fruit and flowers and painted pale green. I sat with my back to a brown marble fireplace, obviously not used as there was a screen of brown paper pasted over the grate. Green paint glistened half-way up the walls, and above it extended red wallpaper with a frieze of convolvulus and pears round the top. We sat at the table, which was spread with a newly ironed cloth spotted with a few blurred and yellow stains.

'And now,' said Arthur. 'Bring on the bubbly.'

'Oo,' said Agnes. 'You do go on.'

What was bubbly? I asked. They shrieked with laughter, tilting back their chairs. It made the evening that I did not know.

A waiter came, a small man, fatherly but obsequious. He carried the menu, a sheet of paper on which was written the choice of food in a large round hand; he could not have written it himself with those gnarled stubby fingers. Edward studied it very grandly, reading aloud the items. Steak. Fried plaice. He hurried over the half portion of lobster saying it was the wrong month, with a certain amount of relief. Mixed grill. Saddle of mutton. Cold beef.

'I'd like a steak,' said Agnes. 'I need nourishing.' I agreed to a steak. I was not hungry and did not care what I ate. 'Four steaks,' repeated the waiter scribbling on his pad. Then cocking his head on one side he remained motionless while the vegetables were discussed. He had waxed whiskers; the shadow of them on the wall was enormous, the end of one point stabbing a pear on the frieze. Agnes ordered a stout with her food. Edward turned inquiringly to me. After my ignorance about the champagne I could hardly ask for lemonade; I tried to appear deep in thought. 'Have a stout?' suggested Edward and I knew he was not deceived. 'That's the ticket,' cried Arthur. The waiter scudded away and we could relax. There was a little silence while we smiled vaguely at each other, savouring the evening.

'Good show that,' said Arthur.

'Wonderful,' I said. It had already slipped into the past. I felt something pressing my foot under the table. Edward caught my eye and smiled, a warm secretive smile. We were both back in the dark, holding hands, alone together in some magic way, despite the crowds of people round us. A little tremor ran through me.

'Cold?' said Edward. His voice was elaborately casual. I shook my head.

The waiter returned with four brimming glasses on a tray. He dusted the table and the liquid swayed in the glasses but did not spill. Three very dark, the colour of a black kitten in the sun, and one brown for Edward. He set them before us, and murmuring confidentially to Edward that the steaks wouldn't be long, he disappeared. There was a thin layer of rich froth on top of my glass. It looked delicious.

'Here's to all of us,' said Arthur, and raised his glass.

I took a gulp and swallowed it quickly. It was horrible.

'All right?' asked Edward.

'Lovely.' How could anyone like it? How would I even finish it? I determined to watch Agnes and drink when she drank.

'I knew you'd like it,' Edward said complacently.

'What would you like most in the world?' asked Agnes dreamily, a moment later gazing into her glass.

'A motor car,' said Arthur promptly. 'With you in it. Driving to Brighton with you.' She flushed and he took her hand.

'Clerks'll never have motor cars,' said Edward scornfully. 'Be lucky to drive in a cab.'

'Everyone'll have motor cars, you mark my words.'

'Only the rich,' said Edward gloomily. Agnes drank again and I raised my glass. There was so much of it.

'Perhaps I won't always be a clerk.'

'Perhaps there'll be an earthquake and we'll all have different jobs.'

'Cheer up, Mr Harris,' cried Agnes. 'This is a party, see.'

'Call me Edward,' he said, and was friendly again.

'Well go on, what would you like?'

'Like?'

'Most in the world.'

'Most in the world,' he repeated slowly looking at me. I buried my face in my glass again. 'I dunno. I'd like to travel, see things, see if everyone has the same social system where a quarter of the population are a bit of all right, and the other three-quarters don't have time to want anything. I'd like to know if it's reading does the trick; or I'd like to know if it's work makes people happy, or if it stops them thinking anything, or knowing what they want. I'd like to find out how many people do what they like; or if they just think it's better to do what they don't like. Smoothes their conscience or something. Things like that.'

'Gloomy aren't you?' said Agnes. 'There's ever such a lot of fun if you take it.'

'I'd like a farm as well.'

'That's better,' said Arthur approvingly. 'She meant what would you like to *have*.'

'Who's she? The cat's mother?' We all laughed. Only a quarter of my glass gone.

'I should like a big house in town and one in the country,' said Agnes. 'And a carriage, and black horses, and lots of gentlemen sending me flowers. And a lot of clothes the latest fashion, from Paris. And a little dog, you know a tiny one that shivers, and furs, and a diamond bracelet, and everyone taking their hats off to me, and a lady's maid, French, and I'd send her to the library, for novels, and boxes of chocolates with pink ribbons, and people taking me out to shows every night, and dancing.' She set down her glass, flushed with excitement. 'I'd marry a foreign count in the end, who'd kiss my hand.'

'Crikey,' said Arthur. He looked unhappy. She looked at him affectionately.

'Go on,' she said. 'That's only what I *want*.'

The waiter brought our steaks, pink and golden with dark edges. There was a little watercress on the top of each, and a rich pile of fried chips on each plate. There were a dish of fresh young beans and two bottles of sauce.

'Everything all right, sir?'

Edward said it was, and the waiter ran away beaming.

'What do *you* want?' said Edward. I had been so fascinated by the others that I had not thought.

'I don't know,' I said foolishly.

'Come now,' they cried, 'that's dull, think a bit, you must want something.'

'Or have you got everything?' said Edward keenly.

'Oh no.' I had not by any means got everything. I wanted so much without knowing precisely what it was. 'Well, I'd like to write a book,' I was startled to hear myself say.

'She's always reading,' Agnes said to the others, showing me off.

They seemed so impressed that I decided to let it stand although I was very much afraid they would ask me what I had written.

'I want to find out about people; feelings.' None of the words felt quite right. 'Living,' I said. 'About living. I would like to be famous. At least I would like to be really well known by someone.' That was absurd. 'I would like to be older and well – wiser I suppose. I don't want things ever to be the same, at least nothing I know. If I found the right things I'd want them for ever. Really I want to be older and know things. Be absolutely certain of them. Now, I don't know much, and I try to make it fit for everything and of course it doesn't. I'd like to be wise enough for anyone's size of mind.' I looked at them, hopelessly incoherent.

'Your steak's getting cold,' said Edward kindly.

'Anyway you want to write a book,' said Agnes.

Heavens, she had finished her stout. I took a deep breath and gulped mine down until the glass was empty except for a drift of bubbles slipping down the inside. I felt hot and light-headed and the stuff didn't taste so bad. We ate our meal, Agnes telling stories of the people who came to change their books.

When he saw that I did not eat much, Edward took my knife and fork and insisted on cutting my meat. I flirted with him, and felt Agnes's approval. She had taken her rose off her dress. The bud was limp, with one petal curled back. She put it in water. 'Looks mopey, poor thing,' she said. 'I love flowers.' Her large blue eyes devoured it hungrily.

I could not finish my plateful but the others did not mind,

seemed rather to admire it as an evidence of my dainty appetite.

We had cold apple tart; and finally little glasses of port, four brilliant red jewels winking on our empty table. Edward smoked a pipe. Did I mind? Mind! I was fascinated. He puffed away, content and well fed. We all agreed that it was a nice little place.

'I wonder what it would be like to be an actress.'

'Wonderful,' I said. The port slipped down my throat like burning balm. It was very sweet and sticky and much nicer than stout. Edward offered me another and I accepted.

'Aren't you a one!' said Agnes admiringly. 'I can't drink any more. I'll have a red nose.' She squinted down it.

'I shouldn't like you to be an actress,' said Arthur firmly.

'Why not?'

'I just shouldn't like it.'

'That settles it,' she said cheerfully. 'I'll have to turn down the offers. Lots of money in it though, I should think.'

'Awful life,' said Edward gloomily, and we all felt glad we were not on the stage.

What a lot Edward knew. I felt sleepy, and all their voices seemed to come startlingly separate out of nothing. They talked and I drank my second port in silence. I did not want it when it came, but I could not be rude when I had asked for it. She got what she asked for, I remembered people saying, and this was what she asked for. Not so terrible as they had made it sound. A wreath of convolvulus and pears swayed suddenly down to hit the top of Agnes's head. My own head was too heavy. 'For he's going to marry Yum-Yum, Yum-Yum,' crawled through my head. Agnes and Arthur were swaying slowly in time to the words. 'She's nearly asleep,' I heard Agnes say, and with a start I realized that my head was on Edward's shoulder and his arm round my waist. I sat up, blinking the blur of lights out of my eyes. 'I'm so sorry.' How awful. What would he think?

'We'll be going upstairs. It's time to go now,' said Agnes.

Edward stood up to let me out and I got carefully to my feet, holding the table as I squeezed past. The floor was a long way down and every time I stepped it was like going downstairs. Agnes took my arm and led the way to a tiny cloak-room.

'How awful of me to go to sleep.'

'It was the port,' she said. 'We're going to see if we can get a cab.'

'What about the bill?' I was very pleased with myself for remembering the bill.

'They're paying it now. Like some powder?' I took it. 'I should wash your face first,' she advised. She had innate tact. She must have known how the cold water would clear my head and revive me but she said nothing. I dried my face and looked in the glass. Agnes was combing her hair over the puffs.

'Been a lovely evening, hasn't it?'

'Lovely,' I said, too emphatically. 'Very nice,' I repeated more guardedly.

'There, now you'll be all right.' She had put on her hat. Where was mine?

'Edward's got it,' she said. 'The pins stuck in his neck.'

We joined the others. They had our coats on their arms and Edward helped me into mine. 'You mustn't get cold.'

'Mind my violets.'

'They'll be all right.' He squeezed my arm.

We went out through a side door into the grey airless street. I stumbled a little until I was used to the light. My head was aching and I could not loosen my tightly arranged hair because Agnes held my other arm. We found a cab and got in. 'Where to?' said the driver. 'Victoria Road,' said Agnes. She knew I lived there. 'We'd better drop you on the corner,' she said. I nodded forgetting that in the dark she could not see. 'All right?'

'Yes,' I said. It was very stuffy and smelt of damp leather and mildew. Arthur lowered the windows. We were off.

'Aren't we nobs, going home in a cab,' said Agnes. 'Laugh at the buses we can.' Dimly I understood that the cab was unusual and for my benefit.

'It's very kind of you,' I murmured.

Edward bent down. 'What was that?'

'Kind of you,' I murmured again. Agnes and Arthur were very quiet. I said something about how quiet they were, and there was a little suppressed giggle from Agnes and some movement in the dark.

'Put your head on my shoulder again,' said Edward. 'I like it.'

How kind he was. My hat was in his lap. I saw the straw gleaming like a neat round nest in a fairy tale. I leaned against him. He put his arm round my shoulders and clasped my wrist. His hand was very hot. We jolted on in silence while I wished that someone would speak, but felt too tired and weak to begin. I sighed, and slowly his hand edged up to the back of my neck, his face loomed over me for a second, so that I saw his eyes in the grey blur, and then his mouth was on mine; his moustache soft and dry in contrast. There was a feeling of a very long time or perhaps none at all: still he was kissing me, with warmth and deliberation, and I lay in his arms unresisting, half stirred. He was not a person to me any more, he was a kiss, the part of myself that I wanted to feel alive. He stirred over me and the hat slipped to the floor with a papery rustle. My neck was aching and I pressed against his hand until I was supported by the corner of the cab. He let me go and then gathered me into his arms again more fiercely, his hands hard on my bones through the thin dress. My arms being limp at my sides, he took them and pressed them round his neck. There were a little chuckle in the dark from Agnes, some whispered protest, and still Edward's mouth urgent, harsh and warm. I was stifled, could not breathe, almost ceased to exist. I was no longer stirred but endured him with a breathless acquiescence with no thought or hope or desire for an end. The jolting slowed into a walk.

'I think we're nearly there,' said Agnes, and her voice sounded small, crushed and unreal.

Edward released me, bent down, picked up my hat, and placed it on my lap. The stopping, the practical neatness of his gesture bred in me a sudden panic, a horror of him and myself, and I had only one thought, to get out of the cab, away from him, from all of them, into the air with no part of my body touching anything but only my feet on the hard familiar pavement. I must have leaned forward groping for the door, for Edward put his hand on my arm and drew me back.

'Don't be in such a hurry. We've not stopped yet.'

I bent my head stiffly over the straw hat in my lap. I felt very sick. I remember the clop of the horse's feet running down slowly like a clock, and the jolt when we finally pulled up into silence. Edward got out, and I followed, my legs shaking so that I could hardly stand.

'Aren't you going to say good night to *us*?' said Agnes with a plaintive emphasis that made the others laugh.

'Good night,' I said, 'and thank you very much. I've enjoyed it most awfully.'

'So have I,' said Edward softly. He was standing close to me.

'Good night,' I said. I could not look at him.

'Say good night to me,' his voice demanded softly. I backed away. 'Why you little witch!'

'Please,' I said. 'I can't.' His arms were round me again and I lifted my face in an agony of surrender and dislike. He let me go abruptly and turned to the cab.

'Hammersmith,' he said, and there was a hurt significance in his voice.

'Thank you for bringing me home,' I called weakly as he was getting back into the cab.

He turned and I felt that he smiled. 'It was nothing. I shall see you again.' And they drove off.

I stood and watched them out of sight, and then hearing, hardly able to realize the relief of being alone. A dry hot breeze ruffled my face; stirred the great trees in the park opposite me and reminded me where I was. A quarter past the hour struck from some distant church clock. The houses round me were dark. It must be very late. I turned shakily and walked back to my home, where a single light gleamed. They were waiting up for me. The memory of my deception and the mood in which I had left the house a few hours before flooded back. I must not think of what had happened. I must get safely to my room. I tapped on the front door and a minute later my sister opened it, with a candle in her hand. She stood aside for me to come in.

'It's after twelve.' Her wrapper fell about her like the folded wings of a moth. 'Where have you been? I was listening and I didn't hear a cab.'

'They dropped me on the corner,' I said, very weary, and started to climb the stairs. I heard her bolt the door and follow me almost noiseless on her bare feet.

'They? Who?' she whispered. We were passing my parents' room.

'I'll tell you about it tomorrow,' I said. She seemed satisfied and pausing at the door of her room she kissed my cheek.

'How hot your face is,' she observed. 'Good night.'

'Good night.'

There was another candle burning on the low table by her bed, before a statue. Goodness, Purity, I thought and stumbled into my room.

I lighted a candle and automatically started to undress. Now I was alone all the nausea and panic crept back. I lived again those minutes lying in the dark; forced to remember every sensation, up to the moment when my sister had finally touched my burning face with her lips. I wrenched off the frock which his hands had crushed. It lay on the floor and I could not bear to touch it again. My mouth was bruised and dry. I remembered the uneasy fluttering and burning of my whole body when I had wanted him to go on kissing me; how I had not cared what he did; how I had lain passive under his mouth and hands, only half conscious of a slow uncertain crescendo within myself. He had kissed me and I had accepted it, and even liked it. In the mirror over my washstand I stared at my face. It was flushed with hectic ringed eyes. My mouth looked rough and pinched.

Suddenly I bathed my face; plunging my arms up to the elbows in the cold water jug, washing Edward from my body, rubbing him off my mouth until it ached. Agnes: had that happened to her? 'I like a bit of fun.' Of course it had. But it was different for Agnes. Arthur was her friend. To me Edward had been a complete stranger. Though he was the first man who had tried to make love to me, I had accepted it with no thought of propriety or his feelings. In bed that night, I still rubbed my mouth again and again with the corner of the sheet.

CHAPTER ELEVEN

The next day I faced the questions and comments of my mother and sister. I had insane gusts of wanting to tell them, or one of them; in order to be scolded and reassured. But most of the time I realized that my adventure was beyond their horizon; that they would be even more shocked, disgusted and unhappy, than I had made myself. And so, pale and heavy eyed, I evaded their probings and promised to help my sister with her stall as a sort of retribution. How fortunate that my parents had refused to allow me to work in the library with Agnes! I took a dreary satisfaction in their refusal having turned out for the best. I was not fit to choose what I did, since I had so easily sunk to such depths of immorality on the first provocation.

I had a great shrinking from seeing Agnes: I knew that I could not endure meeting Edward again, and I had no idea what her reaction would be, although I was afraid that she would be angry with me for an entirely different reason.

It was about then that I got a postcard which said: 'This is where I live. Just the place for you, and I should like to see you here. I believe we called it tea? No matter. I am a very bad painter, and shall expect to see you. Come whenever you like. R.' I put it carefully away beneath clothes in a drawer. Nothing was said about it, although I was sure my sister had read it, for she always read postcards. He must have found my address through the Lancings. I felt a stab of homesickness for the Lancings. They had answered none of my letters and it was impossible to go on writing to a collective silence. The postcard comforted me. He, at least, had not forgotten.

A week had passed since my evening with Agnes and I felt that I could no longer shirk seeing her. I went to the library, choosing the busiest hour in the morning. She was there, and looked just the same, trim and neat and gay.

'Where have you been? Somebody's been asking for you,' she began, and my heart sank.

'There's been a lot to do at home,' I said lamely.

'Well when would you be free?'

'I don't know. You see my parents were furious that I was so late.'

'What a shame! Never mind, we needn't be so late. We can sit in the park. Or what about a Sunday? Edward suggested Kew.' I felt a shudder of the familiar sick feeling I associated with Edward.

'I can't, Agnes. Truly I can't.'

'What's the matter then? Changed your mind?'

'Yes,' I said. 'That's it. I've changed my mind.'

'Well!' She was obviously suspicious and ready to be hurt. 'What's the matter with him?'

'I . . . I wouldn't want to marry him,' I said with desperate simplicity.

She went into gales of laughter, covered her mouth with her hand and said: 'Who said anything about marriage? You *are* a queer one. Don't you like a bit of fun?'

'Look,' I said, 'I'll explain to you. Not here. We could have lunch and I'll try and explain.'

She looked at me for a minute, and then said slowly: 'No, don't do that. I don't think I'd like it really. I'll tell him you've gone away.'

'Thank you. It's very kind of you.'

'I must get back to work,' she said. She was very flushed.

'How's Arthur?' I said.

'He's all right.' She blew her nose on a tiny handkerchief. She was going away to a customer.

'When shall I see you?'

'Oh, we can make an arrangement next time you come. I must get back. Bye-bye.'

I left the shop perturbed and anxious. I wanted badly to explain to her, and yet somehow I knew she was right, that I

123

should not be able to do so without hurting her and myself. For the first time I realized how painful people could be to each other, against both their will and intentions. It made me unbearably sad for the rest of that day.

CHAPTER TWELVE

For several weeks I concentrated on the children and my sister's stall for the Bazaar. The routine steadied and comforted me. In the morning I sewed under my sister's direction. We became better friends sitting in the window of the large dilapidated dining-room with material spread all over the table and linen bags full of scraps on every chair. She was wonderfully neat with her fingers, and her ingenuity and patience in contriving pretty and useful objects out of nothing, made me admire her, and feel less cruelly objective.

I remember asking her one day whether she would like to get married.

'If it comes my way,' she answered mildly, snipping off a thread. She had scissors like Deb's; and in a way she reminded me of her then, so neat and calm and assured. She had much hair and drooping shoulders.

'Do you think things do come one's way?' I asked.

'I'm sure they do. Our lives are very easily filled.'

'But what would you *like*?' I persisted. 'Would you like children?'

She blushed faintly. 'Of course. Two boys and a girl. I should call them Anthony, Richard and Margaret. I should like to live in the country as it would be better for their health.'

So she too had dreams, was not entirely composed of the divine resignations which I had confused with emptiness of mind.

'Go on,' I said. 'What else? What would your husband be like?'

Her face darkened a moment in the effort of concentration, and she said, 'I'm not sure. Fair, I think, but I don't know.' She gave it up.

'But you can't plan your children without a husband.' I was shocked.

She gave me a startled look and said, 'I have not planned them. That's only what I think sometimes. What do *you* want?'

'I want to write a book and get married.' That was the second time I had been asked, the second time I had answered. 'I'm not sure about children,' I went on hurriedly. 'I'd want to be sure of being married first.' It was her turn to be shocked.

'When you are married you expect to have children.'

'Oh well,' I said. 'I'd have them later. I like one thing at a time.'

'You are not likely to have twins.' She smiled at her joke. I don't think she ever laughed. I think she liked my helping her, and her ascendancy over all household matters. She had no one to whom she could show this talent, which obviously meant very much to her.

I went with her on the day that her things were sorted and priced by the Bazaar committee, comprised almost entirely of women. The Bazaar was to take place in a vast house, dark with panelling and draughty along mosaic floors. The stalls were placed round the edges of three large rooms. Two workmen were hammering a small platform, on which the Princess who was to open the Bazaar must stand. The noise was terrific. The hammering and shouting of the men; the excited babel of the women exclaiming over their handiwork; the heat and the rustle of endless tissue paper; and the buzz of bluebottles round the lead-encrusted windows made the scene one of indescribable confusion. There was also an inexplicable smell of bananas and turkish delight.

My sister seemed happier arranging her stall by herself, so with a murmured excuse I slipped away to wander round the rooms. The stalls were made of wooden trestle tables with large white cloths sweeping down to the floor, the corners pinned neatly back. Two women were struggling, scarlet-faced, with a huge pumpkin which they were trying to set up in the middle of their table. The pumpkin wobbled and finally rolled, ponderously juicy, to the floor. There were wails of dismay.

There were packing cases filled with tiny pots of jam; I read Apricot and Strawberry on the labels. A thin earnest creature with a hook nose and brilliant black eyes was painting signs on strips of shiny white paper in one corner of the first room. 'This Way to the Teas'; I read. 'Bran Tub sixpence.' 'Jumble' (in black and yellow). There were little streams of bran like chicken food and the tub had red and green crêpe paper tied round it. There were heaps of raffle tickets on tables; pins and labels, and gaunt pairs of scissors attached to some piece of furniture by string so that one had to crouch to cut anything. Tricks of that kind were what the feminine mind calls 'Organization', I learned. There was a tray of lavender bags belonging to an odious little girl of about fifteen, who was trying to sell in advance to the kind, harassed stall holders. An anxious young curate was engaged in trying to disentangle the lines of a bunch of fishing rods: 'Isn't it dreadful, Mr Beard? I packed them so carefully.'

In the third room I found a woman writing in a notebook. 'Three dozen, no four dozen teaspoons (eighteen Lady Bellamy) in brackets what *can* that mean?' Everyone appealed to Lady Bellamy, who flitted to and fro on incredibly thin elegant feet with a silver pencil pointing outwards in her hand, ordering, directing and admiring her host of followers.

The shadows lengthened on the street outside as the hours passed with no appreciable inroad made on the confusion. A curious way to spend a hot June day. I helped as much as I could, but it was difficult when one knew nobody's names and the help depended very much on a thorough knowledge of them. I carried things to people, counted, sorted, pinned labels, tied parcels, wiped cups and saucers; and simply stood holding one end of string, or with my finger on a knot. By the evening I was more exhausted than I had ever been before in my life.

The following day was the Bazaar itself, of which nothing need be said except that the sum raised was two hundred pounds odd, and that considering the time, energy and patience employed, I think every penny was earned many times over. It did occur to me going home afterwards that it would have been simpler to have had a collection for the money, but seeing my sister's tired, satisfied face I was not sure.

I had bought nothing at the Bazaar. There was at last enough money to buy the material for my mother's dress. My sister, who now knew of the plan, accompanied me to the shop for the purpose of helping to choose. I was faced with bales of material and choice seemed unbearable. There were three possible reds and I was at last able to decide only when on presenting them to my sister she rejected them all on the ground that red was an unsuitable colour.

'Grey,' she said. 'Or a good dark blue would be far more becoming.'

Instantly I was determined on red. I wanted to make my mother rich and gay and full of colour.

'The blue wears better,' said the shopman, sticking his head out and staring at me. My sister agreed that one did not get tired of dark blue as one did of red.

'You don't get tired of it because you never really like it,' I said. 'You can't have any feelings about dark blue. I'll have this one.' And I selected the richest red.

'She never *wears* red,' moaned my sister wringing her hands over the stuff.

'How many yards?' asked the assistant pausing and blinking his eyes.

'Six,' said my sister.

'I'll take seven,' I said grandly.

'Can you afford it?' whispered my sister in a frenzy.

'Of course. I've got enough for the trimming as well.'

I showed her a bulging purse, from which a half-crown fell out.

'Dear oh dear,' said the assistant, darting after it. I could not take my eyes off the silk.

'Could we have a snip to match the trimmings?' I heard my sister ask. She was being very kind. I had completely

CHAPTER THIRTEEN

...t think I was very concerned about the growing
...n Europe. Indeed I do not think anyone was seriously
...ted.

...arly remember my father's agitation over his concert,
...er the concert where his Symphonic Variations were
... performed: his fits of indigestion and depression
...ed us all. One followed very closely upon the other,
...ing the household with nerves and despair. As the
... had never been published, the parts had to be copied;
... when the time grew near, he became anxious at the
...pect of too little rehearsal. We all suffered the mixture
...nxiety and irritation that prefaces a first performance of
... kind. The weather was oppressive.

...On the morning of the concert, I upset a vase of water on
... father's piano. I shall never forget the frightened fluster
... dry cloths, and his almost venomous rage. When the
...amage had been as much repaired as was possible, and I
...as creeping out of the studio, he called me back. He was
...tanding by the piano, his fingers tapping the damp
...lotched case. He did not look at me.

'How came you to be so incredibly careless?'

'I'm very sorry, Father.'

'I don't understand it. You have always been brought up
to respect a piano. You must have known that it was courting disaster in attempting to slide a heavy vase full of water
across it.'

As there had already been an inquest on how I had done
it, and why, this was almost more than I could bear.

'I didn't do it on purpose, Father.'

'I can't understand it,' he repeated still drumming his
fingers. His hand looked yellow in the light. I was starting to
go when he turned on me with a kind of concentrated

disagreed with her and she was still being kind. I squeezed
her arm.

'What's all that for?' she asked.

'I'm excited. Let's choose the trimming.'

'Why not let Mother do that herself?'

'It's my present. I shall choose all of it.'

'Well you have to pay first.'

'You do it,' I said and handed her the purse. I could never
count change and I felt slightly sick at the amount of money
I was spending.

We chose a pale tea-coloured lace, ruffled at the edges with
a coffee ribbon to draw it up. When it was over I had five
shillings left.

'When shall you give it to her?'

'After supper. In the evening.'

'Can you wait till then?'

'Of course. You could,' I retorted.

'We're not the same about waiting,' she replied quietly,
and for a second I wondered what she meant.

The day went slowly and I tortured myself with the fear
that my sister had been right, that my mother would not like
red, or would not want a frock. After tea my mother began
discussing my clothes. My father was trying to read the
paper, a thing he never did well, as his arms were short, and
the paper crumpled and folded the wrong way when he tried
to turn the pages. He grunted and battled miserably and
finally left us with some withering remark about the way
women took no interest in outside events but thought only
of clothes.

'You should have money enough to buy a couple of nice
cotton dresses.' I could see that she was anxious at having
shown no interest in the paper and embarrassed about the
money I earned. She could not get used to the idea. I
mumbled something about the frocks I possessed doing
quite well, and she looked up in relief. 'Ah, you're saving
your money like a good careful girl,' she said.

After supper I gave it to her. 'What is it?' she asked nervously, smiling into my eyes.

'It's for you, a present.'

She gave a little gasp and bent over the string; then looked up uncertainly: 'From you?'

I nodded.

'You shouldn't,' she murmured enraptured.

I had never known how much presents meant to her and my heart beat wildly with a painful excitement. Her fingers trembled over the string until I could no longer bear it. 'I'll help.' We laughed and the string was undone. I sat back on my heels and watched her unfold the brown and white paper until she could see the red silk. She stared at it a moment unbelieving, touched it with her fingers, gave it a little pat, then suddenly lunged forward and shook it out in beautiful rich folds.

'Red,' she cried. 'Red,' and rubbed it softly against her face.

'It's silk,' I said. I was anxious that she should miss none of its beauty.

She became quickly aware of me again and said, 'Is this from you? All this red silk?'

'Seven yards,' I said. 'For a dress. You do like it, don't you?'

She turned her head away from the stuff. 'Darling, it's a wonderful present. You shouldn't have done it. You must have spent so much. All your money. It's magnificent.'

'These are the trimmings.' I gave her the second parcel. I wished now that I had put them together; I found it hard to watch her, she made me feel her pleasure almost too sharply. But she undid the trimmings quite quietly, and laid them on the stuff.

'Do you think they will look all right?' I said falsely. I was sure that they were perfect.

'I haven't worn red for years,' she said, with a hint of doubt.

'Would you have preferred dark blue?'

'No. I – like this very much better. Thank you, darling. It is very sweet of you.' She put her arms round me and kissed me, once, and then again, as though it wasn't enough.

'Will you have it made up soon?'

'I'll have it done in time for
said Daddy when she was happy
present was a success.

'She likes red,' I told my sister tri

'I shan't know you,' was my fath
was unaware of the quick little loo
him.

A few evenings later, I believe it wa
pairing music for my father on the di
mother was mending as usual and my sis
me sorting the battered sheets of Brahm
hot all day and now there was a faint b
tassels on the old green curtains. My fathe
evening paper which he read in unusual si
an organ grinder in the street outside, stopp
again with a violent animation as though
have stopped.

'Anything in the paper, dear?' asked my mot

'Some Archduke or other has been murder
paused, 'at Sarajevo. That's it. Sarajevo.'

'Oh dear.'

The organ grinder stopped and there was pea
estic silence.

disagreed with her and she was still being kind. I squeezed her arm.

'What's all that for?' she asked.

'I'm excited. Let's choose the trimming.'

'Why not let Mother do that herself?'

'It's my present. I shall choose all of it.'

'Well you have to pay first.'

'You do it,' I said and handed her the purse. I could never count change and I felt slightly sick at the amount of money I was spending.

We chose a pale tea-coloured lace, ruffled at the edges with a coffee ribbon to draw it up. When it was over I had five shillings left.

'When shall you give it to her?'

'After supper. In the evening.'

'Can you wait till then?'

'Of course. You could,' I retorted.

'We're not the same about waiting,' she replied quietly, and for a second I wondered what she meant.

The day went slowly and I tortured myself with the fear that my sister had been right, that my mother would not like red, or would not want a frock. After tea my mother began discussing my clothes. My father was trying to read the paper, a thing he never did well, as his arms were short, and the paper crumpled and folded the wrong way when he tried to turn the pages. He grunted and battled miserably and finally left us with some withering remark about the way women took no interest in outside events but thought only of clothes.

'You should have money enough to buy a couple of nice cotton dresses.' I could see that she was anxious at having shown no interest in the paper and embarrassed about the money I earned. She could not get used to the idea. I mumbled something about the frocks I possessed doing quite well, and she looked up in relief. 'Ah, you're saving your money like a good careful girl,' she said.

After supper I gave it to her. 'What is it?' she asked nervously, smiling into my eyes.

'It's for you, a present.'

She gave a little gasp and bent over the string; then looked up uncertainly: 'From you?'

I nodded.

'You shouldn't,' she murmured enraptured.

I had never known how much presents meant to her and my heart beat wildly with a painful excitement. Her fingers trembled over the string until I could no longer bear it. 'I'll help.' We laughed and the string was undone. I sat back on my heels and watched her unfold the brown and white paper until she could see the red silk. She stared at it a moment unbelieving, touched it with her fingers, gave it a little pat, then suddenly lunged forward and shook it out in beautiful rich folds.

'Red,' she cried. 'Red,' and rubbed it softly against her face.

'It's silk,' I said. I was anxious that she should miss none of its beauty.

She became quickly aware of me again and said, 'Is this from you? All this red silk?'

'Seven yards,' I said. 'For a dress. You do like it, don't you?'

She turned her head away from the stuff. 'Darling, it's a wonderful present. You shouldn't have done it. You must have spent so much. All your money. It's magnificent.'

'These are the trimmings.' I gave her the second parcel. I wished now that I had put them together; I found it hard to watch her, she made me feel her pleasure almost too sharply. But she undid the trimmings quite quietly, and laid them on the stuff.

'Do you think they will look all right?' I said falsely. I was sure that they were perfect.

'I haven't worn red for years,' she said, with a hint of doubt.

'Would you have preferred dark blue?'

'No. I – like this very much better. Thank you, darling. It is very sweet of you.' She put her arms round me and kissed me, once, and then again, as though it wasn't enough.

'Will you have it made up soon?'

'I'll have it done in time for Daddy's concert.' She only said Daddy when she was happy and unselfconscious. The present was a success.

'She likes red,' I told my sister triumphantly.

'I shan't know you,' was my father's comment to her. He was unaware of the quick little look of pain that she gave him.

A few evenings later, I believe it was a Sunday, I was repairing music for my father on the dining-room table. My mother was mending as usual and my sister was leaning over me sorting the battered sheets of Brahms. It had been very hot all day and now there was a faint breeze swaying the tassels on the old green curtains. My father came in with an evening paper which he read in unusual silence. There was an organ grinder in the street outside, stopping and starting again with a violent animation as though he could never have stopped.

'Anything in the paper, dear?' asked my mother dutifully.

'Some Archduke or other has been murdered at ...' he paused, 'at Sarajevo. That's it. Sarajevo.'

'Oh dear.'

The organ grinder stopped and there was peaceful domestic silence.

CHAPTER THIRTEEN

I do not think I was very concerned about the growing unrest in Europe. Indeed I do not think anyone was seriously disquieted.

I clearly remember my father's agitation over his concert, or rather the concert where his Symphonic Variations were to be performed: his fits of indigestion and depression affected us all. One followed very closely upon the other, infecting the household with nerves and despair. As the work had never been published, the parts had to be copied; and, when the time grew near, he became anxious at the prospect of too little rehearsal. We all suffered the mixture of anxiety and irritation that prefaces a first performance of any kind. The weather was oppressive.

On the morning of the concert, I upset a vase of water on my father's piano. I shall never forget the frightened fluster for dry cloths, and his almost venomous rage. When the damage had been as much repaired as was possible, and I was creeping out of the studio, he called me back. He was standing by the piano, his fingers tapping the damp blotched case. He did not look at me.

'How came you to be so incredibly careless?'

'I'm very sorry, Father.'

'I don't understand it. You have always been brought up to respect a piano. You must have known that it was courting disaster in attempting to slide a heavy vase full of water across it.'

As there had already been an inquest on how I had done it, and why, this was almost more than I could bear.

'I didn't do it on purpose, Father.'

'I can't understand it,' he repeated still drumming his fingers. His hand looked yellow in the light. I was starting to go when he turned on me with a kind of concentrated ferocity and said, 'Purpose. What do you know about such a thing? Whether you ruin my piano or not is surely a business entirely within your control. You're not a fool. If you had cared enough this wouldn't have happened. What do you mean by "Purpose" – yours or God's?'

'I didn't mean to do it. That's what I meant. I didn't want ...'

'You didn't care,' he accused. I could hear his breath coming in sharp little gasps. I remembered his concert and it saved me from losing my temper.

'I honestly think the piano will be all right.'

'Sit down. I must make you understand this. What you do, what you are, is entirely a matter for you to decide. You are responsible for your future. Nothing else. No one else. If you care to do things, or not to do them, it is possible ...' He was walking about the room picking up small objects, a pencil, a postcard, and throwing them down on a different table. 'You do not seem to me aware of this. Some people think that we are controlled by some destiny or fate. It's utterly untrue. Utterly untrue. Whether we succeed, or fail, our perseverance and the direction we pursue is us. We finish by living the life we have made for ourselves.' His voice stopped suddenly and I realized that he was torturing himself, revealing even to me his own tragedy of failure, a failure because he saw it like that, and a tragedy because to be a failure made him so unhappy. I knew that he needed me to go up to him, touch him, perhaps kiss him; to say something, that would give him some false assurance that I had not understood him, to comfort and deceive. But the old familiar sick hatred for my surroundings and the people trapped in them with me, rose with such violence that I left the room without a word.

My mother's frock was not ready in time for that evening. I remember the concert well: it was the last time I ever went to a concert with my family.

The hall was full, and my father's work was received with a polite, rather uncertain attention. Afterwards, while he was standing on the platform stiff and small in his old evening clothes, I thought of the water on the piano and almost believed that he was right and I had spilt it on purpose. It was a terrifying idea.

We went afterwards to the house of some friends and drank coffee and ate cakes and everyone congratulated my father all over again. The curtains were not drawn; every window was open and even then it was not cool. There were thunder and forked lightning. Otherwise it was still, but in that smoky room people talked about music and exchanged endless personal reminiscences and anecdotes. My father played for a heavy Irish woman who sang, and nobody seemed to mind the ominous rumbling or the brilliant tongues twisting across the sky.

The party broke up very late. My father herded us together and said that we would walk. 'We can pick up a cab by the park,' he said and we all knew, my mother and sister and I, that even if there were a cab we should do no such thing.

The walk was over two miles. As we reached the park there was a tremendous burst of thunder: a few seconds later the rain began, with great angry drops slamming down on to the pavement, and above, branches of the trees swaying from the impact. Instinctively, we covered our heads and started to run. In a few minutes the futility of running became obvious; we had still most of our journey before us and neither my mother nor father was strong. We cowered under an enormous plane tree, hoping, I suppose, that the rain would abate.

'There may be a cab,' gasped my mother.

The drops from the tree gathered and fell with a metallic drip, and beyond the tree it roared. Soon the leaves would be beaten down and we should be no drier where we were.

'It will stop,' said my father, unusually sanguine.

It did not stop. There was another streak of lightning; for a second the sky was lit and we could see the raging clouds hurtling down from their heights. Then thunder, louder than before; I can remember it almost shaking my spine, and the crescendo of rain that followed. The street was empty of anything but the bouncing rain drops, collecting torrents in the gutter.

'We'd better walk,' said my father.

'We'll catch our deaths,' said my mother.

My father shrugged his shoulders and pulled his coat round his chin. There was more thunder and my sister turned to me, her eyes glittering. I knew she was frightened and took her arm as we set off. After a moment's hesitation, my father took hold of my mother and then recoiled with a little grunt saying, 'You're soaked. You'd better have my coat.'

'No dear.' My mother's cloak of old stamped velvet clung round her legs, the ruffles on the shoulders damply flattened.

'Don't be a fool, Evelyne,' said my father irritably as he ripped off the cloak and thrust her arms into his overcoat. 'Can't have you dying of pneumonia.'

We were by a street lamp, and I remember her wan little smile. So, with her cloak over his arm we walked home.

We arrived after one o'clock. My mother suggested warm milk, but there was no milk.

'Tea then.'

But my father, who looked exhausted, snorted and said we'd be far better in bed. He left the room and we heard him sneezing on the stairs. My sister quietly and efficiently filled hot water bottles and we went to bed.

CHAPTER FOURTEEN

Next morning my father was in bed with a feverish cold. He remained there for two days, refusing to see a doctor; and on the third day came down to his studio in his dressing-gown.

He was still feverish and very cross and would not eat the meals we brought in to him, but flew into a rage if we asked how he was feeling or suggested any remedy. He smoked until he began to cough. He was restless, and possessed of a violent desire to tidy all his music and the studio. He pulled everything out of the cupboards and shelves on to the floor; broke a plaster bust of Brahms which nearly fell on his head; and filled the studio with old photographs of people he could not remember. The dust made his cough worse. He would not let anyone help him and became wilder and less approachable as the confusion in his room grew. He left cups of tea, and Bovril made with milk, until they were quite cold and had a film or skin and dust on them. He tore the dead flowers out of the vase I had used, and thrust them head downwards into the bulging waste paper basket with the slimy green stalks in the air and dripping on to the rug. He burned papers in the stove until the air was clouded with crisp black ash. He did not touch the piano. This went on for three days and my mother was almost beside herself. Whenever any of us went into the studio he would demand some piece of music; accusing us in a hoarse strained voice of taking it or losing it or throwing it away. There was a terrible mad feeling in the house, as though we were to expect anything to happen however fantastic or bad.

On the third afternoon my mother gave me his tea to take to the studio, imploring me helplessly 'to try and persuade him to go to bed'. We had already asked her why she did not send for a doctor but she evaded us; she was clearly terrified of my father and utterly unable to manage the situation.

He was scrubbing the mark I had made on his piano, with a curtain which he must have ripped off the pole.

'Here is your tea, Father.' He muttered something and did not look at me.

'Will you come and drink it while it's hot? You have been working so hard, Father.'

He looked up and I saw that his cheeks were a brilliant pink.

'You'll spoil the curtain anyway. I'll fetch you a duster when you have had your tea.'

'Come and look at it. It's *worse*. The damp spreads across the varnish.' He hung over the stain and drawn by some new fear I went to him. He began scrubbing it again furiously. I touched him; he seemed to have forgotten me, when suddenly he whipped round, seized my arm and shouted, 'You did this. You're responsible for this. It's getting worse, I can't use the piano. I can't work unless I have order and you've made that impossible for me. You must have done it on purpose. Look at this room. Haven't I been trying to arrange it for weeks. Look what I've tried to do. You're all against me – all of you . . .' A frightful fit of coughing shook him. It went on and on until he could not see, but hung over the piano still gripping my arm, coughing, an intolerable dry agonizing cough, until I could feel the wracking tearing pain in his lungs, through the frantic grasping of his fingers in my arm. Gradually he stopped; shivered, and whimpered a little, his hair over his face. I pushed back his hair automatically; his forehead was dry and burning. My sister had heard the shouting and was at the open door. Together we led him upstairs. He did not seem to notice us at all.

He collapsed in bed, and my sister went for the doctor. I went back to the studio; I think with an idea that I might tidy some of the chaos. It was impossible. There were letters in grey ink, sheets of music paper with a few bars scrawled in the middle, yellow photographs of singers with bands round their heads and opulent shoulders twisted into coy or smug angles. There were tiny morose men with cellos, and a fat creature with a flute, all of them scrawled with ink that had spurted over the shiny surfaces. To dear Alfred; With kindest remembrances to dear Alfred; To my dear friend – Alfred. Profuse and forgotten affections sprawled over the grey pictures with their faint yellow gloss. There were programmes, with 'First Performance' in brackets under the announcements of my father's works. All the machinery of music lay rampant; even the curtain rail was loose and unbalanced, pointing down across the window, with the rings of the remaining curtain slipping off if anyone slammed a door or a cab passed in the street. There were whole shelves full and untouched. He seemed only to have cleared the less accessible cupboards high up by the picture rail or down by the skirting board. There were ragged press cuttings, unnaturally thin and flat, of concerts I had never heard: it was all a generation beyond me. He seemed to have no present; only a long uncertain past about which I knew nothing; except for the bowls filled with light grey ash and the little contorted stubs of cigarettes. And so while I vainly attempted to arrange his possessions, I sought for some purpose in his life that would comfort me; some joy he had had which I could imagine; some faith or reason which had warmed his heart. I ended by sitting on the floor staring at the rail across the window. My sister came in with a tray on to which she collected the cups and bowls of ash.

'The doctor has come.' She stopped to take a bowl out of my hands. 'Pneumonia. Isn't it odd that he should have said that to mother in the street? Do you remember?' she persisted, pressing the unnecessary drama at me.

'Of course. Is it bad?'

'Yes, it's acute pneumonia of the right lung. We shall have to fight, he will need very careful nursing.' Her face was lit with her energy and resolve. She was one of those people who are most themselves when faced with illness.

'For what purpose?'

'For what purpose?' her shocked voice repeated. 'So that he shall recover.' She set down the tray and came to me. 'I don't think you understand. It's serious. He may die. It would be terrible. Mother would be all alone. I have tried to keep the danger of his illness from her. He will need constant nursing until his crisis. But I can do it. You must help Mother, it is a terrible shock to her. He is delirious.'

I felt the tears spring out of my eyes and put out my hands. 'I don't want him to die.'

'Now you mustn't do that. You must pull yourself together. There's going to be quite enough to do without your giving way. Think how much worse it is for Mother.'

'Or him,' I sobbed.

'He doesn't know anything about it,' she said quickly. 'We must pray for him,' she added seriously.

There was nothing more to say. I got up and followed her, feeling in some curious way deeply ashamed of both of us.

She nursed my father devotedly, until, indeed, there was very little for either my mother or me to do. She sat up with him every night, only consenting to lie down for three hours in the afternoon. She supervised his broths and medicine; cleaned his room, and was always freshly competent for the frequent visits of the doctor. My mother and I sat dumbly in the living-room, starting up almost guiltily if we were called by my sister to perform some minor task.

I think my mother was paralysed all through that time: stripped bare of her daily round, dreary and uneventful as it was, she was revealed in all the unbalance and inadequacy of pure despair, unrelieved by even the warmth of a burning affection for my father. She was simply dependent on him. He was part of her structure, and the possibility of his no longer being in the house was appalling. She was always ready to acknowledge the superior qualities of her daughter. 'Oh no, I am sure he would rather your sister did that.' Her humility was almost unbearable to me. She did not even claim her share of anxiety or grief, effaced herself and her emotions: but I would see her drop her mending and stare ahead, her eyes dull and desperate in her bewilderment, and I imagined two little questions stabbing her mind, 'Will he die?' and 'What shall I do?' just as I found myself endlessly asking, 'What was the use? Have we been worth it to him?

Was there any alternative for him? Does he care what happens to him now?'

I sat with him, one stifling hot night, having persuaded my sister to go to bed for the first time since he had been ill.

He lay on his back, his head propped with pillows, because breathing was a continuously painful effort to him. Occasionally he dozed. I sat in the dim light, acutely conscious in the silence of his irregular rasping breaths, until I leaned forward while each separate gasp was achieved, and the minutes hung heavy and single in the airless room. Then some unknown dream or imagined sound would force him awake, exhausted and querulous. What time was it? he would ask.

The hours struck by the church clock, an eternity apart; ten; eleven; and twelve. I remember him raising himself at the last and asking 'Is it nearly over?' and my not knowing what to reply. He waited a moment then leaned back; an expression of peevish fear like a child flitted across his face. 'Midnight,' he murmured. 'No, it's only just begun.'

'Would you like me to read to you?'

He made a little gesture of indifference with his fingers on the sheet. I searched for a book; those in the room were all about religion (my sister's design). I found a copy of the *Imitation of Christ* bound in white vellum with a rich golden cross, and opened it at random.

'On the contempt of all temporal honour,' I read.

'Oh that,' he said. 'I don't want to consider my death you know.' I looked up startled, and found his eyes alive and appraising.

'Of course not,' I fumbled. 'You're going to get well.'

'I didn't mean that,' he said, and we were silent again, conscious of the chance lost between us.

Part of the night I had an insane desire to tell him that it had been a good thing to devote his life to music, or to have made me, or any of his children; but my own uncertainty loomed before me so immensely that I was prevented. Snatches of his music and aspects of my sister and myself raced through my mind, but they did not help me even privately to any kind of reassurance; and finally I was forced to believe in my separate distant brothers who were expected home at any moment. My sister had written to them, with the result that Tom, the schoolmaster, was coming for one night and Hubert, the embryo accountant, for a week.

And so the night wore wearily away, and I wondered whether it was any comfort to my father to believe that it was as long for me as for him.

He swallowed his medicine, patiently cynical of its properties, and breathed his way painfully through the hours. He did not complain, which made his obsession with time, which was no longer any use to him, more deeply touching.

Gradually a shallow light showed in the window; the street lamps lost their power and stood useless and squalid in the pale grey air; and I was able to tell him that the day had really begun, as though it held some magnificent promise. He slept then, his head on one side, and his short, strong, somehow elegant fingers curved in a little with content.

In the middle of breakfast, my younger brother arrived. He walked straight in, kissed us all in the right order, inquired after my father, and without waiting for a reply, told us that war had been declared on Germany.

'At midnight. Exactly at midnight. We are at war,' he repeated, almost as though he were asking us whether we really were. He was in a state of profound excitement. My mother received the news as a fresh personal tragedy; my sister was indignant (surely something could be done?). I think she minded the deflection from what was, to her, the main issue. To me it meant precisely nothing. I remembered the clock striking twelve, and wondered why, if it had been such an important moment, it had not seemed so then.

'Who will win?' I asked innocently. My brother shot me an exalted, terrifying glance.

'We shall, of course,' he said. 'Thank God, I'm eighteen. They'll need all the men they can get.'

'Oh, Hubert,' said my mother.

'We must keep it from Father,' said my sister, her voice elevating us to more spiritual matters.

Then they started to tell Hubert about father. Hubert walked about the room with folded arms, raising his eyebrows and frowning; asking intelligent questions with a kind of suppressed energy, as though he were really meant for something else.

I went to sleep.

CHAPTER FIFTEEN

Two days later my father died. He died at two o'clock in the morning; none of us had been to bed and we all saw him die. His head just slipped sideways, and my sister in a choked voice said he was dead, although his eyes were open, which seemed very terrible to me. 'Take Mother,' she commanded. We led her away, Tom and I, one limp hand for each of us, and I put her to bed, unresisting and quite silent.

When I went back to my father's room, my sister would not let me in, but told me to go to bed. My brothers kissed me and asked if I would be all right. In my room I sat a long while without crying. Eventually I groped in my chest of drawers until I found Rupert's postcard. I did not read it; just stared until the writing was blurred and my eyes ached. Then I put it carefully away and slept.

The funeral was a slow practical nightmare. Processions of wreaths with shiny cards; piles of letters; and four and a half inches in *The Times* (which considering the war was rather good, said my sister complacently). The house, converted from the silent dread of illness, became crowded with people and their expressions of sorrow. As my mother pointed out, unconscious of the irony, one never knew how many friends he had, until he was no more with us. My sister managed everything with admirable propriety and control. On the afternoon of the funeral, we were all sitting round the dining-room table waiting for the kettle to boil, when the bell rang. My mother began to rise, but my sister motioned her back and went into the hall. She returned with letters and a large cardboard box. 'For you, Mother. I wonder what it is,' she added in the tone with which one encourages a child. 'The letters are all for you, too.'

'Nothing for me?' Hubert relaxed in his seat impatiently. He behaved all the time as though he were waiting for something. Tom continued to read the newspaper, which was blaring with headlines.

I watched my mother undo the string, and remembered that it would be the frock, the red frock she had had made from my material. My heart warmed at the prospect. The lid of the box fell open, and there under the tissue paper lay my present, glowing and beautifully folded. My mother lifted it out by the shoulders and turned to me. 'There, darling, it's come at last,' she said, as though it were mine.

My sister was leaning over her chair. 'It will have to be dyed,' she said. 'What a pity. But it will come in very useful.'

My mother lowered her head, and I saw her hands fall slack on the red.

'What?' I cried. 'It will ruin it. You *can't*!'

'It will have to be dyed,' repeated my sister gently, looking at me.

There was a terrible emotional solicitude hovering in the air. Everyone was very still, watching my mother.

'It is very good material. It won't be spoiled,' said my sister.

At last my mother raised her head, her face covered with tears. She saw us all watching; her shame at being seen to cry broke her shadowy dignity, and she sobbed holding the stuff to her face.

'He never even saw it. He said I won't know you. I can't help it. He didn't see it once.' Her fingers raked in among the silk with an awful comfortless energy.

Swiftly my sister leaned forward, put her arms under my mother's, and lifted her to her feet. 'You are tired. You need a rest. Come and lie down and I will bring you some tea.' With gentle force she led my mother from the room.

I sat like a stone, with grinding pain in my heart for her at the very beginning of her grief; with years ahead, and the poor commiseration by which she was now surrounded contracting until it was just a casual memory, half forgotten and finally vanished. One's own sorrow, I thought then, how bearable, how understandable; but the misery of another person, a separate being, how unimaginably terrible, of what unseen quality, unknown duration, inconceivable anguish! Nobody would feel my mother's suffering even for the years left in her life.

'She's wonderful with Mother,' said Tom, indicating my sister with the newspaper.

Hubert acquiesced moodily and suggested fetching the kettle; at least tea could be made to happen.

'Hey, what are *you* for?' said Tom, and I fetched it.

When I returned, they were both discussing the future, or rather their futures.

Hubert shocked us all by announcing that the chief reason for his anxiety was that he had volunteered for the Army, which meant his immediate departure.

'If they won't have me, I shall lie about my age.'

Tom seemed deeply concerned and implored him to reconsider his decision. 'After all,' he said, 'there's Mother.' It was all exceedingly dangerous and meant putting a terrible strain on her just at this moment.

'She's got you and the girls. I've made up my mind. I've given the matter a great deal of thought.' He frowned deeply, with his eyes sparkling. 'If Father were alive, I should have done it, and it's far too important a business to forgo simply because of Mother.'

'She may not have me. I may feel I should join up.'

'Good Lord, no! This war will be over in a few weeks, or months at the outside. They won't have time to start on schoolmasters. They'll need them where they are.'

'You might not like the Army, Hubert,' I cried.

Both brothers smiled kindly.

'It's not a question of what I should like,' replied Hubert gravely. I noticed his eyes still sparkled.

I poured out the tea. My sister came and fetched cups for mother and herself and retired with them filled.

The brothers were deep in speculations on modern warfare. I wondered desperately what was going to happen to me. The thought started quite casually, like the beginning of rain, but it quickly increased until my mind was full of it, and the need to disperse it amongst the others became too great to overcome.

I remember asking them what I should do. What could I do? I repeated. They both looked at me in astonishment.

'Do? You mean about the war?'

'About anything. About me chiefly.'

'The best thing you can do is to keep the home fires burning.' Tom patted my knee. 'Men do the fighting. All you have to do is to keep yourself fascinating for when we return.'

I think it was coming from one of my brothers that made it such a watery jest.

'But I can't just do nothing.'

'What do you want to do?'

'I don't know. Couldn't I teach or something? If what you said about your being needed is true, surely they will need women for teaching.'

'But you haven't been educated for teaching. It's a serious profession. You didn't go to a school. You haven't passed any examinations.'

'Good thing, too.' Hubert sighed deeply and stared into the fire.

'There's Mother, you know,' I was reminded. 'She will need looking after.'

'*She* does that all the time. There won't be enough for me to do.'

'If Mother sells the house and moves into a smaller one, you will have plenty to do with the move.'

'Tom, you don't understand. That won't last. That's like a – like a Bazaar.'

'Well, you'll get married one day. That's what happens to most women, unless they have some kind of vocation.'

'*She* won't,' said Hubert, and they fell to rapt contemplation of my sister's chastity.

I looked from one to the other in despair. Did they seriously consider me so different from themselves? Did they think that I could live without any of the support they deemed so necessary and admirable? That to prepare meals and clothes and beds in which to sleep was for a woman an end in itself. I stared from Tom's pale moustache to Hubert's shaven cheek and hated them. That was all they need do, trim their moustaches and shave. Their clothes were mended; they did not cook their food or pull back the sheets each morning. They were able to use the means of living as a means: for me they were assumed to be an end.

'It isn't as though you were artistic,' said Tom kindly.

'As though she were what?' Hubert wiped his mouth and put the handkerchief back in his pocket.

'As though she had anything to do with Art.'

'Oh. Good Lord!' he added as an afterthought.

I got up and went to the door.

'What about the tea?' called Tom.

'Clear it yourself.'

I remember feeling inanely proud of that petty little retort. It gave me the courage to lock my door and find the postcard in my top drawer. Some street in Chelsea. I had never heard of it. I must have a suitcase. I crept out into the passage, up the rickety flight of stairs which led to the box-room. The door was stuck; even the paint had melted in the heat. The door yielded, and I had the sense to shut it, for fear of any noise I might make selecting my case. It had been a servant's bedroom, and had white paper striped with watery roses, hanging loose in triangles. The cistern in the passage made horrible furtive noises. I should not have liked to sleep in that room. It was unbearably hot, and the small window was tightly shut. I struggled with the sash until there was a pain in my chest. The sash opened, and a large bluebottle fell out. I turned to survey the trunks. They were all too big and very dirty. There was the black one I had used for my beautiful visit. I unstrapped it almost without thinking, and inside, under the tray, was a small worn case. It had a label marked Bruges on it. It would do. I strapped the trunk and tried to shut the window, but it was jammed. I looked right down into the garden with the weedy square bed in the middle, spattered with nasturtiums. Hubert's bi-cycle was leaning against the wall. Soon I should be away. I should never come back. The thought provoked action. I slipped down and into my bedroom, locking the door carefully. I packed my best clothes and a hairbrush and looked round. There was nothing else that I wanted; I had no precious possession. There was a photograph of my father looking tired and pensive. Perhaps I had better have something like that, although the frame would make my case heavier.

It was finished. I felt almost light headed with calm. I would leave them all. At that moment the whole thing seemed so simple that I could not understand why I had not thought of it before. One just packed a case and walked out of the house. My mind stopped at that point, but I felt no need to consider any further. I washed my hands and put on a coat. A door slammed downstairs and I heard my brothers coming up. They passed my room and I stood motionless until my ears almost hurt with listening. I heard them go into Tom's bedroom and shut their door.

I seized the case and ran down the stairs, out of the house, down the path, out of the gate, and down the road until I was breathless and had to stop. Then an irrational fear of pursuit spurred me on again until I was two streets away. After that I walked, aiming for Gloucester Road; changing hands as the suitcase established its weight. The familiar streets fell away and I became more conscious of adventure. I passed a little girl skipping in a front garden. She did not notice me, but skipped violently, intent on achieving a 'double through', with her pigtails flying up each time she jumped. Her feet on the stones interrupted my plan until I was listening to them as they grew fainter in the distance behind me. I passed the shop where we had bought hoops and tops as children. It was a stationer's, but specialized in a few rare and delightful toys. A faint regret made me stop just past the shop and put down the suitcase. I was in sight of Gloucester Road and a bus lumbered by. Where was I going? I realized that I had neither the postcard nor money. Neither. Not a penny, and I could not remember the address.

Sixteen? six? twenty-four? Any of those numbers seemed probable: indeed, each, when considered separately, invited approval. Four sixes make twenty-four, I murmured frantically aloud. But I had read the postcard many times. I was almost sure that it was sixteen. Perhaps it was simply that my cousin had lived at number sixteen. It could be six. I shut my eyes and tried to see the squat fat handwriting on the postcard. I knew it by heart, but not the number. Not the number. And I had no money. I was trembling and desperately hot. I picked up the suitcase and put it down again. One could not appear at a strange house with no money. I felt foolishly in my pockets. My fingers were merely speckled with stuff like powdered glass. Of course there was no money there. I must think. I could not go on. I could not go back. A man walking on the other side of the street looked at me curiously. Dizzy with chagrin, I staggered up the side streets to the park.

I sat down on the nearest empty seat, with the suitcase beside me. It must look very strange to be sitting there with a suitcase. I pushed it under the bench and out of sight. It was a relief to be still. I was utterly bewildered at my blunderings. That other people or circumstances should prove hostile was bitterly reasonable; but that I should be subject to such an attack from within was beyond my horizon, and I could only feel humiliated and ashamed. If it had not been for my ridiculous and unbusinesslike rush, I should have arrived at the studio by now. Rupert would be painting and there would be a bowl of fat summer roses with loose petals on the table. The room would be very still and golden with the evening light; there would be an unfamiliar smell of paint and another person's house. We would drink milk and I would provoke his admiration by the strength and simplicity of my achievement. Fantastic conceptions of how it would all be, flowed through my mind; all impossibly good and delightful. I remembered my nervous pride in the box-room ('I shall never come back!'), my headlong rush out of the house. Surely I had hardly given myself time to think. Leaving one's home was not so simple it seemed, even when one knew where to go. *Was* it number sixteen? Nobody must know of this abortive attempt. I kicked the suitcase further under the seat. For a moment I was tormented by the thought that other people would have walked, would have found the house by asking at all three numbers. But then I could not have carried the case. It was too heavy for me I decided, and the irony of accepting another weakness escaped me. Perhaps I would take a lighter case. Or perhaps I would pack more belongings and go in a cab. On my way downstairs I had remembered something left out. Hardly remembered. A fleeting thought. It could not have been more than that, or surely I should have thought of the postcard.

I would go home. They would be having supper. There would be cold rice pudding in the pie-dish with blackberries painted on it. I had a peculiar rush of affection for that dish. My brothers would read or play chess and my sister would sew as usual. I wondered whether my mother was better, whether her tears had relieved her, or left her dry and exhausted as tears did me. A sensation which was not hunger, nor fatigue, nor loneliness, but perhaps a blend of all three overcame me. I rose slowly and reached for the case. As I walked out of the gardens, I saw an old woman sprawled back on a seat, underneath which was a parcel wrapped in newspaper. I quickened my steps and still the suitcase did not feel heavy.

CHAPTER SIXTEEN

I excused my shame at the misadventure by making practical arrangements which would conceal my plan from the family. I packed a case with much more care and looked up Beechley Street on a map. I told my mother that I was going to see a friend in Chelsea, implying that Rupert was a woman; and she acquiesced quite readily. Tom had gone back to his school, and Hubert was so obsessed with his own impatience that he took very little notice of me. I feared my sister most, and to her I embroidered the story most cunningly with a long account of this girl's exhaustion from having nursed an aunt who had recently died. I said that I did not want to tell my mother all this, for fear it would distress her. The whole business was arranged with detailed deceit, and was quite undramatic. I finally left at three o'clock, in a cab procured by Hubert, with the family gathered round the door to say good-bye.

A faint disappointment claimed me as I waved farewell and settled back in the cab. This was not really the way to do it. But it was the way that things happened. I was conscious of disliking being overpowered by circumstances, of romance being drained out of the adventure, leaving it as it appears now, tawdry, practical and highly probable. The only pleasant element left was one of surprise. I had not told Rupert that I was coming. This seemed satisfactory to me, and the feeling mounted as we trotted away from Kensington.

I asked the man to put me down at the corner of the street. Somehow I did not want to appear to have arrived in a cab. I paid the driver out of the money I had been given, and walked down the street with my case. It was warm, still and deserted, except for several cats packed between the spikes of railings, or perched on narrow window-sills, with the most belying air of comfort. 'Those artists of position', somebody had once said to me.

I walked past a little row of houses followed by a large block with wide windows, studios I imagined, and next to them an uneven stretch of buildings, all colours and shapes, mostly fat and low, with gay painted front doors immediately on to the street. Here it was at last. A pale green door with a gargoyle knocker. I put down the case and paused. Did one simply say, 'I have come to stay'?

Someone across the road was playing Saint-Saëns on a gramophone. Surely Rupert would understand when he saw the case. Did people often do this kind of thing? Was it generally expected amongst friends? Was one expected to know the friend very well before doing it? Even these speculations were not very practical; but they made my own inexperience painfully clear to me and I realized bitterly how foolish it had been to rejoice in the surprise I was about to spring. He had said, 'Come whenever you like,' but it was hardly the same thing as coming without warning of àny kind. However, I could not go back now. The dignity and authenticity of my departure rendered return impossible. I need not stay very long. And then what? I must have hesitated for several minutes before I lifted the grinning creature's head and let it fall. It fell with such violence that it rebounded, and knocked twice; and I recoiled from the noisy peremptory object. I waited, my thoughts congealing in the silence that followed; even the music had stopped, somebody having taken off the record in the middle. Perhaps Rupert was out. Better knock again. Better count ten first. Very slowly. Somebody had put a waltz on the gramophone now. I counted with my heart beating time as fast. Out: perhaps he was out. Perhaps he was away. What should I do? Almost in a panic I knocked again. Faintly I heard steps. Soft shuffling steps. He must have slippers on, I thought, and my heart was light again. I heard someone fumbling with the door, then it opened, and a girl stood there, staring at me. Her eyes were brown and beautifully set. Her hair was hanging down her back. She was dressed in a flowered wrapper, edged with innumerable ruffles, and feathered mules on her bare feet. We must have stared at each other with equal astonishment for some seconds, a silence from which she recovered first, for she said quite pleasantly: 'And what can I do for you?'

She was almost the first person I had ever heard speak with a foreign accent and I was charmed into smiling.

'Is Mr – ? Does – er – Rupert live here?' Absurd that. But I could not remember his name. 'Rupert Laing' (that was it). 'Does he live here?'

Her eyes narrowed a little as she looked down at the case, and up my body again to my face; but she flattened herself against the narrow wall of the passage and answered that he did, down there, indicating the passage in her voice, without turning her head. I stepped inside, starting down the passage while she shut the door and followed me. We went through a door with stained glass to its waist and out into a little garden, a courtyard, paved, but without flowers, and through another green door, straight into a large studio, with skylights half covered by grey blinds.

'Will you wait here?' the girl said, moving unhurriedly to another door at the far end of the room. 'Do sit down,' she added with great courtesy, so that the phrase seemed new, and the invitation a peculiar honour.

The place was in the utmost confusion. I found a chair with no back and a coffee cup on the seat. I put the cup carefully on the floor and sat down. Flame-coloured sunlight streamed down through the strips of windows (which were also partially covered by blinds) and added to the confusion by vast livid zigzags on the rush matting and black rugs. In one corner was a bed, unmade but strewn with brilliant shawls and scarves. A half empty glass of milk lay on the floor at the head beneath a scarlet corner of fringe, the silken ends of which were poised just above the milk. There was an easel, and canvases were propped against the walls. Three huge orange jugs perched about the room. The paint-work was black, but the walls were a dead pale grey, which, suffused with the violent and restricted sunlight, gave the room a conflicting quality of warmth and cold, of heat and of chill, half midday, half evening, the twilight of some tropical scene. I remembered the girl's black mass of coarse shining hair hanging down her back; it completed the disorder before me, and I had just time to wonder what Rupert would be like, when he entered.

He came through the door at the far end of the room, and stood in a patch of sunlight. I saw him screw up his eyes for a second, as he looked about for me. The moment before a person sees you presents a rare and fleeting aspect of that person, which vanishes after the meeting. It was the first time I had felt it, and I saw him for the first time, tired and defensive and somehow drained.

'It's I, Rupert,' I said.

'Yes, I see you now,' he replied and moved a trifle uncertainly towards me. Then he was standing over me. There was a short silence, and I felt more and more that this was a strange thing to do and less and less able to account to him for my having done it.

'You said I could come when I liked.'

'Yes, of course I did. Do you never warn people when you like?'

'I've never done it before.'

'Of course. You're the person who is always doing things for the first time. Of course.' He bent his head a little to scratch it and saw the suitcase.

'My father's dead,' I said foolishly.

'I'm sorry,' he answered, preoccupied.

I knew he was going at any moment to ask me terrible, practical questions about that case, which pride and resentment rendered me incapable of answering. This was not at all what I had imagined.

'I'm not particularly sad about it,' I said stiffly.

He began to stare at me in a penetrating manner, when the girl re-entered the room. She stood quite still at the door, but Rupert heard her and turned.

'Get some tea,' he said. She nodded. 'Make some toast. Take half an hour over it. I want to talk.'

She moved a step further into the room, standing in the

patch of sunlight (it had narrowed a little now, I noticed), and staring at me inquiringly.

'Go *on*,' he shouted.

'You won't go out?'

'*No!* For the tenth time, I won't go out.'

She nodded again and withdrew.

'Who is she?'

'Her name's Maria.'

'Does she live here?'

'Yes. Does that surprise you?'

'I thought she must live here,' I answered carefully.

'Oh! You did,' he seemed amused, and unhelpful. 'Now, what's the matter?'

'Nothing. I just thought I would come to tea with you.'

'Bringing your suitcase?'

'No – I'm going somewhere else. I had to bring that.'

'Where are you going?'

'To friends.'

'And this was on your way?'

'This was on my way.'

He looked at me again and then said, 'Right. Help me collect some of these cups or we shan't have enough for tea. Wait a minute while I fetch a tray.'

A curious feeling of relief swept over me. I did not then worry at all about the result of my lying, but relaxed now the questions had come to an end. I collected every cup, mug and glass I could see and there were a great many of them.

'Hey! We don't need all those,' he cried. I had ranged them on a papier mâché table. 'Maria can clear them up tomorrow.'

'Does she work for you?'

'No,' he laughed. 'She just lives with me. I suppose it comes to much the same thing though,' he added as though discovering something. 'I don't pay her, you see. She loves me.'

'As though you were married?' I felt intensely curious. The idea was utterly new to me.

'That is a very embarrassing question and one which is not usually asked.'

'Do you love her then?'

'Now you are being very childish and ought to be ashamed of yourself.'

Instantly I felt very impertinent and ashamed and blushed hotly. He took the tray I had filled and kicked open the door.

'Do recover before I return. I keep forgetting how sensitive you are.'

I recovered, slowly and painfully.

Rupert returned and began unwinding the cords which rolled back the blinds so that the windows were clear, and light coloured the room evenly.

Then he said: 'Come and sit on the bed and wait quietly for toast. You must not mind Maria. She is not at her best today, and anyway, she'll try and resent you. She is a – ' he hesitated, and his voice softened – 'a childish creature. She is not very happy today, and she's bad at that.'

'Oh.'

'Perhaps you are not very happy either? Am I surrounded by unfortunate women perhaps?'

I remained silent. I think I was a little afraid of him. Eventually I said:

'Do you like being a painter?'

'More than becoming a doctor, but otherwise not so much as I thought. Doctoring is a disillusioning business. They take years to disillusion you, because they are so scientific about it, of course. Now painting – with painting you can produce a picture in, say, a couple of days, and within half an hour of its completion your friends will flock round it telling you they don't like pink, or nobody has shoulders like that. It is all over in a trice. The most extraordinary thing about painting is the way everyone who sees any picture assumes you are showing it to them solely for the purpose of benefiting by their destructive criticism. They are positively exasperated if they do not at once give vent to some eager ignorant disapproval. After the faint praise, of course. There is very little variety in that.'

'What do you do with them?'

'Take no notice of them. And that is a lonely business. You see one cannot really *afford* their taking no notice of you. It does not make for better painting. I am certain that even the people who survived it would have painted better if they had been needed instead of endured or ignored. People are kind to lovers. All the world loves a lover, they say. It's because they know it won't last. I suppose it is a tribute to the artist when people are hostile to him.'

'Are they hostile?' I was thinking of my father.

'Perhaps hostile is a bad word. They perpetrate a kind of wilful indifference which is just as bad.'

He continued in this strain for some time. At first I thought that he was merely trying to put me at my ease – to avoid any personal subject which might force me to reveal my situation (about which I was sure he had doubts); but then I realized that he was simply obsessed with artistic problems and his own uncertainty, and glad to have a new listener to whom he could talk about them. He finished by saying: 'The other point about people being kind when they know things can't last, is people being lenient about somebody when they know he can't do any more.'

There was a knock on the door.

'Oh, heavens!' He leapt up to open it.

Maria stood there with a tray. She wore a black skirt with a white blouse; but her hair still hung down her back. Rupert seized her hair with both hands, one on each side of her face.

'Listen, Maria. You are not to start being jealous and knocking.'

'There was the tray in my hands.'

He shook her head.

'You know that is not why you knocked. We were talking.'

'*You* were talking,' she interrupted.

'*We* were talking. Weren't we?' He turned to me, his hand on her hair. 'You wouldn't have enjoyed it. You wouldn't have understood one single word.'

This statement was calculated to calm her; as even I could see.

She was trying to frown, to glower at him, but her hair was strained back from her forehead too hard; it was not possible, and only her brows met.

'Will you be reasonable? I shall introduce you from here and if you are not polite and kind, you'll be sorry.'

He introduced us. I was terribly embarrassed; but Maria seemed quite unmoved by the situation. She accepted the introduction with dignity, continuing to frown at Rupert.

'What were you talking about? I *should* have understood,' she added like a child.

He shook her head impatiently again. 'About art. About life.'

'Oh, that,' she said and shrugged her shoulders, so that the tea-cups rattled violently; after which she smiled a magnificent smile. She had the kind of face which seemed correctly arranged when smiling: I remember her small, exceedingly white teeth, and her upper lip curved above them.

'Please may I put the tray down?' He was looking at her; he nodded slowly, running his fingers down to the ends of her hair, and finally releasing her.

We had tea. There were two boiled eggs for Rupert, and one for me. Maria said she was not hungry, whereupon Rupert looked at her with an exasperated anxiety and tried to feed her with egg. She sat on the floor. At the beginning of tea she watched me, but in the end she watched Rupert. I noticed that she treated him with a kind of restrained but agonized attention, that she hated him to see her watch him, anticipated a glance from him and dropped her eyes or turned her head; but even then, I felt her desperate concentration. It was as though his voice touched her, and was unbearable; as though she knew how breathing felt to him; how the eggshell felt to his fingers; these and countless other minute sensations were as if shared by her all the time. At first I thought that he was unaware of this, but as the meal progressed I was less sure. I think in the end we were all affected by it. Apparently we talked easily. We talked about the Lancings: Rupert had not been to see them again, although he had had lunch with Deb and her mother when they were shopping in London; about my family (most superficially); about Rupert's painting (that was when I was acutely sensitive to Maria); about the war (this most vaguely, I being unable to contribute through ignorance, and Maria being vehemently averse to the subject).

'You think wars should be fought, not talked,' I remember Rupert saying to her, when the restraint suddenly loomed enormous before us, filling the room.

'Not talked,' she said.

After tea she lit a cigarette and smoked it very slowly. Almost everything seemed different I reflected. I watched her fascinated, until Rupert asked me whether I would like one, which I hastily refused. When she had finished, Rupert got up off the bed. 'Go and buy something for the pancakes. Enough for all of us. Will you do it now?'

'Won't you come?'

'No. Do it now, or the shops will be closed.'

She left the room without a word. We stacked the things on a tray.

'I'll take this out. I shan't be long,' he said.

'When are we having pancakes?'

'For supper.' He kicked the door and went.

The room was very peaceful. I wondered idly why Rupert had assumed I was staying to supper, but only for a moment. I heard a murmur of voices through the door, and envied Maria, with an abstract impersonal envy, for the kind of life she led. Perhaps, though, it was very painful. She seemed unhappily obsessed with Rupert. He had said she was not happy today, and that she was bad at it. It was strange to be here, not half an hour from my home and yet surrounded by so complete a change. Some of the things Rupert had said came back into my mind, and then, inevitably, I was forced to consider what I should do on leaving this place. It would be worse in the evening. I struggled to enjoy the time I was spending, and still had left to spend. For a long while I stared miserably at the rush matting, going over the insoluble crisis again and again. This unprofitable occupation was broken by Rupert.

'She's gone to buy mushrooms,' said Rupert. He pulled out his pipe and sat on the floor leaning against the bed. 'Now I think you had better talk. You are not an accomplished liar, which is the only possible excuse for being one. You can stay here tonight if you want, but don't bother about lies, because there isn't enough time.'

I was completely silent, shivering and picking the edge of the fringe.

'Has somebody let you down badly? Was this a last resort?'

'No.'

'Poor creature. Were you so desperate then? Had to get away somewhere?'

I nodded.

'Is that yes or no? I can't see.'

'Yes.'

'Your father died – when?'

'Just over two weeks ago.'

'And that was what made you decide to do this?'

'No – not exactly. It's more complicated.'

'I am not asking you from idle curiosity. I might be, but I'm not. Can you go back to your family?'

'I suppose so. Not for a few days. I said that I was going to stay with a friend.'

'Did you tell them it was me?'

'Oh no. They wouldn't have liked it. I said it was a girl who was very tired from nursing someone who'd just died.'

'Very sensible of you,' he said approvingly. 'So that you can go back if you like.'

'Yes.'

'I feel that you are going to cry at any moment,' he said after a pause. 'So I shall just sit here and go on talking to you and asking you questions and we'll both take no notice of you. Why do you hate it at home so much?'

I began to tell him, starting with my brothers at tea, and working backwards. He did not listen in complete silence which would, I think, have frightened me, but threw in small practical questions, which kept my balance for me. In a short time I did not want to cry. I told him nearly everything, the only large exception being Agnes and Edward and *The Mikado*. That I could bear to tell no one, and I was able to persuade myself that it was quite irrelevant.

I came to an end and waited. I think I was certain that he would present me with some solution. At those moments, waiting for someone to speak is rather like the moment before opening a book which one had long desired; or the second at a concert before some new work begins; or the ten seconds before somebody kisses you; or the minute before you open that person's next letter: the almost inevitable disillusionment is far away, indeed it is blessed for the contrast which at that moment it presents. I waited trustfully, expectantly, joyously for that solution; and during those seconds I experienced the complete calm of peaceful certainty.

He had twisted round on the floor facing me and now he suddenly knelt, took my hands and kissed them. Then I thought I knew that he would not be able to help me; and my heart sank down into my hands so that they were heavy and lifeless as he held them.

'Now you will see how very little use people can be to each other,' he said. 'Practically speaking, I'm let out of it. I'm going away tomorrow. Joining the Army.'

'The *Army?*'

'Yes. This war you know. It's going to take up a great many people's time.'

'The Army!' I repeated, dazed. It seemed fantastic. Everyone was in it. Everyone.

'Yes. We can talk about that later. The point is that even if I were continuing here, it would be very difficult for me to be much help. Don't misunderstand me. I think I see your difficulties most clearly, and I am the last person to underestimate them. A purpose in life. I find that hard enough for myself, but for another person, a woman, why it's almost impossible.' He fell silent, staring at my hands.

'Some work,' I said. 'I thought I might be able to do a job of some kind.'

'You might. You might even earn your living. For what?

There is little purpose in earning your living simply in order to go to sleep for the next day's work. And there's very little purpose in marrying someone in order not to earn your living.'

'But I should like it.'

'To marry or work?'

'To work. And marry some day,' I added truthfully.

'Work isn't an end in itself. I know that is a platitude, and so no one really believes it. People are beginning to think of work as an end. I think they may even consider this war as an end. What do you consider the end of a war?'

'To win it?'

He gave my hands a little shake.

'Nobody wins a war nowadays. There is no end to it. War is becoming a compulsory amateur affair. Look at me. I shall be an amateur. That means somebody who does it for the love of the thing. It's not amateur. It's simply compulsory. Once you drag everybody into something, there's no end to it. They muddle along until they're all either dead, or so clearly dying that they can see their own end. Then it stops. It doesn't end.'

'I don't know anything about war.'

'You will,' he said tiredly, and dropped my hands.

I was afraid that he was going to talk and forget me and I was not ready for it. 'I think I should like almost any job as a contrast.'

'Would you?' He looked at me gently. 'I believe you would. What do you want to do?'

'Everyone asks me that. I don't know. But I think that what you said was all very well for people who have a choice, or a talent or something like that, but no use to me. I haven't got any choice, because I don't know what jobs there are, and I haven't any talent that I can see.'

'What, no talent? No talent at all? And you a young lady. Do you not sing?'

'I hate you when you're like that. You won't be serious.'

'I am frequently very serious.'

'Only about yourself, or other things. You won't be serious

162

about my affairs. You think I'm a child. I wouldn't have come if I'd realized . . .'

'If you'd realized how little I could help you. Well, if it's any comfort to you, I don't think anyone else would be much better. Also, and again if it comforts you, I do think you'll get what you want, because at least you do really seem to want it. You are prepared to take some trouble. Now, let's be practical. You have three possibilities that I can see. One is to go home. From there your chances of getting work that you'll be allowed to do are lessened; but you'll be clothed and fed, which can't be underestimated. Another is to try and get some work which means that you'll be living away from home. It limits the work again, because either you'll have to keep yourself or else persuade your family to make you an allowance which gives them some control over what you do. Considerable control. The third is to stay here with Maria if she'll have you, and find your feet a bit. You'll have to do something for your keep as she won't be able to earn enough. My money goes on keeping this place, as the war is not a paying proposition for those who fight it. The third possibility depends very largely on Maria. All right?'

I nodded. 'What does Maria do?'

'She's a model. No you couldn't do that,' he added seeing my face. 'You aren't nearly flamboyant enough to be popular. It would take a good painter to paint you and they are in a minority. Maria gets plenty of work because she's Spanish.'

'And beautiful.'

'And beautiful, too,' he repeated softly.

'How long have you known her?' I wanted to digest the possibilities before further discussion, and I knew he would need very little encouragement to talk about Maria.

'Three months. We met three months ago. She broke the heel of her shoe in the Underground, and when she calmly kicked off the other shoe, put it in her bag, and walked into the street I followed her. It was all very like a play. She was married to a horrid little man who imports wine,' he went on dreamily. 'He told her a lot of lies about England and married her. Then he brought her back to a semi-detached villa in Lewisham with a semi-detached family who hated her. That was last winter. She was cold and homesick. She hated the family, and wouldn't clean the house. One day she left with a man who sang ballads on the Halls. She went to see him nearly every night and persuaded him to take her. She told him she didn't love him as soon as they had left Lewisham and he was nice about it. He told her the address of an Art School, where he thought she would find work. Of course she got it. Now she lives with me. And tomorrow I go away and leave her. She's very unhappy about it. We haven't had time. She's *very* unhappy,' he repeated with emphasis, and I could feel his grief and resentment.

'Are you sorry?'

'Of course I am. I'm very sorry for both of us. It's worse for me although she may feel it more. It's far worse for me.'

'Now you are being sorry for yourself.'

'Well? What of it?'

'I thought you said it was a bad thing for people to indulge in self-pity.'

'I never said any such thing. A little straightforward self-pity never did anyone any harm. It's reasonable and necessary, if you're to feel anything at all. It's when people start eliminating self-pity that they go wrong. They might simply say "this is very bad and I'm unhappy about it," but in fact they nearly always say "of course I'm not sorry for myself, but ..." and then a host of excuses and justifications, if possible vilifying someone else concerned. Does my dogmatic and self-assertive nature strike you?' he asked suddenly.

'I – I don't know.' I was caught off my guard.

'It should. Tonight I am feeling peculiarly defensive. Isn't it odd? Men will consider deeply before they buy a tie or choose a meal; but when it comes to throwing aside their purpose in life, possibly life itself, they do not think at all. They consent to being marshalled, controlled, exposed to unimagined shock, mutilation and death, with barely a tremor, and their reasons for complying, if indeed they have any, would compare most shamefully with their reasons for doing almost anything else. And I am one of them.'

'But surely you don't have any choice?'

'What is that? Ignorance or patriotism? It could easily be both.'

'I mean, you would feel you had to fight in the end, wouldn't you?'

'Oh! Oh, I see. I don't know. But I like to preserve the fragile illusion of personal freedom. You see how I cheat myself. I haven't thought beyond that, at all. There hasn't been time. So I choose to join the Army before public opinion joins me to it.'

'And you go tomorrow?'

'Yes. In the afternoon. Late afternoon,' he added as though the question and the assurance were painfully familiar.

'Where do you go?'

'Can you keep a secret? I go to my family for the night. They live in Norfolk. I have not told Maria. Although a Spaniard she left all her family for that wine importer. She wouldn't understand. My father has not recovered from my giving up medicine. I think this decision will go far to reassure him. If I'm killed it would be better for him to think kindly of me. So I go.'

'Have you a mother?'

'No. She died. I have a father, and an aunt who will knit scarves and revel in the potential crisis.'

'What?'

'My death,' he answered impatiently. 'Oh don't look so anguished. I may not be killed, and you may all live to be sorry.'

Maria came back. Her basket was stuffed with bread and mushrooms and eggs and she seemed very pleased.

'Everything has been bought,' she announced and kicked the door open.

'Come and see the kitchen,' said Rupert.

Once there he became very gay. He sat on the small square table and proceeded to admire Maria for all the things she had bought, whilst I sat primly on a chair and watched them. She said she must peel onions, whereupon he rolled up her sleeves and then changed his mind and peeled them himself. She started to pull her sleeves down again, but he turned round suddenly, the tears from the onions already on his face, saying in a melodramatic manner, 'No don't. I want to remember your arms.'

Immediately Maria burst out crying; he hesitated a second, and then dropping the knife on the draining board, walked over to her, pulled her arm from her face and seated her on the edge of the table.

'Maria, I was not serious. You know I was not serious.'

'I cannot laugh about it. I shall die if you go. It gets worse. I have a terrible pain in my heart about you.' She looked up at him frightened and imploring. 'I have never had that. It won't go. I think I shall not be able to bear it.'

'I shall be back soon. They will give me leave in three months.'

'It is that you go. It is not the time. Don't go tomorrow. Go the next day. No one will notice one day more.'

'It is not the time?' he said, repeating her.

She looked at him speechless and desperate, and for a moment, I, who had sat silent and horrified, could exactly feel her passionate resistance to his reason. It was soon over; he took her hands and led her out of the room without a word.

He returned alone to finish the onions, and for some time we did not speak. He seemed gloomy and uncommunicative and I was afraid and could think of nothing to say.

'Can I help you?' I ventured at last.

'No. She'll come back and do the rest. Women do feel like that,' he added abruptly, as though to reassure himself, 'only she says it.'

'Do women feel very differently from men?'

He looked at me and I saw his bewilderment.

'Sometimes. The devil of it is that you never know when. Come and help me wash up the tea, and we'll discuss your problems again by way of a change.'

So we did. From him I learned that jobs were advertised in newspapers; that the war would probably involve a greater choice of work for women; and that one could live on seven and six a week as far as food was concerned. Presently Maria returned, to begin cooking pancakes with skill and concentration, as though nothing had happened; only perhaps her eyes looked more beautiful and her sleeves were rolled down. Rupert explained that I was staying the night. She accepted this quite calmly. They showed me my room, a narrow strip with a bed and pictures stacked against the walls and space for nothing else. Rupert must be a prolific painter I thought, as I edged my way and started to unpack. The evening cooled. My open window looked out on to another back garden with a studio at the end of it, and I watched the sun sink behind the chimney pots, which were black against the delicate sky, uneven like ogre's teeth. I was cold and hungry. It was half past eight.

We finally ate supper in the studio. The pancakes were crisp and thin and filled with mushrooms deliciously spiced.

'She only cooks pancackes,' said Rupert fondly.

'But I make many kinds.'

'You do indeed. I'm proud of your pancakes.'

'At home my mother cooked with charcoal. It was much better.'

'With nothing else?'

'She made a hole – there was a hole,' she corrected herself, 'in the ground with flat stones on it and the charcoal underneath. Great care was needed to help the oven heat. But it was much better.'

'One day, we'll go and see,' said Rupert, and she shot him a brilliant grateful glance.

After dinner, when we had carried our plates back to the kitchen, we drank a thin, sharp, flame-coloured wine. I was very cautious about it, refusing more than one glass. Maria lit candles in silver branched candlesticks. They were old candles, and had burned unevenly, so that the flames quivered in the air on either side of their silver stems; like someone balancing with outstretched arms on a rope. Rupert made a drawing of Maria which he threw away before either of us could see it. 'I don't really want to draw you,' he said, and frowned at me, twisting the charcoal round and round in his fingers.

'Draw her,' ordered Maria. 'And for a change, I watch.'

'Oh no you don't. You sing. You entertain us.'

A deadlock ensued as Maria would not sing. Eventually I was placed primly on a chair, 'as you were in the kitchen', with my hands in my lap (a most unromantic position I secretly considered). Maria spread herself on the floor against the bed with some sewing, saying that she would sing if the spirit moved her, or words to that effect.

Rupert started to draw, then said that the paper was not wide enough, and he must have a board. He ambled about the room, pulling things from shelves and out of drawers; creating further confusion, alternately swearing and whistling under his breath until he had procured what he needed. I sat all that time tremulously still, my neck beginning to ache with the effort, but not daring to move lest he should swear at me. Returning to his original position, about four yards away on a low stool, he started again. There was silence except for Maria's thread pulled through her material and the occasional squeak of the charcoal.

'Sing the one about the fishermen,' he said after a while.

Maria sang in a small pleasant voice. It was obviously a folk song; a gay simple tune, of the type which is sad in spite of its gaiety. The Spanish words made it irresistibly compelling and attractive.

'Tell her what it is about,' said Rupert drawing hard.

'It is what the women sing when the boats go out on the first day of the season. It is to ask that their nets will be blessed, that they shall safely return, and that good money shall be made in the season and there shall not be storms.'

'It asks a good deal,' said Rupert.

'It simply asks.' Maria shrugged her shoulders.

'Did you like it? You can talk if you want to.'

'Yes. I should like to hear it again.'

'*I* am not allowed to talk when I sit,' said Maria.

'You're different. You're a professional. Besides you move when you talk.'

Maria sulked a little, but most gracefully; and sang again for us, this time a love song about a girl who was renouncing her lover and the world in order to enter a convent as her positon in the family decreed.

The evening wore away, almost unbearably sweet to me. Maria seemed less unhappy; Rupert calmer and less defensive. He did not talk to Maria as he had with me, I noticed, but accepted her presence and was satisfied, did not probe or analyse or work himself into a frenzy over his own words. There was a feeling of private achievement about them; as though they were at least partially contained in each other, and as though this very dependence were a source of joy and peace to them. I was most acutely aware of it, because I was outside and could watch it undisturbed. It was a very lovely thing to watch.

CHAPTER SEVENTEEN

I never saw the drawing. I don't know whether Rupert kept it.

He went the next day. I kept the secret of where he was going from Maria, as he later once more implored me to do. It linked me with them, gave me a responsible share in their crisis. We saw him off at a station, Maria and I, and when the train had disappeared I touched Maria's arm to go. There were so many tears in her eyes that she could not see, and she swayed a little when I touched her. All the way home in the train the tears poured down her face. It was I who bought the tickets, shepherded us through the long tunnels, and into the lifts. She did not speak at all. I do not think she realized that I was there, or where we were going. When we emerged from under ground, I had to ask someone the way to our street. Maria followed me a pace behind. At first I was anxious that I should lose her, but she seemed docile. I think she regarded me as a link with Rupert; as such I am sure she would have followed me any distance. When we reached the door, I turned to her for a key, but she shook her head and then stared at the pavement immobile, so I rapped the knocker as I had done just over twenty-four hours before. After much effort, the people above admitted us. We went back down the passage, through the garden, and into the studio. Maria flung herself on the bed, and after a moment's hesitation I left her.

There was really nothing I could do: her despair was so evident, I had never seen anyone so openly unhappy. I picked a book at random and retired to my room feeling unutterably depressed. I missed Rupert quite enough to start imagining Maria's feelings. I left both the doors open in case she should call me, but the minutes went by and there was no sound. 'Look after her,' he had said in those last self-conscious minutes. 'I'll write when I have an address,' and he had kissed my forehead. Had he known that she would feel like this, I wondered? Had he known the desolation which would break on her when he had gone? I remembered her few tears in his presence; perhaps he did not know. And now, quite suddenly, I was faced with the problem of how to look after a girl from another country, whom I barely knew, who was older than myself (I was young enough for that to weigh heavily in my mind), and whose grief was well beyond the limits of my experience. She will not kill herself, I thought madly; surely she would not do that; but the temptation to creep to the studio door and look at her became overpowering. She lay precisely as I had left her, face downwards, making no sound.

I went back to my room and lay on my bed (it was the only comfortable thing to do in that narrow and congested closet). I tried to review the situation. I did not really know how much Rupert had said to Maria about my staying. Perhaps she knew nothing about it and would dislike the idea very much. It was, of course, Rupert's studio, but it seemed to belong to her, as much, if not more. She had no alternative. The villa in Lewisham sounded worse than my home. But it was impossible for me to go back after one day and night away. If I went back now I should never again escape. Tomorrow I would buy a newspaper and find myself a job. When I had found it, I would go home and explain to them. I would not go home for a week; by which time my brothers should have left, leaving only my mother and sister to persuade. Rupert's warnings about jobs seemed absurd and irrelevant. He had no conception of how tedious life had been in my home, and therefore his ideas of what was stimulating were vastly more ambitious than my own. I would allow three days for finding the job, and then, consulting Maria, I would decide about where to live. These decisions were lighthearted, and based on profound ignorance, but even so, they took some time to achieve.

It was late when I finally reached my conclusions, and there was still no sign or sound of Maria. I looked in the kitchen for food. I found two eggs, some celery, a melon and a small end of bread. Nothing else. There was coffee, but I was not very sure how to make it. I put everything else on a tray. Maria would want coffee. With great difficulty I boiled a kettle on the oil stove, with the eggs in it; taking half an hour over the business. The coffee was in a biscuit tin. I measured three teaspoonsful into a jug, and added one for luck, poured on the water and waited. It was obviously wrong. I added more and more coffee, until the jug was half full of it, and the water slopped over the top turgid with coffee grounds. It was very difficult to prepare anything in other people's kitchens I decided, faint with hunger.

Maria still lay on the bed. When I set the tray on a table, she sat up and stared at me. Her face was quite white, which somehow shocked and astonished me. I expected her to be flushed, with red eyes, but this strained even pallor alarmed me. She had not been crying then, just lying there for these two silent hours.

'I've brought a meal,' I said.

She would not eat, although I tried to make her as hard as my diffidence would allow. The coffee was appalling, but she drank it without comment. I tried to talk; she replied with courtesy to my advances, which soon came to an end, however, when I could think of nothing new to say. The evening dragged on. I do not remember anything about it except the general oppression of complete anti-climax.

She knocked on my door when I was undressing; wearing the wrapper in which I had first seen her, with her hair down her shoulders. It is how I remember her, standing in a doorway, waiting for me to speak.

'Understand me,' she said. 'I do not *at all* mind your staying here. *At all*,' she emphasized, as though aware that she had not perfectly expressed her meaning. Then, before I could reply, she had gone; shutting my door with a gentle decision which permitted no further discourse.

I lay awake for a long time that night, thinking about her and Rupert, and the love people were able to have for each other. There were my parents to consider, but whether they had ever felt deeply about each other at moments like these I could not determine. Perhaps they had not been parted, at least not for a war. Perhaps they had never really had the chance or conditions to be in love. Perhaps parents had to be too much concerned with houses and children and making enough money; so that the initial reason for undertaking all these responsibilities was lost under a morass of material emergencies. Of course Rupert and Maria were not married. I had to think very hard here, because they were to me an exception, and I felt cautious about them. Nearly everyone married, and I had always understood that this was because they fell in love; but according to Maria loving someone was a life in itself demanding all the energy and sensibility that she possessed.

The phrase 'until they've settled down' came into my mind as being one which was often applied to newly married people. Rupert had said that he and Maria had not had time; perhaps that was what he had meant. Then I had only the extremes before me; the end of my parents, and the beginning of Rupert and Maria. This settling down then, seemed an unhappy horrible affair, a disillusionment from which there was no escape or second chance. I did not want to settle down if it was like that, I decided. Perhaps it was merely a matter of selecting one's love with tremendous care. I remembered a discussion between my father and another man about what book they would take to a desert island. I remembered privately selecting my choice, and knew that now I would take no such book because I had changed. One could not manage with any one book on a desert island. Suddenly, like a shooting star in the midst of these depressing conclusions, Mrs Lancing fell into my mind. She seemed happy enough; serene, and surrounded by her devoted family. I turned over to sleep, and the star went out as suddenly as it had come; because try as I would, I could not imagine myself a Mrs Lancing.

CHAPTER EIGHTEEN

I went home. Maria accepted my departure indifferently. She seemed sunk in a kind of stupor. I never saw her again.

I only answered one of the advertisements I read, for the simple reason that it seemed the only position I was capable of occupying. Also, it was the only position that my family would allow; and that I could believe would suit my purpose. I read that a lady living in south-east England, required a young and cheerful companion; light duties, congenial surroundings, etc.; ending with a box number to which I wrote. I was subsequently interviewed in London by an enigmatic but kindly relative of Mrs Border. I had a long argument with my family, which I won through sheer patience and determination; and about three weeks after Rupert had left the studio I set out from my home for the third time in my life.

I realized in the train, that having secured permission to take this step was perhaps my most considerable achievement hitherto. My sister had unwittingly turned the scale by assuring my mother that I should be back in no time at all, and that then I should settle down. That was the phrase she used, with no idea that it was the one utterance calculated to spur me into persistence.

Two men in the compartment were discussing the probable ambitions and state of mind of the Kaiser; but it was a beautiful afternoon and I did not listen. I watched the tightly packed grey houses with gigantic sunflowers in their back gardens; the street children (who never looked at the train, I noticed, for they lived too near the railway); the factories, belching smoke and splayed with advertisement of their products. Then the beginnings of country; or rather the end of London. My thoughts began travelling ahead to the house where I was going, and Mrs Border whose company I was to be paid to keep. The country gradually arrived, and was beautiful. There were enormous patterns of corn stooks curving in lines over the fields; trees laden with leaves declining to a languid yellow; steep fields of stubble and clover; and girls picking blackberries into a blue pail. There were neat green ponds spattered with ducks; hedges sharpened with brilliant berries; rich brown and white cows muddling through a gate; and the sky a pale simple blue, even and cloudless.

What would Mrs Border be like? The relative had said she was lame; had murmured something about rheumatism. I would wheel her in a chair, I thought; she would be certain to possess a chair. I would take her for walks in the afternoons. In many ways I would make her life nicer for her. I wondered what Rupert would say to this adventure. I had not heard from him, although Maria had had a postcard just before I left the studio. She had begun to work again and had promised to let me know about them both, although she never wrote letters. Already the studio seemed distant. I did not mind: setting off to an unknown destination with a salary was an absorbing occupation.

The men were discussing the probable strength of the German navy. They did not agree about anything. They became angrier and more confidential as the stations slipped by. It was a leisurely train. About half an hour too soon I began looking at my watch, struggling with my case, and tucking away the ends of my hair.

A fly met me at the station. At this point I began to feel vaguely frightened. It was not the fly, or the journey, both of which I enjoyed; it was the curious feeling that in a matter of minutes I should be snatched away from myself, be questioned, watched, appraised, be alone with someone I did not know, and utterly subject to her approval. I began to feel sick. Just as the sickness was becoming unbearable we turned into a lane and then a short drive overhung with evergreen trees. It was like diving into a cave.

The drive ended in a small sweep before the house, which had pointed gables and was covered with creeper. The man jumped down and rang the bell, which was immediately answered by a tall elderly parlour maid. She led the way straight upstairs to a bedroom, followed by me, and the driver with my luggage. I was requested to ring when I was ready to be taken downstairs to tea, as Mrs Border was waiting for it, whereupon they withdrew on my presenting the man with a shilling for his services. I hurriedly washed my hands, and laid my jacket on the bed, but even in my nervous haste had time to be struck by one feature of the room. Its walls were covered, literally covered, with water colours, all in precisely the same kind of golden frame, six deep on the walls, with barely two inches between them. They gave the room a curiously crowded appearance, as with the sun from the window, they were reflected in each others' glass, which multiplied their already impressive numbers, and confused their colour to distraction. I rang.

Mrs Border sat in a large chair, very close to a blazing fire. The curtains were half drawn across the narrow Gothic windows and I did not immediately see her face.

'Come in, come in,' she said. 'Come and sit by the fire after your terrible journey. We'll have tea at once, Spalding.' There was only one other chair within polite conversational reach, and that was equally near the fire. However I sat on it.

'Well,' said Mrs Border. 'Let's have a good look at each other. This is the first time you've ever done anything of this nature, isn't it?'

'Yes,' I said. I was looking at her hair which was quite black and most elaborately curled with a waving fringe arranged across her forehead.

'And why are you doing it now? Quarrelled with your family or crossed in love?'

This seemed to me impertinent.

'Neither,' I said firmly. 'I wanted a job.'

'Good. How old are you?'

'Nineteen,' I lied.

'You don't look it. Well, you can take it from me that men are very queer creatures.'

Spalding brought the tea on a large Japanese tray which

she set on a low table between us. It was the most magnificent tea.

'You pour out,' said Mrs Border. 'I should like a quince jelly sandwich, with brown bread.' I poured the tea, and made the sandwich.

The walls of this room also were covered with water colours. I was beginning to realize that they were the work of one artist when I caught Mrs Border looking at me with small grey eyes.

'You were looking at my pictures.'

'Are they yours?'

'I own them and I painted them. I never sell them. I like them round me. After tea you must examine them more closely. Now I should like asparagus with brown bread rolled round it.'

She ate exceedingly fast.

'Help yourself to food,' she said. 'I don't like to know what other people eat; it confuses me.'

She occupied the rest of tea, which continued for a long time, by asking me about my family, and background as she called it. I must have sounded incredibly dull, because after that day she never asked me any more about myself. It was terribly hot in the room. Tea was cleared away, and we continued to sit there until she told me to look at her pictures.

'Start there,' she said, pointing to the door. I assured her that I knew nothing about painting, but she brushed this aside.

'I don't care what you know. I want to hear what you *feel*,' she said.

So round the room I went, admiring what I afterwards counted to be seventy-five water colours.

Sunsets, flowers, churches, buildings, the sea and bits of the room I was in. Many subjects were repeated again and again, particularly the sunsets. The pictures were bad. But apart from avoiding this elementary and final criticism, I could think of nothing to say. There was something almost lovable in her assurance of their quality. Finally, hot and embarrassed, I was allowed back to my seat.

Mrs Border then proceeded to tell me a little about herself, and the life she now led. She lived very quietly, she said; because of her lameness and her unfortunate life she had few friends. I gathered that her uncle had left her the house, or lived in it before her, or bought it for her, and that except for one or two relations to stay, she saw nobody. Very different from what it once had been. Her narration was larded with obscure hints about her past; occasionally, I had the impression that she invited questions, but I was so conscious of my new position that I dismissed this as absurd. Except for going to church three times a year – she would go more often, she assured me, but for the present vicar, of whom she disapproved – she went abroad very little, except to London every two or three years to shop. But her lameness made these visits increasingly exhausting, and also rendered a companion necessary. She was, she said, quite content with her painting and other ploys. She waved her hand vaguely when she said this, and for the first time I noticed an utterly silent and motionless parrot on a perch. I could not think why I had not seen him before. His stillness was as noticeable as the shuffling and squawking I should have expected from such a bird.

'Was he asleep?' I asked interrupting her.

'No. But he only talks at night. He's a night bird, aren't you, Iago?' The bird rolled its curious double eyelids at her but did not move.

We sat there until seven o'clock, when Mrs Border retired to prepare for dinner. I offered, rather timidly, to assist her, but she answered that she did not wish me to begin my duties that evening, leaving me in considerable apprehension as to what my duties would be when they did begin.

Alone, I walked to the windows. They were narrow and upright; fashioned to admit as little light as possible. The light was dying already. Colour had almost left the garden into which I looked. I could, however, faintly discern a brick wall edged with flower beds, a gravel path and a lawn. The size and shape of the garden could not be seen.

I was startled by the maid, Spalding, who made up the fire,

and then drew the curtains, with a purposeful gesture which depressed me. She did not speak, and I could think of nothing to say, although then I should have been grateful for the utmost banality.

I was standing uncertainly in the middle of the room when a shrill little gong rang. I followed Spalding meekly across the passage to the dining-room.

Mrs Border was already seated at the end of a small and elaborately laid table. She was clad in plum-coloured silk and a white cashmere shawl. I apologized for my lateness.

'Dinner is at a quarter past seven,' she replied affably.

We began a long meal, with exceedingly hot soup which Mrs Border drank with alarming speed. Game, sweet and a savoury followed. I found it difficult even to simulate hunger. The room was papered deep red which alone would have produced an illusion of heat; but seemed now to collect the warmth of the fire and throw it back at one from all sides of the room.

We repaired at length to the drawing-room, where we played backgammon until ten o'clock, when hot milk was brought to us by Spalding, which I was emboldened to refuse.

'A little weight wouldn't do you any harm,' observed Mrs Border, and I had the uneasy feeling of my body being appraised by someone I barely knew.

When she had finished her milk, she rose from her chair announcing bed for both of us. She stood for some time, holding on to the tall arm of the chair, and biting her lips as though in pain. I offered to help, but she refused, saying that she was only stiff and needed a few minutes to recover.

Eventually we journeyed slowly out of the room, the door of which was to be left open to afford us light. I stood at the foot of the stairs.

'Up you go,' she said. 'I don't like people behind me on the stairs.' I went, and stood interminably at the top, while she hoisted herself up, step by step.

'Breakfast will be at eight-thirty for you. I have it in my room. When you have finished, I shall require you to come and see me. I think that is all. Good night.' She passed to her room and shut the door.

The windows in my room were tightly closed. I was hot and exhausted from the hours of confined and unfamiliar surroundings. I opened them and leaned out on to the gravel sweep before the house, hemmed in with dark motionless trees. It was still, with no colour or sound; almost secretly quiet with perhaps thunder high in the sky above, which, even now, might be descending, crushing the clouds into rain. I don't know why it should have seemed important but I remember well the certainty in my mind that it would rain, and I was so strung up with the oppressive atmosphere inside the house, that I slept with this notion as a relief.

I woke very suddenly later in the night. It is well known how some grief or fear at the end of a dream can start one into instant wakefulness: the dream is forgotten, and one is left only with the shock of sudden consciousness, and the feeling that something is about to happen, that the shock is only a prelude. I woke like that; every nerve expectant and tense.

All was silent: and then I distinctly heard the most dreadful paroxysm of laughter. It started very high up, dying into a low strangled chuckle, as though whatever was laughing had not breath to subside. It seemed to come from downstairs in the house.

There ensued the most complete and utter silence, during which I heard the blood beating on each side of my forehead, as I lay, frozen and motionless. Whoever had laughed like that could not be sane. Seconds passed while I sought frantically for some solution, however terrible, that could explain it. I dared not move. The sound had come from downstairs; it had been muffled, although distinct; there were walls and stairs between me and it ... Mrs Border ... No, it could not be she ... One of the servants was mad, had laughed in her sleep. In a flash *Jane Eyre* leaped to my mind. The laugh of the first Mrs Rochester wandering about at night, in the dark house. I felt the sweat down my backbone; and still there was no further sound, no sound at all.

With trembling fingers I lit my candle, sinking back on my pillow as the faint misty light filled the room, and I saw my own suitcase, my hairbrush; practical everyday objects lying there to comfort me.

Then I noticed with a return of fear that my door was not shut. Surely it had been shut. It was only just open, just ajar; as though the lock had not been secured and it had sprung back of its own accord. It frightened me, and I could not get up to shut it. I lay and watched it, the long dark slim edge of the door; until the dawn broke or crept into the room, and the candle fluttered, paling in the gentle light. After which I must have slept.

CHAPTER NINETEEN

Spalding woke me with the apparently noiseless efficiency of
the trained housemaid. She drew the curtains, placed a can
of hot water in my basin, covered it with the towel, and retired. The moment she had left the room I jumped out of
bed and tried the door. I opened and shut it. It shut quite
naturally. I found this oddly comforting; and dressed with a
slight feeling of shame at my fears, and relief that nobody
had witnessed them. Perhaps Mrs Border would mention
that one of the servants slept badly – had nightmares. At
any rate, I would say nothing about it.

I breakfasted alone in the red dining-room which, relieved
of its heavy drawn curtains, appeard dank and gloomy.
There was a small rectangular conservatory at one end of it,
which had been concealed at night by the curtains, and
which now added a dense grey light to the room. It appeared
to be filled with ferns. All the glass was edged with a narrow
rim of alternate red and blue.

Immediately after breakfast, I was told by Spalding that
Mrs Border wished me to see her in her bedroom. The door
opposite mine on the landing, I was told.

She was seated in a high-backed armchair drawn close to a
blazing fire that looked so established I could hardly believe
it had only been lighted that morning. She wore a lace cap
with ribbons tied under her chin, a wrapper, a number of
shawls and at least seven rings on her hands. Her hands were
very noticeable, as they were both held out to the fire, the
light of which reflected the jewels as her fingers trembled. A
breakfast tray in a state of abject confusion lay at her feet.
The walls of the room were, of course, encrusted with water-
colours, but water-colours possessed of one different charac-
teristic from the many others I had seen in the house. They
were all paintings of ruins: not always the same ruin, al-

though there was a marked similarity. They were not precisely pleasant or unpleasant, but were very much more compelling than the other paintings; they forced one to look at them when one was in the room, and to remember them when one was not. Mrs Border never alluded to the ruins once, but I was always certain that it was she who had painted them, and surprised that she never attempted to command my appreciation of them as she so frequently did for the rest of her pictures.

I cannot always remember the exact order in which I noticed the many curious aspects of that house. On first entering Mrs Border's room, I was chiefly aware of the intense heat, and my dislike of other people's bedrooms. I stood in front of Mrs Border with my hands behind my back, in the attitude of one awaiting orders.

'Have you had enough to eat?' she asked.

'Yes, thank you.'

'Well now, what am I going to do with you all day?' She regarded me a moment, during which I felt exceedingly uncomfortable. Really her manner was very embarrassing.

'I shall shortly get up. I'm partially dressed as it is. But there are one or two little things . . .' Her voice trailed off into an unexpected silence which was broken by a coal falling out of the grate. 'Pick it up, pick it up!' she cried. 'Not above that sort of thing, are you?'

'No.'

I tried to pick up the coal, but it was red hot, and while I was fumbling for the tongs, she bent down out of her chair and picking it up in her fingers threw it back into the fire all in a moment. I looked at her in astonishment but she merely said, 'I hardly notice heat.'

There was a slight pause.

'Now, I think I'd better tell you what *I* do, and then you can fit yourself in. I shall require you here a little longer, and then, while I am finishing myself, you are to water the pots in the conservatory. I paint all the morning but I like someone in the room when I am working, provided they occupy themselves. There are usually things for you to do. In any case it is not considered good for me to be too much alone. After lunch, I rest, and you may do as you please. Then I like my tea and a little conversation. Is that quite clear?'

'Quite,' I said.

'So you see, you will not have a very strenuous time of it.'

'Oh no.'

'I expect you are fond of walking. There is beautiful country here. What sort of day is it?'

'I am afraid I have not noticed.'

'Go and see.'

I walked to the window. I observed that a little watery sunshine mottled the lawn in the garden, lay on the window sill, the top of the mirror, the dressing-table ... and then I received a very unpleasant shock. On the corner of this dressing-table stood a black wig. It was dull, yet exceedingly greasy, and elaborately arranged in curls and puffs. The parting was unnaturally white; I could see a few grains of dust lying on the coarse sleek hair stretched away from it. I must have stared at it for only a second but Mrs Border interrupted me.

'I wear a wig,' she said softly. 'I have almost no hair, and so I wear a wig.'

I stammered something, and was about to leave the window, but, rising to her feet, she moved towards some curtained recess, loosening the ribbons under her chin and saying, 'Will you lift it very gently and bring it to me? But carefully; we mustn't have it disarranged.'

I lifted the wig off its stand, carried it to her, waited until she stretched out her hands for it, then left the room as I was immediately told to do; and all the time I was filled with the most unreasonable distaste, almost horror. It was no good telling myself that it was ridiculous, even unkind, to be so repelled by something which, after all, the poor woman could not help. I was repelled, and my shame at having been so horrified induced a kind of irritation at Mrs Border herself. There was no need for me to have seen it at all. She was quite active enough to have fetched it herself. Then, as I settled down to the peaceful task of watering innumerable damp green ferns, I began to feel calmer and more ashamed of being so easily startled. Poor Mrs Border. I had read of people enduring some terrible shock or hardship which robbed them of their hair; quite suddenly it went white, or fell out. Perhaps this had happened to her and I should feel only sorry that it was so. But at the back of my mind lingered an unpleasant feeling that she had meant me to be startled, had even, perhaps, arranged it. She had never asked again about the weather.

Mrs Border painted all the morning, or rather applied herself to the business of painting, for although, as I afterwards found, it was her regular habit to paint, it took Spalding and me an hour to produce all the equipment she considered necessary. She sat in her chair while we fetched little tables, pots of water, sketch books, folios of paper, pencils that had to be sharpened to a point where they invariably broke, palette boxes, paint boxes, a most fragile and intractable easel, bundles of brushes tied together with strands of darning wool; all these had to be arranged to her eventual satisfaction. Spalding was dismissed, and I was given the task of unravelling an endless hand-knitted Shetland shawl. Mrs Border painted with great rapidity. One by one the sheets of blistering wet paper were laid all over the floor. The fire was continually replenished, cups of beef tea were brought, and, at intervals, the parrot attacked his sunflower seeds with a kind of weary but vicious dexterity.

Sitting in an overheated room, unravelling an apparently endless strand of fragile and sticky wool in a dead silence only punctuated by sudden alarming and inconsequent questions, was, I discovered, one of the most unpleasant ways of spending a morning, and I was very glad when luncheon was announced. We had what Mrs Border described as a light meal, which consisted mainly of eggs, fish and a very substantial pudding, after which she retired to rest until a quarter past four, telling me I might amuse myself.

'If you think yourself capable of it. You don't amuse me very much as yet. As yet,' she repeated tapping her stick on the dining-room floor. 'However, there's the whole winter before us and people age during the winter as you must have noticed. Run along.'

I repaired disconsolately to the drawing-room; listened until Mrs Border had thudded slowly up the stairs and shut her door; and then partly with the idea of going out, and partly as a prisoner turns to the light, I walked to the windows and looked out. It was pouring with rain; a heavy silent shower, darkening the trees, battering the life out of the Michaelmas daisies and chrysanthemums until they were sodden indistinguishable clumps, sharpening the green complexion of the lawn, and lighting on the odd pieces of slipware and bottle glass in the high garden wall until they winked and glittered.

It was too wet to go out, and I was too oppressed to care. I was about to leave the window, when I heard a tiny click, and turning round, saw the parrot sidling quickly along his perch towards me. He stopped the moment that I turned round; staring at me unblinking and motionless except for the ruffled feathers slowly settling on his neck. I moved quickly out of his reach to the fire, wondering dully whether he had been going to attack me.

The prospect seemed so depressing, I was so divided in my mind between disliking my position and fearing that I should prove unsatisfactory and lose it, that I sank on to a footstool and wept, to the accompaniment of a huge clock on the mantelpiece with a heavy metallic tick. This, not unnaturally, did not last until a quarter past four, and after considering the possibility of procuring a clean handkerchief from my bedroom and discarding it on the ground that I might wake Mrs Border, I searched for a book (there were very few in the room), chose one at random, and tried to read. It was a long and very dull novel and had an inscription inside, 'To Madgie from Dick. Christmas 1889'. Years ago.

I read for what seemed an eternity of ticks, when I heard a door shut and voices. A few seconds later Spalding announced the Reverend Mr Tyburn.

'Don't disturb Mrs Border,' he said. 'I am early, and can very well wait until a quarter past.'

Spalding looked at him disbelievingly, left the room, and was heard to mount the stairs.

Mr Tyburn introduced himself again. I told him my name, and we both stood for a moment before the fire while he warmed his hands. There was a short unavoidable silence; then he straightened himself, and, rather nervously, I invited him to sit down.

'You are paying us a visit,' he said when we had seated ourselves.

I explained my position. He coughed a little, said 'Ah yes' two or three times; then plunging at the subject which he thought most likely to interest me (or, at least, in which he felt I ought to be most interested) asked, 'And how is Mrs Border?' adding hopefully, 'Well, I trust?'

'I don't know really how she was before.'

'Of course,' he replied. 'Naturally. Most suitable that you should be here to keep her interested in things. Not good for people to be too much alone.' He turned to the fire again.

We continued a rather desperate stilted conversation for another ten minutes or so, from which I gathered there were several beautiful walks; that the village was small and straggling (he seemed to resent this); and that the church was in an advanced state of decay (he seemed proud of that). At exactly a quarter past four Mrs Border appeared.

'*You* are punctual at any rate!' he began apologetically, rising out of his chair.

'One of us must be punctual, or there would be no point in time,' she said settling herself.

'Of course,' he murmured as tea was brought.

During this meal she questioned him minutely as to the affairs of the parish; closing his replies either with some alarming contradictory statement, or with a significant silence, implying strong disapproval. He sat there, patient, nervous and conciliatory, with crumbs of shortbread all over his knees, and a cup of cold tea balanced on them. Every now and then he made desperate efforts to bring me into the conversation, and she waited until he had, so to speak, finished with me; then resumed her examination of his business.

After tea she suddenly sent me to post a letter, remarking that the air would do me good, and I escaped.

Outside it was still very oppressive, and I walked down the drive with great warm drops from the trees falling portentously on to the back of my neck. I had been told to turn to the right at the bottom of the drive and to follow the lane until it forked, when the post box would be found a little way up on the left.

On the way back I came across a tall, bony, elderly woman collecting sticks. She walked along the grass verge in little bursts of haste, intermittently swooping down upon a stick which she put in a rush bag, and exclaiming continually to herself until we drew level, when she ceased speaking, stopped, and stared at me in a burning and penetrating manner until I was past her, when she broke out again in some eager but inaudible speech.

When I returned the vicar had left. Mrs Border was seated alone, with her hands spread out to the fire.

'That man's a fool!' she remarked on seeing me. 'The whole parish going to rack and ruin. Wearing out that church of his with tourists and services, until, mark my words, it will be nothing but a ruin. He hardly ever comes, did he ask you anything about me?'

'He asked if you were well.'

'He wouldn't have cared,' she retorted. 'Perhaps you had better read to me. Third book from the right on the bottom shelf.'

It was some novel set in India and had a religious background. I do not know clearly what it was about, because I was told to start half-way through the book; the place, I remember, was marked by a parrot feather.

After dinner when we were seated over the hot milk which I no longer had the courage or heart to refuse, Mrs Border asked me whether I should have behaved as the heroine had behaved (she had, for some reason unknown to me, written a long letter refusing to marry the man to whom she was engaged, and with whom, judging by the subsequent description of her failing health and declining spirit, she was deeply in love); and whether I considered that either she or her fiancé would abide by her decision? I replied that I didn't know why she had written the letter, but that, as it was a novel, I was sure that she would change her mind.

'And what makes you think the girl would behave so differently in a novel?'

'Because I don't think things turn out so conveniently in real life.'

'What, never?'

I hesitated a little, 'Not always.'

'You *have* been crossed in love,' she cried triumphantly.

Blushing deeply, and disliking her not a little, I denied this, and prepared to continue reading, but the page was uncut.

'Mantelpiece, to the right of the paperweight and behind the peacock feathers,' she said instantly.

I cut the uncut page, and began looking for others following it, when she said: 'And what do you think of my knife?'

It was a metal knife, the handle a cobra's hooded head adorned with two red stones for eyes. It was not beautiful and I did not know what to say about it.

'Strange, isn't it?' she said watching the knife in my hands. 'I expect you wonder how I came by that.'

I looked up inquiringly. She was in a gentler mood, and seemed to be thinking deeply. There was a short silence, then she held out her hands for it and said: 'It belonged to my beloved husband. I expect you wonder how he came by an Indian paper knife,' she added a little defensively.

I had *not* wondered, but she seemed to invite a respectful curiosity, so I murmured something and waited.

'He was serving in India you see. He was in the Army.'

'Were you with him?'

'Not out there. I was never out there,' she said hastily. 'He was sent out shortly after we were married. Three months, I think it was. Yes, only three months.'

There was a curious uncertain suspension about everything she said, and also a sense of impending tragedy which I found irresistible.

'He was sent out very suddenly, but he swore that I should join him. We had such a wonderful time. He was everything to me, absolutely everything; everything I had dreamed and imagined in a man. He promised that as soon as he was settled and had found somewhere for me to live I should follow. He wrote to me almost every day, and I waited and hoped and wrote to him. After he had been away a month (it seemed an eternity to me), he said that he had found a home for me, and that I might join him as soon as things were more settled. He said that the situation where he was stationed was very unsettled. He wanted to be absolutely sure that there was no likelihood of trouble to which I might be exposed. Always devoted, you see.'

She had stopped speaking, and stared at the paper knife. I waited a moment for her to continue, but she seemed to have forgotten me, and after a long pause I ventured rather timidly, 'Yes?'

'He was stabbed,' she said. 'Stabbed in the back one night on his way back to the barracks. He had been dining with friends and he left alone at about eleven o'clock. He was found next morning a few yards from their home.' She recounted it all very quietly and without expression, almost as though it were a dream, and I felt tears starting in my eyes at the thought of her dreadful grief.

'I am so ... How terrible for you.'

'It was terrible. No one will ever know what I suffered. I was ill for a long time. For weeks I lay, unable to think of anything else but my great happiness which had so suddenly, so cruelly been taken from me. No one understood. It was simply another young tragedy to them. To me it was my life in ruins. It is very hard for a young person to understand that. You are too young to have suffered. Really suffered,' she repeated unsteadily. 'Or do you imagine,' she continued, 'that you also have suffered?'

'Nothing like that,' I exclaimed. My own anxieties and griefs contracted as I spoke, until I should have been ashamed to admit them at all. She drew in her breath deeply and looked at me, almost as though she were pleased with this admission.

'Well my dear,' she said kindly, 'let us hope you never will.' And there the conversation ended.

The days proceeded, each one seeming so long, so packed with ponderous detail, with monotony and rain and loneliness, that it was sometimes hard to believe that there would be another exactly like it. It was an existence only broken for me by the brief illusion of liberty when at night I retired to my bedroom to undress and sleep. Then, while I shed my clothes, I could enjoy the respite of being alone, without the strain of possible interruption, of a meal, of being told how to spend my time, of being observed while I spent it.

I was frightfully, almost unbearably lonely during that time. I think it was only my comparative inexperience, and perhaps, too, a certain pity for Mrs Border, that made it at all tolerable. I suppose I always thought that something would happen. I know that in my room at night I would repeat endlessly to myself that I was earning my living, that Rupert was away, and that my home was equally monotonous.

The outstanding feature of that house was the sense of complete isolation one experienced when inside it. The affairs of the world, the war, even the village were utterly outside the house, which was fraught with its own daily routine, little tempers and accidents, domestic arrangements and confidences, heat and time and Mrs Border.

Since her revelation to me I was less afraid of Mrs Border. I successfully evaded the question whether I liked her, by a welter of conventional and very conscious emotion about her unhappy life. I felt that my association with her was a precarious and temporary affair, based on mutual ignorance of our natures, on mutual and perhaps tragic need, with an impenetrable gap of generation: she felt that her life was over; I felt that mine had not begun; and in each case we were surprised, and a little resentful that this should be so. I had to be sorry for her, because a great deal of the time I found her repellent, overwhelming, not a little frightening, even sinister. This last aspect, however, did not at first intrude itself. Everything that happened was new to me and for that reason often had very little other significance; it was not until I had thoroughly settled down that I had time and leisure to be afraid.

My fears were precipitated about two weeks after my arrival by my again hearing the ghastly paroxysm of laughter in the middle of the night; again followed by complete silence. I lay petrified as before, and then eventually managed to light a candle. My door was shut, but this time I lay waiting for it to open, to reveal some tall and hitherto unseen figure, dangerous and insane, or ghostly. I imagined the click of the releasing lock, the little blow of air, and the doorway filled with this apparition, quite silent now, but smiling at the remains of the terrible laughter. I imagined the figure pausing, watching me, and then slowly advancing into the room, while I lay, unable to move, even perhaps unable to scream. So I continued the remaining hours of the night, watching the door; my mind a riot of horrible thoughts, until, as before, the grey light suffused the room and relieved me.

The next morning it was hard to believe that I had been so much afraid; the very routine, dull and distasteful (as, for instance, the ritual which took place in Mrs Border's bedroom), belied my fear. I was called; dressed, and breakfasted in the red dining-room which reserved its utmost gloom for me in the morning; repaired to Mrs Border's bedroom (always an inferno of heat and confusion), where she instructed me in my duties for the day, or simply talked at me about what she intended doing herself; and then was dismissed, sometimes having been told to fetch her wig, sometimes without it being mentioned. I found this last particularly unnerving, as I dreaded the office, and the uncertainty of whether or no I would be called upon to perform it somehow made it worse. During the morning I would mend her thick stockings; water the plants in the conservatory; feed the parrot; polish her sticks (she had a number of them, all already highly polished); and fulfil numerous requirements attendant upon her painting. She would often demand painting water, saucers, even criticism (the amateur variety, which it was usually wise to resolve in heartfelt approval). Paper had to be cut to the requisite size with the paper knife, and a significant silence prevailed while I cut it. Flowers had to be arranged: I spent nerve-wracking and wearisome hours moving one flower and then another, and filling the vases to the brim with hot water, a practice upon which she always insisted although the water slopped over if anyone slammed a door.

All these things contrived to make the two frightful nights I had had seem quite unreal and exaggerated. If the servants had ever seemed in the least communicative and human, I might perhaps have confided in them; in Spalding at least, as I saw very little of the cook. But throughout my time there I never got beyond the trivialities which Spalding apparently considered essential to our respective positions in the house. I might, I suppose, have recounted something of my private experiences to my mother or sister, but our correspondence was mutually on the family basis where nobody writes anything which anybody wishes to read. I wrote one stilted and inaccurate letter to Rupert, which I addressed to his studio; but I received no reply, and felt discouraged and too cut off for any further efforts in his direction.

In the afternoon, Mrs Border invariably rested, and if it rained, which it usually did, I read the few books at my disposal (there were no newspapers at all). On the rare occasions when it was dry I went out, trying in vain to discover the walks which Mr Tyburn had assured me existed. I trudged up and down tortuous little lanes sunk low between hedges, and once I actually encountered Mr Tyburn himself.

He was coming out of a cottage. Before he saw me I watched the goodwill slowly ebb from his face as he hastened down the path until, when he reached the gate, it was entirely replaced by a weary and distracted expression which I now saw he must commonly wear. Then he caught sight of me, his face lighted up, and he stood collecting something suitable to say as he waited for me to reach him.

'Are you going up the lane? *I* am going up the lane,' he began, presenting me with a delightful coincidence.

I assented. We trudged up the hill together for a few moments without speaking, then he suddenly said: 'How does she occupy her time these days?'

I was rather at a loss.

'She paints a good deal you know.'

'Of course. And do you paint also?'

'Oh no.'

'I suppose one needs a dexterity of hand and a vivid imagination. Never tried myself. I haven't the time. Oh no.' He laughed cheerlessly. 'Mrs Border produces a remarkable quantity of work. Remarkable.'

'And she does it all out of her head,' I said almost proudly.

'Just so,' he said uneasily. 'Of course one can have too much imagination you know.'

'Not for painting surely?'

'Not for painting of course. Painting is an art. Perhaps for other things . . .' He broke off and glanced at me anxiously: he seemed confused and searching for something to say. 'Have you managed to get her out at all?'

'Well no, I haven't. But the weather has been so bad. She rests in the afternoons,' I added painstakingly. (The thought of suggesting to Mrs Border that she do anything was very alarming.) Nevertheless, although it had not previously occurred to me as strange. I realized that since I had known her she had not once been out of the house, and I began perforce to wonder why not. I was interrupted from this anxious speculation by Mr Tyburn who had sighted a cottage into which he seemed to consider he might reasonably escape.

'Ask her whether a visit would be acceptable next week,' he said, thankfully backing into a fuchsia hedge. 'Dear me, sorry to leave you of course, but I have more business here. I hope yours will be a pleasant walk.' And he disappeared.

At tea-time Mrs Border was in such an unapproachably fractious mood that I did not dare mention meeting Mr Tyburn. We ate muffins and seed cake, and I read to her, frequently interrupted by her commanding me to put more coal on the fire, adjust a screen at her back, or move her footstool further from her chair. She retired earlier than usual to change for dinner, and I was left in the over-heated room with the dreary prospect of playing all the evening with her a game that I disliked, but which I invariably won, with all the consequent bad feeling I had learned to expect from this.

At dinner, however, she seemed in a much happier frame of mind. I had noticed that she always appeared more gracious when wrapped in her white lace shawl. We had a long leisurely meal, during which she expatiated on painting, illustrating her views by many examples of her own work, which she compared favourably (and with an absolute assurance I could not but admire) with many specimens by what I had been taught to call the Old Masters.

From her I learned that 'they' had invariably fallen into a selection of traps from which she personally had escaped. They had painted solely for money; they had indulged in a variety of unpleasant subjects (she was particularly firm on this point); they had copied and even helped each other; they had painted pictures which were too large or too inaccessible; they had painted too much or too little; and, above all, their personal habits and private lives left so much to be desired that in a decent society they would never have been allowed to paint at all. 'They would have been better employed mending roads. The roads abroad are dreadful,' she finished grimly.

As I knew nothing about painting or painters, but very much more of Mrs Border's disposition when disagreed with, I accepted these widespread recriminations whole-heartedly, with the consequence that by the time we were seated again in the drawing-room in front of the backgammon board, she was thoroughly mellow. When I had successfully contrived to let her win a game, I gave her Mr Tyburn's message.

'Where and when have you been meeting Tyburn?'

I told her.

'That man. Messing about in lanes.'

'He seemed to be working very hard,' I ventured timidly.

'Doesn't know the meaning of the word. The only one I know who did his job properly worked himself to death. That's more like it. Died before he was forty. He was a very good man.'

'Did he really die of overwork?' I asked with some interest.

'The doctors called it lung trouble, but I naturally knew more about it than they did.'

She paused, ruminated a while, and then heaving a deep sigh, said, 'Ah well, he was not the only one to suffer, poor man.'

I waited silently, feeling sure that if I did so there would be further revelations; and there were. She made some trifling remark to the effect that surely I wasn't interested in the tragedies of life; and then with the very little encouragement required proceeded.

He was devoted to his work. I never knew another such man. He would hardly allow himself sufficient time for his meals. He was out and about at all hours of the day and night, never thinking of himself, and never thinking that I, who perhaps needed him most, was so much without him. He was never very strong, and naturally, in time (so short a time!) his health was affected. You cannot imagine what I suffered, watching his slow but certain decline, week by week. He did not give up until three months before the end. Then (he was terribly ill with a dreadful cough), we prevailed upon him to rest, but it was too late. All the nursing in the world could not save him by then. He faded slowly away and in three months he was dead. He died when I was not there. I was not with him at the end,' she repeated; she seemed very much distressed by this.

'Were you . . . did you care for him very much?'

'He was my husband. He was my life,' she said simply.
I was aghast.

'What a terrible life you have had!'

'You see that? You see that it *has* been terrible? He was so anxious about me. I tried to conceal my feelings, but he knew, he knew what I was undergoing. He had said he would have to leave me, but I had never really believed it. I clung to every shred of hope, until there was no more left. None at all. Every dream I had had shattered. No one realized what he had meant to me. I don't think he realized himself. Afterwards I cánnot remember very much, I was so paralysed with grief.'

I felt so passionately sorry for her that I could not speak for a moment, but she remained so still, so broodingly silent, that I felt I must say something.

'It seems so desperately unfair. Most people don't seem to have one tragedy, and you have it twice.'

'Twice?' She looked up suddenly.

'Your husband in India and then this,' I faltered. I was a little afraid of her.

'That is over, and I do not wish to think or speak of it,' she cried sharply, and then, seeing my startled expression, added more gently, 'It was an entirely different experience. I was young then but this was the end of my life. You are too young to understand, but to contemplate them both at one and the same time is more than I can bear.'

I tried to say how sorry I was. She dismissed the apology kindly enough, and announced another game before we retired for the night. I was so much upset by this dreadful tale that I was scarcely able to play. She reprimanded me in tones of gentle but courageous reproach; winning the game easily, and eventually even allowing me to help her from her chair, which I was more than eager to do.

I remained awake for many hours that night, bewailing her appalling tragedies; justifying her present eccentricities and tempers; reproaching myself for the lack of sympathy and imagination I had privately used towards her. One could not possibly live through such terrible times and remain totally unaffected. It explained her retired life, her painting and probably much else. It explained the wig. That night I concentrated entirely on what my new knowledge of her explained.

CHAPTER TWENTY

The real difficulty is in attempting to explain how it all
ended. It is hardly enough simply to say that Mrs Border
and that house got slowly more and more on my nerves. I
should have to add that nothing (or nothing very much)
happened to induce any hysteria on my part. How did I
stand it as long as I did, and why should I suddenly find the
situation and atmosphere so hard to endure? I was very
proud, I suppose, and obstinate; I did not want to go back to
my family confessing failure. I think, however, that the
monotony was a chief cause of my increasing nervous
anxiety; paralysing and detailed monotony, where the trouble
lay not so much in nothing happening, but in the endless
succession of tedious and insignificant events, repeated day
by day and week by week, until leisure and freedom became
a kind of mirage. Eventually I ceased to feel free even when
I was alone out of doors. The knowledge that I could only
escape from the house so far as the distance it was possible to
walk in an hour and a half, added to my sense of
confinement and depression. I ceased to go out very much.

Then one day Mrs Border announced that her brother was
coming to stay. She seemed in a high state of excitement and
displeasure at the prospect; making endless arrangements in
the house which she interspersed with vituperative remarks
about his character; 'Dull dog, my brother, never has a word
to say for himself,' or 'Dead lame, and stupid as an ox; can't
think what he does with his time,' and, most frequently:
'Cannot imagine why he's coming at all. Haven't had anything to say to each other for twenty-five years.'

Nevertheless I was set to clearing a spare room of Mrs
Border's paintings (they were stored there, I discovered, in
hundreds, even thousands). The room, being a small one,
contained a mere thirty-seven framed specimens. The un-

framed paintings filled every drawer, every shelf, and at least three dozen large cardboard boxes. They were all signed, quite illegibly, by a scrawl which I could not with any effort of imagination construe as Border. Spalding and I were directed to remove this quantity of genius to the library, which was on the ground floor. I do not know why it was called the library; it contained no books, but boxes of parrot seed, piles of thick white paper, and walking sticks bracketed to the walls. It had a dark green wall paper and black paint; smelled of damp and was unutterably gloomy – the very last place where one would wish to read.

The evening before her brother was due to arrive, Mrs Border favoured me with some startling revelations of his life and character.

'Whole career ruined by women,' she opened unexpectedly.

As we had been in the middle of discussing arrangements for meeting his train, I was thoroughly unprepared for this remark, and said nothing.

'Can't help himself. Perfectly all right for months until he meets some chit of a girl and then there's an outbreak. Loses his head completely. Spends pounds. Careers all over the world making a fool of himself.'

'Is he not married?'

'Not all relationships with the opposite sex end with marriage, you know,' she said bitterly. 'Oh dear me, no. That isn't what most men want at all. My brother, for example. He was not above attempting all kinds of unpleasant things with women who were already married. Ruined his career. It finished him in the Army. Frightful scandals wherever he went. One can't have that kind of thing. He did marry some woman once, a widow, a throughly irresponsible creature, but she left him. I always said that if *she* couldn't stand it, and Heaven knows she was disagreeable enough, nobody would. I was perfectly right. Nobody has. Can't *think* why he's coming here at all.'

'He must be rather lonely,' I ventured.

'Well he won't find himself any less lonely here,' she said

grimly. Then, after a moment's thought, 'A great many young women have considered Hilary to be lonely or *appeared* to consider him so.' She said this so deliberately, and looked at me in so pointed a manner that I felt myself blushing, and at the same time inclined to laugh at the absurd implication.

'Well,' she said, having eyed my discomfiture, 'mark my words. Don't believe a *word* they say, *any one* of them, and never remain too long alone in their company. Unprincipled lout!' she exclaimed, striking her stick on the floor. And leaving her brother at that, we retired to bed.

I woke suddenly during that night, horribly frightened. This time, however, I was certain that I had wakened *after* the laughter; that it had immediately preceded the dead unnatural silence which then obtained. To make matters worse, I found but one match which extinguished itself before I had managed to light my candle from it. Briefly I saw my room in the second's wavering light; then I was forced to lie listening, listening through the dark hours, tense and exhausted with fear. I might, I suppose, have reflected that although I had heard these strange sounds several times now, nothing very alarming had resulted and therefore have learned to be less afraid: but the experience was so unpleasant in itself that each time I expected some horrific sequel; acquired, so to speak, a habit of anticipating something more and worse. I decided that night that I must tell someone what I had heard, if only to have my fears confirmed. The thought of telling Mrs Border seemed so frightening in the dark, that I was forced to discard her as even a possible confidante; indeed I found myself becoming distinctly afraid of her at the mere idea. Then who? Her brother? Mrs Border's description of him made me far from sure that such a confidence to him would be received in a manner conducive to my peace of mind. After much disjointed thought I was forced to fall back (rather uncertainly) on Mr Tyburn. He would, I felt, be discreet and reliable; and possibly reassuring. As soon as I had determined on Mr Tyburn, I spent the rest of that sleepless night persuading myself that I could find no better or more suitable person to tell; these reassurances being punctuated by long periods of almost animal fear, when my mind froze, and straining my eyes towards the bedroom door I simply listened.

I rose at length before I was called, with aching eyes and head, my resolution wavering, shivering in my mind. The practical difficulties were enormous. I was only able to go out if Mrs Border approved my going, or alternatively when she rested in the afternoon. Today, however, she would be unlikely to rest, as her brother was arriving shortly after three. I could say that I required stamps, but in all probability she would tell Spalding to buy them, and then make some embarrassing remark about my eagerness to escape, which I should not, in this case, feel able to countenance.

The problem, however, like so many minor problems (after one has exhausted oneself with anxiety on their behalf), solved itself.

Mrs Border remarked, after breakfast, that she would be unable to take her usual rest, owing to her brother's inconsiderate hour of arrival, adding that I had better take a good walk in the afternoon as she preferred to meet him alone.

'Do you good. You look peaky. You may return for tea. I haven't much to say to him.'

I walked down the drive with a beating heart after lunch, rehearsing what I should say to Mr Tyburn. The whole business had, by then, assumed an urgency, a state of crisis, which I supposed he would resolve, without any clear idea of how he could possibly do so. It was not until I reached the little grey mouldering church with the gaunt unsuitable vicarage beside it, that the frightful thought of Mr Tyburn being contained in neither of these edifices, but out visiting, occurred to me.

I resolved to try the church first, as, if he were there, he would, in all probability, be alone, and nobody would know that I had come. The thickly studded door of the church opened loudly but easily and I went in. A heavy smell of chrysanthemums, baize and damp prevailed, but the church was quite empty. I stood for several minutes, undecided, when the silence was broken by the sound of a door, and shortly afterwards Mr Tyburn appeared from behind the pulpit carrying a bundle of pamphlets. He began moving among the pews with a decorous but purposeful haste, distributing them, and every now and then clearing his throat as though he were about to speak. He saw me, and smiled understandingly, as he mouthed some inaudible greeting. Then he conscientiously took so little notice of me, that I was certain he thought I had been on the point of slipping on to some hassock to pray. As soon as I realized this, it became exceedingly embarrassing not to kneel down to his expectations. After considering the situation, I selected a pew already loaded with pamphlets and knelt in it. He acknowledged this with a quick movement of the head, and began working steadily in the opposite direction. There followed an anxious interval; however, when I judged the pamphlets to be exhausted, I rose to my feet and succeeded in running him down at the main door by which I had entered the church. I was not a moment too soon; his hand was on the latch, he had opened the door by the time I reached it, and I had no choice but to precede him outside. He shut the door, cleared his throat and bade me good afternoon. He had a heavy cold.

'Out on one of your walks I take it.' he added as we walked down the path. I agreed, and murmured something about trying to meet him.

'Ah, yes. Dreadful weather we're having. Going to rain again. Yes, I distinctly felt a drop.'

We had reached the vicarage gate. He hovered uncertainly. I took the plunge.

'Could I possibly come inside for a few moments?' I asked. He glanced at the sky and his face brightened.

'Ah, yes, shelter,' he said. 'Of course.' And led the way.

I followed him up the gravel path to the house. It was built of bright dark red brick, and the front door, which was ajar, was badly in need of another coat of chocolate-coloured paint. The hall was pitch dark; but undeterred, he conducted me into a small room, possessed of a cold fug and a kind of bare untidiness. An enormously fat, old and matted spaniel rose to its feet and lumbered towards us. It smelled strongly, and its eyeballs were covered with a blue film. Mr Tyburn patted it absently.

'Poor old girl. She hears quite well,' he added, with which excuse for the dog's continued existence he motioned me to a chair, sneezed violently, and began poking up the damp uncertain fire, which hissed and proceeded to go out faster than ever. Mr Tyburn sighed and seated himself.

'And how is Mrs Border?' he began. He was a man not lightly shaken from his duty.

'Her brother arrives this afternoon for a visit,' I replied.

'Of course. So you have absented yourself for a while. Very right. I'm sure they must have a great deal to say to one another. Perhaps she would rather I did not come tomorrow?'

'I don't know,' I said. 'She didn't give me any message about it. You see she – I didn't know I was going to see you.'

'Ah,' he said musing. 'Then I wonder ...' He was interrupted by a knock at the door. It opened and what I imagined to be the housekeeper stood there. 'Mr Tickner,' she said. Mr Tyburn rose to his feet.

'Of course. Will you excuse me a moment? I don't think the shower has quite stopped. I shall only be a few moments.' And he left the room.

The spaniel rose again and staggered snuffling after him. On finding the door closed, she stood motionless, pressing her nose against it; then laboriously resumed her corner.

I stared out of the dreary room at the grey sky. The rain had not stopped, but seemed rather to be settling down for the evening. The church clock chimed, and I realized with a shock that it must be a quarter to four. I should have to return. It occurred to me that Mr Tyburn had not grasped that I wanted to see him, and the longer I sat there, the more I shrank from my original intention of telling him about the strange sounds in Mrs Border's house in the night. The notion seemed, as I sat there, to be utterly absurd. What could he possibly do about it? I should only succeed in embarrassing him. But then, if I did not tell him, who should I tell? I sat there feebly struggling with this dilemma until he reappeared.

'I am afraid I shall have to ask you to forgive me,' he said, advancing into the room, and almost falling over the dog which had risen to greet him, 'but I have to go out. Most unfortunate. Perhaps you would like to remain until the rain stops?'

'Thank you, but I am afraid I shall have to go. I don't think it is going to stop.'

He peered at the window.

'I fear not,' he agreed.

He reached for his mackintosh which hung on a peg by the door, and blew his nose. 'We can go together,' he said, trying to make the best of it, and we went.

He wheeled an old bicycle from the black depths of the passage. I opened the door and we hurried to the gate.

'I hope you don't catch anything in this damp as I have foolishly done. I have an appalling cold,' he added unnecessarily. He mounted the bicycle. 'Very damp place. The last man died of a consumption, but I expect Mrs Border has told you that sad story.' And he sped away, waving to me, and then clutching his hat on to his head.

I hurried back, digesting this new piece of information as I went. It had not occurred to me that Mrs Border's husband, her second husband, had lived and died there. It explained her knowledge of the parish; her disapproval perhaps of things being done in a different manner; possibly even her refusal to go to church, which must contain many painful memories. Had she, then, lived in the large dreary house? It was not until I was almost running up the drive (it was raining heavily by then), that Mr Tyburn's remark struck me as at all strange. I was so afraid of being late for tea that I dismissed this strangeness with the rather hasty supposition that Mr Tyburn found that situation, as he seemed to find most situations, embarrassing.

When I had changed, I found Mrs Border opposite the profusely laid tea table.

'You are late. This is my brother. I've told him all about you,' she said almost malevolently.

I apologized and sat down.

Mrs Border and her brother discussed the war during tea. She did most of the talking, while he sat, refusing food, and topping her very general arguments with a few military observations of which she took no notice whatsoever.

He was a very tall man with a soft melancholy voice, melancholy brown eyes, and a curious small round hole in his face just above his moustache. He sat very upright stirring innumerable cups of tea; with one leg stretched stiffly out before him. Mrs Border took no notice of me; but several times I caught her brother's eyes fixed on me in a mournful and inquiring manner. As soon as I could decently be supposed to have finished my tea I was sent to pick flowers from the conservatory for the table.

When I returned, I found the Major standing with his hands behind his back in gloomy contemplation of the parrot. Mrs Border was not in the room.

'They live to the most appalling age,' he remarked, making his way slowly to the fire. I noticed that he had a pronounced limp.

'Has Mrs Border had him long?'

He did not seem to hear. 'Bit quiet here for you I should think,' he observed a moment later. 'No fun, eh? No parties.' Then, with sudden animation, 'Those were the days!' He sighed deeply, and repeated, 'Those were the days. Why, I can remember . . .' He broke off gazing at me sadly. 'Oh well. Even youth gets older, doesn't it?' He leaned forward a little with his stiff bony hands on his knees. 'Or doesn't it?' And then distinctly, and very slowly, he winked.

I thought of Mrs Border's confidence the night before; the wink seemed an awful confirmation of everything she had said. I could make no reply. But he seemed not really to expect one, as after a second he sighed again and leaned back in his chair.

'Has – has Mrs Border had the parrot long? I mean is he very old?' I asked, for want of anything better to say.

'Supposed to have been a young bird when I bought him. Bought him off a ship's steward in Liverpool. Just back from India. Thought I'd better bring Madgie something. Clean forgotten when I was out there don't you know, and had to rake round a bit for one or two little things. Must have been twenty-five years ago. Never liked them myself. Madgie's devoted to it though. Never left her through all her illnesses and everything. Devoted to it. Extraordinary.'

Mrs Border appeared in dining attire. 'What were you two talking about?' she exclaimed.

'About the parrot, Madgie, about the parrot,' he answered patiently. 'Getting on now, poor old chap.'

'He's lasted better than you,' she retorted and led us in to dinner.

After this long and exceedingly uncomfortable meal (Mrs Border was argumentative and fractious, and the Major, bored and almost silent, stared at me in the same gloomy and abstracted manner), we spent an even longer and more uncomfortable evening, in the course of which I remarked that I had seen the Vicar, and that he was coming to tea. This precipitated an avalanche of questions from Mrs Border. I explained about the rain, and his kindness in offering me shelter. I could see she was very angry and I felt so guilty about my private intention (although I had failed to carry it out) that I began to wonder whether she suspected it. The matter was eventually dropped on a very high note of tension. She suddenly announced that she was going to bed and motioned me to follow her. The Major had so thoroughly unnerved me by his staring that I could hardly say good night to him. Mrs Border glanced at us both; I could almost see her suspicion breaking new ground. However, she said nothing until we were up the stairs. Then, after I had waited for her to reach the top she laid her hand heavily on my shoulder. 'It is not at all wise to conceal anything from me,' she said softly, watching me. 'I have a very active imagination you know. I am sure you would not like me to imagine the wrong thing.' And before I could think of replying she had gone, and the door of her room was shut.

My first impulse on reaching my room was to burst into torrents of tears; but they had hardly begun when I heard the shutting of a door below and sounds of the Major hauling himself stiffly up the stairs to bed. I lay choking back my sobs for fear he should hear them, listening while he ascended the flight, paused and stumped slowly to his room. And then I did not want to cry. The events of the day swarmed upon me, disordered, unreal and incomprehensible, a horrible collection of darting inconsequent fears which I could no longer resolve or escape. I thought of Mrs Border's behaviour in the passage; indeed her behaviour throughout the evening, the whole day, and many days before that: her extraordinary confidences; her horrible greasy wig; her solitude and her spite. I thought of Mr Tyburn's curious parting remark; of his obvious embarrassment on the occasions when we had dutifully discussed Mrs Border; of the inexplicable laughter in the night; of the fact that Mrs Border had not once been outside the house during the weeks I had known her. I remembered what she had said about her brother, and what her brother had said to me. I found myself quite unable to remember anything which did not confuse and terrify me. I sat for hours striving to arrange this disjointed flood, these innumerable significances, but without any success, until, shivering, I rose to my feet, groped for my pocket book, and drew from it one pound and fifteen shillings. I had known the money was there, but it comforted me to hold it in my hands. I sat on the bed again, clutching the money as some sort of talisman to a solution. I did not attempt to undress or sleep until the night was over. It was very early morning when I suddenly realized that my fingers were cramped round the money, and that for a very long time I had not thought or felt at all. Then, a little sick with cold and fatigue, I took off my blouse and skirt and slept.

When I descended for breakfast the next morning, I found the Major already seated at the table. He said, 'Good morning,' and made as if to rise to his feet, but I slipped quickly into my place in order to save him the trouble. Spalding brought a newspaper and two letters for the Major, which she placed before him, and then retired to fetch my breakfast. He hardly noticed the newspaper but seized his letters (one I remember was a very large pale mauve envelope), then looked round vaguely, as though he expected something else.

'There were only two,' I said.

'Two?'

'Two letters.'

'Ah yes. Observant young lady. Very observant. I was looking for the thing to open 'em if you take me.'

'It is on the mantelpiece in the drawing-room. I'll get it,' I said quickly.

'Wouldn't trouble you. Don't like messing the thing up though. A knife I suppose.' He looked about for a knife and upset the salt. 'Damned uncivilized mess, I beg your pardon, damned uncivilized.'

Spalding reappeared with my breakfast.

'Clear that up would you and get me the paper knife,' he said, settling to the newspaper. Spalding cleared the salt, then fetching the paper knife she put it beside him and left the room. I suddenly realized how hungry I was, and had begun on my bacon when he put down his paper.

'Hullo,' he said. 'She's still kept this old thing.' He had picked up the knife and was staring at it distastefully. 'Never liked it.'

'It's Indian isn't it?' I faltered.

'Did she tell you it was Indian?'

I nodded.

'No more Indian than you are. No, I bought that at the same time as the parrot. Said I'd brought 'em back with me all the way from India, don't you know, to keep the peace. Clean forgot when I was out there. Memory like a sieve, always have had. Our Colonel had nine sisters and he never forgot one of 'em. Nine!' said the Major with increasing animation. 'He used to bring 'em shawls. Awful business. Good-looking gals, couldn't tell t'other from which. Never remembered Madgie, never.' He slit open a letter.

'Mind you,' he said, 'I wouldn't put it past Madgie to have

known all the time it wasn't really Indian. She'd just tell that little story to impress, you know. Remember when I was wounded. She made a fine thing out of that. Got it in battle saving people's lives. No such thing. A damned native, I beg your pardon, a damned native drove a knife into me when I was walking back one night. Nothing very gallant about that. Been a nuisance ever since. This climate if you take me.'

This burst of confidence ceased as suddenly as it had begun; he fetched out his spectacles and proceeded to read the mauve letter.

I was no longer hungry. The nightmare had begun again, or rather it had never left me. As soon as possible I excused myself and returned to my room. I had only one idea in my head now. All attempts to understand the situation were at an end; I cared not at all for any of them and was obsessed by one problem alone.

I was interrupted by Spalding telling me that Mrs Border was waiting for me.

CHAPTER TWENTY-ONE

That frightful day dragged slowly on; and not for one minute was I alone or free, until, by late afternoon, I began to feel, in an hysterical despair, that I was being watched, being kept. I do not think I was alone in feeling on edge. It was true that I had not slept for the best part of two nights, but Mrs Border and her brother seemed to me almost equally and as much wrought up. They had a number of minor arguments in the morning, during which I was not allowed to leave the room; and at lunch, when the Major in a frenzy of boredom suggested that I go for a walk with him, Mrs Border, quivering with suppressed anger, reminded him that the Vicar was coming to tea and that she was forgoing her rest on his behalf. Then we waited tea for the Vicar, and he did not come. So the day dragged, with the feeling of an imminent crisis drawing nearer and nearer (Mrs Border refusing to allow either the Major or me out of her sight), until I was almost beside myself with fear and frustration.

After tea the Major announced that he would take a turn in the garden. This remark was received in dead silence. He waited a moment, as though screwing himself up to leave the room, then went; and was shortly to be seen pacing slowly round the gravel path in an Ulster and an old tweed hat.

Mrs Border had been playing patience. I was pretending to read a book. but I was so nervous at the immediate prospect of being alone with her, that I read with no idea of what I was reading. When a few minutes later I glanced up from my book, I found her exceedingly bright grey eyes fixed on me, with an unaccountable expression. I looked at my book again, then almost immediately at her. She was still watching me.

'Well, what is it? What is the matter with you?' she snapped.

'What do you mean?'

'You look ill. Why?'

'I – I haven't been sleeping very well.'

'Nonsense. What has he been saying to you about me? What did he say this morning? Or was it last night?'

'He didn't say anything this morning and we talked about the parrot last night,' I answered desperately. I was in no condition for this cross examination, and I think I was more afraid of her than I had ever been.

'I've dealt with plots and conspiracies all my life,' she said almost cunningly, after a pause. 'That is why I'll never have anything happening behind my back. Never. Catch 'em all out at the end. Come now, what is it all about?' She tried to smile at me, but her mouth was trembling so much with suppressed eagerness, and her eyes were so sharp with spite (or something worse), that she hardly ingratiated herself.

'I really do not know what you mean.'

'Has my brother ...? I was always very delicate you know, hardly able to bear the difficult times. I was frequently very ill.'

'He said something about your being ill,' I said involuntarily.

'What? What did he say? A pack of lies the whole story! None of you speak the truth as I see it!' She became very much excited.

'He only mentioned something about your illnesses when he said you were fond of the parrot. That was all,' I said, racking my brains for some means of escape. 'That was all. Perhaps I had better get ready for dinner,' I added hopelessly.

'Or join him in the garden? More talking behind my back?' she suggested.

'Naturally I would not consider discussing you with anyone,' I said, but the words died on my lips. I was no practised deceiver and of late I had considered very little else. 'I do not in the least want to walk round the garden with your brother,' I finished lamely.

'Why not? What is the harm? What has he been saying to you?'

Desperately I seized the only remaining chance of deflecting her. 'He ... I'm afraid of him. He winked at me,' I faltered, feeling dreadfully disloyal to the poor Major.

She drew a deep breath. 'Ah – I knew it. I suppose you fancy you have made a great impression. I know what you will be thinking next. Sentimental old fool! He shan't ruin your life, I'll see to that.'

'Please do not say anything. I am sure he had no intention ...'

'Are you?' she said sharply. 'Perhaps he is not entirely to blame? I know all about young girls and their ridiculous notions. Encouraging him, waiting your chance and encouraging him, that's what you've been up to. So sharp you'll prick yourself. Don't try to deceive me: I see it all.'

This was the last straw. Utterly unable to control myself at this incredible idea, I burst into fits of laughter which I could not stop. My face streamed with tears, so that I could not see Mrs Border. I ached and gasped and laughed, until we were interrupted by the Major returning from his stroll.

'Having a joke? Hope you're not laughing at me,' he remarked affably.

Cramming a handkerchief to my face I fled.

'Too late, too late,' I sobbed in my room. It was dark: I did not feel in the least like laughing any more. the day was almost over and I was faced with another dreadful night. I was by now so seriously driven by the whole situation which seemed to ramify hourly, so utterly out of my depth, and withal so despairing at my recent failure and the uncertainty attendant upon any future success, that for some time I could only weep helplessly. Eventually, at the end of my tears, I summoned the dregs of my courage or desperation, and considered the matter carefully. It would certainly be better, or safer, to appear at dinner as though nothing, or very little was wrong. For one second I visualized the scene which might be taking place downstairs, then, shivering at its possibilities, dismissed it. Whatever had happened I must remain calm, behave naturally, in fact, keep my head. In this spirit I washed my face, tidied my hair, and, wishing for the hundredth time that there was a lock on my bedroom door, planned my descent to coincide with the dinner gong.

I encountered them moving into the dining-room, and was thus spared immediate close scrutiny. We seated ourselves in silence; then Mrs Border remarked; 'Come to your senses, have you?'

She did not seem, however, to expect a reply. Murmuring something inaudible I bent over my soup.

It was impossible to tell what had taken place after I had left the drawing-room before dinner. That something had happened there was no doubt; and the general atmosphere resulting was unexpected. The tension was no less, but I had a strong impression that the Major was in the ascendancy. Mrs Border appeared defensive, almost conciliating; she talked ceaselessly in an uncharacteristically general manner, never mentioning herself; and several times she actually sought her brother's opinion. He was even more silent than before, but watchful; I felt very strongly that he was watching her, and possibly me also. He was studiously polite to me, but underneath this I was aware of a bitter resentment. I endeavoured in my new role of deception to enter into the conversation with a few indisputably harmless remarks; invariably he met them with a soft reproachful glare, coupled with a courteous agreement. It was not a happy meal.

Afterwards, Mrs Border requested me to play back-gammon with her 'as we usually do'. The evening wore on. The Major buried himself in his newspaper and we played; all of us, I think, painfully aware of the ticking clock, I quite unable to keep my mind on the game so that Mrs Border continuously won. All of us were waiting for the evening to end, and with it, perhaps, the conscious suspension of our private feelings; none of us was able to order the finish of the day before its socially appointed time.

The hot milk arrived. I swallowed it, thereby achieving

214

heights of self-control of which I had not known I was capable. The clock struck ten; chimed half past; after which a few heavy minutes elapsed and Mrs Border released us. I put away the game, gave her her stick, and helped her out of her chair. She made great play of being in pain, drawing from her brother some inaudible exclamation of condolence. She stood clutching the high back of her chair and biting her lips.

'Are you coming, Hilary?' she asked, less peremptory than before.

'Shortly, Madgie, shortly,' he replied bristling his paper.

I said good night, and he lowered it to reply, still with the same mournful reproach. Slowly we left the room.

Climbing the stairs as usual, I stood waiting for her, wondering wearily what she would say when she reached me; but at the top she stood breathing heavily, stared at me a moment with steady, almost venomous dislike, and left me without a word.

I sat in my room waiting for the Major to go to bed. There was a little cold sweat in the palms of my hands, which I kept rubbing with my handkerchief. More than an hour passed, during which I sat mechanically listening, until I heard his heavy irregular tread, and bedroom door shut.

I selected the smaller of my two suitcases and began slowly and quietly to pack. When I had put into it everything it would hold, I strapped it and tested its weight. It was surprisingly, impossibly, heavy; I opened it again and set about lightening it, all the while preserving the utmost possible silence. The lightening process took some time, as I was torn between the necessity of a portable case, and my human desire to leave as little as possible behind me. Eventually an unsatisfactory compromise was reached; the case was heavy but not unbearably so. I pushed it out of sight under my bed. After some thought, I changed my shoes, and then packed the other case with the remainder of my things, readdressing the label to my home. This accomplished I looked at the time. It was a little after two. I was very tired and, curiously enough, at that point I could easily have lain on my bed and slept. I was very thirsty and drank nearly all the water in the glass flagon. The cold water was reviving; my senses crept back; and I began with sharpened nerves to consider the long hours which lay ahead, hours during which, however improbable, there were chances of my being discovered. This was so anxious a thought, that I peered cautiously through my curtains for light. But there was not enough for my purpose: I was afraid of losing my way, or, perhaps worse, that I should stumble and make some sound, which would easily attract attention in the black silence. It was the dead of night; a time when it was easy to feel that sleep and death had been contrived to kill these hours; that to endure them awake and alive was a private, dangerous ordeal. I lay on my bed a short while but I was afraid of sleep and rose reluctantly. I spent some time disarranging the bed to look as though I had slept in it. I counted the pictures in the room and lit my remaining candle from the little guttering pool of its predecessor. I did not consciously think of my situation at all, I was not even afraid of hearing the laughter, but simply concentrated on passing through those few dark hours as I had never concentrated on anything before.

A little after five, as the venture loomed in sight, I became more and more restless and began to be anxious lest the boards should creak, or I should be too clumsy with fatigue; lest it be still too dark in the house for me silently to find my way. This anxiety increased to a positive terror; my bones melted like the candle, the blood thudded in my head; I began to imagine myself fainting, falling down the stairs. And still there was nearly an hour before the dawn. Even if I succeeded in getting down the stairs, I reflected desperately, there remained the door, with a key to be turned and two bolts to be drawn, and then the gravel drive. I took off my shoes and tied them together, trembling that I had not realized this necessity until now. Suppose I had never realized it? I looked repeatedly through the curtains, but there did not seem to be more light. The candle was now very low. I prayed that it would last until six o'clock. I should need matches, I suddenly realized, if I was to find the bolts on the door; but how could I contrive to carry matches, with the suitcase and my shoes? I tried hanging the shoes round my neck, but the laces were too short; I was afraid that they would fall. I put the matches in the pocket of my coat, but the box was half full, and they rattled. Eventually I separated the matches from the box and put them in different pockets. It was better, but hardly satisfactory, as I was by no means sure that they would not prove necessary on the stairs, and I was without a free hand to guide myself.

The moment for which I had waited so long was nearly arrived, but now I dreaded it. At a quarter to six I dared wait no longer, as with every minute my courage crumbled away until I was on the edge of panic. I moved the cases into the middle of the room and put on my coat. I blew out the candle and gently drew back the curtains. It was barely light. My room was near the staircase, and I hoped the uncurtained window would help me down the stairs. I felt in my pockets for the box, the matches and my pocket book. I arranged the case and shoes in one hand and moved slowly towards the door. It opened easily, and pushing it wide I listened. There was no sound. I waited a moment, until my eyes were accustomed to the gloom, and then started for the staircase. The shoes bumped softly against each other; I was forced to transfer them to my free hand. The carpet in the passage was thick and rich; I made no sound. Elated by this, I proceeded to descend the stairs.

The first stair creaked loudly; instinctively I stood frozen; then realized that it would creak again when I transferred my weight to the stair below it. I waited again, my heart pounding loudly in the silence, and then moved. The second creak seemed tremendous, but the stair below it was silent, and somehow I reached the bottom with hardly another sound. The front door was only a few yards away. Leaving the suitcase I felt for the box and a match, and then, as I withdrew them, I thought I heard a sound. I listened, could hear nothing, and was about to strike the match (it was almost entirely dark) when I heard it again. A muffled indistinct murmur. Someone was awake and talking, on the same floor as I; in the drawing-room, I quickly realized; and then realized almost as quickly that it was the parrot gabbling away in the room. The shock had been so sudden, the relief so immediate, that a moment later the incident hardly remained in my mind. I turned feverishly towards the door again. There were small windows on either side of it, and I was inspired to draw one curtain on the right-hand window. I turned the key, slipped back the top bolt, and, with more difficulty, the one at the bottom.

A minute later I stood in the grey delicious air, suitcase and shoes in hand, and the door closed behind me. The gravel was damp and painful to my unshod feet, but I crossed the sweep and continued down the drive until it curved, when I turned back to look at the house. Even that last glance revealed something strange. There were no curtains over the window of Mrs Border's bedroom, which was suffused with a warm glow of flickering light. Her bedroom fire, I thought, and knew then that it must burn throughout the night. Spalding invariably lighted it before Mrs Border changed for dinner; kept it in until she retired, but certainly did not rise to clear and relight it at six in the morning. 'She never sleeps; she does not go to bed,' I thought with the old familiar dread and revulsion. Seizing the suitcase, I stumbled running down the drive, hardly caring any more what noise I made, until I reached the gate, where I put the shoes on my soaking feet.

I must have walked the best part of a mile when a milk cart overtook me, and upon it I secured a lift to the station.

An hour later I sat in a train. My feet were wet, I was very hungry and unbearably tired, but I had escaped. From what? Almost immediately I found my mind struggling feebly with this (under the circumstances) exceedingly tiresome question. Surely it was enough to relax and be thankful that I had planned and achieved the whole difficult business; but ironically I found it impossible either to relax or be thankful. In books, I found myself thinking bitterly, in books, the character would not at this point be in any doubt whatsoever. If he or she had escaped, it would be from some explicit danger or discomfort. I had escaped, but, I realized, without any clear idea of why I had done so. It was true that I had disliked and been afraid of the house and its occupants, but for what reasons? Mrs Border had never been positively unkind to me. And now, without warning, I had fled; leaving more than half my possessions behind; almost as though I had been in danger of my life. Instantly, my divided mind rushed to excuse this apparent foolishness. I have lived cut off for weeks with an old woman who wore a black repugnant wig; who never went out of doors; who had, for no apparent reason, invented two husbands. But perhaps she had *not* invented the second husband, the clergyman. I had no evidence beyond Mr Tyburn's curious remark that: 'Mrs Border will have told you that sad story.' Possibly the man to whom he alluded had not been her husband; but there might have been another consumptive clergyman who was. This seemed improbable, however, and I concluded that she had invented both husbands. But what if she had? In books, I felt again, there would have been some conclusive circumstance or event, sinister or reassuring, which would have left me in no doubt as to what I should do and why. Then I remembered the parrot, and was filled with shame that I had not before realized that he was the author of the frightful fits of laughter. He had not, of course, uttered a sound during the day, but I now remembered Mrs Border's remark about his talking at night. That was satisfactorily about to explain that, when I reflected with renewed alarm or relief (it was really impossible to be certain which) that parrots do not usually talk and laugh like human beings unless they have either been taught to do so by one person, or been so much with them that they learn to mimic of their own accord. If her brother's account of the parrot was true, Mrs Border was the only person from whom the parrot could possibly have learned to laugh as he did. It had been with her through all her illnesses, the Major had said. This, again, presented Mrs Border in an unpleasant light. Perhaps she had only laughed like that when she was beside herself with grief, or during those mysterious illnesses. Well then,

Mrs Border was eccentric, even a little mad, but did that justify the terrible night I had spent, and my subsequent flight?

A week later I received my second suitcase. Inside, on the top was an envelope. It contained a cheque for my salary. No note accompanied it. I never heard anything more.

CHAPTER TWENTY-TWO

At home it was hard to believe I had been away so many weeks. Everything in my room was exactly as I had left it. My sister had plunged herself into packing parcels for the Army. My mother helped twice a week in some Officers Club. They did not ask me many questions (I do not think they were really at all interested), and I told them nothing. My mother had sold one of the pianos.

My mother and sister as the months went by became more and more obsessed with the war: they could talk of nothing else. They did not discuss the outcome of the war (it was assumed that we were to win it), but simply food and dressings and hospitals; the gallantry of the Belgians; the cruelty of the Germans; the appalling casualty lists; the probability of further battles; and, of course, Tom and Hubert, particularly Hubert. I think they existed in a kind of dramatic vacuum about Hubert, who they were sure would be killed. Tom was at some gunnery school and seemed likely to remain there; but Hubert was in the thick of it. They awaited his letters as though his life depended on them, read each when it came as though it were the last, and generally treated him as the family God of War. However, perhaps Hubert liked it. They were probably better for him than many families were.

Then ultimately I met Ian. I had not seen him since the Lancings' years ago. I had been sent by my sister to buy tickets for a theatre, to which she and my mother intended taking Tom on his leave. I remember that it was very cold, and that I did not want to buy the tickets, being unable to go myself, as I was working for the Red Cross and there being some function which I felt bound to attend instead.

There were a great many people trying to buy tickets. When I had eventually secured them and turned from the box office, I came face to face with him. He was wearing uniform, and looked much thinner and older. I did not immediately recognize him, as he did me. I think it was the first time in my life that anyone was really glad to see me, and I felt a warm rush of gratitude to him for it.

'Yes I do perfectly well. You are Ian. Ian Graham.'

'I say, that's most awfully good of you. To remember my name I mean.'

'You remembered mine.'

'Oh *well*,' he murmured, and was about to move away with me when I said: 'What about your tickets?'

'Oh. Oh yes.' He looked at the box office and at me, hesitated, and then went to buy them. He was some time, as there were people ahead of him. I saw him cast an anxious glance in my direction, as though he were not quite certain that I should wait.

'I suppose you are awfully busy,' he said as we walked slowly out of the theatre.

'No. That is, I do part-time work.'

'What do you do?'

'I pack parcels and help in a canteen.'

'Oh yes. Everyone is doing something, aren't they? Nobody seems to have much time.' We walked on for a few minutes of indecisive silence.

'Are you on leave?'

'Yes. My first for ten months.'

'You must have looked forward to it.'

'Oh, rather.'

We reached the end of the street. He saw me hesitate and said, 'I suppose you are hurrying back?'

'I'm going home.'

'Home,' he repeated; then, frowning slightly with the effort, said, 'I suppose you wouldn't care to have a cup of tea with me somewhere?'

I answered almost automatically, 'I'm afraid I ought to go home.' There was so reason at all for me to go home, I reflected, but now I could not change my mind, I should have to go.

'Shall I get you a cab?'

'Oh, I think I shall take a bus. I go to Kensington.'

'Where do you catch your bus?'

I pointed. We crossed the street together. I considered, for one moment, the possibility of asking him to come home to tea with me, but rejected it. I hated anyone to see my home.

The first bus was full, and although he raised his stick to stop it, it lumbered by.

'No good, I'm afraid,' he said, and as he smiled at me, suddenly I felt how desperately unhappy he was. It was such an overwhelming discovery that I was almost embarrassed by it; and began talking at random to cover my dismay. I asked whether he had had a good leave. 'Ripping,' he said, and repeated himself to impress upon me that he knew the right answer. It was nearly over, I learned, only three days remaining; he had been unable to go home for it, as his home was in Scotland and had been turned into a convalescent hospital. His father was away. 'Not much point, you see,' he said politely. His father was at the War Office all day and most of the night, he added. He answered all my questions patiently, as though he had answered them many times before, and always at the end of a sentence he met my eye with a kind of deprecating reserve.

Several buses had passed us. When I had exhausted my stock of inquiries I turned again to the road, but changed my mind and said I *should* like to have tea with him.

'Would you?' he said, and the colour rushed into his face. He raised his stick, stopped a cab into which he handed me, said something to the driver, and we set off.

'Where are we going?' I asked.

'Where would you like to go?'

'I don't know.'

There was a short silence. Then he said rather stiffly, 'I have told him to drive once round the park first. I intensely dislike hiring a vehicle solely for the purpose of arriving somewhere.'

I looked at him with some surprise. He seemed entirely different. We drove round the park in complete silence, and I had a curious feeling that he was all the while passionately conducting a continuous private conversation with me of the utmost importance, although I neither knew nor could I imagine what we were talking about.

Ultimately, we arrived at Rumpelmayer's.

Inside, he indicated a table in the extreme corner of the room. As I followed him, I realized suddenly that I had enjoyed the drive in the cab and his silent company, and began to dread talking with him. Nobody can live up to their own silence, I thought, although he had at least refrained from apologizing for it.

At tea, however, he began talking of Scotland, about which he was remarkably well informed, and I entirely ignorant. He talked with an easy intimate devotion about the country, the people, their politics (he was a Scottish Nationalist, I discovered, discovering Scottish Nationalism); their literature; their predilections for law suits, and learning, and alcohol, for devils and witches, and sculpture and travel. He set out not to impress or inform, but to entertain me with his knowledge, and I think he knew that he had succeeded.

We had been drinking chocolate and the pot was empty. He was about to send for some more, when he recollected himself, frowned, and said, 'Perhaps I should tell you that it is a quarter to six.'

'Oh.'

'Will you allow me to take you home?'

'Thank you.'

We were seated again in a cab. After a long silence he said, 'Would you care to go to the theatre with me this evening?'

I answered, 'I am supposed to be working in the canteen tonight.'

There was a brief pause. I felt him collecting himself. Then he said with some effort: 'You see I have only three days left. I cannot talk to you as though it were only three days, I cannot behave to you as though it were so short a time, because it would arrange everything I said in those terms. There would not have been time to drive round the

224

park – ' he stopped abruptly – 'a kind of emotional short-hand – ' he stopped again – 'I have never in my life – I am in love with you, and that is all the time I have.'

We did not look at each other. The cab rumbled on until very distantly I heard myself say: 'I will come to the theatre,' and turned to find him regarding me with a kind of anxious excitement.

An expression of extreme gentleness crossed his face; then he shivered and said, 'I do not know where you live.'

I told him and he told the driver. We did not speak again until we were almost arrived at my house when he said: 'May I come and fetch you at seven o'clock?'

He saw me hesitate and said quickly: 'Half past seven if you prefer. The theatre is not until a quarter to nine, but I thought we should need something to eat first. Do you like oysters?'

'I don't know.'

He thought a moment and said, 'I think you will like them, but if you do not, there will be something else. You are not doomed to oysters.'

The cab stopped outside my house. We stood on the pavement a moment while I repeated the hour at which we were to meet; and parted.

The house was quiet. I went up to my room: I had just over an hour. As soon as I shut the door it dawned on me that I had nothing to wear; he would expect me to change and I had absolutely nothing. I had only the pink frock he had seen me wear at the Lancings'. I dragged it out of its cardboard box. It presented the indescribably withered appearance that party clothes achieve when they are not worn. It was old-fashioned, girlish and jaded; utterly impossible. I pushed the box under my bed and looked wildly through my wardrobe. I should have to wear my new dark grey jacket and skirt; they were the only presentable garments I possessed, but I had nothing to wear with them which did not lower them to the drab and disreputable status of the rest of my wardrobe. I hung the jacket and skirt on the back of my door, and stared at them. The skirt was well cut, the jacket charmingly braided; the ensemble possessed a large grey tam-o'-shanter to match it; but all was lost unless I could procure a blouse.

I had known that I should probably be forced to do it, but it was with desperation bordering on despair that I eventually crept to my sister's room, knocked and then entered to find it empty. She had for some time been engaged upon making herself a new blouse to wear at the Annual Church Bazaar, but I was not even sure that she had completed it. For the second time in my life I opened her wardrobe, searched and discovered her new confection. It was an extravagant affair of soft cream-coloured lace and net, beautifully made, achieving an elaborate and fashionable air wholly inconsistent with the rest of her nature. I seized it, shut the wardrobe and fled.

I then proceeded to dress with an utter concentration I had never formerly achieved. I did not think of Ian: he did not once enter my mind. I did not even consider the canteen where I was supposed to be that evening, or worry about my mother or sister returning to discover me. I simply dressed; with a care and thoroughness, a pleasure even, which had never before seemed necessary or possible. My hair came down and went up again perfectly, there seeming not one hair too few or too many. I changed my stockings, my shoes, my camisole; then slipped into the exquisite blouse. The collar was high and boned, surmounted by a crisp frill which just touched the lobes of my ears. The sleeves were a fraction too long, but otherwise the thing fitted perfectly. I hooked up my skirt and buckled the shining black belt my mother had given me as a birthday present. I had by then achieved the dignity of a small powder box, from which I powdered my nose and forehead. I washed my hands and scrubbed my nails. I selected a pocket handkerchief, and an exceedingly pretty bag of brown and grey beads, into which I put the handkerchief and a little money. I had no scent, and no gloves fit to wear. In a moment of inspiration I remembered my mother's small round brown fur muff, which was all that remained of what once had been a cape she had been given on her marriage. I knew where it was; but a second raid was an unnerving prospect. I looked at my watch; it was a quarter past seven. Only fifteen minutes remained in which to secure the muff.

This time, however, I met my mother coming out of her room.

'I have just met someone I knew at the Lancings'. He's a soldier,' I said. Her face cleared a little. 'I've promised to go to a theatre with him, he is just going out again.'

'What about the canteen?'

'I haven't missed a single evening before. I do so want to go to the theatre. Only I haven't any gloves, I was wondering whether . . .'

'Is not that your sister's blouse you are wearing?'

'It is, it is. Please don't tell her. I'll explain to her in the morning, I really will. I haven't had a party for so long,' I said, simulating a pathetic gaiety which I hoped would divert her from the immediate situation.

She smiled, patted my shoulder, and said: 'I hope you are not going to be late, and he is a suitable young man. I won't tell your sister, unless she asks me about it.'

'Do you think I could possibly borrow your muff?'

Going to her room, she returned with it.

'It will look much better than gloves,' I cried.

She put it into my hands and said: 'You had better keep it, darling. Have you enough money?'

'Oh yes. Oh thank you.'

'Don't be too late.'

'No, no. I won't be. I promise.' I kissed her, almost hysterically; I could think of nothing to say.

'Have a lovely time,' she murmured.

'I am awfully grateful for the muff. I *am*,' I repeated and ran back to my room. She had been so kind. She had made no difficulties. She had not even asked his name. Suddenly I remembered that he would be coming; the whole evening opened out before me, and I stood inside my clothes, trembling, with my heart on the brink of the hours ahead.

I sat on my bed to wait, remembered the tam-o'-shanter,

227

and heard his cab. I immediately resolved to meet him on the doorstep, or at least to open the door a moment after he had rung the bell, as he would not then see more than a glimpse of the hall, which was anyway almost pitch dark with only one gas lighted. The bell rang as I reached the bottom of the staircase, and, hearing footsteps upstairs, I almost ran to open the door.

As we walked to the gate he said: 'I am so very glad you have come. It isn't kind of you, is it?'

'Why should it be kind of me?'

'You *are* kind. I thought perhaps it might be.'

He put me in the cab and we drove away. I wanted to ask why he considered me kind, but did not dare. He told me about the theatre to which we were going, and asked me if I liked plays and whether I went often. I answered truthfully that I did like them, but went very seldom. Every single thing I said to him sounded unconscionably dull; but he listened carefully, intently, and gave no sign that he considered them so. I had the impression that he was feeling for my mind, for the best in me, as though he expected to like what he found; and I began to find it easier to talk. In Knightsbridge the cab stopped.

'Will you wait a moment?' he said, and jumped out.

He returned a minute later with two small bunches of dark red roses.

'One for your jacket, and one for your delicious muff,' he said, and the cab drove on.

I sat staring at the roses in my lap, so delighted that I was unable to speak. When I looked up to thank him, I found him watching me intently and could think of nothing to say, nothing which would express this agonizing painful delight.

'There are pins,' I heard him saying, 'but I expect they are inadequate.'

'Would you pin a bunch on my muff?'

'I will try. I don't think I shall be very good at it, but I'll try.'

When they were pinned, I did thank him and said that I

loved them. 'I have never had roses before,' I added as general explanation.

'I have never given roses before,' he answered seriously.

I looked again at the little fiery patch of roses, like hot velvet on the fur; and it was as if my senses were slowly returning to me, or perhaps arriving for the first time, to pain and delight me. Then suddenly I felt bound to ask, 'Why did you do this?'

He was silent.

'So much trouble . . .' I murmured, a little afraid of him.

'I thought perhaps they might please you,' he answered at length. 'You see, I want to please you, or at least I want you not to be so unhappy.' Almost at once he began to talk about flowers and trees, and where they originally came from. England was soon a vast forest of oak, and we reached the restaurant before there was time to plant anything else. 'In any case, I don't know nearly enough about it, so your ancestors must make do with oak,' he finished, helping me out of the cab.

A moment later we were seated in a tiny room with green walls, on a red plush seat placed in an angle between them, with a narrow table before us. A pale yellow wine was brought, sharp, light, exceedingly delicious. It reminded me of Agnes and Edward, and Arthur who said: 'Bring on the bubbly.' I asked Ian whether it was champagne.

'No. Would you prefer champagne?' And he looked at me rather doubtfully.

'No, no, I would not prefer it. But you see I am very ignorant in these matters, and once some people laughed at me because I didn't know what champagne was called . . .' And I told him about the party and *The Mikado*. He listened so well that I began to enjoy the tale; to enjoy being interrupted for more detail, further description, and even an impersonation of Agnes telling one of her stories. The oysters arrived before I had finished. I stopped to eye them rather anxiously.

'Some people do not like them, and you may be one,' he said, 'but you must not decide until your third oyster. I will prepare them for you while you finish your story. I want to hear what you wanted most in the world.'

'I didn't know. I made it up and said that I wanted to write a book.'

'Do you write?'

'Sometimes.' I remember blushing.

'What else did you tell them?'

'I can't remember. About wanting to know things, I think.' I watched him squeeze lemon on to each shell. 'Then I went to sleep. It was dreadful of me. They were very nice about it.'

'And then what happened?'

'They drove me home in a cab.' I felt my face beginning to burn.

He was silent, and suddenly I told him about Edward kissing me in the cab. I had never told anyone before: it had seemed a small shameful experience; the kind of thing one hugs miserably in one's mind; at the best with the poor comfort that one knows the worst of oneself, and at the worst blushing at one's secret and unique capability for second-rate behaviour – curiosity and half-baked sensuality and the like. Now when I told Ian, it seemed a small and unimportant thing, reflecting little, revealing less.

'Oysters,' he said when I had finished, and pushed the plate over to me with a friendly smile. 'Some people swallow them.'

I looked at them with horror.

'Only experienced oyster eaters,' he said and began eating his.

'I *do* like them,' I said a minute later.

'I am delighted,' he replied.

The rest of the meal slipped away and I was startled when he said that we must go.

'The theatre,' he said, and then seeing my dismay, 'What are you thinking?'

'How fast the time has gone.'

His face clouded, then became expressionless. But he only said, 'Yes, I know.'

All the way to the theatre he was very silent, and, I

thought, but I was not sure, very unhappy, almost as unhappy as he had seemed while we had waited for the bus; but because I was almost certain of this, I did not dare to ask him why.

We sat in a box; another delight for me, as the only occasions on which I had ever done so in the past had been at concerts to which I had not wanted to go.

'Are you very rich?' I asked.

'Oh, enormously rich,' he replied gravely.

'Of course. Rupert said you were.'

'Rupert? Oh Rupert Laing. Did he?'

'At the Lancings', where we met. Have you seen him since?'

'Yes – as a matter of fact we trained together. He told me he'd seen you.'

'Did he tell you about my trying to run away?'

'Yes. Yes, he did tell me that. Do you mind?'

'No. What else did he tell you?'

'That you were too sensitive,' he said, staring at his programme.

'What did he mean, too sensitive?'

'Too sensitive for your own peace of mind, I think. He said that unless you could record it, or use it, he probably said express it, you would be unhappy.'

'Oh.'

'I would always try not to hurt your feelings,' he said in a low voice. 'Always. That isn't much, but many people don't attempt even that. I love you and I would like to be very gentle with you. I would like to spend a great deal of time learning about you, being with you, and loving you more. I have always believed in the importance of love, that it should be searched for, delighted in, and treated with seriousness, and now I have precisely two and a half days before I go away, and because I cannot say everything, there is nothing worth saying, and the two and a half days seem no time at all. You see?' He made a hopeless little gesture with his hands. Then the lights went down, the orchestra struck up, and we saw the first act of a musical comedy that had been running for over a year.

All the while until the interval, I sat trembling, wondering, trying to adjust myself to the incredible idea that the man sitting by me loved me, or thought he was going to love me. I was unwilling or unable to consider my feelings for him at all: as whenever I attempted to do so, my mind shied away in a kind of ecstasy of nervous excitement, back to his feeling for me, his caring for me or not caring; my incredulity and his conviction, his solitary imagination of me as I began to think it must be. I stared resolutely at the stage. I did not want him to divine my thoughts; which revolved in a dull complexity incomprehensible to me. I think that I must have become more sunk in apathy and unhappiness, more hopeless of experiencing any desire, even more of attaining it, than I knew. At any rate those few hours succeeded in shocking me into some sort of life. I was quickened; my heart beat, seemed almost to enlarge itself; and my locked and silent sensibilities streamed forth, an almost unbearable torrent flooding my mind.

In the interval we turned to each other. He smiled and said, 'Would you like some lemonade?'

I nodded and he left me.

When he returned with the glasses I asked, 'How long have you – when did you think . . .'

'That I cared for you? When you left the Lancings'. No, I suppose not really until Rupert talked about you. I had thought of you often, but it was not until then.'

'But *why* do you care for me?'

'Do you mind not asking me that yet?' he replied gently, then added, 'I want to say one more thing. I do not expect you to love, to care for me. I do not want you to be anxious and disquieted. I should very much like . . .' He stopped and smiled at the inadequacy of his words, 'Well, I should *very* much like you to like spending as much of my two and a half days as you can with me. That is all. I am asking you to believe in my sincerity to that extent at least, and I should like the benefit of any doubt you may have. I am very serious, and shall not abuse it.'

'You will not be unhappy if . . .'

'No. I shall not mind what you do. It will make no difference to me what you do.'

His last words gave me a sense of infinite release. I felt vulnerable, but less exposed to being hurt; calmer, and more simply at ease with him and myself. After the theatre he took me home, having arranged that I should meet him at eleven o'clock the following morning at the place where we had drunk chocolate. He seemed to know that I did not want him to enter my home, and accepted this without surprise or resentment. When we reached the house, he took my hand and kissed it, turned it over and kissed the palm, then looked at me. 'You have such very beautiful eyes,' he said. 'If you had nothing else they would be sufficient reason for loving you. Thank you for coming.'

I entered my gate, and then stood listening until I could no longer hear the cab. It was a clear night with a frost; my feet sounded sharply on the paving stones. 'It will be fine,' I thought and longed for the next day.

I put the roses in a glass of water; they seemed soft and darker, but they were not dying. I lay in the dark trying to imagine his face, but I could only remember his eyes; his eyes and his voice matched each other with an immense kindness, perhaps an affection for me. Affection, I thought, must be a very rare thing between people, since I had lived all this time without it.

CHAPTER TWENTY-THREE

The next morning I said I would be out all day, and went before my mother and sister had time to inquire or disapprove. I went straight to the place where we had had chocolate. I was early, but he was there. We drank coffee. I remember he smiled and said 'I have not seen you in the morning for nearly four years.'

'And I look the same?'

'No, entirely different. You do not look the same for ten minutes together. When I have tried to remember your face, a hundred faces appear, a hundred expressions, each of them part of you. If I see you for a whole day I shall put some of them together. Am I to see you for the whole day?'

'If you like.'

'Oh, I should like,' he replied solemnly. 'Shall we go to the country? Walk and have lunch and come back when the light goes? Do you think you would like that?'

'Yes.'

He stared at me a moment in a penetrating manner, then said, 'You *don't* think you would like it; nevertheless, *I* think you will. I'll risk it and look at you carefully now and then to see which of us is right.'

We took a cab and drove to Marylebone. I had never in my life gone anywhere so simply and suddenly, and there was, I discovered, a delicious sense of freedom, of lack of responsibility about it. I think he must have planned the day before we met, as we caught a train immediately on our arrival at the station. He stopped at a bookstall, and asked whether I wanted to read in the train. When I said that I didn't, he bought a bunch of black grapes in a round basket. He selected an empty first class compartment and handed me into it.

In the train we ate grapes, and he asked me a little about

my home. At first I did not want to tell him, fearing he would be bored; but he had, as I had already partly discovered, a great talent for listening, for making everything I said seem absorbing. I told him about my mother, and the death of my father. I explained about there being very little money, about my wanting to work in a library, and about minding children instead. Then I again suddenly felt that everything I had to say was dull and fell silent.

'You should write,' he said. 'You observe things very well.'

'Is that the most important thing about-writing?'

'No, not really. But I think it is for women who write. Observation is their strong suit. They seldom write out of their pure imagination.'

'Do men?'

'Oh dear. Perhaps *they* don't. But perhaps they observe more what one does not expect them to observe. And sometimes they use their imagination. Or mix the two more cunningly.'

'Do you write?' I asked.

'No, not really. Everyone writes a little at University,' he added almost apologetically.

'Do you always live in Scotland?'

'No, not all the time. I like it best there.'

I wanted to hear about it.

'It was a castle,' he began, 'but now it has degenerated into a mere house. Fires, and battles, and countless men who could not leave well alone, have so altered it, that only from one aspect does it still resemble a castle. It stands on a very green hill – the turf is so unnaturally green that there is a story to account for its greenness – and there are peacocks and red deer and wild daffodils and, of course, a ghost.'

'Have you seen it?'

'Oh yes. Not very often. It only comes when there is some crisis in the family. Some crisis or festivity. It is quite indiscriminate. It comes into the dining-room after the women have left the table and always sits on a special chair which is kept for it. The Ghost's Chair. Once when I was small I wanted to sit on it and my father was very angry.'

'Does it, does it speak?'

'Oh no. It simply listens and then goes away.'

He went on to tell me more about his house, and as I listened I watched his face, so that I should not again forget it. He had that very fair skin which flushes easily; a large and rather bony nose; blue eyes not in any way remarkable except sometimes for their expression; and a high broad forehead with the skin very white where it stretched over the bones. Then I saw that he was watching me, and turned to the window in some confusion, wondering whether, even now, I should remember his face. We talked easily by then, as though we knew each other much better than we did; only halted occasionally by some little shock of ignorance in each other, some taste, some phrase, some feeling that we had not encountered before.

We arrived and had lunch at an hotel. It was not a very good meal (things being bad by then in the way of food) but I do not think we noticed it very much. After lunch we walked. It was a fine, still afternoon, with no wind, and a large orange sun shining flatly on the tall bare trees. We walked up a cart track and then along a chalky ridge fringed with beeches. Their elegant leaves lay thick on the ground, pink and brown; our feet shuffled sharply among them. Below us the country seemed a mysterious and endless purple haze. After some time we came to a gap in the line of trees where several had been felled, and Ian proposed that we sit on one. We had not spoken for a long while. His voice startled me out of my private thoughts, and I wondered whether he had been bored by or disapproved my silence.

' – For a little while, unless you will be cold,' he was saying.

I shook my head and we sat on a smooth tree trunk.

'You look deliciously flushed,' he said. 'You like it?'

'You were quite right. It is lovely.'

'It is very good country for this purpose,' he said. 'One can come here easily, enjoy it, and go away again without regret. You do look happy.'

'I should like to do this again. The moment I am happy I start worrying that it will be the last time. Then I think perhaps it is whatever I am doing that makes me happy, and worry about being unable to do it.'

'Perhaps you are not often happy.'

'That is my fault, isn't it?'

'Not necessarily, and in any case not entirely. It is not easy to be happy now.'

'How long will the war last?'

'I don't know. Some people say a few months and some say much longer. I don't know. I think it must end soon if we are any of us to retain our sanity.'

'Is it – is it very frightful?' I asked. I had never dared to ask anyone before.

He turned to me and I saw the anguish in his face.

'Much worse than you can imagine. We all behave most of the time as though it were a boyish nightmare, an heroic tragedy, but it is long past human enduring. It is really that. More frightful than any creature can stand. Each single thing is too loud, too bloody and frightful for the nerves and heart and brain of anyone in their senses to bear. Many of them die of it, stretched till they break by the impossible demands made on them. But most of them will return, and God knows how they will manage to live with the people who were not there. There may not be another war, but this war ends more than war. To me, it seems to end almost everything. Unless,' he added, 'unless this war creates another species inured to its exigencies. I suppose it may do that.'

'Is it all like that?'

'No. I suppose not. It is only like that where I am. Don't believe what people say. Don't believe the books that will be written, the papers that are printed, the men who were not there. Believe me. It is the only thing I know.' He looked at me and then said, 'Perhaps not the only thing. I do not really want to talk about it. And I do *not* want to distress you.'

'You haven't distressed me.'

'You look unutterably distressed.' He paused. 'You cannot imagine how glad I am to have met you at that theatre,' he continued. 'You cannot possibly imagine it. I had thought about coming back for so long and then when I came, it seemed a kind of solitary marking time, painful and point-less; until I saw you again. I had ceased to make any plans with my time; to use it at all. I walked by that theatre, and then went back to buy a seat at random.'

'But we had a box.'

'Yes, but that was afterwards. I got that while you were changing.'

'Have you no friends in London?'

'Nobody I could bear to see. I don't want to sound pathetic. Of course there are people; relations, and a few odd friends left if one looked hard enough for them. I did at first, but then I had nothing to say when we met. It cuts you off, this business, you know. When I saw you, you looked so un-happy, so thoroughly in despair that you seemed more cut off than myself. I thought then that perhaps we are not so very different from the people at home. I had always imagined you as I used to see you – in large contented houses, surrounded by numbers of happy confident people. I used to think of you like that.'

'I only stayed with the Lancings for two weeks. I have not been there again,' I said.

'You were happy then?'

'Yes. Oh yes. I didn't expect to be, but I was. And then I have no cause, no reason, to be unhappy as you have. It isn't the war with me, at least I don't think it is. It's just that – well that I go on living and I didn't see the point of it.'

'Once you think like that you are lost. Most people don't think it so young. It does not usually cross their minds at your age.'

'But it is dreadful,' I persisted, wanting him to admit it.

'Of course. The war acts for me as a kind of safety valve. One is inclined in war to wonder what is the point of all these people dying? You have reached the stage where you wonder what is the point of all these people living.'

'I'm afraid I don't think it often of other people,' I said. 'I did think it of my father, when he was dying. I wondered about him then. But generally other people do seem to me to find some reason or contentment in life. It is only I who failed.'

'You are failing less – today?'

'Perhaps.' I did not want to pursue the matter. 'Once I sat in a wood with Rupert,' I said. 'He was very frightening about life, and I did not much understand what he said.'

'He was probably showing off.'

'No ... Perhaps he was. I think he meant to be kind.' There was a slight pause.

'Many men,' he said, 'many men need a kind of affectionate passion, but you, more than most women, seem to me to need affection, passionately, passionately.' When he finished speaking I found myself shivering violently. I pressed the palms of my hands together in a vain effort to stop. I turned to him to ask him whether – but one could not ask any such thing. I wondered desperately whether I should ever stop shivering. Then he held out his arms, I threw myself into them; and for the first time in my life I wept bitterly about nothing, and everything I knew, before someone else.

For a long time I wept and he did not speak, but held me, bent over me silently, stroking my head a little, until gradually I ceased weeping and lay quietly in his arms. Then he said: 'Shall I give you my handkerchief?' and after a moment gave it me.

'I haven't cried for a long time,' I said.

'No,' he replied reassuringly.

I did not feel I need say any more. I felt light, exhausted and incredibly relieved. After a while, I made some slight movement, and instantly he released me. The sun had disappeared, I noticed; the sky was grey and pink; there was no sound except a bird rustling about the trees; the air smelled dry and cold. I gave him back his handkerchief.

'Are you ready to go?'

'Yes.'

'It will soon be very cold.'

He pulled me to my feet and we walked back across the ridge, on down the cart track, where we could see the very end of the brilliant swollen sun sliding away. It was already cold, and we walked fast down the track corrugated with frozen ridges. I slipped a little, he put out his hand to steady me and I asked, 'Why are there cart tracks up here?'

'Charcoal burners most probably,' he answered.

On the station platform there was a crowd of soldiers. They all looked incredibly overloaded with rifles and kit; they were pink and panting, very young, and rather self-consciously noisy. An officer stood alone at one end of the platform. He was making entries in a large black notebook and I saw Ian begin to raise his hand as we passed, and then lower it again.

'What are they doing?'

'A draft. Going to London, and then on, I should think. We'll go the other end.'

We made our way back past the officer again. His luggage was polished like toffee, I noticed. He shut his book, and stuffing it back into his breast pocket, began slowly to walk behind us towards the men. They ceased shouting to each other, but shuffled noisily with their kit, each man trying not to look at us, at each other, or the officer. Somebody muttered something and there was a burst of suppressed laughter. Ian walked faster until we had reached the other end of the platform.

We sat alone in the train, opposite one another, watching the country pass our windows. He leaned forward and said: 'I had meant to give you tea, but then I thought we should catch this train. So now I want to take you to my house in London. You shall have tea there.'

'Yes.'

All the way in the train I sat, cold and peaceful; contented just to be sitting in a train, with him opposite me; to be moving together in the freezing fading light to his house. All my life, everything contained in my experience, seemed so past and done that it might have belonged to someone else. I knew all about it, without caring in the least. I was not unhappy, not ashamed; I had no mother, no sister; I knew nobody, I was not young or old, or afraid or beautiful. I had no plans and nothing to remember or forget; I was utterly contained in each moment, so that when it slipped and I lost it, there was another isolated moment, another little separate time alone with him in the train. Sometimes I looked at him, and he gave me a small steady smile. Sometimes I felt that he observed me as I sat with my face turned to the window, but this no longer frightened me: I felt almost as if he were I, and I he. I *wanted* to be him, I realized. Perhaps *he* had no past and no future; perhaps his heart was suspended as mine; perhaps I saw with his eyes and lived in his mind. All the pity I had felt for myself I had given him to feel for me. Then the affection he had felt for me, was, perhaps, also exchanged. Suddenly I wanted to lean forward and say, 'My dear, my dear, my very dear Ian.' I leaned forward ... but perhaps he was not mine at all, not my dear; but only kind, and without any object on which to bestow his kindness.

He had leaned forward and was saying: 'My house, you know. It is shut up, and empty. No one lives there, but I want you to come to it. I thought we might get some food and eat it there.' He seemed almost to be pleading with me, as though he half expected me to refuse. But I assented. I did not at all want to join crowds of other people. I wanted to continue to be alone with him without anything changed.

His house was a tall stucco building facing a park. I remember the trees on the other side of the Terrace, but it was dusk, and we had driven about so much that I had no idea where we were. We had stopped at three places; where Ian had each time disappeared, to return at length with some packet or basket. 'There will be drink,' he had said. 'We need only concentrate upon food.'

Now we were arrived, the cab dismissed, at his empty shuttered house. He opened the door and we entered. Inside it was dark and smelled of china tea. 'I think we will go to the drawing-room,' he said. 'Give me your hand. You are awfully cold. I did not know you were so cold.' I liked to hear him talk as we climbed the stairs, and I also liked being led by his deliciously warm hand. On the first floor he stopped and fumbled for the door handle.

The drawing-room was a very large L-shaped room: the tall windows were shuttered, and when Ian had produced some light, I saw that the piano, the sofas and chairs, almost all the contents were covered with white sheets; the carpets were rolled back and the surface of the mirrors was glazed with dust.

He led me to the fireplace; set down our packets; and stripping the dust sheet from a large sofa, pulled it over to me, inviting me to sit on it. 'No, lie on it while I light the fire,' he said. The fire was already laid, I noticed.

'Does this seem an impossible venture to you?' he asked a minute later, as he knelt before the fire.

'Very nearly.' He looked at me, then looked as though he were about to speak, but said nothing. 'What were you going to say?'

'Would you let down your hair?' he replied. 'I should so much like to see you reclining on white velvet with your hair down.'

'I shall need a comb.' Instantly he handed me a small yellowed ivory comb.

'Do not watch me then.'

'No.' He turned again to the fire and began building it up with pieces of wood and lumps of coal whilst I unpinned my hair.

'Would you like another cushion?' he asked after a time.

'Yes.'

He rose and delved under the cover of another sofa, returning with a large yellow silk cushion.

'Oh yes,' he said, placing it behind my head. 'I knew you would look beautiful like that. You should be painted. Thank you for letting down your hair. Now I am going to leave you alone in the firelight while I collect things for our meal.'

'Shall I not help?'

'No. I like to think of you lying there in your dark grey skirt. You may watch the fire. I shall come back and find you.' He walked to the door, then turned back and said: 'You will not be bored or frightened by yourself? I am only going downstairs. You will be all right?'

I nodded.

242

He shut the door. I heard his footsteps descend the bare stairs; and then there was silence. I lay watching the flames, and the shadow of the flames on the gold encrusted ceiling; the richness of my white velvet sofa in the gentle restless light; the strands of my hair lying on the glowing cushion; and the way the parquet floor looked almost like plaited hair stamped on the ground. I could still detect the closed scented smell which had seemed to fill the house. I was content just to lie there watching the room. There were pictures, and a mirror hanging above the piano. I began counting the pieces of furniture, the dim white lumps placed all over the room; even in the furthest corner they could be discerned . . .

I woke to find his hand on my hair.

'It really *is* an improbable venture,' he was saying.

'I didn't intend . . .'

'I like you to have slept,' he said.

There was a little round table beside me with food spread on it, laid upon a knotted lace cloth. There were knives, plates and two glasses; and a black bottle wrapped in a white napkin. There were also two small steaming pots.

'I did not even watch the fire. What *is* in the pots?'

'Soup,' he said proudly. 'I bought it in a jar and I've made it into proper soup. There are biscuits. There was a little sherry. The fire is all right. I was not very long, you know, but I had to keep unlocking things. My father has a passion for locking everything. He carries an enormous ring with all the keys of all his houses on it; he is unable to unlock anything in less than half an hour.' He sat on a stool beside me and gave me some soup and a biscuit.

'Now, you are starving and you must eat, or the food may vanish.'

The soup was very hot and good.

'Any soup tastes good with sherry in it,' he said, but I think he was secretly very proud of his concoction.

'Does your father not live here?' I asked.

'No,' he said, 'he prefers to live in his club. He works incessantly, and he says he is too tired to combat a large empty house at the end of each day. So it is shut up except for a caretaker who comes in to clean it, and make sure that nothing has been stolen.'

'Have you been living here?'

'No, not really. I come here a good deal, and I spent the first night of my leave here, but it was not the same as it is now. It needs another person.' He gave me a second biscuit. 'I shall have to go and see him again.' He fell silent and I felt all his life that I did not know crowd into his mind.

He gave me a plate on which were half a cold bird, some potato salad, and sprig of watercress. He poured some wine into the glasses. Then he said, 'I shall drink to our happiness. Your happiness.' He drank.

'May I drink to yours?'

He gave me a glass of the red wine, looked at me, and then said in a bantering facetious manner which ill became him: 'You may drink to my old age. My happy and prosperous senility.'

I repeated the toast uncomprehendingly and without much enthusiasm and drank to it.

'And now let us return to this evening. We are not old, and you are not, I think, unhappy.'

'I think,' I said cautiously, 'that I am very happy.'

'Do you? Well don't think any more about it than that. Of course you know you deserve to be. You took an awful risk. You might be utterly ruined by now, in floods of tears, or white and silent and desperately bored.'

'Why?'

'Because,' he said solemnly, 'wicked men and worse still, dull men, frequently collect young women outside London theatres, feed them on grapes and oysters, and carry them off to some deserted house. I tell you this, because you do not seem to realize how fortunate you are that I am not wicked and hardly at all dull.'

'But how are the men to know about the women? Suppose they are dull?'

'In these cases that is seldom a primary consideration.'

'I knew that you were not dull – or wicked.'

'My upbringing,' he said sadly. 'The bad thing about that

244

was that although it presented a fair chance of my being dull, it made no allowance for wickedness whatsoever.'

'Tell me about your upbringing.'

'I should like to hear about yours.'

'I don't think I was brought up. I just drifted.'

'Probably a very good thing.'

'Yes, but I'm still drifting. I don't know how to stop. I have no talents, and hardly any friends.'

'I am your friend.'

'Yes, I ...'

'What would you *like* to do?' he interrupted to relieve me.

'What would you suggest?'

He thought for a moment and then said, 'I should imagine that in a better world you are well equipped simply to live. You would not need a reason for doing this. But at the present time people have all to be doing something more or less frightful in order to justify their being alive. Everyone labours under a kind of unorganized mass guilt. When they start to organize their guilt the trouble will really begin.'

'Will they?'

'After this war they might. As long as we can think the Germans are even a little worse than ourselves, and the Germans can think that they are a little better than us, we shall rub along as we are, killing each other. But when the war is over and we are forced back on to comparing ourselves with other members of the family it will not take very long before we see, or think we see, that we are all equally wicked. Then we shall organize ourselves to compensate for this feeling. Work for work's sake, and so on. I don't think you've reached that stage.' He gave me more wine, and then continued: 'I think you should write. I cannot think of anything else. Have you ever tried?'

I nodded: 'But it was no good, and I stopped.'

'Start again. I shall expect to be sent some results.'

We finished our dinner with exquisite pears. Then he asked me to play to him.

'I cannot play to people.'

245

He walked to the piano, uncovered and opened it, and came back to the fire.

'I am not people,' he said. 'I cannot play, and it would give me so much pleasure to hear this piano again.'

After some minutes' indecisive silence, I rose from the sofa, went reluctantly to the instrument, and played an Allemande from the English Suites. When I had finished I turned to him, but he was staring into the fire and did not move or speak. After a moment I suddenly remembered a sonata of Scarlatti and played it.

'What key is that in?'

'B minor.'

'It is most hopelessly sad. The epitome of despair. Like the beginning of the end of something. Would you play it again?'

'The end of love,' he said when I had finished it.

I played a slow movement from a B Flat sonata of Haydn, and then shut the piano.

'Who was that?'

'Haydn.'

'All people you like?' he said.

'Yes.'

'Thank you. Please come back now.'

When I was again back on the sofa he drew up his stool, and took my hand.

'I am already so much devoted to you,' he said. 'Will you remember how devoted to you I am? Will you tell me one thing? Has anyone made you very unhappy?'

'No one.'

'Good.' He enclosed my hand in both of his for a moment and then said, 'Now I suppose I must take you home.'

'I must put up my hair.'

'Oh yes. Stay here and I will fetch you a mirror.'

He returned with a mirror and ivory brush, which he placed on the table beside me. 'While you do that I must extinguish the fire.'

'What about the remains of our dinner?'

'That will vanish of itself,' he replied.

I remember that as we opened the front door, we were assaulted by the biting moonlit air, and a thin distant howling.

'The wolves,' he said. 'They often howl at night. I had forgotten them. Do you mind walking until we find a cab?'

'No. I do not mind anything,' I replied.

'Does that mean that were you in the mood for objecting, you would object to walking for a cab?'

'No.'

We discovered a cab, and began the long quiet drive to Kensington which was the very end of our entire day together.

I think it was then that I first clearly realized that the next day was his last: it was then that I began dreading it, not very sure what precisely it was that I dreaded, not even certain that I was not simply afraid that *he* dreaded it. I knew, at least, that he was thinking about it, and realized suddenly that he must often have done so since I had met him outside the theatre – very much more often than the few occasions when he had spoken about his three remaining days. Now it was one remaining day, perhaps not even that. Perhaps he had meant that he was going away in the evening. It seemed absolutely necessary to know this. I asked him.

'Very early in the morning the day after tomorrow.'

'Oh.' There was one whole day left.

'I am awfully afraid that I shall not be free until after lunch,' he said. 'My father arranged at the beginning of my leave that I lunch with him on my last day, and he is not free at any other time excepting the evening, which I would like to spend with you. I should like to meet you immediately after lunch, if you would. If you would,' he repeated, and looked at me.

'Where shall I meet you?'

'Meet me just inside the National Gallery at half past two,' he said quickly.

He must have considered the matter, I thought, as I agreed to this arrangement.

We were silent again, unable to think of anything which did not render us more silent.

'Tomorrow night,' I remember thinking, 'tomorrow night I shall drive back like this with him for the last time,' and wondered what would become of me.

'At any rate, we have decided that you are going to write,' he said, almost as though he were interrupting me.

'I shall try.'

We had reached my home. He did not kiss my hand, but helped me out of the cab and then led me to the gate.

'Will you get in?'

'Oh yes, I have a key.'

'I adored your hair. You are a kind and beautiful creature.'

'I meet you at two-thirty?'

'Two-thirty. Inside the National Gallery.'

'Yes.'

'Good night my dear,' he said and returned to the cab.

I slipped into the house and up to my room as silently as possible; stripped off my clothes and endeavoured to choose my thoughts, or at least to collect the incidents of the day and savour them. I knew that it had been a wonderful day. I *knew* this without in the least being able to count the joys, because I was filled with vague but tremendous anxieties which could not be counted. All I could count were the hours I had left before he went, and I counted them carefully while I unpinned my hair. Eight hours at least; and he had said that he adored my hair. It had seemed a strange word for him to use. No one had ever adored anything about me. It did not anyway seem a word to which he was accustomed. I adore your hair, I said to myself, hearing his voice; and experienced a sharp nervous thrill. Tonight I should be able to sleep with my last thought that I should see him tomorrow; but tomorrow night – tomorrow night was like some disastrous precipice, towards which I was inevitably propelled and on the edge of which I was inevitably forsaken. Now I should not see him until half past two, which seemed so many hours away, that the ensuing hours with him must seem long also. He does not want to go; and I think he does not want to leave me, I thought, knowing that also. Then I lay down with the false childish little hope that perhaps something which we both desired so intensely not to happen, would not happen.

CHAPTER TWENTY-FOUR

I spent a long dreadful morning, evading my family, struggling with my share, and more than my share (for I had a guilty conscience) of the family chores, watching the time, and finally attempting to eat lunch under the watchful family eyes. At ten minutes to two I escaped to my room, at two left the house, and then was so afraid of being late that I took a cab. In consequence of this I arrived early; but once more he was there.

'I am very glad that you are early, because we are going to a theatre,' he said almost at once. 'I have a cab waiting.' He took my arm and led me down the steps again.

'I am sorry to be peremptory, but I have thought this out very carefully,' he said as we drove away. 'I thought we should have tea, and then dine in my house. Is that all right?'

I nodded. The slight disappointment I had felt about the theatre dissolved as he continued the plans. I surrendered myself to the third day in his company so completely that the morning vanished; there was nothing beyond going to his house, and I was able utterly to concentrate upon the hours between.

Curiously, I can remember almost nothing about the theatre we visited. It must have been a comedy, as I remember us both laughing; on one occasion turning to each other, ceasing to laugh, and turning back to the stage again, with the play knocked out of our minds.

Afterwards we had tea. Ian had again bought me dark red roses, which smelled of more roses than could possibly be contained in the paper. 'Do not unwrap them,' he said. 'I want you to wear them in your hair at dinner.'

'In these clothes?'

'I assure you they will be perfectly suitable. You have very good hair for the purpose. Like the Empress Elisabeth. She preferred diamonds, but you will have to make do with roses for the present.'

'Did she always wear diamonds in her hair?'

'Invariably. But she wore a top hat when riding in order to conceal the diamonds.'

He proceeded to tell me about the Empress Elisabeth: of her beauty; her passion for adventure; her terror of growing old; and her incredible hair. 'Of course, being an Empress she was able to make the most of it,' he concluded as we rose to go. 'Shall we walk a little? We have now to collect our dinner.'

I agreed. We proceeded to St James's Street.

'Do you arrange about food?'

'Yes. I wake very early, and that is how I employ the time. We are going to my club first, where I am afraid you will have to wait for me.'

As I waited, I reflected that this was, after all, not so difficult as I had previously imagined it would be. We were not tense or strained, either of us; we were simply two friends spending the day – spending it perhaps in a slightly less usual manner than many friends who spent time together (I was thinking of the empty house and the private meal we were collecting); but that was all. That really seemed to be all, I repeated to myself.

It began to rain a little. We collected the rest of the food in a cab, and then drove to his house. Here the same ceremony took place as before. Ian lighted the fire, uncovered the white sofa (everything in the room had been restored to the state in which I had first seen it), and then announced that he was going to prepare the meal. I offered to help him; but he declined, and I felt certain that he did not want me to see the rest of the house. When he had left me I wandered round the room.

Hung on the wall there was a large portrait of an extremely fascinating woman. She was wearing a riding habit: her beautiful hands palely clutched the heavy folds of her skirt, as she gazed out upon the room above the severe gloss of her high stiff collar, with an expression at once imperious and immature; smiling a little curling smile, which conveyed nothing of the humour in which she was painted. Possibly she was Ian's sister, although he had never mentioned a sister. But then, I really knew very little about him. I replenished the fire; then, without thinking very much, wandered to the piano and played.

I found myself totally unable to remember any piece of music completely. This was not customary with me, and I found it unreasonably frightening. For what seemed hours of panic and futility, I struggled; always breaking down at the same place or within a few bars of it; until I was eventually interrupted by Ian.

I did not hear him come into the room, which increased my alarm and mortification. I rose from the piano, wordless and shivering, and moved to the sofa avoiding him.

'You have not used your roses,' he said.

'No.'

I made no move towards them, sat with my hands stretched out to the fire, as though they were cold and I must do nothing but warm them. I felt him regarding me; my unaccountable tumult of feeling rose to the pitch of anger. I discovered that my hands were freezing. He indicated a stool where I might sit nearer the fire, and I moved to it with my back to him. 'If he imagines that I will unpin my hair and play the piano, he is wrong,' I thought viciously, longing for him to give me the chance of denying him either of these things. 'I will do nothing of the kind.' I wanted to sit there until he was as angry with me as I was with him; there was nothing else that I *could* do now, I realized quickly. It is very easy to reach a point where one's next action is so dependent on pride and so confined by emotion that one is driven on to ungraciousness and everything fast becomes intolerable. It was intolerable to sit on the stool, unable to speak, refusing the roses, and waiting for him to be hurt, but it was all I was able to do. And a few minutes ago everything had seemed simple; until he had come into the room when I was trying to remember the music.

All this while I heard him arranging things on the table. Eventually he said: 'Would you like to eat where you are?'

I felt that he was trying to accommodate me, and knew that if I were to continue hating him at all, I must comply. I turned round, and he offered me a steaming bowl as he had done the previous evening. For some minutes we sat in silence, while I attempted to drink the soup, but long before it was finished I knew that I should be quite incapable of sustaining the meal. I put the bowl on the table in order better to struggle with myself. Then I heard him set down his bowl, looked at him, and suddenly, covering my face in my hands, was shaken with sobs. He got up after a moment and led me to the sofa. I think he knelt before me, holding my hands, asking me why I was sobbing. I shook my head. I was so ashamed and so unhappy that I did not know or care why.

'Did I frighten you? Was it because you dislike anyone hearing you practise? Or because you do not want to unpin your hair?' I heard him trying all these possibilities with patient credulity, prepared to believe anything I told him. So I told him the truth; that I did not want him to go away, most passionately I did not want it. It was the only thing I knew.

'I think I had better hold you in my arms,' he said.

'No. I am dreadfully sorry.'

'Why are you sorry?'

'I cannot manage any of my feelings at all. I simply weep. I wept yesterday.'

'That was different,' he said reassuringly.

'Yes. But this is much worse. I will try to explain. I do not love you, at least, surely if I did love you I should not be so utterly unhappy. Even if you were going away, surely I should not be so much in despair?'

'I do not know,' he said after considering this. 'Perhaps not. Perhaps you wish you did love me.'

'I wish I knew you more. I do not want you to go and never to see you. I know nothing about this. I cannot compare myself, or you, with anyone or anything else. I simply want to choose more: and not be forced into your going away. Must you go?'

'Yes, I must go.'

'Well, do you really believe that you love me?'

'Yes, I know that.'

'If you stayed, I might know that I loved you. Wouldn't that be what you would want?'

'If I were staying, I should do everything in my power to induce your love,' he replied.

'But you cannot possibly stay? Even a little time?'

I saw that he began to suffer but he reiterated steadily, 'No, I must go.'

We stared silently at each other; and then, with a tremendous effort, my heart devoured my imagination of him, and my half-conscious dream of our gentle slow-moving love. I believe I only touched his hand; but it was as though our hearts touched, lay quietly together and returned to us. If he had stayed many months I think there might not have been such another moment. They are the only moments when more than one person is beautiful: when each mind is unfolded to the other like some marvellous map of a Paradise: when each also loves the self equally because it is the lover of the beloved. They are the moments of life which continue it: the vindication of all the desolate hours and days and years that each one spends searching.

He was holding my hand again now; and still we watched the glow from the first exquisite shock die in our eyes; and the lovely amiable ease which followed.

'Who is the portrait at the end of the room?'

'My mother. It was very like her, I believe.' She was killed, he continued, in a riding accident when he was a child. He barely remembered her.

We talked very quietly for a time, hardly aware of what we said, and then he rose to his feet.

'Don't leave me.'

'I was proposing to sit on the sofa with you,' he said.

I remembered the roses.

'May I have your comb?'

'Yes, of course.'

I held out my hand. He gave it me. I walked to the mirror over the fireplace, and he watched me let down my hair.

'Don't cut it, will you? At least, not yet.'

'Why do you ask that?'

'Many women have cut their hair. I am not sure that it would become you. I should have to know you better.'

'I will ask your opinion before I cut it, but it is very heavy.'

'It is very romantic and beautiful,' he answered seriously. 'Shall I comb it for you?'

'Yes.'

'Sit on this cushion and give me the comb.'

He was very good at it and I said so, with some surprise. 'Have you combed many women's hair?'

'Would it not be better for you if I had?'

I reflected. 'Yes, I suppose it would.'

'Well then, I am an extremely experienced hair comber.'

'Of course you might be instinctively good at it.'

I felt that he smiled as he said: 'Perhaps that is what I am. Now, where are the roses. I presume you intend wearing the roses.'

'As I am without a single diamond, I have no choice.'

'I should have bought diamonds as well. It is dreadful to have no choice.'

'You are not meant to give me diamonds! I didn't mean that.'

'I think I should enormously enjoy giving you diamonds. It simply had not occurred to me.'

'Give me the roses. I want to unwrap them myself.'

'Now,' he said, when the roses were finally arranged. 'Come and recline on the sofa. I think it will entail taking you in my arms. For our mutual comfort,' he added when I came.

For a long while I lay on the sofa with his arms round me. There seemed to be so very much to say, and conversation of any kind was delightful to us both. We talked, we reassured one another (I did not at first perceive his need of this), we discovered, or bred, a crowd of new perfections in one another: and all the while, time, the hours, raced, galloped, fell headlong into the night. Then, when he suggested that we eat the rest of our meal, I did ask him the time. We found that it was well past eleven. I was so appalled that I did not notice him, as the relentless situation closed in on me again with frightful force. I should have to go, in less than an hour I should have to go. I turned from any hopeless attempt to eat; determining this time thoroughly to control myself, unconsciously clinging to him until he said: 'My poor darling. We are neither of us very good at this.' I saw his eyes filled with tears, and was overwhelmed with an agony of tenderness for him, with a passionate desire that he should not feel so much or so painfully as I. I put my arms round him and kissed him; held him in my arms as though I were the lover; and for a moment the imminence of our parting ebbed away. I remember thinking quite quietly to myself when I had kissed him: 'No, I cannot bear this, really I cannot bear it. Something must happen to stop, or at least defer my going, because this is more than I can bear.'

Then, almost immediately, he said: 'I have to go very early in the morning. Would you stay here with me until I go?'

'I will stay with you.'

'What about your family? Will they not become anxious?' He was very still, watching me steadily.

'I told them I should be late, and I have a key. I don't think they will know until tomorrow morning.' I wondered why he continued to watch me, as though he were trying to understand me. I repeated almost angrily, 'They won't know until the morning, and then I shall be back.'

'You want to stay?'

'I don't want to leave you. I think I must love you very much indeed. I want to lie on this sofa all night, talking with your arms round me.'

'That is what you want?'

'Yes. Is that wrong?'

He touched my hair and then dropped his hand. 'No,' he said, 'of course it is not wrong. That is what you shall have. But first you must eat.'

We ate: the morning seemed very far away. We even discussed the plans for his departure, and they none of them seemed in the least real to me. He must leave at seven, he said, in search of a cab, but he would make tea before he left; therefore we must, if we slept at all, wake at six-thirty.

'Shall we sleep?'

'I expect not,' he said, 'but we might.'

Fetching a small clock, a kettle and two large cups; he set them on the table, which he moved away from the sofa whereon I lay.

'Should I do anything?'

'No, I will make up the fire and join you.'

He knelt before the fire, began to replenish it, and then suddenly exclaimed: 'Oh my darling!'

'What is it?' He was sitting back on his heels regarding me.

'I have a sudden access of anxiety for you. I do not want to make you unhappy. I do not want you to suffer because of me.'

'But you are not making me suffer.'

'I am in no position to love anyone,' he said. 'Perhaps you least of all.'

'But – but you do not want to go away?'

'You know that I do not want to.'

'Well then I do not understand. It is not you who are deliberately making me unhappy, but the situation, which is no more yours than mine.'

'Then you *are* unhappy.'

'Oh – not more than you. I think, perhaps less. I am simply filled with feelings I have never had before. I no longer know precisely what I feel. I do love you,' I added.

'I desire you,' he said quietly. 'I want you, because I love you so much. Most of all, I have wanted to tell you. I don't want you to answer me, but it eases my mind to tell you this one thing. I know quite well that you are not ready to love me as much as you must love me before I could possess you. But telling you makes it possible for me to love lying on the sofa with you in my arms; my beloved creature. You do not mind my saying this? In other circumstances there would be no need to say it. I love you.' He turned back to the fire again.

'I suppose,' I said uncertainly, 'that it is I who am a step behind you.'

'Or a step ahead. It makes no difference.'

'Then do we never meet? Do not people ever feel the same at the same moment?'

'Sometimes they do. I think that at the beginning and at the end of love there is always a kind of dishonesty; it is inevitable, and should not be resented, even when it is painful. But in the middle, the centre, there is a brilliant pure streak, when honesty is merely another joy. Then people meet.'

All the remainder of the night we lay, wrapped in one another's arms, furthering our love, spending the precious time like gold, that we, as misers, were forced to spend. We lay with the small clock evenly distributing our hours, striking them off by a single impersonal note, so that we began each hour in trembling silence.

Very early in the morning he slept for a short while. I watched his face by the light of the dying fire. I moved to touch his head, and he woke, instantly alert, as though he never slept more deeply.

'Is it time?'

'No, no I do not think so. I am sorry I woke you.'

'I did not mean to sleep.'

We would make tea now, he continued, and talk while we drank it. He put the last pieces of wood on the fire: the room seemed cold and I looked at the time. It was a quarter to six. The roses in my hair were bruised and wilting. I unpinned them.

'I should like one,' he observed.

He produced a black pocket book, like the one the officer on the station had had, and tucked the rose away. The flames from the replenished fire leapt higher up the chimney and the kettle began to throb.

'I can see the lovely bones of your face in this light,' he said. He came to me, and traced them with his finger.

'Will you remember my face?' I asked.

'Of course.'

'I do not think it is so easy. I had great difficulty in remembering yours, even when I had just left you, and wanted to remember it.'

'Perhaps I have not a very memorable face, or perhaps you tried to remember the wrong things. But I shall remember you.'

'The wrong things?'

'I shall remember you by your square forehead: it is almost completely square; and by the ledges of bone under your eyes; the way your whole face tilts into your small neat chin; the heavy enchanting curve of your eyelid; and your enormous tears. One should not try to remember people in order to describe them to someone else. In doing this one loses everything of significance. If I said that you had long grey eyes, a white complexion, and heavy dark brown hair, no one would be very much the wiser; but I should have made a public image of you which could be anybody, and which would slowly obscure my private idea of you. All of which proves, my darling, that love should be a very private business. In communicating any of it to society, one literally gives something away, and one does not get it back.'

We made and drank the tea and then I asked Ian whether I might wash my face.

'The water will be cold. Shall I boil some more?'

'No. I want cold water.'

He took me up the stairs to another landing where there was a large bathroom, and I bathed my aching eyes in icy water, resolving, as I did so, that when the moment arrived for him to go, I would employ self-control.

The moment seemed to creep towards us in a measured remorseless manner, more calculated to destroy our sensibility than any sudden unmeditated parting. We were reduced to sitting silently by one another, he holding my hand, exchanging little shadowy words of comfort, the ghosts of our grief.

'You will write to me?'

'If you will write to me.'

'Yes, I promise.'

'You know where to write?'

'Yes.'

'Shall I come to the station with you?'

'No. I have to collect some luggage on my way.'

Eventually he rose, and went out for his cab. I heard his steps go down the stairs and the door shut, as I sat holding the sides of my forehead in my hands. He had said that he would be five minutes, perhaps longer. I remembered that my hair was undressed, and, glad of employment, put it up. Almost as soon as I finished doing this, I heard the cab. It was ten minutes to seven. He did not immediately come into the room; I imagined him putting luggage into the vehicle. Then I heard him, and turned to face the door. He came quickly into the room shutting the door, and walked over to where I stood.

'Do you mind very much if I leave you here? I should prefer it to anything else.'

I shook my head.

'You need only walk out of the house. Leave everything. I should have asked you before. You don't mind?' He was gripping my hands.

'No, I don't mind.'

He took my head in his hands, bent a little to kiss me, stared at me for a moment and went. He shut the door; again I heard him descend the stairs; the front door slam; the cab door slam more faintly. I heard the cab drive away. Then there was complete silence. I was alone. For some seconds I stood, frozen and trembling, where he had left me; my throat aching intolerably. I imagined him leaning back in the cab, watching more and more streets separate us. Then the little clock struck seven and I turned blindly to the fire with some idea of extinguishing it.

I did put out the fire, and covered the white sofa and the piano; but the sight of the table with two cups still faintly warm from their tea was almost too much for me so that I decided not to touch them. All the time I had been doing these things, I had thought that my one desire was to leave the house as quickly as possible. Now, however, when everything was done, going out of the house seemed infinitely worse than staying within it. Here, no one could see me: I was afforded some kind of protection. I moved to the covered sofa and sat on it, still shivering, and quite unable to do anything which required more initiative. Now, I thought, he will have collected his luggage and be driving to the station. I would sit there until I felt better; until the ache in my throat subsided and my legs did not tremble so much; and then I would go. It seemed to have come so suddenly in the end: he had held my hands and kissed me – and gone in a moment without saying a word. I had never asked him when I should see him again; there was an utterly unknown stretch of time between his kissing me and the next time we should meet. Why had I not asked him that simple question? But perhaps he would not have known. At any rate he would have been able to tell me the longest time that he would be likely to be away. Perhaps when he wrote – *if* he wrote. I began to be uncertain even of his writing, and felt much worse. Then I suddenly remembered that a caretaker came to the house, and began to worry that she would arrive and discover me. I must go. I looked carefully round the room in order to remember it – and then my eye lighted on the clock.

It was six minutes past seven. He had only been gone six minutes. He would not even have picked up his luggage in all this time, which was only six minutes.

CHAPTER TWENTY-FIVE

I went home and remained in my room most of the day. Being very tired, I did not want to speak to my family. When they tried to make me come down for lunch, I said that I had been dancing all night and only wanted to sleep. I do not know what they made of this tale, but they left me alone. I lay on my bed and imagined the other room – wondered whether the caretaker had been to it; had taken away the cups, and cleared the fire: wept a few unrelieving tears, and slept, imagining his arms round me.

For fifteen days I existed in a kind of double life, half of which consisted in my job of packing parcels, cutting sandwiches at the canteen, and living with my family: and half of which was centred round Ian's absence; his absence and his silence. Whenever I was alone, and sometimes when I was not, my mind revolved round the three days I had spent with him. I remembered and then elaborated and invented conversations I had had with him or might have had. I thought of everything there was to remember about him, stretching and spreading it thinly over my entire mind. I tried to imagine what he was doing; and took to reading newspapers in the vain hope of discovering. I longed for him to write to me, and speculated endlessly on the reasons for his silence. On at least two occasions I began writing to him, but found this so difficult (I was afraid to express my feelings, and nothing else seemed worth expressing) that I tore up the paper before I had covered it. Sometimes I almost hated him for not writing, or I would imagine that he had done so and sent the letter to the wrong address, or that the letter had strayed, or that he had simply forgotten my address. Sometimes I would reason with myself that it was absurd to expect a letter so soon; that for all I knew, he might be so placed that he was unable to write to anyone;

and that it was mad to mind so much about so small a thing. And sometimes I would simply weep and comfort myself with the hope that he would write the next day. All the fifteen days I fell more in love with him, and each day I grew more afraid that perhaps, after all, he did not love me. Then on the evening of the sixteenth day a letter arrived.

There is, for the first time since I last saw you, the promise of an uninterrupted hour, when I can write to you and think of you continuously, instead of having you swept from my mind by the interminable demands made on one by this life.

I should really like, my darling, to carry you off to some island on the west coast of Scotland, to begin even a small new world with you, as I do not feel that we shall either of us much like the remains of the old one. But perhaps you would not like that? Will you write to me and tell me what you would like? At least write to me. Do you realize that I have not a piece of paper with your writing on it?

I continue to imagine more about you than I knew after three days of you; until now, after twelve days without you, you are probably quite different – excepting your beauty. That is indelibly fixed in my mind.

I admire and love you for spending the end of my time with me. I do believe that I might make you happy, and sometimes I almost believe that you will allow me to try.

This letter is, after all, constantly interrupted, and none the better for it.

I want to hear about your life, but I do not want to write about mine ... and I think I am afraid, my darling, that I have rushed you, with your kindness and sensibility, very much more than I had any business to rush you. I am very much content if I may love you, and you will be my friend. A letter here would be like a little water in a desert.

You see, I began this in the most feverish confidence, and line by line I have become more apprehensive about you, until an island seems a presumptuous mirage: and a letter more than I deserve. Many people are happier if they get less than they deserve, but I am not one of them. I shall be happier when you have written to me.

I am totally unsuited to what I am doing, but so is almost everyone else. I find this has a generally paralysing effect; so that one expects not to do anything well, nor to like doing it, but to have to do it again. Any qualities I possess are drawbacks, and the qualities I am considered to have are a humiliation. The effort to retain self-respect, and at the same time the respect of many more unhappy people who are forced to believe in me and God at the same time, is a severe strain. I have not an illusion about this business, not one. I have only your beauty to sustain me, and that is not an illusion, but an unhappily distant reality. I love you and am entirely yours.

IAN

P.S. Write to me, I beg you.

He did love me. I read the letter three times to be sure of this, and then, a little ashamed of myself, read it again, in an attempt to discover anything else he felt. But except that he was unhappy and that the letter was constantly interrupted, there seemed to be nothing.

'He does love me,' I repeated endlessly, smoothing the thin paper with my fingers and imagining his hand moving along it as he wrote. I examined and adored his writing. I folded the paper and put it into the envelope. 'He does love me, and he did not forget my address.' I withdrew the letter again from the envelope, and tried to imagine the bare paper, before he had covered it with words and sent it to me. That he should be able, so far away, to tell me on a piece of paper that he loved me, and then send it to me, seemed miraculous; waiting fifteen days for such a joy a mere nothing. And this letter was now in my possession, so that never again should I have to wait with nothing to comfort me – I should never again be so desolate.

I collected writing materials, and, no longer afraid of expressing my feelings, started to write to him. I told him that I had received his letter, that I loved him, that I would go anywhere with him; and after that words poured out of my heart; everything that I wrote seemed to add to my love, although never exactly pronouncing it, so that in a frenzy I wrote and wrote, tearing the sheets and beginning again, until, very late in the night, I had completed my letter, addressed it carefully (he was a captain in some Scottish regiment I discovered), and sealed it. Then I read his letter again and slept. I think it was then, reading his letter in my nightdress, that I began to desire him. At least I lay down remembering his hands and aching to be touched by them.

I posted the letter in the morning, on my way to the large dreary house where the parcels were packed. All day I packed with a feverish exhilaration which provoked the official gratitude of the Organizer; a weary little man, whose private feelings appeared to be worn away by responsibility and lack of supplies (or what he called suitable matter) for parcels, and who seemed to consider himself solely as an institution. He did not remember who I was, or what precisely I had been doing; but he thanked me, employing the faded rhetoric he used on these rare occasions; this last implying that the parcels provided our boys with more than material inspiration in their task of ending all wars, but that they could not be inspired, materially or otherwise, unless a steady flow were maintained. 'A steady flow,' he repeated, glaring at me from watery eyes and backing away as he spoke, conscious of having achieved the personal touch so important in an institution.

This incident was of the kind recounted by my family at meals. I was not usually possessed of such a crumb, and I resolved as I walked home that I would make the most of it. It was the kind of thing that made my mother laugh: my sister never laughed. Afterwards I would escape to my room and read Ian's letter again, and perhaps I would write part of another letter to him. I stopped on my way to buy writing paper. If this new and tremendous private life was to be restricted to letters, they should at least be written with extravagant care; they must at least attempt perfection. I bought a quantity of pale green paper, a box of new nibs, and a roll of purple blotting paper. I almost ran home with them.

At dinner I told them about my day and the remark of the Organizer. My mother did laugh. My sister allowed us to treat the matter lightly for a moment, then remarked that he was perfectly right, and, to change the subject, began to speculate on the possibility of Hubert obtaining Christmas leave. With a rush of excitement that brought tears to my eyes, I thought of Ian coming back; but reflected that this was really too much to hope for, when he had so recently had leave. On the other hand, Hubert, my mother confirmed, would very likely be coming. Still, I had had a letter.

The conversation staggered on to the shortage of butter; my mother remarking that there was a very good letter in the paper about it. My sister agreed that the shortage was unfortunate, but pointed out that it was better we suffer than our men, adding rather unexpectedly, that we must remember what Napoleon said. My mother looked up inquiringly, went faintly pink and said of course, but surely things were rather different nowadays, with trenches and modern warfare. 'We must march to Berlin!' cried my sister inspired; and that seemed to settle the butter shortage. I asked, as was then my custom, whether I might borrow the paper. 'Of course, darling,' said my mother, 'you can read the letter yourself.'

'There is nothing *happening*,' complained my sister, collecting the table mats. 'I thought you might help me with the studio curtains.'

I promised that I would do so the following night. Thus ended the meal; like so many hundred meals I had eaten in this dreary despairing house, whose inhabitants all seemed so utterly cut off from each other and from anything that life seemed to me to offer on the few occasions when I had succeeded in escaping from it and them. Now that I was presented with a means of escape, I was filled with remorse: that I had not been kinder, or made more attempt to impart some energy and interest to the house; had not encouraged the people who came, to do so again; which would at least have given my mother pleasure, if no one else. I resolved to do all these things, as I shut my bedroom door and my secret life with Ian consumed me.

My room possessed a small table, on which I had hitherto kept a pile of books, a framed photograph of my father, and, while they had lasted, Ian's roses. I decided that I would write my letters on it in future, and rearranged it accordingly. I then settled down to the long delicious evening of reading and writing. I began by reading his letter again, but now that I almost knew it by heart I found myself lamenting its brevity and thirsting for more of his handwriting. Perhaps he would reply to my letter. Whether he replied or no, the desire to write to him again was overwhelming; even if I refrained from sending the letter immediately, I must write. So I wrote four pages on my beautiful green paper, addressing the envelope with joy at writing his name. Afterwards, disinclined either to sleep or to read anything which absorbed my attention to the exclusion of my love, I began casually to search in the paper for the letter my mother had enjoined me to read. It was then that my eyes fell upon the list of fallen officers, and I as casually discovered that Ian had been killed three days before.

CHAPTER TWENTY-SIX

At least I was spared any uncertainty about Ian's death.
There was enough in the paper to leave me in no doubt. He
must have died even before I received his letter. I supposed
he must always have thought that he would be killed, and
that was what he had meant when he had said that he was
in no position to love anybody and did not want to cause me
suffering. He had never mentioned the possibility, however,
and oddly enough, it had never been in the forefront of my
mind. I had lived so much cut off from the war as to be
almost unaware of its perils and tragedies. I simply picked
up the paper, and that is what I read. I think it was the
unobtrusive and incidental manner of his death which most
horrified me. He had gone out there, loving me, hating the
life he felt bound to live; and then, quite suddenly, he was
dead; wiped out; all his heart and life were stopped, and of
no account to anyone. A little notice in the paper finished
him off and the war turned to the next man.

After that, I suffered agonies from those long, tightly
packed lists of unknown names. I came to imagine that no
one of the people who went returned. The tragedy of somebody dying is that they only die for themselves; never for
the people who love them. To those who love them they
remain, poised on the last moments before the last farewell.
They leave a room or a house, shut a door or a gate, and
disappear; but they do not die.

That was the end of it. I never told anyone about him. The
last remaining comfort was that no one should know. He
had said that communicating love to anyone but the beloved
diminished the feeling. I clung to this; enduring the weeks
that followed, until the gradual paralysis of my sensibility
(which was only sharpened by an unreasoning fear that I
should forget something about him), slowly crept round my

aching heart; and I was left in the nerveless insensible state which is called normal.

I worked very much harder during the next months. I worked blindly through Christmas, and the dreadful spring when our armies retreated, a time when the gallantry of our soldiers was insisted on in a way which meant, I knew by now, that thousands more of them were being killed. I threw myself into the dull and probably useless work upon which I was engaged, because I had nothing else. Sometimes when I was very tired (the food available to people like my family was patently insufficient), I would read the letter from Ian, and for a short while abandon myself to the rush of feeling it invariably induced. Once, I remember weeping helplessly because I had torn the letter a little. It seemed the last unbearable bitterness that even the paper should perish.

My family went away in the summer to stay with relatives of my mother, who, since my father's death, had relented towards her for what they considered her initial folly. I refused to go with them, and remained during the hot dusty months alone in the house, except for the servant who consented to 'live in' while the family were away. I worked all day, slept heavily at night; and weeks passed when I spoke to no one outside the house where I worked and the house where I slept.

Then the tide turned, and the almost forgotten end was in sight.

On the evening after the Armistice, my sister distinguished herself by making an unprecedented scene. I never knew the real reason for her behaviour, but remember that it started quite quietly over some minor disagreement with my mother, when I took the latter's side. She was in the habit of treating our mother as a tiresome child, and on this occasion, not her remark, but her implication, was more than I could bear. It ended, however, by her declaring passionately that no one understood her, no one; that she should like anyone to tell her what on earth she was supposed to do now; and that she wished she had never been born. She then left the room, slamming the door, and in tears; leaving my mother and me alone, staring disconsolately at one another across the dining-room table.

'Oh dear,' said my mother at last. 'I wonder if I should go after her.'

'I should leave her alone.'

'If only your father were alive.' She always said this when she meant 'if only that hadn't happened'.

'I wonder what is the matter with her?'

'Of course, her work will come to an end. I think she is rather upset about that,' my mother said. 'I suppose you will have to stop too.'

'I suppose so.' I had not considered this aspect of the Armistice.

'Anyway when your brothers return, I expect they will take you both out a bit,' she continued, as though reassuring herself.

'I shall get some other job.'

'Yes, but you never have any fun, darling. I often feel that is my fault. You ought to be out enjoying yourself tonight, like everyone else.'

'And what about you?'

'I should enjoy you enjoying yourself. I used to have awfully jolly times before I met your father.' Then, a little defensively, she added: 'And afterwards, of course. But we see so few people now that I often feel you don't have a chance.'

'A chance?'

'To be light-hearted,' she said quietly, 'and perhaps to love someone.'

'Oh . . .' I began to be afraid of being hurt. 'I suppose you mean marriage,' I said aggressively.

'I suppose I do. After all, it does give one someone to live for – I mean, it does fill one's life.'

'Do you think women need someone to live for?'

She looked up, a little startled. 'Of course. They cannot *really live* by themselves.'

'Well wouldn't anyone do? Or anything, for that matter.'

'I should not like you to live for me, and a pile of parcels.'

She said this so bitterly that I was astonished. It had never entered my mind that she could regard my wartime occupation so objectively; and I asked immediately: 'You think my packing parcels for soldiers was foolish?'

'Not exactly foolish. But often when I see people, many people that I do not even know, doing things, I find myself thinking "surely they were not born and reared merely to do that". I think one cannot help expecting the people one knows and loves to do something much more significant.'

I could not help interrupting. 'Most people seem to have been born and brought up merely to get killed.'

She eyed me thoughtfully and then said: 'Yes. And one person is usually the death of another. But when they are dead one cannot go on expecting them to do anything significant. One has to put them back where they belong, with all the other people.'

With a great effort because I was terribly afraid that she knew something about Ian, I said, 'I am not dead.'

But she answered: 'Oh no. I was thinking of your father.'

I stared at the broad expanse of table between us, and realized how very little we knew about one another. She was still speaking.

'Your father believed in music, and I believed in your father. By the time he died, I don't think he believed in anything, and now I find it very difficult to believe in him.' She screwed up her eyes as though she were trying very hard to imagine something. 'What I really mean to say is, that if something should happen, and you are presented with any kind of opportunity – I cannot think at the moment what it might be – you should take it. You should not worry about me. I do not know really what makes me think of such a thing,' she continued hurriedly, 'except that, soon after your father's death, your sister told me that she would never leave me, even to marry: and although I should feel grateful I know, and she meant nothing but good, it made me feel more useless and bereaved than anything else. Sometimes things do happen by the merest chance.'

'Bad things happen too.'

'Oh yes. But you know, I have come to feel that they do

not happen by chance.' She looked at me almost timidly. 'Do you know, since your father died I have come to feel increasingly that they are organized.' She gave a little laugh. 'That is almost like your sister, isn't it? Only she would say that I pretended to understand the things, and presumed to call them bad. I cannot believe in something I do not understand. And now, I am sometimes afraid that I never understood your father.'

'I suppose, however, that my sister would say she understood God.'

She rose to her feet. A rare smile flitted across her worn face. She looked suddenly endearing and rather wicked as she said: 'Oh undoubtedly. It is very clear that they have mutual interests.'

She had walked round the table, and now she laid her hand lightly on my head.

'Good night, darling,' she said. 'I do hope that you will soon be happier.'

She left the room, and it was almost as though she were saying good-bye to me, as she never again talked to me in this manner, although on several later occasions I tried to induce her to do so.

CHAPTER TWENTY-SEVEN

A month later I let myself into the hall, having returned from an unsatisfactory interview with a Society to whom I had applied for work of some kind, to hear the steady rise and fall of a man's voice in the studio. I immediately assumed that one of my brothers had returned without warning, and slipped upstairs to my room, resolving at least to wash my hands before encountering him. I had almost nothing in common with either of my brothers and had been dreading their return for weeks, as I knew it distressed my mother if she thought that we were not perfectly in sympathy; and with Hubert, at least, once he had settled in the house, it seemed utterly impossible to conceal from her that we were not. I had barely, however, taken off my coat, and was fetching a jug of tepid water from the bathroom geyser, when my sister sped along the passage, looking flushed and important.

'When did you return?' she cried on seeing me.

'A moment ago. Is Hubert back?'

'Gracious no. I should hope he would give us some warning.'

'Thank God for that,' I thought. 'Anyone is better than Hubert.'

Then she said: 'A man called Mr Laing has called to see you. He says he knows you. He says he met you at the Lancings' before the war. He's been wounded,' she added in tones of rapturous solicitude.

'Why on earth has he come here?' I found myself repeating as I went down to the studio. 'Why on earth come *here*? He could have written,' I thought with a sudden rush of anxiety and irritation.

I opened the studio door, and found him sitting in the leather arm-chair, drinking tea with my mother. He made some attempt to rise when I entered the room, but my mother motioned him back: I saw that one of his legs was in plaster, and that a crutch lay on the floor by the tea table.

'I told Mr Laing that you wouldn't be long,' said my mother.

'My sister told me you were here. How are you, Rupert?'

'As you see, a little the worse for war,' he replied.

'I'll fetch you some tea, darling,' said my mother and before I could stop her she had flown tactfully out of the room.

'I really think,' observed Rupert, 'that your family expect me to propose to you on the spot.'

'You'd better propose to me then. Having exposed yourself to my family, you must not disappoint them,' I said crossly. I was still annoyed at the manner of his arrival.

'All in good time,' he said, staring at me. 'You have grown up. I should hardly have known you.'

'You haven't changed at all.'

'Are you not in the least glad to see me?'

'I really don't know. Yes, I suppose I am.'

'You should be, you know. You should always be glad to see a soldier back from the wars. As I did not, so to speak, invoke the King's sympathy for my leg in the shape of a medal, I do feel entitled to a little feminine consideration.'

'I am sure my sister provided you with all you were entitled to.'

'Your mother likes me. I do think you should try and be polite to your mother's friends.'

'I did not think you were principally one of my mother's friends.'

He replied in an utterly different voice: 'I had forgotten about that. I'm sorry. I have been away so long that I had forgotten the details. I have reached the stage where I really only notice whether someone is alive or dead. Anyway I like your mother.'

'I like her. But that isn't the point.'

'No. I am sorry,' he said again. 'Will you have dinner with me tonight?'

I considered this for a moment. 'If you like.'

'I don't like your sister,' he said. 'She gave me *exactly* what I deserved about my leg. Is this where your father worked?'

'Yes.'

'Will you play the piano to me?'

'No. I cannot play the piano to people.'

'I am not people, and it is such a long time since I heard a piano.'

'*No!* I said no.'

'I wondered where your sensibility had got to,' he observed. 'I've lost mine. That is one reason why I *should* like to dine with you. Do you think your mother is going to bring you tea?'

'I don't know. I'll go and stop her. Do you want me to change?' I was glad of a chance to escape.

'Well, I cannot *honestly* say you look very nice as you are, but I doubt my being worth any very radical alteration. I seem to remember you in a pink dress.'

'That was for dancing when I was sixteen.'

'Ah yes. And now you are not sixteen, and you don't dance.'

'No,' I said patiently. 'Do you want something to read while I am away?'

'I'll find something. I am perfectly capable of rising to my feet if no one is watching and trying to help.'

I rose to go, and he said: 'I am not really so tiresome as this. At least, I do not mean to be, and do not enjoy it when I am. I shall desist with the undergraduate backchat, when I have spent a few hours alone with you. Please have dinner with me. I am sorry about appearing in the bosom of your family.'

So I had dinner with him; without any strong feeling one way or the other. He seemed to have disintegrated in the most alarming manner, and was quite incapable of concentrating on anything, even to the end of a sentence. He asked me about myself but did not listen to the end of my replies; and he talked a great deal, without hearing, or, it seemed to me, caring, what he said. He was irritable and self-conscious about his leg; and alternately boastful and depressed about his future. He continually reminded me of things we had said or done together, but he never remembered them accurately, and lost interest when, at the beginning of the evening, I tried to correct him. 'Did we?' he would say.

Drumming his finger on the table he remarked, 'My father has offered me the management of his estate, just like that. But of course, it doesn't really offer much scope. I could do it with one hand tied behind my back, and still have time to think. What's your opinion?' Without waiting for a reply he continued, 'I'm no good at painting really, and even if I were it will be impossible to make a living out of it. I should end up by drawing on pavements, though you know, I was never any good with chalk. I'm no good with anything. I've spent so many years trying to make the best of a bad job. That is enough to finish anyone. Do you remember that walk we went with Deb? I wonder how she is getting on.' We had never walked anywhere with Deb, but I did not interrupt him to say so, as he continued, 'She's married, you know. They've asked me down there for Christmas. I know, *you* come too.'

'I have not been asked.'

'That doesn't matter. I'll ask them. They always make a good thing out of Christmas. No tinned puddings for them. Please come. My first Christmas home. You remember what fun we had?'

Suddenly I became infected with the desire to go. My beautiful visit. I wanted badly to get away.

'Will you ask Mrs Lancing whether she'll have me?'

'I'll ask her now. Waiter! I want to send a telegram. Could you manage that for me do you think?'

The waiter hesitated, and then, looking at Rupert's stiff white leg, said that he would do his best. Rupert wrote out a message on the back of an envelope, and gave him money. And that is how I came to spend a second Christmas with the Lancings.

CHAPTER TWENTY-EIGHT

The day before my departure, my mother insisted that I buy at least one new garment. When I protested, she pressed on me the considerable sum of ten pounds, imploring me to spend it. My sister offered to accompany me, in order to help me choose something sensible; but this I hastily declined. I took my mother, and we purchased a new black skirt, a coffee-coloured shirt and a very superior mackintosh cape, the outside of which was dark green velveteen. We ended the afternoon with tea out; my mother seeming to enjoy the whole excursion hugely. Even I began to view the prospect of Christmas in the country with pleasure. 'You've looked so *pale*, darling,' my mother kept saying, implying, rather optimistically I thought, that never again should I look pale.

Rupert was to fetch me in a cab at eleven o'clock the following day. I packed my clothes, and began to wonder about the Lancings. My mother and sister wondered (aloud as much as they dared) about Rupert. 'Such a pity he has been wounded,' said my mother, and mechanically I agreed; wondering what else was the matter with him.

My sister implied on the eve of my departure, that I was behaving in the most dissipated and selfish manner imaginable. Either I was missing my brothers' return; or, in the event of their not returning before Christmas, I was leaving her and my mother utterly alone, as she put it. She seemed unable to decide which was worse. She did not succeed in shaking me from my purpose, but she managed to make me feel exceedingly sorry for my mother, who continued, however, pathetically anxious that I should go.

We left London shrouded in fog, which resolved to a white mist in the country. Rupert had brought innumerable papers which he strewed, half read, all over the compartment, while I stared out of the window, unable to forget the last occasion on which I had been in the train.

'I ought to be spending Christmas at home,' Rupert suddenly remarked, some half an hour after the train had started.

'Why?'

'Oh, because it is expected of me. But having done what is expected of me for more than four years, I feel entitled to a little personal choice. They talk about nothing but the war. You would think they had been through it. I can't stand it. Give me the Lancings any day. Life will be just the same there as it used to be – you'll see. Gerald was killed though,' he added. 'You remember Gerald,' he said when I remained silent.

'Yes, very well.'

'Although really they've come off better than most families. All those girls. Better to have girls.'

'Who has Deb married?' I asked, to change the subject.

'I really don't know. Some chap who lives quite near them. He has a job in some Ministry or other. Nice for Deb. She's got two children, but that won't have changed her. How I hate journeys!' he exclaimed. 'I never want to go anywhere again. Just shut myself up in a little box, and have the box moved from time to time without my being aware of it. It's all the machinery of movement that bores me.' We hardly spoke again until our arrival.

We were not met, so we took the station fly.

'She's certain to have muddled the trains, bless her,' observed Rupert; and then, stretching out his leg, he exclaimed, 'By Jove, it's good to be back. Something to come back to which won't change.'

We both leaned forward as the fly rounded the drive and revealed the house. It was very quiet, and smaller than I remembered. The shutters (still crooked) had been repainted, but not the fading stucco of the house. When we stopped, I heard the peevish rhythmic wail of a baby crying. Our driver, after glancing back at Rupert's leg, jumped down and rang the bell. 'How he must hate these glances,' I thought, 'or perhaps he does not notice them'; but he said irritably, 'Go on, out with you. Don't wait patiently for me.'

We were met in the hall by Mrs Lancing herself, armed most incongruously with a hammer.

'My dears,' she said, looked at Rupert's leg, and kissed us both.

'My dears – Come along – I knew I was right about your train.' We followed her, past the bowl of lavender, to the drawing-room.

'Wretched fire – Parker will not dry out the logs,' she exclaimed; looked doubtfully at the hammer; and laid it down on a small table covered with chestnuts.

'Where is everybody?' inquired Rupert when we had seated ourselves.

'Some people are collecting holly for the church. Richard has been crying all the morning. That is darling Deb's youngest child. Alfred is writing a letter to *The Times*, but he meant to write it last week. Now I'm going to give you some sherry and hear all your news.'

Rupert proceeded to furnish her with his news, interpolating some general remarks about the war; upon which she interrupted him, saying, 'That is exactly what Gerald always said. You know, of course, that we lost him.'

Rupert began to murmur something, but she continued as though he had not spoken. 'March 1917. He was hit by a bullet, and died at once. His Commanding Officer wrote me a very nice letter. He said Gerald was killed instantaneously while attempting most gallantly to hold a position. He was killed instantaneously; no pain.' She accompanied this last statement with a little social smile of reassurance; her face contracted again, and I realized how very much older she seemed. She raised one of her hands to touch her hair: I noticed that the hand was trembling, and that her hair was grey and lifeless.

'Tell me about the others,' said Rupert cheerfully. I looked at him in some surprise; to see that he was leaning forward smiling at her, almost loving her.

She pulled herself together. 'The others. Well, darling Deb

is married – Aubrey Hurst – such a nice man, who has been doing something very clever at the Foreign Office. She has two babies. Charles, who is a lamb, and no trouble at all, and Richard, who has a very strong character. Alfred adores them. They have made all the difference to him. Of course Nanny is here with them . . .'

'How's Toby?'

'Dear Toby. He's had a horrid attack of bronchitis this term and he's growing so fast. I'm afraid he isn't too dreadfully strong, but Alfred says I worry too much.'

The door opened and a tall rather colourless girl came in.

'They've arrived,' cried Mrs Lancing triumphantly. 'You remember Elinor.'

'But I've just sent Parker to the station. You said twelve forty-five, Mother.'

'I know I did, and here they are. Even earlier!'

'Shall we try and stop Parker?' said Rupert.

'It's too late, I saw him leave.' Elinor smiled at me. 'Has Mother shown you your rooms?'

'No dear. We were drinking sherry and I was telling them about – everybody. And Gerald. They wanted to know about Gerald. But you show them their rooms. Lunch is at a quarter to one because of Toby.'

'I don't want to see my room,' said Rupert. 'I want to hear the letter to *The Times*. And more sherry.'

'You need the bandage on your leg re-doing,' observed Elinor, with more animation than she had previously shown.

'Oh no I don't. You leave my leg alone.'

'Dear Elinor can do anything!' exclaimed Mrs Lancing, rather as though she wished dear Elinor couldn't.

I had the same bedroom as before. When Elinor left me, I laid my jacket on the bed, and stared out of the window at the lawn, the river, the park and the copse. It seemed unchanged; even the rooks and moorhens jostled and slid across my view as they had done before. 'I suppose they *are* different rooks and moorhens,' I heard myself say aloud; but it was hard to believe that they were. I wondered what Deb would be like; and whether Lucy and Elspeth were in the house, but I was in no great hurry to satisfy these curiosities. I unpacked my clothes, without any anxious speculation as to their quality and quantity when compared with those of the others, and was combing my hair when there was a knock on the door, and Lucy entered. Except that she was taller, and that her hair was knotted in a tight sleek bun, she had not changed at all.

'Hullo,' she said. We stood observing one another. Then she said, 'I'm so glad you've come. It will be just like it used to be at Christmas. It was awful all through the war and one couldn't even *pretend* it was the same. The hunting's wonderful, and we're going to have a dance. Elspeth's coming, and she's bringing two strange *new* men with her. We don't know them at all. Have you got everything you want?'

While I answered her, she stood regarding me with her kind eyes and eager smile; the tip of her nose a delicate pink, as though she had been out.

'I've been exercising. Deb won't do it. Would you like to see her babies? Deb hasn't been out all the morning. Some mornings she lies in bed till the lunch bell rings, and father gets furious. He likes everyone to *scald* themselves with soup. And some mornings she is up before any of us and gets through two horses by twelve o'clock. Simply wears them out, and doesn't cool them off or anything. They come back covered with sweat. She won't say where she has been.'

'Is she as beautiful as ever?'

'*More* beautiful,' said Lucy, with a kind of triumphant despair.

She led me down the passage, stopped at a white door, and opened it. I had thought it was going to be the nursery, but it was simply a rather empty little white room.

'Gerald's room. You know he was killed – Father can't bear talking about it. It's just the same as when he had it. I wanted it for my room, but they wouldn't let me. Even his brushes.' The windows were open, and the curtains floated over the silver-topped brushes on the dressing-table. An old tweed jacket hung on the back of the door. It was very cold.

'I put flowers in here,' said Lucy. She had become very white and a tear rolled down her face.

'I thought you would like to see his room,' she said, watching me anxiously, lest I feel as unhappy as she.

I nodded. She was still the kind transparent creature who judged everyone more exactly and honestly to be like herself than anybody I had known.

In the nursery, Nanny was seated in a basket chair feeding one infant on her lap while an older and more responsible baby sat strapped in a high chair beside her, eating something brown and sloppy with a short-handled spoon.

Nanny greeted me in a courteous, but abstracted manner. It was plain that she was engrossed in her charges.

'He hasn't stopped since a quarter past eleven. I don't know what it is, I'm sure. Not a tooth in sight . . .' Then to the baby in the chair, 'Put it in your mouth, Charles.'

'Can I feed him?' said Lucy.

'Give the young lady a chair and you can finish him off. Give her the spoon, Charles, there's a good boy.'

Charles watched me to my chair; but when Lucy approached him he dropped the spoon, and seizing the bowl before him turned it carefully upside down over his head. In the commotion which followed, he remained impassive, staring at me in a gentle, reproachful manner, with broth streaming down his face.

'Showing off at meal times,' muttered Nanny, as she carried him, stern and indifferent, into the night nursery.

Richard, cheated of his bottle, began to cry. He began quietly, in the manner of the real expert, and worked himself slowly up to a shattering volume, arching his back and screwing up his toes, in spite of Lucy's frantic efforts to appease him.

Then the door opened, and Deb appeared. Her hair was elaborately dressed; she wore the most ravishing and ethereal negligée, edged with swansdown. When she saw me, she smiled, walked over to the fender, and began talking to me as though nothing was happening. She was incredibly beautiful.

'Oh, Deb – I can't stop him,' cried Lucy almost beside herself.

Deb looked at Richard.

'He's a bore,' she remarked, picked him up, and threw him over her shoulder. Instantly he stopped, and began picking at the swansdown round her neck, cramming it into his mouth, choking with laughter.

'You can always stop him. I don't know how you do it,' said Lucy, half resentful, half relieved at the peace.

Deb with her back to Lucy, met my eye for an instant. She was smiling, but there was a faintly ironical, almost bitter expression in her smile. She did not reply.

A gong boomed for lunch.

'I'll take him,' said Lucy. 'Father will be so furious.'

'Why we should have the entire household upset for a little boy I fail to see,' observed Deb.

'It is only a quarter of an hour early. He has to rest afterwards. If we have lunch later there isn't time for him to get to the Westons',' pleaded Lucy holding out her arms for Richard.

'All this resting is absolute nonsense, anyway,' said Deb, and, ignoring Lucy, dropped Richard on his back in a blue cot, where after a shocked silence, he instantly began yelling again. 'I shall now get dressed,' Deb said calmly, and left the room.

Lucy cast agonized glances at Richard, the open night-nursery door and at me. Finally she gasped: 'We'll *have* to go. Can't all be late. Father has got much *fiercer* since the end of the war,' she explained, as we sped down the broad shallow staircase, almost colliding with Rupert at the foot.

'Hullo, Rupert. Frightfully sorry.' Then seeing his leg, '*Frightfully* sorry,' she repeated.

Toby was already sitting at the table. 'I had my place laid round me,' he said, 'I've been waiting ages.' He was not fat at all now; he seemed to be about twice as tall, and his face was finely powdered with freckles. 'I say, did you fly an aeroplane?' he almost shouted at Rupert.

'I did not.'

Mrs Lancing arrived, to settle Rupert and me next to each other and near her. Gradually the remaining members of the family appeared. Aunt Edith supported by Elinor; Mr Lancing with a sheaf of papers in his hand – all of them except Deb. When we had been greeted and everyone was settling to the very good hare soup, Mr Lancing inquired: 'Has anyone informed Deborah that we are lunching?'

'She was kept by the babies, Papa,' Lucy said. 'Richard has been crying,' she added.

'Ah.' Mr Lancing's expression softened to one of almost professional concern. 'It is my considered opinion that the child should be fed earlier.'

'Dear, we've tried that, and it throws the whole routine out, and poor Nanny doesn't get a wink of sleep.'

'Feed him when he's hungry. He knows when he is hungry.'

'But dear Alfred, one must consider his digestion.'

'Nonsense. When I was a child I was fed when I howled. I howled when I was hungry. Nothing wrong with my digestion.' He launched forth on a long and complicated story, the gist of which was that he had even eaten Stilton cheese and herrings at the age of eleven months and thrived on them.

'Have you *ever* flown an aeroplane?' persisted Toby.

'Never once been in one.' Toby fell back.

Half-way through the second course, Deb appeared, entirely and charmingly dressed in brown.

'Hullo Rupert. 'Fraid I'm rather late.'

'You are very late, Deborah.'

'Is Richard all right now?' asked the loyal Lucy.

But Deb answered, sweetly perverse, 'I don't know. I left him when you did. I expect so.' She yawned elaborately, and began on her soup.

Rupert had sat very silent, but now he began to talk to Deb, admiring her, as he had done before, in tones of mock despair. '*Why* didn't you wait for me?' he finished.

Deb lifted her head. I noticed the faintest blush, but she replied evenly, 'You never asked me.'

'What does this dreadful Aubrey *do*?'

'Something deadly dull in an office.'

There was a chorus from the others of 'Oh, *Deb*. Poor Aubrey – Really, Rupert.'

'It *is* deadly dull,' persisted Deb. 'So, poor Aubrey, I suppose.' She seized a piece of brittle toast, and began crushing it between her fingers.

'Have you ever been in a submarine then?' asked Toby. Rupert spread out his hands and shook his head. 'What a waste.' Toby was thoroughly disappointed. 'I'm going to fly an aeroplane in the next war.'

Everyone, in the brief pause which followed, instinctively looked at Mrs Lancing, and then, baffled by her immobility, and perhaps a little embarrassed by the discovery that they were not alone in their glance, looked away.

'There isn't going to *be* another war, anyway,' Lucy explained to Toby. Mrs Lancing drank a little water. The tension snapped.

After lunch, there was the usual discussion round the table of what everyone was going to do until they met for the next meal. Toby must rest for an hour and a half before he repaired to the Westons', who, I gathered, were possessed of a fives court, in which he and the younger Westons were to roller skate. Mrs Lancing was going to finish off invitations for the dance. Elinor offered to help her.

'What about a walk?' suggested Lucy.

'Where to?' said Deb; and Lucy, taking her literally, proceeded to outline a walk. Deb yawned again, stretching her hands over her head. 'There's no point in going out.'

'I think,' exclaimed Mr Lancing looking firmly at Rupert, 'that you would be interested in my collection of letters to various newspapers. If you have nothing better to do, I propose to show them to you now ...'

This left Lucy and me for the walk.

'Would you like that?'

I said I should like it. During lunch I had hardly spoken at all, not because I had been frightened, but because I could think of nothing to say. When I had stayed with them before, I had been nervous lest I prove unable to fit in with their very different and to me extremely hectic and glamorous existence; but after this fear had shown itself to be unnecessary, I had been able to throw myself into this Lancing life-in-the-country-house-at-Christmas and I had been very happy. I had, so to speak, poured myself eagerly into their large and decorative mould. Now, I was stiffened with experience, no longer nervous, but isolated in some curious manner by the reality of my own struggles from the reality of theirs. They were not to me any longer the easy happy collection of a family I had known; but they were not, so far as I could see, aware that they had changed. Gerald's death was the only change they were aware of that I could understand, and in some inexplicable manner this merely accentuated their apparent notion of the sameness of everything else.

During our walk I asked Lucy more about her family, and she, without any hesitation, told me all she knew. Deb had married very soon after my first visit, and everyone liked Aubrey. 'They have a house about twelve miles away, but Deb wants to live in London. Aubrey doesn't like London, he says he works there and that is quite enough, so I don't know what they will do. I think she would miss the hunting. It'll be London in the end I suppose. Aubrey's terribly kind, he does anything Deb wants. She's frightfully lucky because Aubrey didn't have to leave her at *all* in the war. Deb's rather – different these days. I think she must miss Gerald.' I had never noticed any particular feeling in Deb for Gerald, or indeed for anyone except the Roland she had not married. Perhaps he also had been killed. I did not want to ask.

We had been walking across the park, up the hill to the copse or little wood: the walk I had taken with Lucy and Elspeth on the first afternoon when we had made the house out of twigs. I wondered how many hundred times Lucy had walked this way, and whether she ever grew tired of it and wanted to walk somewhere else. I reminded her of the house; she remembered more about it than I did, and suggested making another. But I shrank from making another house.

I asked about Elspeth.

'She's an heiress,' said Lucy gravely. 'Her father died and left her all his money, *and* two houses. She lives with an uncle who lets her do anything she likes. She was supposed to have gone abroad you know, but the war stopped that.'

'Will her uncle let her go now?'

'I don't know. I believe he considers her ideas folly. But she's coming. She's bringing these men for the dance. Father says she is being spoilt,' Lucy added rather unexpectedly. 'Would you like to walk through the wood?' she continued. 'I expect you'd like to see the place where we made your little house. Do you know what Deb said when she heard you were coming?'

I did not know.

'She said, were you engaged to Rupert!'

'Oh.'

'Of course, she thinks rather a lot about that sort of thing.' Lucy seemed rather apologetic.

'Well I'm *not* engaged to Rupert,' I felt bound to add.

'Of course not. Why should you be? I'm twenty-one and *I* don't intend marrying anyone for years. Elinor does though. She is younger than you, and *she* has always wanted to marry someone. Well, since she was ten. She was awfully in love with a man she looked after in the war. She is a V.A.D. you know, but he died. He was frightfully badly wounded,' her voice trembled, 'but she doesn't mind that. She says there will be an awful shortage of people to marry and she doesn't mind looking after someone who has been wounded, so she'd better marry one of them, because someone who *doesn't* need looking after won't want to marry her. I suppose there are a lot of people like that? I mean you don't think she is very unusual, do you?'

'I don't think so,' I said doubtfully. 'I don't think many people are so honest – well, candid, about it.'

'Oh, she's frightfully honest. She was Head of her School in the end. She wanted that, too.'

'What do *you* want?'

Lucy seemed rather at a loss.

'Oh – I don't know. I should like another horse, and I wish my hair wasn't so straight. I wish Gerald was alive, most of all. I wish he was alive, and everything was exactly the same. Like it was last time you came.'

'Isn't it the same, Lucy?'

'Except for Gerald it is. But somehow, *nothing* feels right without him. Such a beastly way to die!' She suddenly burst into tears. 'I must tell you! I haven't had *anyone* to tell. He had a friend who was at school with him. Peter ...' She was crying so much now that she was unable to walk, and leaned against a tree. I made some gesture inviting her to sit, but she shook her head and struggled to speak, streaming with tears. 'It doesn't matter what his name was. I can't tell you his name. He loved Gerald; they went out together. They had an awful job to stay together. When Gerald had leave, he took me to a theatre and told me all about Peter, and asked me to write to him. He said Peter was the only person he really cared about except me. After Gerald was dead he wrote to me, Peter did I mean, and said he wanted to see me. I went to London. He was dreadfully unhappy, he *cried* about Gerald. We went for a walk; he told me about him and then cried. Then he said he had to tell me about him properly, because he couldn't bear it by himself. That letter Mummy had was all a lie. He didn't die quickly at all. He was hit by a shell in his stomach. Peter found him after the attack. He was so bad Peter couldn't move him. He tried, but Gerald just shrieked and shrieked and – there was a lot more about it. I can't tell you, it is so awful, *so awful*. Peter tried to get help, but there wasn't a stretcher. He tried to give him some water, but whatever he did he said Gerald just went on moaning, and if Peter touched him, he shrieked, and stared about, as though Peter was trying to torture him. So Peter shot him. He had to. He said if he hadn't Gerald would just have gone on in that agony until he lost consciousness, and that might have been hours later. He had to do it. He kissed him, and told him he loved him first, but he said Gerald didn't know who he was. He said when he got out his revolver, he thought Gerald understood about that, because he tried to keep still and shut his eyes – Oh, I shouldn't have told you.'

I said, 'I do not think Peter should have told you.'

'He had to,' she cried fiercely, 'it was too much for him to bear. *He's* dead now, too. So I am the only one left, and Mummy goes on and on talking about it, and Papa can't bear talking about it, and they both say I take it too much to heart. I try not to think about it, but when I'm alone I remember Peter telling me, his voice, and the exact words, and it seems as though I was there – I meant not to tell *anyone*, truly I did, but it doesn't matter with you, does it? You won't tell anyone, will you – You won't?'

I assured her that I would not. She wiped her eyes. 'Most extraordinary thing,' she said, 'when other people talk about him it feels as though my heart is trying to break out. It's like a sudden burn; that sort of pain. I don't expect you know what I mean. But I like to talk about him sometimes.'

'I do know,' I said. The contrast of her pale and tear-stained face, with the appearance she presented to her family, and indeed, until a few moments ago to me, was infinitely touching. I wanted badly to comfort her, I felt she was a creature young enough to be comforted; but the things she had told me started such horrible fears in my own mind, that I dared not say anything. I took her hand and held it in mine. I had been so stunned by the fact that Ian had been killed, that I had never until now imagined the circumstances of his death. I felt sick; my legs seemed unable to support me. I sat on the ground, pulling Lucy down with me. For one moment I considered telling her about Ian, and then I knew that it would make no difference to me to tell anyone. I looked at poor Lucy. It was she who was so unhappy with her first grief. Nothing would ever be so painful for her again; but, I reflected, I could hardly tell her that, she would not believe it. She would not even believe that she would recover at all from this. Better tell her that, though. I told her.

'I shall never forget it,' she said.

'No, but it won't hurt so much.'

She stared at me disbelievingly, and then said, 'Of course I do get better at concealing it from the others. But not to myself. Never that.'

I searched desperately about for some other consolation, eventually saying feebly, and at some length, that I was sure Gerald would hate her to continue so despairing on his account. He was so gay, I added, he would think her wrong to grieve overmuch.

Lucy said with shining eyes. 'It's perfectly true. He would hate it. I will remember that. Thank you for telling me.'

She *was* capable of being comforted. She made me renew my promise to tell no one and we continued our walk.

'I suppose,' I said casually as we walked back down the park, 'that hundreds of people died like that, or something like it?'

And Lucy answered with her eyes fixed on her home: 'Hundreds I think. Of course not everybody. I don't suppose we shall ever really know how many.' She seemed calm again, calm and almost happy. 'We're going to have tea in the nursery,' she said. 'I love that.'

It was exactly as though she had handed her grief over to me, to take care of until some little circumstance should force her again to suffer it. As we entered the house, I wondered which of the spurious and meaningless little clichés would have comforted me, and when it should have been uttered, and by whom. Comfort, of any kind, seemed the most random affair.

CHAPTER TWENTY-NINE

On reaching the house, we went straight to the library where we discovered Rupert and Deb. They were sharing a large volume of *Punch*: Deb seated in one of the leather chairs, and Rupert perched rather uncomfortably upon one of its arms. A fire burned; but there was no other light, and the room was deliciously warm and dusky.

Lucy flung herself into a chair. After a moment's hesitation, I selected another. I felt we were intruding, and Rupert, at least, made no effort to conceal it. Deb had lifted her head when we entered the room, had seen me and smiled, then continued to turn the pages of their book.

'Aubrey not back yet?' asked Lucy, breaking the silence.

'I don't know whether he is back,' answered Deb.

Rupert reached out for his crutch and rose to his feet. 'I had forgotten the mysterious Aubrey. I really think it is rather forward of you to ally yourself to a man I have not even seen.'

'None of us really saw him until after she was engaged to him,' said Lucy cheerfully. 'Good thing he's so nice. He'll probably be back for tea. He usually is.'

'He invariably is,' said Deb. I knew that she was angry with Lucy. She shut the book, let it slide to the floor, and left the room. After a moment, Lucy followed, saying she would call us when tea was ready.

Alone with Rupert, I remained very still, staring into the fire. I had a sudden desire to ask him whether he knew anything about Ian; but I could not think how to do so without arousing his suspicion, or at least his curiosity.

'You are very silent here,' he said at last. 'What do you think about all the time?'

'About them. I – I am not very used to living with a lot of people. I think it makes me dull.'

'You are not dull. Although, when one thinks about you, one cannot imagine how you escape appearing inexpressibly dull. You sit and watch everyone, and hardly say a word. You also sometimes look extremely tragic. How did you get on with Lucy?'

'Very well, I think. I like her.'

'Which is more than her sister does.'

'Has she said so?'

'Oh come, sisters don't do that. No, she has not actually said anything. She says remarkably little, don't you think?' Then, without waiting for a reply he went on, 'Are you glad you came? Are you going to like it?'

'Are you?'

'Of course. I like anything new.'

'But this isn't new. It's old,' I cried.

'Oh dear. Has the gloss worn off? Are you bored?'

'No. I wish you would not ask me these questions.'

'But seriously, do you only enjoy things or people who are entirely strange to you?'

'I don't think so. If I found the right people, or things, I don't think I should want to change them.'

'But you haven't found them? Or found them and lost them?'

I did not reply.

'Well, if you think I am the person you knew, you are wrong. I am entirely, almost entirely changed, and not even used to myself. I find the most extraordinary ideas running through my head, which have nothing to do with what I was. You know, I don't think they like each other.'

'Who?'

He said ignoring me: 'But if you want change for the sake of it, here I am.'

Before I could reply Elinor put her head round the door.

'Tea is ready. In the nursery. Who lit the fire?'

'Deb lit it.'

'Oh, Deb – she lights them all over the house and never stays in one room and it makes so much work. Servants have been very difficult,' she explained to me, as we slowly ascended the staircase behind Rupert.

The day nursery (in which I had spent very little time on my previous visit), was quite unchanged, except that it showed signs of more use. The bears and dolls, which had before sat primly in rows on the seat round the bay window, now lay on the floor in various attitudes of abject and clownish helplessness. The high brass fender was hung with innumerable white garments. The rocking horse pranced well out in the room, instead of behind the screen covered by Mrs Lancing in her youth with scraps. For the rest, it contained the same pictures: Reynolds's cherubs, Millais's Ophelia, and various Henry Ford dragons and fairies; the same cracked white paint, pink curtains, and wallpaper covered with fat blue buds and pale yellow butterflies; the same bright brown chairs and table with Nanny's sewing machine; the same yellow nursery cupboard containing everything one could possibly want for a rainy afternoon, a sickness, accidents, boredom, or yet another baby. All this had not changed: only Nanny had shrunk a little, I noticed, her hair was whiter, her face more like a walnut, and her feet, which pointed outwards when she walked, bulged more painfully in her sharp black shoes. She was folding paper napkins on to each plate laid round the table when we entered the room. Lucy lay on the floor, building a tower from some bricks which she drew from a large canvas sack. Charles sat on his heels beside her taking no notice. Nanny seemed delighted to see Rupert, whom she placed in a large wicker chair between the fire and the tower of bricks. Elinor fetched a plate of crumpets to be toasted in front of the fire. I offered to help her.

'I have to put the forks out of reach because of Master Charles,' said Nanny wrenching open one of the drawers in the yellow cupboard.

Lucy finished the tower, and called us to admire it; but immediately we turned round from the scorching fire, Charles put out his hand, and with one casual sweeping gesture reduced the tower to ruins. Lucy said he was unkind (I think she was really disappointed), but he sat quite still smiling gently at her and not uttering a sound.

'You'd better wash your hands, Miss Lucy. Take him with you. He always breaks them down, don't you, Charles?'

'I cannot think why babies are so destructive,' cried Lucy. 'Come on, Charles.'

Charles rose to his feet, and as she bent to pick him up he flung himself on her, his arms round her neck and his legs round her waist so that she was unable to stand upright.

'That's his new trick,' said Nanny, prising him off the unfortunate Lucy as though he were a limpet. He opened his mouth to howl, when Deb appeared, and he changed his mind. Brushing Nanny aside, he staggered across the room to his mother, and repeated his new trick. Deb, however, seemed perfectly equal to it, as she made no move to pick him up; and after clinging to her legs for a few moments, he gave up, wheeled round, and made for the nursery at a heavy dangerous trot. Lucy dashed after him. 'I shall never manage to wash his hands.'

We had finished toasting the crumpets and sat at the table.

'Where is your mother?' asked Nanny, the steaming kettle poised in her hands over the gigantic tea-pot.

'She has gone over to Charrington. Lady Voyle sent a message.'

'There, Miss Elinor, and you never told me. Well there is nothing to keep us is there? I am sure you won't say no to your nice hot tea,' she added kindly to me. 'To tell the truth, I'd be glad to start before Master Richard wakes up. That's right, Miss Deb, you pour out for us.'

Deb who had also seated herself at the table, made a little *moue* of horror when she discovered that she had placed herself before all the tea cups.

'The big one is for Mr Hurst. He likes a good big cup like all the gentlemen.' Nanny was clearly in her element.

'What about me?' cried Rupert. 'Aren't I a gentleman, Nanny?'

Nanny bridled and burst into a peal of dried-up laughter. 'There, Mr Rupert. So many people I was forgetting.'

'He'll have to have a mug,' said Deb.

'Anything so long as it holds a lot.'

Elinor fetched a mug from the yellow cupboard and put it in front of Rupert.

'Goosey Goosey Gander, whither shall I wander, Upstairs and downstairs and in my lady's chamber,' Rupert read out, turning the mug in his hands. 'Will you fill my mug for me?' He handed it to Deb. Their eyes met for an instant, and Deb, after a moment's hesitation, put the mug on the table.

'All in good time.' She began filling the cups.

Lucy and Charles emerged from the night nursery pink and speechless.

'He's sort of washed,' said Lucy.

Nanny stuffed him into his high chair, strapped him in, and tied a huge feeder round his neck. Then she placed a piece of bread and butter in front of him cut in fingers.

'Take no notice of him and he'll eat his nice tea,' she commanded.

We all ate our nice tea. Deb immediately asked me about London, and what I had been doing. I felt that she expected me to have led a delightful life of continuous gaiety, and was at a loss how to answer her. I explained that I had been out of London much of the time, stretching the weeks I had spent with Mrs Border into months, but that did not do.

'What were you doing in the country?' asked Lucy.

'Oh, looking after an old lady.'

'How awful! Did she die or something?'

'No, she didn't die.' For a moment my mind flashed back to the dense hot house, and my terrifying employer. I realized, with a shock, that that life was probably continuing, with my successor, whoever she might be.

'Was it fearfully dull?'

'Yes. Fearfully dull. So I left.'

'And came back to London?' persisted Deb.

'Yes, and got a very dull job.'

'Oh *work*.' She managed to convey worlds of contempt

when she said that. 'But the evenings. Did you not dance a great deal? Even Elinor had hospital dances.'

'Only for the convalescents,' Elinor put in.

'I didn't, you know. My father died, and somehow we didn't go out much after that. I used to go to the theatre sometimes.'

'Deb has a romantic view of London which she can only preserve by absolute ignorance of it,' observed Rupert. I think he thought these questions were embarrassing me, but they were not (although they would once have reduced me almost to tears).

'I do go to London. *When* I go, I have a very gay time,' Deb retorted, like a child.

'I should think it is perfectly possible to have a very gay time,' I said.

'Well! Of course I remember you were very serious about things, like music,' said Deb. 'Perhaps that makes a difference.'

'I cannot think what you *do* in London,' said Lucy, helping herself to cake.

'Hand it round, Miss Lucy,' said Nanny, who, having no interest in the conversation, was well able to preserve the proprieties of nursery tea.

'Sorry. Cake anyone?'

Charles stretched out his arms for the cake. When Lucy handed it to him, he paused, picked off a cherry, and swallowed it whole.

'Just like his mother,' said Nanny hastening to bang his back. He choked; the cherry came up intact, and bounced across the table. Lucy put it back on his plate, where he regarded it with an air of stately disapproval. Nanny chopped up a small piece of cake, whipped the cherry away, and told him to finish his tea. 'He'll get hiccups if he goes eating cherries,' she explained severely to Lucy.

Rupert suddenly began the most fantastic stories about London in war time. After a few minutes, nobody took him seriously, and there was a good deal of laughter, in the midst of which Aubrey appeared.

My first impression on seeing Aubrey, was amused admiration that Deb should have discovered, and then married, someone who seemed so exactly designed to pair with her. He was tall, dark, discreetly handsome; and, as I was very soon to discover, he invariably made the right remark at the right moment. (Afterwards, one realized that it was rather an obvious remark to make; but at the time he produced it with such a charming air of modesty and kindliness – this is only a small white rabbit, but it is all I can find in my hat, and perhaps it may please you – that one could not but be charmed.)

Now, he begged not to interrupt; managed to be introduced to Rupert and me; to salute his elder child; to inquire respectfully of Nanny after his younger; to meet Deb's eye with intimate admiration; and to seat himself at the table next to her with the kind of appetite Nanny would expect of him: he managed all this in a few moments, and then steered the conversation back to Rupert's imaginary exploits in London.

Nanny insisted on making a small special pot of tea. It was plain that she adored him, that he dazzled Elinor and pleased Lucy. It was only not plain how precisely he affected Deb.

Rupert concluded his tale by turning to Aubrey and saying, 'That was solely for the benefit of your wife, who seems to have an incomprehensible passion for London.'

'I know she has. I have quite enough of it myself, but I expect we shall all end by living there. If Nanny doesn't desert us. But she doesn't realize,' he continued, having secured Nanny's devoted denial, 'how expensive London has become for a beautiful woman, or that I am only a poor struggling minnow at the Foreign Office.' And he smiled brilliantly at Deb.

'I only want a small house.'

'Yes, darling, and a motor car, and four servants – But you shall have them all so soon as anyone will buy my very inexpensive soul.'

'You might get sent abroad somewhere,' said Deb.

'I might,' he said, anxious to agree with her.

'You easily might,' repeated Deb.

'I'm sure you would be able to go too,' said Lucy.

'The climate might be very unsuitable for the children,' said Elinor.

'Why?' Deb stared at her. 'There are surely very few places where children do not live; and Aubrey would have to be a great failure to get sent to one of them.'

'Children have to be born in places to live in them. Sometimes even that isn't enough.'

'One surely is not expected to have one's entire life arranged by children . . .'

The atmosphere suddenly became unbearable; then Aubrey cleared his throat and said: 'In any case, I think you would enjoy a year or two in London first, as you missed your season; and after that, I hope I shall be in a position to select somewhere, within reason, which would be suitable for all of us, including Nanny.'

'That's right, Mr Aubrey, we must all cross our bridges when we come to them,' said Nanny approvingly. 'Drink down your nice milk, Charles.'

After tea, we all played musical bumps, ostensibly for the benefit of Charles, who hit his head on the corner of the rocking horse, and didn't enjoy any of it. Rupert worked the gramophone, and Aubrey nearly won, being left at the end with Lucy and Deb. The latter was defeated by the gasping triumphant Lucy. It was then clear that Aubrey intended to give Lucy a good run for her money, and let her win. He did this, from his point of view, extremely well; so that Lucy was convinced that he was fairly beaten, while at the same time it was perfectly clear to at least Deb, Rupert and me, that he lost intentionally.

'I'm beaten!' he exclaimed in good-tempered distress. 'Your aunt has beaten me, Charles! Never mind, I shall win next time.' And I felt that, in the interest of family diplomacy, he probably would.

After dinner, while Rupert and Aubrey played chess, the rest of us spent the evening mending, with glue, needles, cotton and other oddments, the large and battered collection of Christmas tree ornaments. 'We *must* use the same ones,' Lucy had said at the beginning of the evening.

The whole family apparently agreed with her, for they spent, and I helped them, hours of patience and ingenuity, on a multitude of fragile tarnished objects. I remember suddenly looking up to see Lucy sticking the dry yellow hair on to the head of a fairy doll; watching her intent, and happy, and disproportionately serious, and wondering whether I had dreamed or imagined her passionate outburst in the wood. But then I felt that when I had first known her, she would not have been quite so serious about the doll, and I knew that I had not dreamed.

She had divulged her secret. I was imprisoned with mine, and the new fear which accompanied it. In the dark of my room I wept for Ian; resolving that it should be the last time I wept for him; that I would leave him dead, would not consider how he died, would not try to think of him apart from myself. For a moment I allowed myself to remember him bending his head and kissing me, then walking away; the two doors slamming; the cab, and the silence. I endured the silence until I slept.

CHAPTER THIRTY

For the week before Christmas we all ate and played and slept, and generally fulfilled our functions in the house. We saw few people outside the house, and too much of each other, since the Lancings all tended to drift together for any arrangement. We saw too much of each other because for the amount of time involved, we communicated remarkably seldom. A man will pick his friend for some common interest; the friendship will flourish largely as the interest flourishes. A woman will pick her friend for some more or less intangible sympathy, emotional or compensative; and this friendship flourishes, dependent on continuing sympathy. But a family does not pick its component parts. It is marched down the aisle, and gradually born. It becomes so used to itself, it is so dependent upon regarding itself as a whole, that its individuals must find it increasingly difficult to have any emotions unrelated to other members; because if they *do* give vent to these emotions, the family, that public private life of its own, is threatened, and re-retaliates.

The Lancings were far gone in family life. They had reached the state where the real desires and feelings of each one of them were hidden from each other one. Nevertheless I, being outside the family (in a sense, more outside it than Rupert, who wished to identify himself with it), was increasingly aware of the private underlying tensions. These were not, perhaps, very significant, the Lancings having well developed the capacity of concentrating upon the many communal diversions with which they provided themselves, but they did exist; and I, unable to throw myself into the diversions with the abandon I had previously enjoyed, had very little else to do but watch the small personal struggles of temperament against the settled environment.

It was almost immediately clear that Deb was not happy,

and that she was consequently not kind to Aubrey. Aubrey, however, seemed genuinely unaware of this. The rest of the family protected him as best they could, and pretended not to notice. Deb roved about the house, beautiful, discontented, capricious and, above all, bored. She obviously intended to appear all these things, and it was some time before I realized how unhappy she must be. Then I noticed that the more time Rupert spent with me, even if he did not spend it exclusively with me, the more distant she became; until she was so positively rude that I felt it could hardly escape notice. I think Rupert noticed it (he seemed very much attracted to her), but no one else did, or, if they did, they were relieved that she was not being rude to Aubrey. I formed the conclusion that she was in love with Rupert, or very near it, and that he was aware of this and frightened by it. It upset his notion of a jolly family pre-war Christmas. He pursued me with a kind of relentless desperation, aware that the Lancings viewed this with approval. I also began to suspect that Elinor was quietly and hopelessly in love with Aubrey. It was always she, I observed, who flew to his rescue when Deb attempted to disconcert or embarrass him, to puncture his modesty and good temper. He was more the great man with Elinor, more the possessor of brilliant inside information: he knew more than he could possibly tell her, while with Deb he knew less than he dared admit.

I reached all these conclusions amid a whirl of secrets and presents and general Christmas plans, and, much of the time, it was difficult not to think I was merely dramatizing or enlarging situations which barely existed. But then I would see Lucy breathless with tickling Toby on the sofa; or clamouring to ride Deb's devilish black mare; or pink with importance over packing her Christmas presents: I would remember her leaning against the tree, her frantic outpourings of what must have been to her the most horrible story conceivable, and the infinitely touching manner in which she had said that when other people talked about Gerald, her heart broke out. And sometimes, when Mrs Lancing mentioned Gerald (which she seemed unable to help doing at every possible opportunity), I would see Lucy flinch, and try to smile, or simply smile. Then the chasm between the family and each member of it yawned suddenly. I would watch Lucy withdraw from it, trembling over the skates that she would once have given Gerald and would now give to Toby; would watch her feverishly trying to decide whether to tie the parcel in red ribbon or green; watch the chasm close up again, as her mother approved the red ribbon and she scrambled to hide the skates because Toby had entered the room.

Toby suffered a little, perhaps, from being too much the object of Mrs Lancing's passionate anxiety and care, but for a greater part of the time he remained unaware of this, and of almost everything else. His life was rendered full and complicated by the fact that he considered roller skates superior, if not necessary, as a means of transport. He and several noisy and dangerously accomplished friends spent hours building ramps up and down steps and staircases, rolling gravel paths, and indulging in the most appalling accidents. Sometimes, however, I would see Toby submit with uncharacteristic docility to his hair being ruffled by his mother; or to a long and tiresome rest, so placed that, as he would sadly explain to anyone else present, it ruined his day.

Mr Lancing lived, so far as I could determine, an extremely exhausting life of leisure. That is to say he ostensibly did nothing, but was perpetually occupied with the most exacting and onerous self-employment. He, alone of all the family, spent much of his time without them. On fine days he would swallow his breakfast and stump into the hall, where he would collect a large and intricate tape measure designed by himself, an old tweed cap, a villainous knobbly stick, and a small nervous little henchman called Salt, who was largely composed of long drooping moustaches and frightened faithful eyes. He would disappear for the day, occasionally sending Salt back for sandwiches. What he actually did remained a mystery. I noticed that Salt carried a large notebook in which be wrote down, or attempted to write down, everything that Mr Lancing said. This, as Mr

Lancing appeared when alone with Salt to talk incessantly on an endless variety of subjects, and usually when standing or walking at great speed, was naturally a somewhat difficult task, but Salt, with a spare pencil behind one ear, stuck faithfully to the job. We would sometimes watch Mr Lancing stride off, shouting information down the drive or across the park, Salt trotting behind him, the pages of the notebook flapping. On wet days, Mr Lancing would be discovered reorganizing the gun-room or repairing inexhaustible quantities of broken wine decanters, reputed to be his own wedding presents; and Salt was nowhere to be found. Any tidying or mending Mr Lancing did involved a chaos which, temporarily, at least, almost stopped the entire household. His most peaceful days were occupied in writing immense, abusive and erudite letters to newspapers. From all these pursuits he emerged at meals, and occasionally in the evenings, calm, silent and benign. He was devoted to his grandchildren, the elder of whom he frightened horribly, largely because in its presence he insisted on impersonating a lion. Charles could hardly be expected to know this, and invariably retreated, howling, to the nearest woman. This caused Mr Lancing great disappointment. He persisted, however, certain that Charles would see the joke in the end.

CHAPTER THIRTY-ONE

Just before Christmas Elspeth arrived with the two entirely new men. The latter, called George and Nicholas, were quite unremarkable in any way; but Elspeth, with whom the two young men were evidently in love, was certainly remarkable. She was now eighteen, and where she had been precocious, was now fascinating, where she had been an oddly attractive child, was now an unusually beautiful young woman. Her once long hair was now bobbed, and lay sleek and shining on her head; her clothes were expensive, and unlike everyone else's, in their neatness and severity; and she was possessed of a high, perfectly clear, voice, which in some way crowned her distinction. Altogether she imparted a glamour, an elegance to the household, which was badly in need of stimulation. She arrived with a small quantity of luxurious luggage, and an Alsatian dog who followed her everywhere, but on whom she bestowed almost no attention. She greeted everyone with enthusiasm, and at dinner, when we were all dressed in various depressing frocks ranging from beige lace to blue velveteen, caused a minor sensation by appearing in a white silk shirt, grey tie and sleek black skirt.

'Is this what young women are wearing for purposes of education?' inquired Mr Lancing. He pretended to disapprove of her, but was in reality fascinated.

'Oh no, Uncle. It is merely what this young woman wears for amusement.'

'Are you terribly educated?' asked Rupert.

'Terribly terribly educated. It is really the result of my darling uncle worrying for years about my spare time. He has educated me so much that nobody could possibly marry me and so that I know how difficult everything is and how little I know. And now he's stuck, poor lamb. It is frightfully sad for him.'

'What *are* you going to do?' asked Aubrey. He seemed very much amused by her.

'Well, he's got a new plan. He's trying to make me very very frivolous. He keeps sending me to the most awful parties with lots of paper streamers, and buying me yards of lace and pearls and things like that. He says if only I could giggle it would help tremendously.'

And then, as though she was suddenly aware that this kind of conversation, dominated by one young girl, did not suit the Lancings, she relapsed into a vital silence. She listened to conversation about the coming dance, fixing her lovely rather serious eyes upon each speaker, occasionally producing an intelligent reason for someone else's suggestion. Long before the end of the meal I noticed that Deb did not like her, although it was clear that everyone else did.

After dinner it was suggested by one of the two men (who had not previously spoken) that we dance. Everyone was enthusiastic. As before, Rupert offered to work the gramophone and everyone remembered his leg. In the end we all flocked to the big room, rolled up the carpet and danced. Rupert did work the gramophone. The two young men immediately revealed their talent. They were virtually speechless, but extremely good at dancing. Elspeth was the only one of us capable of following and entering into their intricacies. They danced with us, but it was only with Elspeth that they could abandon all pretence of conversation and let themselves go. They danced with stern concentration: Elspeth danced with a little rapt smile. Deb, who was unable to manage the latest steps, wanted older and more familiar records, but she was in a minority, only obtaining a few waltzes which she danced with anyone but Aubrey. She spent most of the evening lounging against the gramophone with Rupert. Aubrey danced conscientiously with Lucy, Elinor and me, and once with Mrs Lancing, who came to implore us all into bed. We were, indeed, very much later that night than we had ever previously been and crept up the stairs whispering and laughing and suppressing each other.

The following day a ride had been planned, but Deb upset the arrangements by announcing that she was taking Rupert out for the day in the trap. This, as Aubrey had secured Christmas leave from the Foreign Office starting from that morning, was extremely disconcerting. He suggested that he join the driving party, whereupon Deb rose from the breakfast table and left the room without a word.

'Well, the horses will be round in half an hour,' announced Mr Lancing abruptly.

Aubrey said: 'As a matter of fact, sir, I'd clean forgotten it, but I ought to ride over to old Stebbing; so I'll join you if I may.'

Everyone looked much relieved at this fragile excuse, and then Rupert made matters worse by saying rather heavily, as we left the dining-room, 'Sure you don't mind, old man? I had no idea your leave started today.'

And Aubrey replied: 'My dear fellow, of course not. Damned bad luck you can't ride.'

Mrs Lancing and I saw the riding party off. It consisted of Aubrey, Mr Lancing, Lucy, Elinor, Elspeth, the two young men, Elspeth's Alsatian and a red setter. After much noise and confusion, shortening of stirrups and loosening of curb chains, they clattered off down the drive in the brisk golden air, and we turned to the house, I, at least, wishing very much that I was able to ride.

Half an hour later Deb's trap was brought round by Parker, who adored her whatever she did, and who plainly considered now that she was forgoing a beautiful ride in order to give a wounded man some pleasure. From a landing window I watched them depart. Deb looked particularly charming in a buff-coloured driving cap and large fur hat. They were settled in the trap. A rug was tucked round them by Parker, and they were off. I watched the red ribbon on the whip glide round the bend.

I had said that I had letters to write and an alteration to make to my dress for the dance: nevertheless, I could not help feeling bored and rather desolate at the prospect. I should have liked a drive, and to see Deb's house; although I felt that my presence in the trap would have been unwelcome and embarrassing. Really, I thought irritably, Deb does behave in the most extraordinary manner, and the certainty that she is unhappy does not stop one feeling cross. In a sense, I thought, the more you know about people, the less you can possibly blame them for their behaviour; and their being irreproachable implies a hostility in fate or circumstance, which becomes very frightening when applied to oneself. I really prefer to blame them, I concluded, as I began rather viciously to rip up the hem of an old and dull party dress.

It was a tiresome day. I broke my needle, and was forced to borrow one from Nanny, which involved a long and depressing conversation on the relative merits of Richard and Charles. I wrote to my mother, but found myself without a stamp. Mrs Lancing was sure that she had one, although it could not be found.

After lunch I was settling down to a book in the library, when Mrs Lancing appeared, armed with a trug and huge wrinkled gardening gloves. I was kindly forced into electing to garden with her. The gardening consisted, as I find it usually does, of weeding an interminable path, down which nobody walked, which was why, as Mrs Lancing pointed out, it was so thick with weeds. For two and a half hours we toiled with horrid little knives, with increasingly sore fingers, with aching backs, with frozen feet. Mrs Lancing weeded with relish; regarding each successful struggle with a daisy or dandelion root as a personal triumph. She was a woman who talked exclusively about what she was doing all the while she was doing it. My weeding conversation ran out in the first hour; and I was left to make miserable inadequate rejoinders to remarks like 'Got it, the brute,' and 'It is amazing the *hold* they get, isn't it?'

Eventually I was released for tea, for which everybody returned, except Rupert and Deb, about whom elaborately nothing was said. I had a bad headache and the depression which usually accompanies it; and after tea managed to escape, more or less unobserved, to my room with some aspirin. I took off my skirt in order to lie on my bed in the darkness.

The aspirin must have sent me to sleep, as I was awakened some time later by pent-up voices, which seemed to come from the next room.

... 'Why did you marry me, then?' I heard Aubrey say.

And Deb answered: 'What an impossible question. You ask as though I was solely responsible for everything that happens. I'm not! I'm not responsible for anything. I don't want to be. I tell you I don't want always to know what is going to happen!'

I began to wonder drowsily why I could so easily hear their voices, when I heard a rustling of paper, and starting up at the sound, saw that the communicating door to the dressing-room was ajar, was neatly edged with golden light. I could hardly get up and shut it; nor could I light my gas, since obviously neither Deb nor Aubrey had any idea that I was in my room.

Then Aubrey said, with deliberate good temper: 'Well, all I can say is, I completely fail to understand you. I give up Christmas in my own house in order that you may spend it with your family, as you have always done ...'

'Exactly!'

'Isn't that what you wanted?'

'It is what my family wanted.'

'Surely that is the same thing. However, if it is not, and you seem to me to be in such an incalculable state of mind that perhaps it isn't, why didn't you say so, and we would have planned to stay at home?'

'Because it does not make any difference whether we spend Christmas here or in your house, and I loathe all plans. You love them. You even planned to marry me. To "fall in love with me"!' It is impossible to describe the scorn with which she said 'to fall in love with me'.

'Well one cannot marry without making some sort of plan.'

'Then you did plan it.'

'Plan what?'

'To fall in love with me.'

'Don't be so ridiculous, of course not. What I cannot understand is why you persist in sulking and being positively rude to Elspeth and that other poor girl, and making everyone feel uncomfortable as you did this morning.' There was a pause, and then he added: 'Do you want Richard's golliwog to go into his stocking, or is it a separate present?'

'In his stocking.'

Then he said: 'I don't mind your taking Rupert out, but I cannot see why you had to wait until today, that is all. You knew my leave started today.'

'I like Rupert. He is different.'

'Yes, but ...'

She interrupted. 'I thought marriage meant *more* freedom, not less. I didn't know it meant years of plans, and having children, and sitting by myself all day.'

Aubrey answered gently: 'It doesn't necessarily mean that.'

'It does necessarily mean that. It means that I know what I shall be doing in five, ten, twenty years' time.'

'If you know that, it means that you also know you will be surrounded by at least three people who love you.'

'Is *that* all there is to choose?' she cried passionately.

'You don't really love me,' he replied sadly.

'It is you who do not love me. You don't want to be loved. You want to be looked after, cared for. You think that that is what I want – I think you think that is love.'

'Isn't it? Listen my darling. Just before I married you I was offered a job, abroad and much less well paid but with the prospect of greatly increased responsibility, far more than I have now. I didn't take it, because of you.'

'Did you *want* to take it?'

'Oh yes. Of course.'

'With much more responsibility and less pay?'

'It would have led to something better, far more quickly than my present work is likely to do.'

'Well why didn't you take it?'

'Because I had other responsibilities. You, and now the children.'

'But don't you see that regarding me principally as a responsibility, you cannot love me?'

'No, I do not. How can I make you understand? I chose you. Because I loved you. I loved you more than my career. Now do you see?'

'I do not think that loving someone can be compared with anything at all,' said Deb. She sounded very unhappy.

'I don't believe that you mean serious love. You mean flirting, and being admired. You are furiously jealous of the other girls, because they can do this without censure.'

Deb answered wearily, 'I expect I do.' And then, gaining spirit, 'And what if I do? If I am so beautiful, are you to be the only man to tell me so? There seem to me enough certainties in our life without that one.'

'What do you mean, certainties?'

She answered: 'Whatever we do I know that at the end of every day you will empty your money out of your pockets and spill it over the dressing-table and undress. You will open the window, draw back the curtains, and made some remark about the night. Then you will climb into bed with me and we shall lie side by side in the dark. Then either you will say that you have had a frightful day and kiss my forehead, or you will make love to me. It all happens like that.'

There was a long silence, and then Aubrey said: 'Do you love Rupert then? Do you think he would be so different if you were married to him?'

'I do not want to discuss Rupert.'

'But I want to talk about him.' He seemed angry now.

'Do you think he is in love with me?' she asked.

'Of course he is. Any man would be in love with you. Are you in love with him?'

There was a pause, and then she said: 'No, I am not in love with him. He will marry that silent creature in the end; and she will be the you, and he will be the me. She will want security and affection, and he will want excitement, uncertainty and love. I know much more about people than I did. But there is far less to know than I imagined.'

Her voice broke a little and I think she was crying because a minute later he said: 'I cannot bear you to be so unhappy. You are so beautiful and I *do* love you, my darling. I am sorry about Rupert. I should not have asked. I cannot bear to see you cry. My darling Deb.'

She said: 'Kiss me. Don't try to comfort me. Kiss me now ...'

There was a short silence, and seconds later he murmured something. I heard them move about the room. Then he said: 'The children's stockings! We did not finish them – No darling, we must do that first ...'

She gave a little choked laugh, or sob, and I heard her running past my door down the passage.

'Oh damn,' Aubrey said. A few moments later he put out the light and left the room.

As soon as they had gone, I lit my light to examine the door. It had always been shut; without trying it I had assumed that it was kept permanently locked, but now I saw there was no key. But why it should have been open on this particular occasion, I was unable to determine until I remembered that on several evenings lately Toby and his friends had been engaged upon some noisy and frightening game in the dark, which had involved the top floor landing and many of the rooms. I concluded that they must have opened all the doors and removed the keys.

At least neither Aubrey nor Deb had known I was there. I was no sooner congratulating myself upon this, than I became beset by serious misgivings. Perhaps, when I first heard them, I should have announced my presence, either by telling them, or by lighting my light. Or perhaps I should have attempted to creep out of my room without being heard. The last idea seemed impossible, as even if I had managed to get off the bed and open the door without their hearing me, I could hardly have wandered about the landing without a skirt. No, there was nothing else to have been done; embarrassed though I was at the prospect of facing Deb and Aubrey at dinner, I felt that to have faced them when I woke, at what was obviously not the beginning of their scene, would have been, for all of us, unbearably embarrassing. The whole situation was one which I simply had never experienced before, and I was at a loss how to deal with it. It was easier to feel sorry for Aubrey, but, without knowing precisely why, I felt more sorry for Deb, in spite of the fact that she did not appear to like me very much. At least Aubrey knew what he wanted, even if he was not getting it; while she, like I, was consumed with an aimless desire for something just beyond her own imagination. Then I remembered her weary certainty that I should marry Rupert, and a wave of irritation overwhelmed me, which was quickly followed by panic at the prospect itself. How could she be so sure that he would ask me? Why did I not know whether I wanted to marry him or not? 'I suppose that, if he is going to ask me, it will be at the dance,' I thought. 'I shall be wearing my horrible dress, and I shall be expecting it, and what could be worse. The fact that I hate my frock, in which I shall look dowdy, and that everyone else seems to be expecting the proposal, far outweigh the rest of the situation (a dance, Christmas and an eligible young man asking me to marry him). Perhaps they are all wrong, and he will not ask me,' I concluded. But that was not a very invigorating alternative.

CHAPTER THIRTY-TWO

At dinner, Rupert sat next to me, but I could think of nothing to say to him. Mrs Lancing asked whether the babies' stockings had been filled, and Aubrey answered, No, they were not quite finished.

After dinner someone suggested that we play a game in the dark. Mr and Mrs Lancing agreed to being shut in Mr Lancing's study for the evening, in order that all lights on the ground floor might be turned out. The game, which was so complicated that no one really understood the rules, was then inadequately explained by several people at once, who did not appear to agree with one another, and the lights were turned out. I was rather afraid of the dark, and having no idea of what I was supposed to do, groped and crept my way to the library.

The door of the room was wide open, and after entering I stretched out to shut it and thus cut myself off from the rest of the party, when my hand struck someone, who must have been standing stiff and motionless behind the door. I gave a little gasp of terror, and the next moment I was seized, felt arms thrown round me, and was passionately kissed on my mouth. The kiss continued until I had ceased to be terrified; indeed the dark, the man's suddenness and intensity shocked me into a kind of irresponsible excitement. For seconds I clung to the unknown, as though he were the most dearly loved and desirable creature in the world. Then, with an abrupt movement, he disengaged me. I thought he had stepped backwards, but he cannot have done so, as when I instinctively stretched out my hands, I felt nothing but the smooth leather spines of the books on the shelves.

As soon as I realized that he had left me, I began to wonder who he was, and then, who he thought *I* was. It could not be Rupert, I realized, as he was incapable of such silent mobility. I decided to retreat from the library altogether. If I was not to know who had been standing behind the door (almost as though he had been waiting for someone), then I would not give myself away by remaining foolishly for everyone to see when the lights were turned up.

So I left, encountering nobody else; nor, at the end of the game, could I determine who it had been. We were supposed to give some account of our movements; but no one, man or woman, admitted to having been in the library, and I followed suit. The game appeared not to have been a success, and we did not play it again. After a little desultory conversation (among the men the topic was where they had all been in 1914, and among the women what they were going to wear for the Christmas dance), we broke up. Elspeth and Deb, Lucy and even Elinor, it appeared, all had new confections for the occasion; but when I was asked, I was forced to admit that I had only the blue dress they had already seen.

It was no use caring, I reflected drearily in my room: I would somehow never achieve their easy innocent glamour. It would take very much more than a Christmas dance in the country to transform me. I fell asleep, wondering what it would take. It is curious that I should have wondered that: I certainly had no idea of how to set about procuring the circumstances necessary to effect the transformation, although I had some dim idea that I should, by now, know something of the ingredients. However, beyond the fact that they must be new, I had no very clear thought. Perhaps they must simply be new, I concluded, very drowsy.

Christmas was spent in the traditional manner; we were exhausted with presents before midday, and exhausted with food after it. The tree stood mysterious and glittering in the hall; the dining-room was littered with red ribbon and crumpled tissue paper; and secrets exploded all over the house, with little shrieks of delight and excitement. Charles was given a stuffed monkey which plainly frightened him even more than Mr Lancing impersonating a lion; but otherwise there were no regrets. They were very kind to me.

After lunch we walked. I wanted to walk with Elspeth, but she was so hemmed in by her men and her Alsatian that I soon gave up the attempt. She was always friendly, but, unlike the others, did not seem to recall my previous visit, and behaved all the time as though she were someone else, almost as though she were playing some part for the benefit of the Lancings – as though anywhere else she would be really quite different.

I had avoided Deb as much as possible since overhearing her, but she seemed almost to be seeking my company; she spoke to me more often – once, even, asked my opinion.

After an early tea, embellished only by the Christmas cake, which defied description, in its icy unapproachable magnificence, we retired, as I remembered I had done before, to our rooms, to rest and then to dress.

I was interrupted by a hurried tap on my door, which opened to reveal Deb. She *did* know I was here last night, I thought, with a sinking heart. She was very pale.

'Will you come to my room?' she began, and then added nervously, 'Do come.'

I followed her along the landing to her room. It was empty. She motioned me to the chaise-longue before the fire.

'I wanted to ask you something extraordinary . . .' she said, and then stopped. She was standing before me, twisting the heavy gold wedding ring round and round her finger. She did not look at me.

'Yes?' I stared at her timidly.

'Don't think that I am being patronizing or anything so absurd,' she began again in an arrogant manner, and then, catching my eye, she smiled, and slipped, with a rustling movement, on to her knees. 'Will you promise to do something for me? And will you promise now, before I tell you what it is?'

'But it might be something I could not possibly promise.'

'Against your principles? You look so serious that I always imagine you to have principles. *I* have none. I was not sneering at you. I am sure you think I was, but I was not. One must make some impression on everybody. But this is for

315

your good. To help you. It is nothing really, the smallest thing . . .'

'You said it was extraordinary . . .' I interrupted.

'Extraordinary for me to ask, but nothing for you to promise. Don't you trust me? Do you think that I dislike you?'

'I did not think that you liked me very much,' I said.

'I suppose not. I feel as though I don't *know* anybody you know, and that makes it difficult to like them. Or perhaps as though I knew everyone, but no one very well. I even know what I am going to do, so I find myself monotonous. Nothing ages women like monotony you know.' She delivered the last remark like someone in a play, who did not really believe what was said. I realized that she was saying anything that came into her head, in order to put off revealing what it was I had to promise. 'You always sound as though you have a very dull life. I am really sorry. I know what a dull life means, and I also know how little one can do about it. Now do you see that it cannot possibly harm you to promise?'

I promised.

'You said last night that you had only your old blue dress to wear tonight. Well, now you are to wear this.'

She rose to her feet, went to her wardrobe and drew out of it the most extraordinary dress. It is impossible to describe the very few garments one ever comes across that suit one. It was certainly not fashionable, but I knew instantly, as Deb held it before me, that dressed in it I should become more myself than I had ever been.

'I have never worn it, and I think it will become you,' she was saying.

'Were you not going to wear it tonight?'

'Oh no. I am wearing my wedding dress. It has been altered slightly, so that everyone will know it is my wedding dress which has been altered slightly. Will you put this on? The bodice will be very tight. I have lengthened the sleeves for you. You see now, why it was better to promise.'

'Yes, I do see.'

To my astonishment the dress fitted well. I looked remarkable in it. I really did: I think even Deb was surprised.

'It is extraordinary what a difference clothes make,' she said, 'but I cannot wear that colour. Your complexion is just right.'

There was a pause, a slight feeling of anti-climax while we surveyed me in the dress. Then she began unfastening it. Why was she doing it, I wondered, why should she care in the least what I wore for the dance? She seemed to think it very important, but why? I felt I must know why.

'Don't you think it is important?' she countered.

'I cannot see why it should be so for you.'

'Sometimes one knows when certain occasions are going to be significant,' she said. 'One cannot prepare when one does not know, but this is different.' I stared at her. 'Of course it is. You know perfectly well what I mean. But when I was in your position, nobody knew but I, and there was nothing I could do. Aubrey proposed to me in the waiting-room of a railway station. We were both afraid my train was leaving without me, and the whole thing was hurried. No point in caring about the accessories. But this is different. I thought I would help to make it a wonderful time.'

I started to speak, but she interrupted me. 'That is not all. I am afraid you must think very poorly of me. I am sorry. There is something, perverse, I suppose, about me, that cannot bear the steady arrangements, the forgone conclusions. I want to alter things; then I know I can't really, and wish that I had not tried. But I have not really tried to take him away from you. I have made no difference at all. I think I minded that. I thought it meant that nobody would ever care for me, but I was wrong. It is simply that life stops when one is married, and one ought to take care that it stops in a very good place. I thought perhaps that the least I could do was to help make it perfect for you. I thought perhaps this would help. You are too serious to consider such aspects; it takes frivolous people like me to do this sort of thing well.' She was very breathless, and stopped speaking suddenly, not as though she had finished, but as though she could not bear to go on talking, uninterrupted.

'Did Rupert tell you he wanted to marry me?'

'No, no, he didn't say anything about it.'

Deliberately, in order to gain time, I resumed my seat. 'Why do you think that he wants to marry me?'

'Oh don't be so tiresome! He brought you down here. It is obvious.' She was standing by the fire, her arm on the mantelpiece, and now she kicked a red coal as she spoke: 'I knew it the first day that you arrived.'

'But not that I wanted to marry him.'

She swung round, genuinely startled. 'But you *must* want to marry him . . . You must!'

'Why?'

'He cares for you. He needs someone who understands about his being a painter. You surely know about that. He will want to lead an adventurous life, and one cannot do that successfully alone. At least men cannot. He has had a bad time, I think, but he is awfully talented and all that sort of thing, and you could probably make him a tremendous success. He needs that. I thought perhaps you met many people like him, but you don't, do you? He is the only one. Heavens, if it is obvious to me, of all people . . . Anyway, what will happen to you, if you don't marry him? You surely do not intend spending the rest of your life doing those dreary jobs, do you? With all your family. Don't pretend you haven't thought about that.'

I had *not* thought much about it, but it was useless to say so, and in any case I immediately began thinking about it. 'I cannot understand why you should so much want us to marry.'

She made a gesture of indifference, but there was something strained about it. 'Of course I do not care what you do. But if you *are* going to marry him I thought . . .' Her voice tailed away.

'Yes?'

'That it ought to be,' she searched for a word, 'well, that it should matter very much. That it should be memorable. Aubrey said . . .' She cleared her throat. 'Aubrey said that I did not care for other people. He meant that I didn't care for

318

him, that I was heartless. And there is nothing I can do about it. I only care for things that people do not think important. Doing the small things really well; the things most people think are not worth doing at all.' She stopped.

'Does Aubrey know about this?' I indicated the dress hanging beside her.

'Of course not. No one knows. Naturally I should not have made you promise to wear it if anyone knew.'

'Are you very unhappy?' I asked.

She turned her head towards me quickly, as though she hated me. Her eyes were full of tears. 'Why do you ask that?'

'I'm sorry. I shouldn't have asked.'

'No, I am not unhappy, or happy. I am nothing at all . . .' A pulse in her throat began to beat violently. She seized the dress from its hanger and crammed it into my arms.

'Take the dress, take it. That is why I wanted to see you. Take it now. No one knows that I have it. I shall hate you, if you tell them. I shall hate you,' she repeated.

At last I began to understand her. I took the dress without a word, as I knew she wanted it taken, and fled from the room. I just heard the gentle subsidence of her skirt sinking to the floor as I shut myself out.

I had no sooner reached my room than the dressing bell sounded. I laid the dress on my bed, and then sat beside it in an agony of indecision. I had tried to pretend that I knew what I should say to Rupert; but Deb, unwittingly, had shaken up the inertia of my mind on this point, until it was now a shattering, urgent uncertainty. I felt my life depended on it, but for the life of me I did not know what to say. It seemed useless to pretend any longer that Rupert was *not* going to ask me to marry him. Wrong though Deb was about some things, I felt she was right about this. I began feverishly to count the times when Rupert had shown the slightest sign of preferring me to anyone else. I gathered these up like a few little bare bones, and I thought I could remember them all. He had sought me out, brought me here, had said that I was not dull; and several times I had caught him looking at me, with tired watchful eyes, as though he had wanted (but not very much) to know what I was thinking. That was all, and really it did not argue any very pronounced attachment. But perhaps he was reserving his feelings for this evening.

There was a knock on my door, and Mrs Lancing's maid appeared to inquire whether I wanted any help. I accepted her aid gratefully, because we could then concentrate together on my appearance; I need not think of anything else. As I put on the beautiful dress, I did think of poor Deborah and her gesture; but my mind shied away from her despair, because, in some way, I could not help relating it to Rupert, about whom I did not wish to think. 'You look a picture, Miss,' said the maid, when I was finished.

Even this casual routine remark warmed me. I sent the maid away in order that I might collect myself in peace. I had meant to come to some decision, but my unusual appearance so fascinated and overwhelmed me, that I simply stood foolishly before my mirror, abandoning myself to a detailed and intimate appraisal of my charms. I seemed to myself to have infinite possibilities ... Then the second bell rang.

CHAPTER THIRTY-THREE

I sat through dinner with the extraordinary conviction of being someone else. I found it easy to talk; to amuse them; even to astonish them. They admired the dress, they all admired it, and some of them asked why I had kept it so secret. Rupert said nothing. When I had entered the drawing-room he had been stretched out on the sofa, admiring the other women, and drinking sherry. He had not immediately looked at me, as I advanced rather nervously, wishing that he would turn round and say something before everyone would notice what he said. Lucy had spoken to me; he had turned his head, and ceased to smile. He had not said anything at all, but simply stared without speaking, while I walked to the fire and accepted my sherry; and then, when I had turned towards him with the glass in my hand, looked away, whereupon conversation, which had virtually ceased, began again.

After dinner the women clustered upstairs for a final prink, before awaiting the first guests. Following Deb as we ascended, I accidentally trod on her stiff white satin skirt, from which the train had been cut a little (although it was still much longer at the back than was usual or fashionable); and she turned to see that it was me. I apologized. She shook her head, signifying that it was of no importance. I have a final picture of her there, half-way up the red staircase; very pale, all eyes, and throat, and dark massed hair; trembling a little from the cold, and with nothing left to say to me.

When I came down again, I found Rupert waiting for me in the hall.

'Will you, as I am unable to dance, allow me to take you in to supper?'

'Yes. I cannot bear to think of supper now, but yes.'

'You are not compelled to eat,' he observed.

He had dispensed with his crutches, and was using a heavy but elegant stick, given him that morning by Mr Lancing. We walked to the big room together, at the door of which Lucy met us with a bundle of dance programmes. Rupert declined one but Lucy insisted.

'Of course you must. You can write down all the people you are going to talk to.'

'Give me your programme then,' said Rupert to me. 'I shall enter your one sedentary appointment in it.'

'May *I* come and talk to you, Rupert?' said Elspeth.

She was rather unexpectedly wearing yellow chiffon. Rupert and she continued talking, while I was swept away by Mrs Lancing, who always felt that it was a mistake for people who knew each other, to talk together at parties.

'Here is someone you *don't* know!' she announced triumphantly. 'Mr Fielding. He is devoted to music.' And she abandoned us.

I remembered that I had met Mr Fielding before, but he did not seem to recollect me; and on the point of reminding him, I restrained myself. I must have altered beyond recognition, I reflected with sudden pleasure.

'I don't know why Mrs Lancing thinks I like music. I don't. Never have. Are you very musical or something?'

I assured him earnestly that I was not, and he seemed relieved.

'That's something anyway,' he said, and then, aware that he had not said what he meant in the most tactful manner, added, 'I say, I didn't mean that. "Things that might have been expressed differently," what? That's a ripping dress. I mean it,' he added, anxious to reassure me. 'Look here, shall we set the ball rolling? Someone has to make a start.'

So we danced. There were twelve dances before the supper interval; and I was never without a partner. It was very odd, I reflected; on my previous visit I had been overwhelmingly anxious to be a success, had been disposed deeply to enjoy it if I were, or passionately to despair if I were not; but now, I floated through the evening with the utmost ease. I seemed not to *be* myself, but simply a successful reflection of all my partners. This, I found, generally speaking, constituted success.

I discoursed eagerly about fox hunting with one partner; and as vehemently deplored it with the next. I adored London; I loathed it. I agreed that dancing had disintegrated into something utterly ungraceful; I wearied of the old waltzes and longed for even further developments of ragtime. I was devoted to animals and interested in their welfare; then thought that far too much fuss was made of them which could be better devoted to people. Many of my partners considered me intelligent, and frankly said so. When I thought at all, it was about Rupert and the supper interval, which was divided from me by fewer and fewer dances, and which I had begun to dread.

When the moment finally arrived, Rupert was nowhere to be seen, and glad of a few minutes alone, I slipped away from the dancing, along the passage to the library, which was not being used that night, except as a depository for men's coats. A light was on in the room, but I entered it without thinking. I found a fire burning, Rupert seated on a stool before it, and a small table covered with supper for two people beside him.

'I'm sorry, I didn't know you were here,' I said foolishly.

'Has the supper started? I meant to come to fetch you on the stroke of eleven. Now, in fact,' he said, as the clock struck.

'Yes. I came here . . . I just came.'

'Very good thing. Shut the door, and come and eat.'

'Is that for us?'

'Of course. I made it for us. Wild with jealousy, I have limped about preparing a pathetic repast. Are you touched?'

'You meant to amuse, not touch me,' I replied moving uncertainly towards him.

'And I haven't done either. Do I ever?'

'Amuse or touch me?'

'No don't answer yet, until you have had some wine.' He poured it into two glasses.

'What is it?'

'Champagne – especially good champagne for us.'

At last I was drinking champagne, I thought, and remembered the two occasions when I had not.

'*Now* what are you thinking?'

'Nothing. I have never drunk champagne before,' I said.

The whole situation, the firelight, the little table, the slightly unexpected seclusion, was a shock to me, and I was uncertain whether I could sustain it.

'Do you feel like eating?'

'Not very.'

'Nor do I.' He suddenly drained his glass. 'I have the uneasy feeling with you that while I am quite ignorant of what is in your mind, you know exactly what I am going to say. Do you?'

I raised my eyes to him. 'I think I know what you are going to say; but I have not the smallest idea why you are going to say it.'

'Isn't that rather coy of you?'

'It wasn't meant to be,' I said, and in my embarrassment drank the rest of my champagne.

'Well, perhaps I had better attempt some sort of explanation; although I may as well warn you it will be neither explicit nor particularly illuminating. You have always, to me, ever since I first met you, seemed possessed of a potential capacity for life which I am quite without. I did not value this when I met you here, because I did not know myself how much I was without it; nor when you ran away to my studio, because then I was obsessed with my own problems. I just thought you over sensitive but delightful. It seemed to me that you wanted to get away from your home much in the spirit that I wanted to stop being a doctor. Things were simple for me then; not pleasant, but simple. I stopped being a doctor because the dazzling alternative was being a painter. I then found that this in turn produced the less dazzling alternative of becoming a soldier. That is how I saw it then, you understand. I was sorry for you when you came to the studio, but I felt quite unable to do anything about you;

324

and also slightly afraid that you would depend on me if I did. Painting was not at all what I had expected it to be, and so becoming a soldier did not seem, on the face of it, too bad a prospect. It took me about a year to discover how much I hated the whole thing; and by then I couldn't get away from it. I mean *I* couldn't. I hadn't the initiative to walk out, or the kind of desperate strength of mind to stop a blighty one. I just hung on, and lost my self-respect. At first I thought we should win quickly; then not for a long time; and finally that we should lose, but long after it didn't matter. I didn't care in the least. Nearly all my friends got killed, or worse, and then I had this leg trouble. Weeks and weeks of cheerful quiet and filthy smells, in a hospital. In hospital I began to think about you, and wondered whether, in order to escape your home, you had become a nurse. That would finish her, I thought, just about as much as soldiering's finished me. If you do a job for months and years which shatters the sensibility without in any way strengthening the intellect (and most people do that, war, or no war), you really are not worth more than the creature comforts a government or an employer accords you; down to the shortest possible telegram announcing your death, or everyone getting drunk for a night because you have survived. Anyhow, for some weeks I lay in bed, thinking a little about you, and concluding, quite wrongly, that you had probably been reduced to the same state as I. I suppose I wanted to think that. That is why I arrived at your house. I didn't expect you to mind. I talked to your mother, who didn't seem to know anything about you, but was obviously very relieved to see me. She seemed to regard me as the answer to a mother's prayer. Then you appeared. I couldn't understand you then, and I don't now. At first, I thought that *you* had been very unhappy, and then I changed my mind. You would not have come here for Christmas, where you had not seemed to enjoy yourself very much before, if you were very unhappy. Then I thought that perhaps, although you had not lost your sensibility, you had begun to lose hope about escaping from your dreary home. And then I began to see the least I could do about it. And now we are sitting here, and I am asking you to marry me.'

There was a silence; during which I wondered where to begin. I felt he had not told me anything at all, anything, at least, that I wanted to hear. And a good deal of what he thought about me was simply wrong. No point in telling him that.

'Well?' he asked.

'I am afraid I still don't see why you want to marry me.'

'I told you my explanation would not be very illuminating. You do not seem very surprised, by the way.'

'Did you expect me to be surprised?'

'No,' he said, after a moment's thought. 'No, I suppose not. Well, if you can think of anything more to ask me, I'll try and answer honestly.'

'What do you propose to do, if I marry you?'

'I have considered that very carefully. I shall give up painting and accept my father's offer. It means living with him, but it is a large house and there would be plenty of room. I very much doubt my ability to earn enough money for two people as an artist; and in any case, after staying here, I am sure it is better to live in the country. Life is much simpler, safer too, I think. And better for children. Do you know Norfolk at all?'

'Not at all,' I answered politely. We really might have been two complete strangers conversing in a train.

'It is very flat where we should live. On the edge of a salt marsh. The country stretches flat to the sky, and green, greener than any other part of England. There are small ridges beside the dykes, and windmills standing about, and long narrow roads running dead straight; but otherwise, it is simply miles and miles of soft wet green marsh, with geese in winter, and cows all the year round. To the people who know it well, it is the most beautiful county of all.'

'I don't know it,' I repeated. I was not in a frame of mind receptive to the emotional appeal of landscape.

'I thought you minded so much about painting,' I added. I

remembered his outburst to me in the studio; it was almost impossible to believe that this was the same man.

'Oh yes,' he laughed shortly. 'I expect I was very fluent and intellectual about art when we met before. That should have warned you. Good artists are seldom good at talking about it; they simply get on with the job. Perhaps they have a larger share of animal intuition than most, but very little intellect. If they start talking about it, start relating it to life in any more than the grand, emotional, or intuitive manner, there is trouble at once. They start analysing their work, and find that there is nothing there. And then they are confounded.'

'Of course there are exceptions,' I said.

'Of course there are exceptions. There are, fortunately, always exceptions. They are the only thing which prevents anyone knowing everything about anything. I was talking about the kind of artist which I might have aimed at being. And you see, it's no good. I've done too many other things and talked too much. I'm not single-minded enough. My mind is too divided.'

'So you would not paint anyway?'

'What do you mean?'

'I mean you would not paint whether I married you or not.'

'Oh I see. No. No, you need have no fear that you are corrupting a fine artist into a breadwinner. None of that. Have some more champagne?'

'Thank you. But you still have not, so far as I can see, produced a single reason for wanting to marry me, more than anyone else.'

'Isn't the fact that I am asking *you*, and not, shall we say, Elinor, sufficient reason?'

'I don't think it is. Why not Elinor? Why not Maria?'

'Maria died of tuberculosis nearly two years ago. It's all right,' he continued, as I was about to interrupt. 'It was probably the best thing that could have happened to her. She could never have gone back to her family, and she was the kind of woman who loved the kind of man who left her. She

327

found someone else about four months after I joined up. She would have been all right until she had begun to get fat, and then she would have had a bad time. Her family would never have taken her back after the wine importer, as she would no longer have been marriageable.'

I remembered Maria, and how much she had loved Rupert, and how much he had loved, or seemed to love, her; and suddenly felt frightened. But I said nothing.

'Elinor? Well not Elinor, because she would marry anyone who asked her. I should not feel that she had any particular feeling for me.'

'I think that is how I feel.' I was almost surprised at the boldness of my own voice.

'There is one other point,' he said, as though he had not heard me. 'And that is *your* position. You don't like living with your family ... I take it that you have not changed in this respect?'

'I have not changed,' I answered steadily.

'You have made several abortive attempts to get away from them. I remember you once wrote to me from Sussex where you were being companion to some boring old woman. You have not discovered some great career for yourself?'

'No.'

'Well, here I am, offering you a peaceful life, independent of your family.'

'But you used to be so much against marriage.'

'You do remember things, don't you? I was. I was against marriage, against democracy, and I did not believe in God. That is all very well until one is, say, twenty-five or thirty. One can seriously imagine that there are better alternatives to all three propositions until then. Until then, living is rather like beginning to learn a foreign language. It is exciting, and not nearly so difficult as one imagined; and then, quite suddenly, one either has to go and live in the country where the language is spoken, or one has to sweat for hours, learning declensions of verbs until one is blind with fatigue, and knowledge of the language seems hopelessly unattainable. I prefer to live in the country. That is to say, I prefer to marry, in a church, and become a Liberal.'

There was a silence, which he broke by saying: 'But *you* were not against marriage?'

'No. But I never thought of marrying someone I didn't love.'

'I was waiting for that. I know you do not love me.'

'More than that, you do not love me.'

'Really, I think I am the best judge of that.'

'I think *I* am the best judge of it.'

'You attract me,' he said angrily, 'and I like talking to you. Also, I've told you, I don't know what you are thinking all the time, and with most women, one knows exactly what they are thinking. I *want* to marry you. I tell you it would be a success.'

'Not unless I felt at least some of those things for you.'

'Don't you? Don't you feel any of them?'

'None of them,' I said.

'Why did you run away to my studio then?'

'Really, your own opinions have changed so much since then, that you can hardly blame me for any alteration in mine. Besides, I had nowhere else to go.'

'I think you would have married me then. If I had swept you into my arms, and said "Darling be mine", you would have been mine.'

'I was seventeen then. And I had never been in love.'

'Are you in love now?' he asked quickly, and I saw he flushed.

'No.'

'But you have been in love. Poor thing. Did it all end badly?' He was eager and gentle now. I did not reply. 'Well, could you not accept me as a second best?' he said, and for the first time it occurred to me that he really did badly want to marry me.

'I am afraid I could not do it in such very cold blood.'

He winced at this, but continued: 'A great many marriages start like this. More than you would think. It is not necessarily a bad way to begin. We are both honest with one another. We neither of us have any very brilliant alternative ...'

'I am sorry, Rupert, but I could not do it. I do not want to marry you.'

We had been sitting opposite one another over the table of untouched food, and now he slumped on his stool a little. I thought he had accepted my refusal, but after a moment he drew a deep breath, and said: 'Look here. I am serious about this. If you like, I didn't know how serious I was until just now. Also, if you like (and this is very honest of me), I did not expect you to refuse me. Will you think it over? Perhaps you have not thought seriously about it, and really need more time. I'll ask you again in London.'

'I do not want to be asked again, in London or anywhere else.'

'But damn it, I love you! I've banked everything on your marrying me! I've thought of very little else since we have been here!'

'I don't believe it.'

'Well what do you expect me to do? It is no good my making violent love to you. I should think you would be awfully difficult to make love to ...'

'It would not make the slightest difference,' I said, quite uncertain what difference it would make.

'Of course it would make a difference, but the wrong kind, I thought, with you. What *do* you want? Would you marry me if I remained a painter, and lived in disreputable squalor?'

'No.'

'Would you simply live with me in disreputable squalor?' I shook my head. I could think of nothing more to say.

'I suppose I've done this very badly,' he said. 'There must be *some* way of proposing to you which you would feel constrained to accept.'

'If I loved you, it wouldn't matter much what you said; and as I don't love you, it doesn't matter what you say either.' But I could see that he did not really believe I should refuse him in all circumstances; that he was still considerably startled at my refusing him at all. The picture he had drawn of my life was certainly accurate, but the idea that I would marry him simply because I could think of nothing better to do, touched my pride, and I resolved, there and then, that I *would* find something to do. Anything, I reiterated to myself.

'Are you having to determine not to marry me?' asked Rupert.

'I was determining something else. I think I will go now.'

'May I say, gratuitously, that you look positively enchanting in that frock?' I did not reply. Then he said: 'By the way, do you remember my rich friend Ian? He asked after you, when we were at camp together. You know he was killed of course.'

I rose to my feet. 'I read it in the newspaper.'

'The title has gone to his rather unpleasant cousin. All the best people were killed. You know you will eventually have to make do with some realistic chap like me.'

I was sure that he knew something and hated him, but his face was expressionless. He, too, rose to his feet. I turned to the door.

'No, don't go yet,' he murmured, and seized my arm. I knew that he desperately wanted to kiss me; remembered Deb's envious romantic plans for us, and was suddenly filled with extreme revulsion, partly because of her, and partly because I was certain that he had meant to probe me about Ian. We stared at each other, until he dropped my arm and said: 'I am very sorry. That was unpardonable of me. Please stay and have supper with me. I won't talk any more about it ...'

'I'd rather go.'

He watched me for a minute, and then stooped, picked up our two glasses, and flung them into the grate.

'Most people get more out of their first champagne,' he said.

I left the room.

CHAPTER THIRTY-FOUR

Two days later I left the Lancings, and went back to London alone. They were very kind to me right up to the end, although I think they had begun to sense that I was not one of them or ever likely to be. I told them I had to go because of the imminent arrival of my younger brother. I put the lovely dress back in Deb's room, with a note thanking her. She gave no sign afterwards that she had received it, and her behaviour to me was utterly commonplace. Mrs Lancing asked me to come again. Lucy begged me not to go. Rupert wavered between extreme silence in my company (arguing embarrassment or hostility), and various efforts to secure it. He repeated his intention of again asking me to marry him when in London.

Lucy and Elinor accompanied me to the station.

'There is a compartment with a woman in it,' said Elinor as the train drew in.

Lucy flung her arms round me with anxious vehemence. I knew we were both thinking of her revelations in the wood, that she wanted to ask me for the last time to tell no one, that I wanted to assure her I would not; but we neither of us said anything.

'Do come back. Or it would be lovely to see you in London. Come every year,' she said, and I answered: 'Thank you. You have been very kind and I've enjoyed myself tremendously.'

In the train I waved to both of them until the train had begun to hurry and they had begun to turn away.

And that was the end of my second visit.

CHAPTER THIRTY-FIVE

My mother opened the door to me and said: 'Well, darling?'

And that was only the beginning of it; I did not immediately perceive what she meant, but five minutes with my sister left me in no doubt. (I escaped my sister in rather less than five minutes, unable to bear the exasperating vulgarity of her inquisition.) They had both clearly been certain that Rupert had carried me off for Christmas with the express intention of proposing to me. The worst of it was that they were right. It was the kind of point on which I was very bad at deceiving them, although I did what I could. I wrote to Rupert asking him never to arrive in my home, particularly without warning. I quelled my poor mother by preserving an obstinate and forbidding silence on the subject of my visit. I think she was rendered more sympathetically silent by my sister's persistent and increasingly hostile curiosity. My sister, I reflected, after three days of unrequited tension, was certainly very odd about the whole affair. She followed me about the house, appearing suddenly in my room for no ostensible reason; her conversation at these and other times consisting in discourses alternatively on her hard life, and my selfish ingratitude and want of confidence in those nearest me. As we none of us had anything whatever to do, she had ample opportunity for this kind of thing. In front of our mother she contented herself with a series of repetitive and double-edged remarks about marriage, and other peoples' friends.

For about a week I racked my brains for something to do. Eventually I hit upon the not very brilliant notion of part copying for orchestras. I told my mother that I was going to do this; she looked at me sadly and acquiesced. 'Don't try your eyes, darling,' was all she said.

The work, with my father's connections, was easy to acquire. I copied slowly, but with extreme neatness: however, people underpaid me, and were satisfied.

Two weeks after I had begun this work I received a letter from Rupert. I came in and found it lying on the hall table. It suggested that we meet somewhere and 'discuss matters'. I was reading it in my room, when, without any warning, my sister entered.

'You have had a letter from him!' she cried. 'He never comes here, but you meet him, and he writes to you!' She was panting as though she were hardly able to breathe, and as she finished speaking she put one hand to her side.

I stared at her in some astonishment.

'What has it to do with you?'

'Why don't you tell us about him?'

'Do you mean whether he asked me to marry him?'

She nodded, but her eyes never left my face.

'I do not understand . . .' I began.

But she interrupted me: 'You go off with him to those people at a moment's warning, leaving me here doing what I can to make poor Mother's Christmas brighter for her, and then you come back without saying one word. It's *awful* for her. Simply selfish and unkind. I know you meet him. This copying you do is just a blind. You're too jealous to have him here. Afraid of what he might think. It's wicked of you. We all go on day after day as though nothing were happening, and it *is* . . . it must be, only you won't say. How can you be so deceitful!'

'He has asked me to marry him,' I said. I was very angry. 'I have refused him. I have asked him not to come here because I don't like it.'

'But he has asked you to meet him elsewhere!'

'Did you open this letter?'

She stared at me without replying, but a slow painful colour suffused her neck and then her face.

'You opened my letter?' Suddenly I was so angry that I could not see her standing in front of me. I lunged forward. I think I must have struck her. I realized that my hand hurt and I could see her fallen back upon the door, supporting herself by its handle. There was a broad white mark across her face; she seemed scarcely to breathe at all, and the letter lay on the floor between us.

Before I could say anything, she began talking, so quietly that at first I could hardly hear her. I don't think she cared whether I heard, it was simply her own mind let loose, she barely knew herself what she said.

'I thought when he came, that he would want to marry you. He sat in Father's chair with his poor leg, and I felt so sorry for him. You went away with him, and I steeled myself to face your coming back ... engaged. I am older than you, and Mother has no one. If you married and went away I should be left. Then I thought that he might have friends and, and ... but if you do not marry him you've no right to prevent me from doing so. I've nothing to look forward to now my war work has ended. If *you* married, you would go away and leave us; but if I married, I should take Mother with me and it would all be exactly the same as before. It would be so much more ... *sensible* if I married.' She rambled on, explaining herself, and giving herself away, unconscious of her dishevelled unattractive appearance, which had never, perhaps, been so dishevelled before.

When she had nothing more to say, I took her hand and led her to the only chair in my room. Then I sat on the bed facing her. She was pushing the hairpins back into her thick slippery hair, and staring at me with a haggard, somewhat vacant expression.

'You cannot,' I said patiently, 'simply marry someone because you see them and want to be married. You do not know this man. You might not like him.'

'I have not had a chance with him. I have never had a chance.'

'But he might not like you. He might not in the least want to marry you.'

She flushed again. 'You've set him against me!'

'Don't be foolish. We have not discussed you.'

'I suppose you are so sure of him,' she said. 'I suppose you do mean to marry him in the end.'

'No, I do not. I don't want to marry for the sake of marrying.' As soon as I said this and heard how smug it sounded I felt rather ashamed.

'How do you know that he doesn't?' she asked suddenly.

It was the first acute remark she had made. I was taken off my guard and said lamely: 'I *don't* know.'

'Well, why won't you help me? It's not very much to ask. If you really don't want him yourself, why shouldn't you at least ask him here so that I have a chance to see him again?'

I was trapped. I had already said that Rupert and I had not discussed her, so I could hardly say now that the only remark he had made about her had been far from flattering.

'I'll think about it.'

'You are trying to put me off,' she said and began to cry.

'He might not want to come here now he knows that I won't marry him.'

'The letter,' she sobbed, 'you know what he says in the letter. Oh I wish I were dead! Everything happens to you and nothing to me. It is you who go off and find people and do things, and I can't. I'm not made that way. I thought I could lose myself in work, but now there is no work, and Mother does not need all I have to give. I'm sick of this house that is too big for us and trying to find things to do. I want a nice little home: with Mother, of course; and children, and everything arranged by me.' She pulled out a little handkerchief embroidered by herself, and wiped her eyes. 'Do you know, I have never even had a letter from a man? Of course Hubert used to write to me sometimes. But even he doesn't seem very anxious to come home, and he is only a brother, after all. Men don't recognize the lasting qualities in women. You are hopeless in the house and yet he wants to marry you! How can you refuse him!' she added inconsistently. 'What do you mean to do instead?'

'I don't know.' I was becoming very tired of this question, because even on the rare occasions when other people were not asking it, I was asking myself, and I never had any satisfactory reply.

My sister stared at me morosely. 'You must be mad,' she said at last.

'I am sorry I struck you,' I said awkwardly.

'Oh. Of course I forgive you,' she replied. She did not apologize for opening my letter.

Nor was that the end of it.

My sister and I avoided each other for the rest of that evening (she had left the room when she had forgiven me, still pressing the embroidered handkerchief to her eyes); but next day she resumed her attack. When was I going to ask Rupert to tea? Why had I not already asked him? Why did I not at least *ask* him? In the end, worn down by a series of little urgent private scenes with her I gave in, and wrote asking Rupert to tea. She posted the letter herself, and was then unaccountably irritable for the rest of the day.

Rupert accepted the invitation; my sister made various absurd and pathetic preparations; and I dreaded the whole thing so much that I felt sick when I thought of it. One preparation of my sister's consisted in manoeuvring our mother out of the house. She did this by the simple expedient of telling our mother that *I* did not want her there; but I only discovered this afterwards.

Rupert was due to arrive at four o'clock, but at half past, when he still had not appeared, we received a telegram to the effect that he was unable to come.

My sister, who seemed in the most alarming state of nerves, broke down completely at this. She wept, became hysterical, and finally accused me of conspiring with Rupert against her. After a useless interminable scene, I got her to her room with aspirin and lavender water and a handkerchief round the lamp. My mother returned and, when my sister did not come down for dinner (she had locked her door and would not answer me when I tried to fetch her), I learned why my mother had gone out.

I had been thinking very hard since the end of the scene with my sister, and after dinner I took the plunge and told my mother what I intended doing. She listened to me carefully, and made no objection, which was worse, of course, than even the most selfish or unreasonable opposition. She even offered me a little, a very little, money, which was, I am sure, more than she could afford. I explained that I was out of sympathy with my sister, and that I thought the situation was likely to get worse. My mother did not understand me. She suggested hopelessly that perhaps things would be better when my brothers came home, although she admitted that Tom would go straight to his school and Hubert showed no signs of appearing at all. Then she reverted to worries about money. One by one she enumerated my own fears, and one by one I pretended to explode them. She believed me. By the end of the evening she was quite full of light-hearted admiration for the scheme, or pretended to be.

I fell asleep stretching thirty pounds over twelve months so thinly that the weeks showed through, and I had to make shillings of the pounds.

CHAPTER THIRTY-SIX

The end of it was that I found, after much searching, a room in which I could live by myself. The search took several days, partly because I had no idea how to start anything of the kind, and partly because even when I had learned something about it, there was the problem of finding a respectable room that I possibly dare afford.

I began by crossing Kensington Gardens to Bayswater and searching the streets at random for houses with signs about letting rooms. I did find one or two, but their landladies were expensive and disproportionately suspicious. One of them, who raised my spirits by being much cheaper, scratched herself furiously while I told her what I wanted, and then, withdrawing her hand from the small of her back, laughed so much that she broke two exceedingly dirty milk bottles which had been propped on her doorstep. She kicked the pieces of glass into the area and slammed her door.

As I neared Paddington station there were more and more houses with rooms to let. I became very used to ringing the bell at some gaunt house, to the door being opened (generally by a pasty-faced girl with half her wits about her and a cold), to explaining what I wanted, to the girl shouting 'Mum!' or 'Auntie!' or 'Vi!', to the appearance of some woman who was invariably too fat or too thin, and to whom I must explain all over again what I wanted, and then either to being turned away, or to being shown some attic which was damp, dirty or dark, and very often all three, and finally to the long silent descent of the house after I had fabricated some excuse for declining the room – and then the street again.

The first day was utterly abortive; on the second I discovered the invaluable assistance of local newspapers; on the third, the still more invaluable assistance of newspaper shops. It was in one of these that I found, approximately, what I was looking for.

I was scanning the rows of miscellaneous advertisements stuck to his window with stampedge when the shopkeeper himself beckoned to me.

'Thought I might help you. I know them cards off by heart,' he began. 'What is it, a little dawg, or yer Mum's tiara?'

I told him, and he whistled.

'Don't know London, do you?' he said. 'You want somewhere quiet, and respectable, *and* cheap. I know. Just come off the train you 'ave.' He nodded knowingly. 'Now, let's see, what 'ave we? We got everything 'ere,' he said after a minute's fruitless search in a large greasy blue book. 'Ah! Here we have it. Mrs Pompey. Number sixteen.' He scribbled something on a card and pushed it across the counter. 'Schoolmaster's widder. You say I sent you. Williams is the name. Tell 'er 'er ad's lapsed. Turn left outside the shop, keep straight on down and then right turn. Orlright?'

I thanked him gratefully.

'You can get yer papers 'ere,' he called cheerfully as I shut the door.

Number sixteen was in the middle of a terrace of tall thin houses, but was quite noticeable, being painted a rich apricot cream with a black front door. (The door was newly painted.) There was nothing to say that rooms were to be let. However, I rang the bell. Mrs Pompey answered the door. She was a little woman with no neck and a strong Scottish accent. I explained who had sent me, and what I wanted, while she surveyed me keenly.

'What do you want to pay?' she said.

I nervously stated my maximum figure.

There was a short silence.

'It's not very much, is it?' she said.

I added another two shillings to my price.

'I have one room I might let you have at that,' she said. 'Will you step inside while I close the door?'

I stepped into a hall which was pitch black when she shut the door.

'Will you follow me up, then?'

One floor from the top she halted and unlocked a door. At the same moment a loud bell rang twice from somewhere below us.

'Perhaps you'd step inside and be looking round you a minute. I shall be back.' And she hastened away.

The room was small, rectangular and clean. It was not very light, although possessed of a fair-sized sash window. The window, I discovered looked squarely out on to a sooty brick wall of a neighbouring house, which stood but three yards away, and which was broken only by olive green drainpipes. There would never be very much more light, I realized, although the afternoon was a dull one. I turned to the rest of the room. There was a black iron and brass bed, covered by a flaming slippery counterpane. The walls were covered in streaky buff paper which was heavily laced with mauve wistaria clinging to a darker buff trellis. There were a small gas fire and ring, a washstand with huge pitcher, a large highly polished wardrobe with an oval mirror set in its door, a comfortless armchair bristling with horsehair and little vicious round buttons, a stained oak chest of drawers. There were two pictures on the walls, one of which was entitled 'First Love'. I did not have time to examine the other before Mrs Pompey entered the room.

'Well, have you decided?' she began. She was a woman, I discovered, who went straight from one point to the next, wasting no time at all.

I started. I had been surveying the room with a minute, objective interest, but I had forgotten the purpose for which I was surveying it.

'You will see there is a gas ring, and the bathroom is across the passage. I change the linen once a week and you have your own keys. No visitors after seven, and one hot meal a day for an extra consideration. This is a respectable household and I wouldn't take gentlemen if they paid me.'

I did not feel that she would take anyone who did *not* pay her. However, I said nothing.

'What is your opinion?' she pressed after a moment.

I looked wildly round the room. It was not in the least what I had imagined, but I had searched for three days now, and did not seem likely to procure anything better.

'I should like to take it, please.'

'One month's rent in advance, and when would you be coming in?' she said instantly.

'Tomorrow. I have to fetch my things.'

And so the bargain was concluded. In the end I obtained the room and the meal for the original price she had agreed to. I paid the rent, and she hastened away for a receipt, while I waited in the dark hall.

I left with the keys, and strong, but very mixed feelings. By the time I had reached home, however, the situation settled itself into a romantic attitude of escape and a new life. I told my mother that I had a clean and cheap room with a respectable landlady, and that I was leaving the following day. I was so intent upon concealing my anxieties and fears that I succeeded in sounding merely callous about the whole thing; but my mother tried to enter into the spirit of it, helping me to pack, bringing me little pots of jam, and encouraging my optimism (assembled for her benefit) as much as she was able. My sister absented herself from these preparations in a marked manner. She had made one remark to the effect that I should soon return, after which she had ignored me.

'You will come back if you are ill?' asked my mother when we said good night.

'I'll come back anyway, in two days' time, for tea,' I replied. Her face brightened.

No, it was not really an escape, I reflected, but it was a new life.

CHAPTER THIRTY-SEVEN

I left my home at three o'clock the following day. By half past three I was back in the room facing the brick wall, with the door shut, and my trunks beside me. I found the speed with which I had effected this a little disconcerting. It did not seem very adventurous to leave one's home and reach the new destination in merely half an hour. The room was exactly the same as when I had left it except that there was a coarse white net cloth on top of the chest of drawers, rather like the cloth I had at home. I tried to think that that was far behind me, but half an hour did not seem very far. I decided to unpack and arrange all my belongings.

It took me about an hour to do this. I discovered that the wardrobe door swung open with a creak if I did not wedge it with a piece of paper, and that almost none of the drawers would open or shut unless I employed great ingenuity or strength or both. The first real trouble presented itself when I realized that I had no table on which to do my part copying. I should have to speak to Mrs Pompey. I would go and buy the food and other necessities required before broaching Mrs Pompey, I thought.

I bought bread, sausages, butter, margarine, apples and milk, in the street containing the newspaper shop. I did not feel able to run to the luxury of a newspaper, but I had decided to keep a diary, and, remembering that the man sold stationery, resolved to buy an exercise book from him for this purpose. He was very cheerful, and asked if I was fixed up, and whether I had reminded Mrs Pompey about her ad? I promised to remind her that evening, and he sold me a fat exercise book. 'Going to write yer life?' he remarked, expertly tying the string. 'That'll be something for us all to read. My eye!' He rolled them both skywards. 'Come back when you get to Vol. Two.'

After him, and a brief interlude with Mrs Pompey, who produced a small table, I did not speak to anyone for the rest of the day.

I cooked my supper, started the first page of my diary, and then, although it was only nine o'clock, went to bed. I could think of nothing else to do. The light was not strong enough for copying, and I was disinclined to read. The bed had noisy springs, but was quite comfortable.

The next day I rose, made myself toast on the fire (which required an alarming number of pennies to keep it alight), and settled down to work. I was interrupted, however, by an old woman who intended 'doing' my room. She was amiable, but so inquisitive that I fled, walking about the streets for nearly an hour, by which time I deemed my room should be clear of her. It was. It was also clear of three shillings which I had left on the writing-table with the intention of getting them changed into pennies for the fire. I was somewhat discouraged by this, and searched anxiously through my things to see whether anything else had disappeared. But she seemed to have the simple immediate kind of mind that takes only money.

I copied until a quarter to one, when an absurdly dignified gong rang. I ate stewed rabbit and semolina pudding in a room with seven tables and four other lunchers. They muttered occasionally to each other, but they mostly ate, with gloomy concentration, the not very appetizing food. Then, one by one, they left in a portentously silent manner, as though they had something important to do but the remainder of us must not be disturbed. After lunch I automatically went to my room. What should I do now? The thought of copying even more music was intolerable, as was the alternative of darning my stockings. I wrote to my mother; and then, as an afterthought, to Lucy, asking for Elspeth's London address.

Friends were essential to this sort of life. I wondered what they were doing at home. I could walk over and see them. I resisted this idea with some difficulty, and posted my letters instead.

There were sausages again for supper. The bathroom geyser required a shilling, and took even longer than the one at home. I wrote the diary again, and was disappointed in the shortness of the entry and its repetition of the day before.

A week passed, in which the only events were a self-conscious visit to my home, and a friendly but very short letter from Lucy containing Elspeth's address.

Even after a week I realized that the money I made from part copying, and the money my mother had given me, were not going to be enough. The food, and most of all, the fire, raced through a third as much again as I had calculated to spend on them.

I went to the newspaper shop and asked the proprietor to put a card in his window to the effect that a young lady would teach music on pupil's own piano. We worded it together, and he told me how much to charge. 'Can't be much in these parts,' he said, shaking his head wisely. 'You won't get them to pay for it. I should say five bob a lesson is about the mark, or maybe half a crown.' We settled on three and six.

I wrote to Elspeth asking whether I might come and see her. There was no reply. I went every day to the newspaper shop, but nobody seemed to want piano lessons. Then one night after I had eaten my bacon, and tried to write the listless monotonous diary, I broke down and simply wept. It did not seem to matter how hard I tried, life continued blank and impenetrable like the black brick wall outside. I seemed to have no friends. Elspeth did not reply, and even Rupert seemed to have given me up. I had no talents and no money. I was not starving. I had what unsympathetic listeners would call a good home. And a young man had asked me to marry him. I flipped through the pages of my diary with their sparse uninteresting information, tore the written sheets from the book and threw them away in fragments. What was the use of writing the same thing day after day all through this thick book? Then I remembered the newspaper man telling me to come to him when I got to Vol. Two. If I

345

had always kept a diary, there would have been Vol. Two by now, and after all, things had not always remained exactly the same. They had not, I remembered more sharply, as an engine whistled at Paddington, and I recalled my first journey to the Lancings, to whom my father had seen me off. One could not keep a retrospective diary, however, and it was just my luck that I should choose this moment to begin. Then I suddenly wanted to write about my first journey to the Lancings diary or no diary.

And that was how I came to write this book.

CHAPTER THIRTY-EIGHT

I wrote the book. I continued to live in my room in Paddington; to copy music, and to eat my lunch in the dim room on the ground floor, crowded with cruets, with sauce, and with tables, in fact with anything but people. I bought food; collected shillings and pennies for the geyser and my fire respectively; went home to my mother once a week (she did not ask to see my room, and I did not invite her); mended my clothes; and occasionally went for walks when I had music to return, as the concentrated confinement was making me more than usually pale. Every hour when I was not occupied in the above employments, I wrote.

I began by writing about the first visit to the Lancings, and then realized the necessity of describing my home which provided such violent contrast. After the earlier part was completed, I related every incident subsequent to the first visit, that seemed in the least worthy of narration. I found the whole business incredibly arduous, but I was no longer lonely or bored. I only stopped to consider whether I had remembered the things that had mattered to me at the time; the right things, and enough of them. When I began, I found this difficult; but after one painful month my past life consumed me, and I had no trouble in projecting myself back into each experience as its turn came.

I told no one about my writing. Even Mr Williams, the newsagent, with whom I had become very friendly, when selling me a second fat exercise book, laughed about my 'life' because, of course, he did not really believe in it. I began to write every afternoon except on the day that I went home; continuing until eleven or twelve at night, with a break for the inevitable sausages or eggs or bacon. I ate them in rotation by now, but I had ceased to notice them very much; I had ceased to notice anything. It is only now that I realize how difficult it is to live, observe and feel; and to write. Living and writing at once were almost impossible to me. For five months I did not live at all; that is to say, almost nothing happened to me, and when it did, I made no effort to enjoy whatever it was, I hardly noticed it, and resented what I did notice. I simply wrote. It was a curious business. I had no very clear idea of why I was writing, or even, as the months went by, how I was to end the whole thing. This last point became for some time a very real problem. Everything connected with the book had by then become real, and everything else a drab boarding-house dream. The underlying problem in my life became the end of my book; the most immediate problem, my increasing lack of money.

Several weeks after I had begun writing, Mr Williams hailed me from his shop as I was passing (I had ceased asking him about the advertisement, which indeed I had forgotten).

'Lidy with too many daughters wants you to call. Any afternoon this week. Here's the address. 'Tisn't far. What ho! looks as though yer luck's turned, hey?'

I agreed that it probably had, and hastened home for my music. Now I was faced with it, the prospect of teaching little girls the piano was rather appalling. I had lived without a piano for some time, and had not practised seriously for years. Also, if there were a *great* many daughters, my writing time would be seriously depleted. However, I had paid for the advertisement, and I needed money.

Having selected several pieces like Somervell's Rhythmic Gradus, 'The Harmonious Blacksmith', a little very early Mozart, and some Czerny, I set off that afternoon to Mrs Garth-Jackson's house. It was, I discovered, another boarding-house, of the more genteel and expensive variety. It had a chinese lantern in the hall, and an intricate piece of furniture bracketed to the wall, which pigeon-holed all the inmates' letters in alphabetical order. There was also a smell of soap and burnt rock cakes which assailed me the moment the door was opened by a stolid young woman of about

348

eighteen who conducted me to a room leading off the hall, and then abandoned me. There was a piano in it, an extraordinarily ancient Erard.

Mrs Garth-Jackson had an exceedingly thin stiff nose, like a placket jammed between two pale grey buttons which were her eyes. When she smiled, which she did all the while she was talking, she displayed bulbous ingrown teeth, which were so large and so numerous that they seemed almost to be falling out of her mouth. She wore a hideous overall spattered with huge orange flowers, and over this, to show, I suppose, that she wore real clothes underneath, a large lapis lazuli and mother-of-pearl cross on a silver chain.

'I am Mrs Garth-Jackson,' she began. 'You must excuse my greeting you like this, but I have everything to do myself, and all my large family have home-made food. Today is my baking day and you couldn't have caught me at a worse moment, but never mind. Do sit down. Be at home. Now then. I have three daughters who all require lessons, but I'm afraid I cannot run to the figure you are asking as I am a war widow.'

This did not seem a very promising start. However, I smiled, wanly sympathetic, and she continued: 'One of the things I rescued from the Wreck, was the dear old piano which nobody has played on since I can remember. So all we need is a nice sing-song in the evening with one of the girls officiating.'

I summoned enough courage to ask: 'Have your daughters received no previous tuition?'

'Dear me no. Of course I see that if you had been contemplating *advanced* tuition your price was perhaps not so ... but these girls are right at the *beginning*, and only the most elementary teaching is necessary. That *does* make a difference, doesn't it?' She smiled harder than ever.

Panic stricken, I attempted to consider the difference it made. But she allowed me no time for this.

'You look very young to be a teacher of any kind. What are your qualifications?'

I explained, as impressively as possible, about my father. She seemed satisfied, but not impressed, and continued to talk about her daughters.

'You will find them eager to learn, and not, I fancy, ungifted. Their great-uncle used to play the viola; so you see there is music in our family, too. They are available any afternoons that you wish, but perhaps it would save your time and my money if you taught them together, shall we say for an hour and a half at the figure you mentioned?'

She was still smiling, with her eyes boring into my face as she exploded this last awful suggestion. I was about to grasp weakly at the only straw in sight, when she continued: 'I see you have brought music with you. Quite unnecessary, as a matter of fact. I have got something suitable for each of them.'

I found my voice. 'Have they any knowledge of musical notation?'

Mrs Garth-Jackson laughed.

'No idea of notes from A to Z. That is your job, isn't it?' Here is the music. I will fetch the girls while you peruse it.' She laid three thin leaflets on my lap and hurried purposefully out.

The leaflets contained three songs: 'Tipperary', 'Roses in Picardy', and one I had never heard of called 'Moonlight on My Dreams'. I stared at them aghast. I was still staring at them in a kind of petrified trance, when the three Miss Garth-Jacksons followed their mother into the room. The daughters were all alike, and exactly like their mother. The first shock, however, was in respect of their age. They all looked, in spite of their girlish and identical clothes, considerably older than me. I realized by their expressions, that if Mrs Garth-Jackson had not constantly smiled, she would have looked morose and stupid. On the whole, I still wished she would not smile. Meanwhile four sharp noses were directed at me, and three pairs of pale grey eyes stared with expressionless intensity into mine.

'This is Muriel; Mildred; and my youngest, Mabel. Now as I think we were agreed upon terms, supposing you begin now, and when I have finished my weary round of household duties, I shall be able to join you, and I hope also profit.'

The next moment I was left facing the unprepossessing and silent trio. Divested of Mrs Garth-Jackson's smile, the atmosphere became frankly gloomy, even desperate. Stiffening my sinews, however, I began, with assumed confidence, which did not for one moment deceive any of us, to examine the extent of their knowledge. This was easy. They knew nothing, and, I felt, cared less. I realized with horror that teaching them the names of the notes was going to be no easy task. Nevertheless, I began to attempt this.

I opened my book of Czerny and they shuffled up to the piano. The situation was made worse by the fact that some of the notes of the piano never sounded at all, many others were erratic, and all of them were out of tune. With every minute I felt my pupils grow more bewildered and hostile. They never spoke to me, but muttered an occasional disparaging remark to each other. My position was only relieved by their apparently despising each other more thoroughly even than me, although they clearly had no very good opinion of me. In half an hour I had made no progress at all. Their minds did not exactly wander; quite simply they did not seem to have any minds. I endeavoured to remain bright and patient, but I was clearly very bad at teaching. I could not remember when I had learned this particular aspect of the subject myself. I seemed always to have known it. So I dare say my methods were hopeless.

Mrs Garth-Jackson's reappearance, which I had formerly been dreading, came as a relief.

'What *have* you been doing?' I haven't heard a sound,' she began.

'We haven't been learning the songs you said,' announced, I think, Mildred, but I was so bemused by their noses that I am not very sure.

'Although I know all the chunes,' said another daughter.

'We *all* know the chunes,' said the third crushingly.

That was the beginning of the end. In vain did I try to

explain the elementary principles that must be grasped before any playing might proceed. I was too depressed to be very persuasive.

Mrs Garth-Jackson succeeded in getting rid of me as a charlatan and without paying me. I went with all the dignity I could muster, inadvertently leaving Czerny behind me. I withdrew my advertisement and gave up all thought of teaching anybody anything which I could not remember learning myself.

I resolved to cut down my meals, at least until I had finished writing.

CHAPTER THIRTY-NINE

I discovered that exercise and fresh air made me hungry. Sitting in my room and drinking a quantity of cold water, however, did not. I was far from starving, but subsisting mainly on the monotonous tepid luncheons provided by Mrs Pompey, reinforced by bread, apples and cocoa in my room, required a certain adjustment of the mind if one was occupied in successively copying music, writing and, worse still, worrying about a book.

One afternoon, however, having some music to return, I decided to walk back to Paddington. It was a beautiful day; one of those rare single perfect days, with balmy air and exquisite colour; the whole inlaid with a seductive, but treacherous sense of timelessness. Tomorrow it would probably rain, but it was impossible to think so today.

I turned reluctantly from the edge of the Park towards my sunless room, and the copying which lay before me. The door of my room was unlocked. I pushed it open – and there was Elspeth.

As I opened the door she rose from the chair in which she had been sitting. She was dressed in a costume of vivid yellow, which seemed to illumine the room. I think I gasped: tears of amazement started into my eyes.

'I have been waiting for you,' said Elspeth. 'You must have thought me so rude in not answering your letter that I decided simply to come.'

I shut the door. Curiously, seeing someone, a friend in this room for the first time, where I had spent so many solitary hours, my loneliness rushed out on me, enveloping me.

Elspeth said: 'Can we light your fire? I cannot make it work.'

'It needs pennies.' I went to the little box in which I kept them, on the mantelpiece.

'Have you been waiting long?' I asked when the fire was alight.

'Not very long. Your landlady put me in here. Is this where you live?'

'Yes.'

She stared at me thoughtfully for a moment, and then said:

'I have been abroad. Uncle does not forward letters. So you see, I have only just had yours. I got back two days ago.'

'I am very glad to see you,' I said. 'Shall we have tea?'

'On the bed there is a paper bag full of meringues,' she observed.

I made tea. We talked about the Lancings, and she a little about Paris. There was a kind of constraint upon us; neither of our minds was employed in our conversation, as we wondered about each other, our eyes occasionally meeting in a spasm of amiable curiosity.

When the tea was poured she said suddenly: 'Tell me why you are here? Has something dreadful happened since I saw you last?'

'No. I couldn't bear living with my family any more, so I left.'

'But why here?'

I looked at her shining trim head with small ear-rings glinting at the edge of her hair (her actual ears were invisible), and answered carefully: 'I have very little money. I couldn't afford anywhere else.'

'Do you work?'

'I copy music. I don't earn very much.'

'Are you not very lonely? What happens when you've finished copying music?'

'Nothing. I get some more.'

'So much music as that?' She made an extravagant little gesture with her fingers. 'What did you dislike so much about your home?'

I tried to tell her, but somehow, since I had written about it, I had no more to say on the subject, and found it difficult even to be convincing.

'I see,' she said. I do not think she did. 'But what do you intend doing? You surely cannot copy music all your life?'

I was becoming hardened to this question and countered: 'What do *you* intend doing?'

Her clear serious eyes widened a moment but she answered casually: 'Oh, I have some sort of plan.'

'Well I have none,' I said flatly. I knew from experience that this kind of conversation only made me thoroughly unhappy for long afterwards.

'I remember you once said that you would write books and keep a small Zoo,' I added.

'How do you remember that? I remember thinking it, but I do not remember telling you.'

'I was thinking about it the other day. Well, are you doing either of those things?'

'Good heavens, no. At least, not at the moment.' The corners of her mouth flitted upwards and then down again as though she were smiling alone to herself.

'You see?' I said. 'It's no good planning anything. Anyway, what could I plan?'

'I suppose you could earn more money. That would make a difference.'

'It would certainly make a difference. But I am not trained to do anything. I have no vocation or talent, or whatever it is people need.'

'How did you learn to copy music?'

'That doesn't count. I was brought up on music. It is like words; only a little more complicated.'

'And do you do it all day?'

'Yes.' I did not want to tell her about the book.

'All the time?'

'Almost all of it.'

'That's better,' said Elspeth calmly. 'I am afraid I know that you don't.' She indicated my writing-table with the back of her head. I saw that my second vast exercise book lay open upon it, and felt violently angry and stupid.

'I have not touched it. You must have left it there. Generally you lock it up, but today you forgot.'

'How do you know that?'

She leaned back a little in her chair.

'That is what people do. The locking up and the forgetting.'

'Do you write?' I asked politely.

She frowned. 'I cannot. I have done enough of it to know that I cannot. It is a bad situation.'

I did not know what she meant, and did not reply. Suddenly she leaned forward and said, very charmingly: 'Do *you* find it difficult? Will you tell me about it?'

I stared at her, hopelessly incoherent. 'I haven't finished,' I said at last.

'It's about you, I suppose?' Elspeth said.

I nodded.

'What are you going to do with it?'

'Do with it?'

She laughed. 'Extraordinary creature. You don't plan anything, do you? Look here, I want to read it. I read very quickly and shall not lose it,' she added.

'My writing ...' I began faintly. I suddenly felt sick at the thought of anyone reading it. There were all kinds of things.

'Am *I* in it?' asked Elspeth sitting bolt upright.

'Yes. So you are.'

'So I am,' she smiled delightedly. 'I'll read it in one day, or perhaps two. Yes?'

I hesitated, knowing she would win. 'It isn't *finished*,' I said again.

'We'll invent an ending,' said Elspeth. 'If I have time we will. I shall have to be quick because of ... Why it might make you famous!'

I had the feeling that she said this to prevent herself saying something else. We did not talk about it any more. Nor did we again mention the Lancings. I felt that for quite different reasons we had neither of us liked staying with them and that we neither of us wanted, by discussion, to find out how different our reasons for not liking it were.

She left in a short while, carrying the exercise books, with the promise that she would return with them two days later.

She left me in a tumult; about her and about the book. I lay for hours that night imagining myself an accepted and successful author. Gigantic fantasies rioted with wholly improbable simplicity; clear unpractical dreams filled me to the brim; my ambition was as boundless, as limitless, as my illusion, and I indulged them both in the privacy of my dark room for hours and hours.

CHAPTER FORTY

The next day, of course, I had to battle with the depression which results from any orgy of private and imaginative optimism.

In thinking of Elspeth reading my books, I fell to thinking of Elspeth herself. I realized that I knew almost nothing about her, since on each of the three widely spaced occasions when we had met, she had seemed an entirely different creature. Nor could I, except by the wildest unsatisfactory conjecture, connect these three people, although they all had something in common. She had on all occasions given the impression of being only partially contained in the immediate situation, as though the most vital part of her was withdrawn, intensely active, but withdrawn. If she had some private life of which I was ignorant, it did not seem dependent upon her environment. I felt she carried it about with her; and since ignorance is conducive to envy, I envied her.

Her appearance was also perplexing. She had dressed on this last, and the previous occasion with an extreme, but elegant, severity, although her face, her habitual expression of grave preoccupation had altered remarkably little, I realized, since she was fourteen. She had looked too old for her age then; now she appeared, not precisely too young, but imbued with a curious mixture of sophistication and youth. The effect was certainly startling, but it was impossible to be sure whether or not it was conscious.

In spite of the feeling I had so strongly about her divided nature, I felt that there was no situation to which she would prove unequal, possibly *because* of her essential division. She had, I felt, what many people call (and I can think of no better way to describe it) some secret purpose in her life.

Fortunate Elspeth, I thought, having successfully

simplified her situation without knowing anything about it.

I spent the whole day alternately resolving to put Elspeth and the books out of my mind, and impatiently waiting for her return and her conclusions. I spent an almost sleepless night in the same condition.

She arrived exactly when she had said she would. She was carrying a small suitcase. I had prepared tea for us, and proceeded to dispense it, confidently expecting that she would of herself broach the subject of my book. But she seemed wrought up and unusually silent. It had been raining, and she arrived buttoned to the chin in an unusually long and heavy mackintosh, although she was bareheaded.

'I had better hang it somewhere,' she observed, after standing restlessly in it for some moments. She was wearing an equally businesslike shirt and tie; together with a beautifully cut grey costume, the skirt of which reached to her ankles.

'I'm so sorry.' I unwedged the piece of paper in the wardrobe door, and produced a hanger.

'Do you always have to do that?' she asked.

'Use the paper? Yes. Otherwise it swings open.'

'Bore for you,' she remarked and flung herself into a chair.

'Do you know what struck me most forcibly about your book?' she said suddenly after a very long silence which I had not known how to break. I drew a deep breath; she was coming to the point.

'No? How should I?'

'It struck me so much that I thought you might also have noticed it,' she replied, ignoring the tea I had placed beside her.

I waited.

'It is that after repeated efforts to shake off your family atmosphere and environment, you have finally succeeded in eloping with it . . . in carrying it off, and bringing it here.'

'This is not in the least like my home!' I cried.

'No? It is considerably less comfortable, and much more solitary. Otherwise it seems to me to be very much the same.' She said this almost aggressively, but her eyes looked calmly out of her pale serious face, and I saw that she really meant what she said.

'What I want to know,' she continued, 'is whether, if presented with the opportunity, you would be prepared to leave all this behind, and *really* get away? Would you, do you think?'

I struggled hard to adjust my mind to the new and brutal conclusion she had put forward.

'I suppose *if* the opportunity really arose, yes,' I said slowly, my dreams of authorship rapidly fading under her practical and unexpected attack.

'But you do not believe in the opportunity?'

'I find that difficult,' I admitted.

'Is that because you really want an unadventurous kind of life, or because you simply haven't had the chance to try anything else?'

'You've read the book,' I said stiffly.

'What sort of shape do you believe the world to be?'

This question really shook me so much that I answered quite simply: 'Round.'

'Entirely round? Spherical?'

'Er . . . yes. I haven't thought much about it.'

'My uncle has thought of almost nothing else for the last twenty-five years,' said Elspeth.

There was a short silence.

'I am beating round the bush, but there *is* a bush,' she said at last. 'It is not so much that I believe in *it*; but I believe in *him*, and he is too old to find out for himself.'

'Could you explain a little more about it?' I asked.

'The point is that I am not talking nonsense. This has something to do with that book you have written. I should not have said anything if I had not read it. First of all: do you think you would be prepared to leave all this for something utterly different? I cannot say very much more than that until I know myself.'

I looked round the drab crowded room.

'Don't you think I should be foolish to refuse?'

'*I* think so. Now look.'

She picked up her plate, turned it in her hands, and put it down.

'No,' she said. 'It would be easier if I get my suitcase.'

Thereupon began a most improbable exposition. It was her uncle's theory, she said, and although a few people upheld it, they were totally unprepared, or unable, to do anything to promote it. Her uncle was rich, he was old, he was infirm, and above all he was obsessed with his idea. He left it to her, and she was determined to do everything in her power to prove or disprove the thing. She required someone who was able to record her findings, accurately, and at the same time, with imagination. 'The two are indivisible. I have discovered that,' she said. I must divulge the idea to no one, but she thought that I would fulfil this particular position admirably. 'There will also be a lot of hard work,' she said. 'Harder, I think, than you have ever known.' She looked at the exercise books. As soon as she had finished speaking, she rose to her feet and announced that she was going.

'Write to me about it,' she said. 'There is not very much time left. I should be glad to know as soon as you have made up your mind.'

So she left me.

It was not a difficult decision. It was really one of those decisions which are instantly decided; until the sheer size of it forces one to rally a few faint objections, in order to flatter one's initial judgement. I knew, the moment Elspeth had gone, that I would gladly leave this room. I could assure myself with a kind of triumphant self-pity that I had no ties beyond it, or, if I had, they were ties I could easily break. I wanted just then to think of myself spinning away round the earth, unbreakable and separate from anything that I touched. Round the earth was, perhaps, hardly the way to describe this desire.

I wrote to Elspeth that night.

CHAPTER FORTY-ONE

Two weeks later we left. The days were so hectically crowded with practical preparation and emotional spilt milk, that I was not able to record them. I spent most of the mornings and afternoons ordering things, choosing things, buying things, fetching things, and having things altered. There were to be three of us; but the third was not to join Elspeth and me until something obscure had been arranged between Elspeth's uncle and some mythical eccentric elsewhere. Elspeth displayed remarkable ingenuity and intelligence, together with her customary incomplete presence of mind whenever I saw her. The whole business was transacted efficiently, and with a comfortable disregard for money which made even the suppliers of our varied and incongruous requirements treat us with astonished awe.

I spent the evenings alternately with Elspeth and my family. The family evenings were extraordinarily difficult. I had been pledged to a complete silence on the real reason for my departure, which made the venture frivolous, incomprehensible and almost disastrous to my mother. I told her I was going to write: she looked suddenly anxious and said: 'Not music, darling?' I answered: 'No, only words,' and she seemed faintly reassured. She did not feel that composing music was a very happy career, she said: for a woman, she added. She was unhappy about my going: I felt helplessly sorry for her, but I knew that I should go. How long would it all *take*? she would inquire at intervals. I did not really know.

Eventually, the day before we were to leave London, I left my room in Paddington, and walked with a single light suitcase out into the street. Although I was leaving my room for ever, I felt quietly unreal about it, as though my departure were merely imaginary (I had come very close to my im-

agination during the recent months), as though there were
no real question of my leaving at all, in spite of Mrs
Pompey's brisk decisive farewell.

I went home to sleep the last night in my old room.
Having kissed my mother and sister (my sister seemed to
feel that the solemnity of the situation required this), I lay
awake in this earlier bed that I knew so well, with the unknown prospect of the journey flooding my mind. In spite or
because of the knowledge that I must rise at six o'clock the
next morning, I slept very little.

I quelled the alarum-clock almost as soon as it rang, but a
minute later my mother stood in the door of my room,
shivering in a faded pink dressing-gown.

'I was awake anyway,' she said. 'I will get tea.'

This was the worst time to attempt any kind of social departure, I reflected, struggling into the garments the
arduous labours ahead of me required. It was the time when
memory is sharp, everything is remembered, but there is
nothing to say. The worst possible time.

When my mother returned with a tray she gasped faintly
and said: 'Darling! Are you going like that?'

For a second we both looked at my clothes, and then, both
aware of the hopelessness of any argument or explanation,
looked away. *She* had always prepared me for any previous
journey, I knew we were both remembering.

We said the things we had said the night before; of course
they did not console her. When she had asked whether I
should come back soon, and I had reassured her, she said:
'We shall hardly know you.'

Would she have felt like this if I had been marrying? I
wondered. No, she would regard my marriage as a logical
continuation, she would comfort herself with that. She
would not regard this venture as either logical or lyrical; nor
could it seem a continuation of anything at all.

We drank the warm metallic tea from the thermos. I swallowed a piece of bread and butter to please her. The cab
arrived. The man blustered silently with my trunks in the

hall while my mother hovered miserably on the stairs, catching cold and trying not to cry, not to utter one word against me.

Kissing her, saying good-bye, was a curiously formal affair. I felt very like saying: 'Thank you for having me', the kind of thing one says after a long disappointing visit. I simply kissed her again and went. The feeling was no more than a shadowy echo of what I had felt before embarking on a fortnight in the country. But this was not a fortnight in the country.

In a few racing silent moments my home was left behind; the little span when there was no present, and I was strung between the last moments of my family and the enormous mysterious future, was endured in the cab, until, meeting Elspeth, it began to be my present again.

The journey by rail to the ship took ten hours. I had to read most of the time, a manuscript of technical and, in consequence, chiefly incomprehensible notes.

I imagined that on arrival we should board our (unexpectedly small) vessel and relax. I was utterly wrong about this. The boarding itself took three hours with all our equipment, and the suspicious hostility of all customs officials to be contended with.

On board, a great deal of unpacking was necessary. I was given a cabin to myself with a good small table for writing.

Elspeth is next door, which is a good thing as she seems to know much more about every aspect of travelling than I. I found we had missed dinner, but were provided with sandwiches and soup. Elspeth has gone to bed, and I am writing this, although I am too exhausted to do more than make notes now.

Tomorrow, however, I shall start my new book. I am so tired that I cannot see the lines on the paper, but I have finished the second exercise book from Mr Williams. I am very cold, and work on the floor, wrapped in Elspeth's magnificent rug.

The new book in which I am to write has no lines.

I have opened it and written the title across the first page.

I am calling it 'The Four Corners of The Earth'.

Joan Lingard
Sisters by Rite £3.50

*Enclosed in a playtime world, three children mingle their blood in
eternal alliance . . .*

Through the blackout of wartime Belfast Cora, Rosie and Teresa
cherish their ties of blood. But Rosie's family are Protestant, Teresa's
Catholic, and it is only through Cora, the daughter of Christian
Scientists, that their friendship can flourish.

Betrayals and breakdowns threaten the childhood pact as they travel
through adolescence: to the awakening of sexual love, religious
doubts and political commitment.

Spanning three turbulent decades, from the ominous shadows of a
world at war to the divisive bitterness which heralded the beginning
of 'The Troubles', *Sisters by Rite* is an unforgettable portrait of Irish
womanhood – as three women grow up in a society torn apart by
prejudice and hatred . . .

'She is both shrewd and perceptive; her characters believable and
painfully accurate' IRISH TIMES

'Ms Lingard's voice is quiet, it is wise too, funny and sharp'
SUNDAY TELEGRAPH

'She has a beautiful feel for the texture of life'
ALAN MASSIE, THE SCOTSMAN

All Pan Books are available at your local bookshop or newsagent, or can be ordered direct from the publisher. Indicate the number of copies required and fill in the form below.

Send to: Pan C. S. Dept
               Macmillan Distribution Ltd
               Houndmills Basingstoke RG21 2XS
or phone: 0256 29242, quoting title, author and Credit Card number.

Please enclose a remittance* to the value of the cover price plus £1.00 for the first book plus 50p per copy for each additional book ordered.

*Payment may be made in sterling by UK personal cheque, postal order, sterling draft or international money order, made payable to Pan Books Ltd.

Alternatively by Barclaycard/Access/Amex/Diners

Card No.   ☐☐☐☐☐☐☐☐☐☐☐☐☐☐☐☐☐☐☐

Expiry Date   ☐☐☐☐☐☐

——————————————————————————
                            Signature

Applicable only in the UK and BFPO addresses.

While every effort is made to keep prices low, it is sometimes necessary to increase prices at short notice. Pan Books reserve the right to show on covers and charge new retail prices which may differ from those advertised in the text or elsewhere.

NAME AND ADDRESS IN BLOCK LETTERS PLEASE

....

Name _____

Address_____

_____

_____

_____

                                                    3/87